I thought I had already experienced my greatest fears, but what was happening now surpassed them all. As I drove away from the house, leaving my children in the care of others, I had no idea what our next moves were going to be. I glanced at Emelia. "Do you have plans beyond tonight?"

"No."

"I can't leave my children for so long—I won't. You must figure out a way we can be together again."

"That may not be possible for a while. We must ensure that no one can get their hands on the children, especially Santan. If anything were to happen to his son, Basarab would lose all focus. If that happens, the Dracul family will lose control and humankind will be annihilated."

"I could help protect them."

Emelia reached out and laid her hand on my leg. "No ... no, you cannot protect them because you will need protection, too. Only our kind can fully save them from harm now. If the wrong individual gets hold of you, you will be expendable. The count will not care what happens to you—leastwise, not above his duty to his throne—and you can be assured, Radu and Elizabeth know that."...

I had an idea growing in my head, but it would take some planning. I glanced at Emelia and felt a twinge of guilt...

I tiptoed from the building and headed to the car. Just as I was putting the key in the car door, I heard the sound of a motor approaching up the driveway ... Around the corner came a familiar red Volkswagen ... The car came to a halt behind my vehicle, blocking my exit. Randy jumped out, and ran to me ... and then, Vacaresti approached us. "What are you doing, Virginia? Why is Emelia not with you?"...

My feet felt like lead as I walked back to the office ... my plan had failed...

# *Night's Return*

*Fear not night's return*

*Mary M. Cushnie-Mansour*

# Books by Mary M. Cushnie-Mansour

## Adult Novels

***Night's Vampire Series***
Night's Gift
Night's Children
Night's Return
Night's Temptress
Night's Betrayals
Night's Revelations

***Detective Toby Series***
Are You Listening to Me
Running Away From Loneliness

### Short Stories
From the Heart
Mysteries From the Keys

### Poetry
picking up the pieces
Life's Roller Coaster
Devastations of Mankind
Shattered
Memories

### Biographies
A 20th Century Portia

## Children/Youth Titles

### Novels
A Story of Day & Night    The Silver Tree

### Bilingual Picture Books
The Day Bo Found His Bark/Le jour où Bo trouva sa voix
Charlie Seal Meets a Fairy Seal/Charlie le phoque rencontre une fée
Charlie and the Elves/Charlie et les lutins
Jesse's Secret/Le Secret de Jesse
Teensy Weensy Spider/L'araignée Riquiqui
The Temper Tantrum/La crise de colère
Alexandra's Christmas Surprise/La surprise de Noël d'Alexandra
Curtis The Crock/Curtis le crocodile
Freddy Frog's Frolic/La gambade de Freddy la grenouille

### Picture Books
The Official Tickler
The Seahorse and the Little Girl With Big Blue Eyes
Curtis the Crock
The Old Woman of the Mountain

# Night's Return

Mary M. Cushnie-Mansour

**CAVERN OF DREAMS**
PUBLISHING

# NIGHT'S RETURN

Copyright © 2014 by Mary M. Cushnie-Mansour

All rights reserved. No part of this publication may be reproduced, distributed or transmitted in any form or by any means, including photocopying, recording, or other electronic or mechanical methods, without the prior written permission of the publisher, except in the case of brief quotations embodied in critical reviews and certain other noncommercial uses permitted by copyright law. For permission requests, contact the author through the website: www.marymcushniemansour.ca

Publisher's Note: This is a work of fiction. Names, characters, places, and incidents are a product of the author's imagination. Locales and public names are sometimes used for atmospheric purposes. Any resemblance to actual people, living or dead, or to businesses, companies, events, institutions, or locales are entirely coincidental.

Ordering Information:
Books may be ordered directly through the author's website: www.marymcushniemansour.ca or through booksellers. Contact:
Cavern of Dreams Publishing
43 Kerr-Shaver Terrace
Brantford, ON  N3T 6H8
1-519-770-7515
Discounts are available for volume orders.

**Library and Archives Canada Cataloguing in Publication**

Cushnie-Mansour, Mary M., 1953-
[Novels. Selections]
    Night's vampire / Mary M. Cushnie-Mansour.

(Night's vampire trilogy )
Contents: bk. 1. Night's gift -- bk. 2. Night's children -- bk.
   3. Night's return.
Issued in print, electronic and audio formats.
ISBN 978-0-9868169-1-8 (bk. 1 : pbk.).--ISBN 978-0-9868169-2-5
(bk. 1 : bound).--ISBN 978-0-9868169-5-6 (bk. 2 : pbk.).--
ISBN 978-0-9868169-6-3 (bk. 2 : bound).--ISBN 978-0-9868169-9-4
(bk. 3 : pbk.).--ISBN 978-1-927899-00-7 (bk. 3 : bound).--
ISBN 978-0-9868169-3-2 (bk. 1 : epub).--ISBN 978-0-9868169-7-0
(bk. 2 : epub).--ISBN 978-1-927899-02-1 (bk. 3 : epub).--
ISBN 978-0-9868169-4-9 (bk. 1 : audiobook).--ISBN 978-0-9868169-8-7
(bk. 2 : audiobook).--ISBN 978-1-927899-03-8 (bk. 3 : audiobook)

    I. Cushnie-Mansour, Mary M., 1953- . Night's gift. II. Cushnie-Mansour, Mary M., 1953- . Night's children. III. Cushnie-Mansour, Mary M., 1953- . Night's return  IV. Title.

PS8605.U83N53 2013        C813'.6        C2013-905509-6
                                                                 C2013-905510-X
                                                                  C2013-905505-3

*Do not dismiss your dreams*
*To be without dreams is to be without hope*
*To be without hope is to be without purpose*
~
*To my niece, Bethany,*
*who has been by my side throughout*
*the writing and editing of the*
*"Night's Vampire Trilogy,"*
*brandishing her red pen over my pages,*
*keeping me on track and focused to the task at*
*hand… "you are the writer; I am the editor" was*
*one of her favourite sayings as we went over and*
*over the manuscripts, bringing each one to an*
*amazing conclusion!*

# Acknowledgements

Thanks to Bethany Jamieson for all the hours you spent helping me with the editing of *Night's Return*. Remember the night I called you and told you I had found so many little things wrong, and we needed to get everything fixed, and you panicked, wondering what you had missed—and then you laughed at me and said most of what I had found would never have even occurred to the readers—and then you took my red pen away from me! Your hard work and staying power when dealing with the ever-changing mind of the writer, (that would be me), is heartfelt. You are amazing!

Cover design by Terry Davis @ Ball Media, Brantford, ON Canada—Terry you did another amazing job!

Cover picture of wolf and girl by Elena Dudina. Photograph of model by Cathleen Tarawhiti. You can check out their amazing profiles, (under their names), on Facebook.

Winter scene picture of Wynarden was provided by the Talos family.

Special thanks to: Brenda Ann Wright, Judi Klinck, Mariette Havens, Eleanor Bahry, Tracy Bucholtz, Heather Cardle, Joan Jenkins, and Myra Houston for taking the time to read *Night's Return* and for giving me such wonderful testimonials.

It was a pleasure to work, once again, with Randy at Brant Service Press. Over the years, he has been an amazing support whenever I called upon him for my printing needs. Another great print run!

One more time, I must thank the Talos family for allowing me the continued use of photos of Wynarden for the book cover. You have been an amazing support throughout my writing journey. Wynarden was built in 1864 by the Yates family, and over the years it has often been referred to as Yates Castle. In the 1920s it came into the hands of the Talos family. It is a prominent, historical landsite in Brantford, Ontario.

# Night's Return:
# Cast of Characters
*indicated turned by original` family member—not full blooded

## The Dracul Family

Count Basarab Musat
Teresa * (Basarab's wife)
Count Attila (Basarab's father)
Mara (Attila's wife/Basarab's mother)
Count Vlad Dracul—(referred to as Dracula)
Mihail and Vlad (Dracula's sons)
Radu (Dracula's brother)
Zigana (Dracula's bastard daughter)
Ponquor * (Zigana's husband)
Vacaresti (Attila's half brother)
Emelia * (Vacaresti's wife)
Stephen (The Great) and his wife Evdochia
Kerecsen and Laborc (brothers—Evdochia's cousins)
Kate * (Kerecsen's wife)
Melissa * (Laborc's wife)
Ildiko and Gara (twins—Basarab's cousins)
Farkas (Father of Ildiko and Gara)
Bajnok and son, Kardos
Lardom, Tardos, and Sebes
Uros and his wife Aliz

## Basarab's & Virginia's Children

Santan and Samara

## *The Humans*

Virginia
Randy
Adelaide and Alfred (Emelia's friends)
Carla (Adelaide's adopted daughter/doctor)
Sean (Basarab's source for blood supplies)

## *Radu's Rogues*

Elizabeth Bathory
Jack "The Ripper"     Delphine LaLaurie
Peter Stumpp          Thomas Cream
Renata                Orsolya

## *In Dracul Family Service*

Max and his wife, Lilly
Count Balenti Danesti (doctor)

## *Gypsy Witches*

Tanyasin
Angelique

# Virginia

## Chapter One

The past few minutes of confusion had weakened me to the point of collapse; yet, somehow, I managed to gather strength enough to stand my ground. Maybe, the strength came from my two young children, Santan and Samara, who were clinging to me as they tried to hide from the monster that had invaded the room. My eyes flitted between the three women in my presence. Ildiko, Basarab's cousin, stood frozen in a trance-like state. Angelique, who had been going to help me escape, stood between me and Tanyasin, the Gypsy responsible for the curse on the Dracul family. Tanyasin had said she was here for Basarab's son—my son.

As the words sputtered out of Tanyasin's mouth, in the strange, yet familiar language, I tried to back away, keeping my children, well behind me. "There is no escaping me," Tanyasin cackled. "I care not what happens to you—you are irrelevant—it is the children I want. And, how lucky I am ... I thought there was only one, yet here I stand gazing upon two!"

The sound of footsteps in the hallway drew closer. Tanyasin cursed again and spun around, turning her back to us. Taking the opportunity, Angelique lunged at her sister. Tanyasin must have felt her movement because she sidestepped, and Angelique crashed into the wall. "Fool!" Tanyasin guffawed.

Angelique quickly regained her feet. She whirled and grabbed Tanyasin by the arm. "Let them go, sister, they are innocents."

Tanyasin pulled her arm from her sister's grip. "Not one who carries *his* blood is innocent. You may have a bleeding heart for *his* kind, but I will never forget the sight of my guiltless family and what that monster did to them! My precious husband ... my innocent son ... no, I shall never forget the blood dripping from their open wounds, nor the rattle of their final breaths! Don't speak to me of compassion."

"But these children are not Dracula's."

I sensed Angelique was doing what she could in order to try and save me and my children from her sister. I felt small fingers gripping my legs. I would have closed my eyes and prayed for a saviour to sweep into the room and save us, but I dared not. For, as much as I was afraid, I knew I needed to keep my eyes open and my wits sharp.

Tanyasin appeared empowered. She gazed briefly at me, and then returned her attention to her sister. "You were the obedient child, Angelique—the favoured one—when we were children. You thought you had power over everyone. But it is I, Tanyasin, who has the supreme power now!" She turned her head as the commotion in the hallway burst through the doorway.

I breathed a sigh of relief when I saw Emelia, Adelaide, Alfred, Carla, and Randy. Suddenly, Tanyasin lunged at me, almost knocking me off my feet. I staggered against the counter, which saved me from tumbling to the floor. Before I could stop her, though, she grabbed Santan up in her arms, pushed past Angelique, and entered the main dining room. She stood in the centre of the room, a defiant look on her face, as though she were daring anyone to come close to her. Despite what was happening to him, Santan remained calm. Emelia raised her hand, motioning the others to stop when she saw what was happening.

"Ah, Emelia," Tanyasin's voice grated with evil. "Have you told your beloved nephew, Basarab, he has a second child? Does he know of the girl?"

"No, he does not," Emelia took a step forward.

Tanyasin hissed. Emelia stopped. "Do not come any closer! I am taking this child and leaving. You can have the other one. I shall not tell Basarab of her until after he gives me what I want, and for what I desire, one child will do." She laughed hysterically.

Unexpectedly, Samara stepped out from behind me. It was as though she were in a trance as she waddled toward the centre of the room where Tanyasin was imprisoning Santan in her arms. Samara began to sing...
*Come hither, don't dither, come around to me*
*On bended knee, for your life you must plead*
*Free the one you hold in your arms*
*If to yourself, you wish no harm...*

Tanyasin stared at Samara, surprise written all over her face. I held my laughter in check as this child, my child, who could barely walk, stood up to Tanyasin. Unfortunately, the old Gypsy recovered quickly.

"Go and suckle your mother's breast, baby! You do not scare me!" she screeched.

Santan's voice rang out clear and strong. "You should fear her, Tanyasin. You should fear my sister! Would you like me to allow her to unleash the demon that possesses her?"

I noticed the strange smile on Santan's face, and the shocked look on Tanyasin's. I watched as Angelique walked toward her sister, reaching out her arms. "Give him to me, Tanyasin. You are no match for the forces in this room. Leave the children to me and go and do what you must with Radu. But, once again, I must warn you that he is only using you. If he leaves you alive and you come to me for help, I will still embrace you…"

"I want not your embrace, Angelique," she sputtered. "Don't even dream I would come to you for anything, not even if the breath was leaving my body and I could only crawl!" She paused, and I noticed a thoughtful look on her face, as though she were weighing her alternatives. Slowly, she released Santan and set him down on the floor, ignoring Angelique's outstretched arms.

It surprised me that he did not run immediately to me. Instead, he looked up at Tanyasin and charged her with the following words: "You should listen to Angelique, Tanyasin, for she speaks the truth. Radu is only using you. My great-uncle is an immoral man; he cares not whom he harms in his quest for the throne. I also tell you that he will never gain the throne he covets. My father is all-powerful; those around him are more faithful to him than those who surround Radu and Elizabeth Bathory!" With that statement, Santan turned and walked to me. "Also, you would be wise to release my Aunt Ildiko from the spell you have cast on her," he ordered, his voice ringing out loud and clear in the room.

My son's statements floored me. How did he have such knowledge of the family? Who had been feeding him this information? Or, did it flow to him by a river of dreams, sent by his father? It appeared there was still much I had to learn about my children.

Tanyasin hesitated. She glanced around the room, especially at the two children who had just thwarted her plans. Slowly, she raised her hands in the air with a sweeping motion, mumbled some words under her breath, and then took a few hesitant steps toward the doorway.

Ildiko, realizing she was free, shook her head and roared. She looked at Tanyasin and charged. Angelique stepped between them, blocking the assault. "Not now. We must leave here as quickly as possible. Tanyasin is the least of our worries at the moment."

Ildiko did not look pleased, but she backed off. I moved forward to greet Emelia and the others. I had noticed a strange look on Randy's face as he took in the scene that had just unfolded, and wondered how much he knew about the reality of what my life was like. Santan, as though noticing Randy for the first time, raced to his friend and jumped into the arms that opened for him. Tanyasin must have slipped away during the commotion, for when we turned around, she was gone.

"We should go after her," Ildiko spat.

"No, let her go. She can do us no harm now; but, others are on their way. You should fear them more than Tanyasin," Emelia stated. I noticed the panic in her eyes. She motioned to the table and chairs. "We need to go over our plan to get the children and Virginia to safety; however, Angelique is right ... we need to do so quickly."

Ildiko turned to Angelique. "What are you doing here?" she demanded. "It is the middle of the night. Did Vacaresti send you? Or Basarab?"

Angelique drew in a deep breath. "No, I came for Virginia and the children, to get them to somewhere safe. Elizabeth has already realized they are not in Montreal. I am sure she will be on the next available plane to Toronto. And, she is furious. I have a feeling this will be the first place she will look for them."

"I can handle Elizabeth," Ildiko spoke with a bold bravado.

"Are you sure? My sister overpowered you quickly enough. Even if you can deal with Elizabeth, what will it cost? She has others with her: Teresa and a woman named Delphine LaLaurie, one of her recruits. Delphine is not the nicest individual, and she would not think twice of torturing, or even murdering whoever might get in the way of her mistress." Angelique drove her point home.

Ildiko hesitated for a moment. "Vacaresti told me to watch over them until he returned, at which time we would take the children to their father in Brasov. I know not what his plans are for their mother. I will do what it takes to honour Basarab's wishes and return his son to him." A strange look crossed over Ildiko's face. "Did I just hear you say that Teresa is with Elizabeth?" The words spewed from her mouth.

"Yes…"

"So, the filthy Gypsy has betrayed my cousin?"

Angelique reached out to lay a hand on Ildiko's arm, to try to calm her, I assumed. "No, she did not betray Basarab. They had a plan that you were not privy to. Few were. Teresa was trying to get information for Basarab, but the events that unfolded had gone dreadfully wrong. Elizabeth found out about Santan, and she also discovered that Emelia had not only assisted Virginia in her escape from the count, but had given her the child. Teresa did everything in her power to ensure Emelia got out of the country before Elizabeth could reach her. Emelia was smart enough to throw a red herring on the trail by booking a flight to Montreal, but not getting on it. Instead, she flew to Toronto."

Angelique turned to Emelia. "You are later than I thought you might be; did something happen on the way?"

"A traffic jam on the highway delayed us," Emelia informed. "We also decided it best to wait until dusk so we would be able to move the children safely." Emelia turned her attention to Ildiko. "You must listen, Ildiko; Vacaresti would want it this way, too. He would do whatever he deemed necessary to protect Basarab's children."

Ildiko still looked as though she was ready to explode. I glanced over at my son who was sitting quietly on Randy's lap. Santan's eyes were aflame with a red ring of fire consuming the iris. Samara had found refuge with Carla. My daughter's eyes danced with fire, as well. I sighed, feeling lost and alone.

"There is more," Angelique continued. "Not only is Elizabeth coming, but Radu has sent one of his *special* men to keep an eye on her. Thomas Cream is not nice. It is rumoured that he is a rogue of the worst kind—one not to be reckoned with."

"How is it that you know this, when Basarab does not know of these whom you speak of?" Ildiko's words were rank with ridicule.

"I have been watching over your family for many centuries, Ildiko; you know that."

Carla cleared her throat, and then spoke up. "We have a plan. We were going to stash the children in a cottage I own in Port Dover, about a forty-five minute drive from here. We brought along some belongings for the children. Emelia's friends and I will stay with them. The plan was to have Emelia take a different route with Virginia, with the hope that Elizabeth would follow their trail first. We figured she would assume Virginia would not separate from her children, and Emelia would stand a better chance of eluding such a force as Elizabeth."

Angelique looked to be considering the plan. "It might just work, at least for the short term. You will have to figure something else out, though. Possibly a few moves to keep well ahead of Elizabeth. Unfortunately, I must return to Transylvania, to ensure all is well there. I hope, now that Emelia is here, you will be safe ... at least she will be capable of buying some time until we can think of something better."

I decided to speak up and voice my opinion. Everyone was talking as though I had no say in what was to happen to me and my children. I felt I was the best one to protect them. After all, I believed I had done an admirable job, at least until the other night when Vacaresti and Ildiko had knocked on my door. I wouldn't be so willing to open my door next time ... if there were a next time. And, I would have an emergency escape plan in place. I had thought that by staying in Brantford, I would throw him off my tracks—Basarab would not expect me to be that foolish. In reality, though, it probably wouldn't have mattered where I went, he would have found me.

"I don't feel comfortable separating from my children," I stated firmly, looking straight at Carla. Carla's face twisted into a grimace, and I noticed the muscles in her face twitch. Was that anger I saw reflected in her eyes?

Emelia intervened. "There is no other way, my dear. Elizabeth will never think you would separate from your children. She probably knows, by now, that I outfoxed her, and she will follow my scent, thinking I would be the one getting you and the children to another hiding place."

"But, if your plan doesn't work, if Elizabeth discovers where Carla is taking the children—excuse me for being brash—what power does Carla, Adelaide, and Alfred have to overcome Elizabeth Bathory and this woman that Angelique says is with her?"

Emelia's voice was soft as she spoke to me. "They will do whatever they can in order to protect these children. Besides, once we know they are safe, and if we have thrown Elizabeth off the trail, we can make our way to the cottage. At the moment, this seems the most feasible plan."

I glanced over at Randy, wondering again just how much he knew. "What of Randy?" I asked. "Is he not in danger, just by association?" I noticed how dishevelled he was, and the worry lines on his face—too many for such a young man.

Randy looked over to me. I could see the despair in his eyes as he forced the words from his throat. I felt his pain. "I'll be all right, Virginia; don't worry about me. You've got to listen to Emelia and Carla; they know what's best for you. I'm going back to our place; if these others show up…" Randy didn't finish his statement, but I could guess what he might have been thinking he would do to the vampires—at least like to do.

I felt the flush of fear flutter through my chest when Randy mentioned delaying the others. He had no idea what these creatures were capable of! I saw the love in his eyes as he stared me down.

"You are no match for them, Randy." I barely heard my own voice.

Ildiko spoke up. "I will go with him, Virginia, to ensure his safety."

I was shocked. I had not known Ildiko long, but during that short time, she had never displayed any signs of unselfishness. I had to wonder at her motive. Her goal had always been to rid Basarab of his wife, Teresa. She hated Teresa with a passion. She hated anyone who might come between her and the goal of becoming the vampire queen. Another thought occurred to me—the probable reason she wanted to accompany Randy. Teresa would be with Elizabeth; what better way to remove her arch rival from the equation! If she had any fears about where Basarab might stand with me, the mother of his two children, well, I was a human and could be disposed of easily when the time came. Still, I felt it would be advantageous for Randy to have someone like her with him. He would never be able to fight the vampires on his own.

Angelique must have picked up on my thoughts. "I believe it is a terrific idea that Ildiko goes with Randy. I feel it in my bones that we are going to be inundated very soon with visitors, first to Randy's place, and then to here." She turned and spoke directly to Ildiko. "You and Randy should get to the apartment as quickly as possible. Make it look as though Virginia left in a hurry with the children. Get her van out of there; that way they will not suspect someone else might have taken her; or, at least, if there is no time to remove it, say the van belongs to Randy. Do whatever it takes to allow Emelia and the others to have as much time as possible to get away." She turned to Emelia. "Where are you planning to take Virginia for tonight?"

"My office in Hamilton," Carla replied for Emelia. She pulled a set of keys from her pocket and removed a couple keys from the ring and then handed them to Emelia. "The key with the red rubber cover fits the back door of my office. There is a small sitting room down the hallway, on the left, where you will be able to make yourself comfortable. I wouldn't stay there for long, though; it is too close to here. The longer the trail is that you create for Elizabeth to follow, the more time we will have."

Angelique stood up. "It is time to go. Get the children in the car, Carla. Are their belongings in your vehicle?"

Emelia nodded affirmation.

I felt wretched inside. I reached out to my children, one last effort to keep them in my arms. Santan climbed off Randy's lap and came to me. Samara snuggled closer to Carla. "Please, don't separate me from them," I choked on the tears that were trapped in my throat.

Emelia took hold of my arm. Her voice was gentle. "Virginia, this is the only way. You must come with me now. Hopefully, Elizabeth will pick up our track, giving Carla time to get the children safely to the cottage and out of harm's way. The children are still young enough that their vampire scents will be faint, and when it mixes with human's scents, it may not be detectable at all."

I still hesitated. Emelia reached for Santan, tugging him gently from my arms. Before he released his arms from around my neck, he whispered in my ear. "Everything will be okay, Mama. We will see each other soon."

Emelia set Santan down, and he went directly to Alfred and took hold of his hand. I fought the tears back as I watched my children leave with Carla, Adelaide, and Alfred, not knowing when I would see them again. I sighed deeply, and then followed Emelia out of the house. Within a few minutes, we were all going our separate ways.

## Chapter Two

I thought I had already experienced my greatest fears, but what was happening now surpassed them all. As I drove away from the house, leaving my children in the care of others, I had no idea what our next moves were going to be. I glanced at Emelia. She was staring out her window.

"Do you have any plans beyond tonight?" I asked, hoping Emelia had thought of some magical solution to reunite me with my children, sooner rather than later.

"No." Emelia did not look at me.

"I can't leave my children for so long—I won't. You must figure out a way we can be together again."

"That may not be possible for a while. We must ensure that no one can get their hands on the children, especially Santan. If anything were to happen to his son, Basarab would lose all focus. If that happens, the Dracul family will lose control and humankind will be annihilated."

"But why can I not stay with the children? I could help protect them."

Emelia finally looked at me. She reached out and laid her hand on my leg. "No ... no, you cannot protect them because you will need protection, too. Only our kind can fully save them from harm now. If the wrong individual gets hold of you, you will be expendable. The count will not care what happens to you—leastwise, not above his duty to his throne—and you can be assured Radu and Elizabeth know that." She turned away again.

I had an idea growing in my head, but it would take some planning. I glanced at Emelia and felt a twinge of guilt; however, I felt I had no other choice. When we arrived at the address Carla had provided us with, we got out of the car and used the key to enter the back door. We located the room Carla had told us about and settled down. I let Emelia have the couch while I took the chair and footstool. Emelia lay down and folded her hands across her chest. Within minutes, she was asleep.

Quickly, I got up and headed to the office where the filing cabinets were located. I looked around on the desk, searching for the address of Carla's cottage. I carefully looked through the papers on the desk, the desk drawers, and the Rolodex. Nothing. From there I dug through the filing cabinets, which were filled with rows of patients' files. *My, you are a busy girl, Carla.* Finally, in the bottom drawer of the last cabinet I looked in, I saw the deed to the cottage in Port Dover. I wrote the address down on a piece of paper and stuffed it into my pocket.

I crept back to the room where Emelia was, to make sure she was still sleeping. I thought to leave a note, but changed my mind. I tiptoed from the building and headed to the car. Just as I was putting the key in the car door, I heard the sound of a motor approaching up the driveway. I turned, wondering who would be coming here at this late hour. If I hadn't been of stronger character, I would have had a heart attack. Around the corner came a familiar red Volkswagen. There were three people inside, the driver I recognized immediately—Randy. Sitting beside him was Vacaresti. I couldn't see who was in the backseat, but it appeared to be a woman—maybe Ildiko?

The car came to a halt behind my vehicle, blocking my exit. Randy jumped out of the Volkswagen and ran to me, sweeping me into his arms. "Thank God, you are okay." He leaned over, as though he were going to kiss me, but straightened up at the last minute. He must have noticed the warning look in my eyes.

Vacaresti approached us. "What are you doing, Virginia? Why is Emelia not with you?"

I purposely ignored Vacaresti's first question. "Emelia is resting inside," I said, hoping my feeling of frustration would not resonate in my words. "I will have to unlock the door for you." My feet felt like lead as I walked back to the office. My plan was failing, but I was happy Vacaresti did not pursue what I had been up to. I could tell by the look on his face, though, he probably would return to his question at a later point. As I was about to put the key into the lock, I heard a car door slam shut. I had almost forgotten about the third person in the car. I turned and saw Teresa. She did not look happy. "Teresa," was all I could manage to say. She was the last person I wanted to see right now.

"Virginia." Her voice was unpleasantly cold—emotionless—suggesting that she was not thrilled to see me, either.

I led the way into the office, and then stepped to the side. Once everyone was through the door, I shut it and fastened the lock back into place. I pointed to the room where Emelia was sleeping. "She is in there," I said. Vacaresti headed down the hallway.

Teresa put her hand on my shoulder and spun me around to face her. I noticed Randy tense. "Where were you going, Virginia?" She gave me a piercing look.

There was no use lying; they would find out soon enough. If I didn't answer Teresa, Vacaresti would ask again, and for sure, once Emelia found out what I had been doing, she would want to know, as well. "I was going to my children."

"Oh yes … your children." Teresa's eyebrows rose sarcastically. She glanced over at Randy. "Is he your other bastard's father?" I sensed the irony in her voice.

I knew Teresa was jealous of me; and, I had also sensed when we were at the house that she hadn't genuinely cared about Santan. She had put on an ambitious pretence, trying to play the perfect mother when Basarab was around. She was too selfish to be a devoted mother; however, she had gone too far by referring to Santan as a bastard. I hoped Vacaresti and Emelia had not heard her—for her sake. *Then again…*

"No," I finally answered. "Randy is not the father of my second child. The count is—a little gift he left me on that final night in the house. You remember that night, don't you? Me, on the floor, weeping—you and the count in the hallway, laughing at me. Nevertheless, it is I who has given your husband another child, something you were never able to do," I sneered.

Teresa's face clouded with anger. I had hit a nerve, just like old times. I smiled. I had meant it to be an inward smile, but it crawled across my lips without any consideration of possible consequences. Randy cleared his throat, reminding me that he was still present. I looked away from Teresa when Vacaresti and Emelia entered the room. Vacaresti did not seem pleased at what he had obviously heard.

"Now is not the time for this," he commented as he and Emelia approached us. "We have more pertinent matters to tend to. Emelia tells me the children are safe, for now." He turned directly to Teresa. "I need to know everything that has transpired from the time you left the hotel in Brasov until I found you at this young man's apartment."

Teresa looked disgruntled. "There is much to tell, do we have the time?"

"Tell it quickly, Teresa. We will not be able to leave just yet because the sun will be up soon." He paused and turned to Emelia. "I have a sense that some of your story and Teresa's is intermingled."

Emelia nodded. "Why don't I start, then?" she stated.

Vacaresti nodded, and motioned for us to return to the room where the couch was. He sat on a chair, facing Emelia and Teresa who had sat down on the couch. Randy and I looked around for other places to sit. Finding nothing, we sat on the floor at the end of the couch.

Emelia breathed in deeply, and then began. "There is not much for me to tell. Teresa showed up to my door and told me I needed to get out of Brasov and go to wherever Santan was living in order to protect him. At first, I was hesitant because I knew how she actually felt about the child, and I also knew how she hated Virginia; however, she was convincing enough that I decided to go with her." Here, Emelia turned to Teresa. "I still did not trust you. That is why I waited for you to leave the airport before I went through the gate, and why I purchased a ticket to Montreal, but took a train to my friend's house instead."

"And this friend was Adelaide?" Vacaresti interrupted.

A look of surprise crossed Emelia's face, but she recovered quickly and nodded. "Yes ... Adelaide and her brother, Alfred. They insisted on accompanying me and helping me to get the children to safety. Carla, the young woman who has done some occasional doctoring for our family members, met us at the airport. We drove straight to Virginia's apartment, but found only Randy there. He told us Virginia and the children had been taken by someone, he didn't know who. Carla came up with a plan of where to hide the children and of how to throw anyone else off their scent. Of course, the plan could only have been initiated if we were able to rescue the children from whoever had taken them."

"And they are where, now?" Vacaresti asked.

Emelia glanced at Teresa and didn't answer. I had the feeling she did not trust Teresa with such vital information. As though Vacaresti understood her thoughts, he turned his next question to Teresa. "What transpired after you left the airport? Elizabeth found out somehow that Emelia had purchased a ticket to Montreal—did you tell her?"

Teresa shook her head. "No. I went straight to the hotel to talk to Basarab, but he was gone. I found my father and filled him in on what had transpired. Max tried to insist I go to the caves. He was worried Elizabeth hadn't actually gone to her lair, and that she had followed me instead."

"Were you not afraid of the same thing?" Vacaresti questioned.

"Yes, but I think I would have picked up her scent. The plan Basarab and I had come up with needed to be kept up. I felt I was making progress. I assured Max everything would be okay; I would go to Elizabeth and tell her Emelia had already left the hotel, but I had been lucky to see her getting into a cab, so I followed her to the airport where she disappeared into the crowd. I headed back to Elizabeth's apartment and waited for her return.

"I crawled into bed, to give Elizabeth the impression I had stayed in. It worked. She appeared shocked." Teresa breathed in deeply. "Elizabeth told me we were leaving in the morning for Montreal, but she had to go and see someone first. I asked what was in Montreal, and she said she had business there. As we were walking, I tried to get some information about the rogues out of her, but she became testy and suggested I might not be trying to settle a score with my charlatan husband—maybe, I was seeking revenge on his behalf. I dropped my line of questioning after she told me it would be most unwise of me to deceive her."

"Where did she take you?" Vacaresti leaned forward in his chair. "Who did she meet with?"

"Radu."

"Do remember the building you were in?"

Teresa shook her head no.

"Think, Teresa … this could be very important."

Teresa shook her head again. "I am sorry, Vacaresti. I was not paying attention. I guess I was too anxious. All I can tell you is that it was a club of some sort … in downtown Brasov … we hadn't walked too far from her apartment building. We were greeted at the door by some rogues who licked their lips when they saw me. Elizabeth ordered them to back off. As we walked down a hallway, Elizabeth told me to stay close to her; the rogues had thought I was a fresh meal, which she sometimes brought them. Then, she had laughed hysterically. I began to suspect I might not be taking the trip to Montreal—that Elizabeth had other plans for me. I also began to think it might be Radu we were going to see, and my hunch proved correct."

I noticed a scowl cross over Vacaresti's eyes, and, once again, he interrupted Teresa. "So, Elizabeth took you directly into Radu's lair? Do you think this site is his main headquarters?"

Teresa hesitated. "No … no, I think not. Possibly one of his locations, but not the main one. Too small."

Vacaresti leaned back in his chair. "Continue, then … what happened next?"

"Radu appeared happy to see Elizabeth, and surprised to see me. He questioned me as to why I was not with Basarab. Elizabeth was quick to fill him in—how Basarab had beaten me, how he flaunted his whore cousin, Ildiko, in my face, how he treated me as though I was nothing more than a servant, not as his queen. She told him how I had finally defected, arriving at her door bloodied and bruised. I don't think Radu believed a word. He approached me, ran his finger down my cheek, leaned over and stared intently at me with those horrible eyes, and asked me why his nephew would want to destroy such a treasure. When I didn't answer, he shrugged and turned to Elizabeth, and suggested they get to the business at hand."

"Were others in the room?" Vacaresti intervened.

"There were others, but they were silent."

"Did you recognize any of them?"

"No."

It was the way Teresa said no that made me actually look up and observe her body language. At the mention of the others, she had become agitated, wringing her hands nervously. I decided to pay closer attention. I glanced at Randy. He appeared captivated by Teresa's story.

"There was one man, though," Teresa's voice began to shake. "I don't think anyone would forget him once they laid eyes on him! He is the biggest man I have ever seen—ruggedly wild. His eyes, deep-set as they were, glowed like an inferno, and I am sure he did not miss a thing as he watched all that passed between Elizabeth and Radu. He noticed me looking at him, and his tongue flicked across his lips as he half-grinned at me. I focused my eyes elsewhere … the man was repulsing."

"There have been rumours that Radu has a right-hand man who is more vicious than any creature that has walked or crawled upon this earth," Vacaresti stated, a serious wrinkle on his brow. "It is also rumoured this man is the true power, the counsel in Radu's ear. Continue, Teresa."

"It was at this point that Elizabeth informed Radu of Basarab's son. Radu demanded to know the child's whereabouts––knowing that having such a possession in his hands could deliver the throne to him in a heartbeat. But, that was one piece of information even I was not privy to, so Elizabeth was not able to say. However, she did tell Radu that Emelia had played a role in all this and had left Brasov, heading for Montreal. Elizabeth told Radu that she had procured two tickets for Montreal for us, and we were catching the early morning flight. Radu praised her for a job well done, and told her that her rewards would be numerous if she returned with the child." Teresa paused. "I observed something strange, though, throughout the conversation

… Elizabeth appeared submissive to Radu, unlike the woman I had come to know over the few weeks I had been meeting with her."

Emelia spoke up. "Maybe that is the woman Elizabeth prefers Radu to see," she suggested. "Radu may well not realize everything she is up to. I cannot see one such as her sitting beside any ruler. I might suggest she toys with our cousin, which is something that just might work to our advantage in the long run. As long as we can keep Elizabeth and Radu from getting their hands on Santan and Samara, we stand a chance of winning this war."

I was surprised when Vacaresti chuckled. He reached over and laid his hand on Emelia's knee. "Did you ever think we would not win this war, my love? The family of the Dracul bloodline is all-powerful—you know that."

"But you must remember Radu is of the same blood," Emelia reminded her husband.

"True … but, he is not of the same heart."

Vacaresti stood and stretched. He gazed around at us, resting his eyes on me for a moment longer than I thought was necessary. I pondered what might be going on behind the mask he wore. What I knew of Vacaresti, so far, was that he seemed to be a truly fair man and that he loved Emelia—even beyond what might be considered a normal love between a man and a woman—despite what she had done for me, and how she had hidden some of her friends from him over the years.

"Carry on, Teresa … what happened when you reached Montreal?" Vacaresti asked, returning to his seat.

"We were met by Elizabeth's friend, Delphine. Delphine appeared to be to Elizabeth what the huge man in Radu's room was to him. I noted the mutual respect between the two women."

"What did she look like?" Vacaresti enquired.

"Tall and slender … olive complexion, as though she is of mixed blood—or maybe of French heritage. She has short, black hair that is full of tight, wiry curls, and a crafty look in her eyes, I'd say."

"How old would you say she is? And, what kind of accent did she have?" I thought these were strange questions for Vacaresti to be asking, but his next statement enlightened me. "Your information may give us an indication of where this woman is from, and possibly how long she may have been with Elizabeth. If the relationship is as close as what you say it appeared to be, then this woman is not a new recruit, which might also be another indication that Elizabeth has her own plans when it comes to who will be sitting on the throne beside her when this is all over ... if she makes it that far, I must add."

"She had a strange accent," Teresa informed. "But not European ... that much I know for sure. I believe I heard something similar to it when Basarab and I travelled in the southern part of the United States. I remember laughing at how the people drawled their words. As for her age, I am unsure ... assuming she is a rogue, possibly middle-aged at the time of her turning."

I glanced over at Randy, again, and noticed how heavy his eyes were. "Are we boring you, Randy?" I needed Randy to be alert during these revelations, for my own reasons. When I started to put the pieces of the puzzle together, later, I wanted someone else on the same page with me—someone whom I could completely trust.

Randy jumped and smiled guiltily. "Sorry ... no ... not boring at all. I'm just tired." He straightened himself up and nodded to me. "Okay, I'm listening."

"You should have let the poor boy sleep, Virginia," Emelia chastised gently. "His brain is on overload with everything he has been exposed to over the past few days."

I grimaced.

Randy came to my rescue. "Its okay, Emelia; I should be paying attention." He blushed when he glanced at me. I noticed his reaction had not gone unnoticed by Vacaresti, or Teresa.

"What happened next?" Vacaresti leaned back in the chair again and folded his hands under his chin. He seemed to be digesting and studying every word that came out of Teresa's mouth.

Teresa continued. "Delphine had secured an apartment for us. She told Elizabeth that she hadn't been able to glean any information about Virginia and the child; it didn't appear they were in Montreal. She suggested Emelia had duped them. Elizabeth questioned me, then, as to if I thought Emelia might have led us astray. I reminded her that no one had actually seen Emelia board the plane, and it had been her own inside informants who had told her of Emelia's destination. I don't think Elizabeth was impressed with my tone of voice because she turned to Delphine and asked her if she thought I was being truthful.

"I have to admit, I was scared when Delphine asked Elizabeth if I had always been honest with her. Then, Elizabeth placed her hands on the arms of the chair I was sitting on, levelled her eyes with mine, and asked me if I had ever lied to her. She demanded to know what truths I held in my head. I had to give her something, so I told her that Virginia might still be in Brantford, where Basarab and I had lived. Elizabeth smiled knowingly and asked for a description of Virginia.

"Finally, Elizabeth said she was tired and would like to lie down. Before doing so, she offered me some refreshment. I never even thought to question the blood she handed me—I was famished. I downed the first glass in seconds, and Delphine quickly refilled it for me. Then, the two of them took their glasses and headed to the bedroom. It was when I stood up to take my empty glass to the kitchen that I felt the wooziness creep over me. I knew I was being dismissed from Elizabeth's service.

"When I awoke, they were gone. I was desperate as to what to do, knowing I needed to get to Brantford immediately, especially since Elizabeth had the house address. I had been smart enough to stash some extra cash in my suitcase, and I checked to make sure it was still there before I headed to the airport. It was when I was buying my ticket for Toronto that I sensed I was being watched, and not by a human. I turned around, and there he was, leaning up against a pillar, staring at me. The red gleam in his eyes gave him away. I grabbed my bag and headed toward my departure gate, but he stepped in my way.

Up close, I realized he was one of the men who had been in the room with Radu the night Elizabeth and I had been there. I realized the magnitude of the game, then, between Radu and Elizabeth. This man had probably been sent to keep his eye on Elizabeth, and somehow she had given him the slip. I would be the next best person to know where she was headed. He waved a ticket in my face, and I noticed his destination was Toronto—he gave me no choice. I thought it better to play along with him. I couldn't take the chance on either him or Elizabeth actually getting their hands on Santan…"

"So all of a sudden you developed a conscience?" I burst into the conversation, not being able to help myself. "You never showed any love for Santan when he was born; why would you now?" I sneered. I noticed the worried look on Emelia's face, as though she were remembering the old days at the house when Teresa and I had always been at each other's throat.

A sardonic grin spread slowly across Teresa's face, parting her lips enough for me to take notice of her fangs. "On the contrary, my dear Virginia, I would see no harm come to the child. He is my husband's son, and family protects family. You, on the other hand…"

"Enough!" Vacaresti's voice cut Teresa off. "There is no time for this discord between you two; I thought I had already made that quite clear, earlier. Finish your story, Teresa."

"Well, as I was saying before being so rudely interrupted," she threw me another nasty glance, "I decided it best to go with this man. On the way to Brantford, he wasn't much for small-talk, but he did tell me his name—Thomas Cream—and that he was one of Radu's chosen men. Plus, in a tone of voice that didn't sit well with me, he added that he was a bit of a ladies' man. As he said that, he reached over and laid his hand on my leg. I slapped him away, and without thinking told him my husband would not be pleased another man had tried to take such a liberty with me. Of course, he was quick of wit, picking up on my slip, and he confronted me with the obvious fact that it was not my husband then that I was deceiving, but

Elizabeth, and he couldn't wait to inform Radu of that little tidbit of information.

"When we arrived to the Toronto airport, the place was abuzz with police cars. They had cordoned off the area around a taxi. Thomas sniffed the air, and then said that whatever had happened there, Elizabeth had been involved. We hailed another cab and gave the address for the house. To our surprise, the driver told us his friend had taken two other cab fares to the same address that night, and his last customer had been a real crazy woman who had made him follow some tire tracks to a big old house near some cement factory. The last message this cabbie's friend sent to him said that two women had gone into the house, three had come out.

"Thomas decided to check out the house, anyway. He ordered the driver to secure the address of the place where he had taken the women, we would be right back. When we returned, the driver was visibly distraught. He informed us that it was his friend who had been murdered around the time he had delivered his last passenger to the airport, his throat ripped open as though he had been attacked by a vicious animal. Thomas showed no empathy, just ordered the driver to take us to the address he had procured, and when we arrived there he ordered him to wait.

"When we entered the house, it was quiet as a tomb. I took note of the heavily-lined curtains. I saw a photo with two children, and recognized Santan to be one of them. They looked very much alike, with the exception of their hair colour. Thomas cursed when he realized there was no one in the house, and then we heard the car motor revving. By the time Thomas got to the door, the cab was halfway down the lane. I mentioned that maybe we should try and get some rest since the sun was just beginning to emerge—we could decide what to do later. He became enraged at my suggestion, and asked if I was trying to get him to go to sleep so I could sneak out and run to Basarab. And then, he grinned and began to circle around the room, advancing on me like a slithering snake. I sensed his intention, and I was ready for him when he attacked. He was powerful. I missed my target, but he didn't. I felt his fangs beginning to sink into my neck … that is when Randy burst through one door and knocked Thomas off me … and then, you, Vacaresti … you know the rest."

　　Teresa breathed in deeply. She looked drained. Vacaresti appeared thoughtful, digesting all that Teresa had just revealed.

## Chapter Three

Several seconds ticked away on the clock on the wall. I hadn't noticed before how loud it was. Finally, Vacaresti stood and directed his first words to Teresa. "You and I will return to Brasov as soon as we can secure a flight. Basarab must be informed of all that has transpired here. It is time to put an end to Elizabeth and Radu, once and for all."

Teresa pointed to me and Randy. "What do we do with these two; we can't take them with us." I noticed she was glaring right at me, not Randy. "And what of your wife?" she added.

I glanced at Randy and could tell he was becoming agitated with the situation. His face was blushed, and his Adam's apple was working overtime. However, Emelia intervened before either I or Vacaresti could give Teresa an answer.

"I think it best that they go to the cottage and stay with the children," Emelia suggested. I noticed she didn't comment as to where she would be going. "Carla cannot remain there for long; she has her practice here to look after. Adelaide and Alfred mean well, but they are older, and human. In reality, if it came down to the crunch, they would not be able to escape with the children if such an immense danger were to present itself."

Vacaresti nodded in agreement. "Wisely said, Emelia ... and, if I might add, as much as I don't want to leave you behind, you should accompany Virginia and Randy—a little extra protection. Once Teresa and I fill Basarab in on what is happening, it will be his decision what to do about the children— keep them hidden here in Canada, or take them to Brasov so that they are directly under the protection of the entire family."

Randy stood up. He shoved his hands in his jean pockets and cleared his throat. "There is something else we need to remember ... Elizabeth has Ildiko. Will the count not try to negotiate for her life?"

I glanced at Teresa, trying to read the reaction on her face at the mention of Ildiko's name. Her voice sounded bitter as she answered Randy. "I am sure my husband will bargain something for her, but I do not think he will risk his throne! In fact, I know he won't!"

"She is his cousin, and I am certain he would not see her harmed in any way," Vacaresti pointed out. "However, now, we cannot worry about Ildiko; we need to move forward with our plan to keep the children safe." He turned to Emelia. "Do you have the supplies you need?"

"No. Adelaide managed to get me some before we left for here, but not enough to last for more than a few days."

"I have some in my bag in the car," Teresa mentioned.

"Good." Vacaresti ran his tongue over his lips. "I am assuming Carla is able to get you more when you need it?" he enquired, turning to Emelia.

"Yes, being a doctor, she should have no problem." Emelia turned and headed to the room where she had been sleeping. "I'll just get my things." Vacaresti followed her.

Randy headed out the door, mentioning that he needed to make room in the trunk of his car for my and Emelia's cases. I lingered in the hallway outside the room where Emelia and Vacaresti had gone. I heard them talking, but even though they kept their voices low, I managed to catch much of what they were discussing…

"How did you know where to find us, Vacaresti?"

"I have known many of your secrets for a long time, my dear wife. Did you think you could hide such goings on from me?"

"Do any of the others know?" I detected fear in Emelia's voice.

"About Virginia and the children?"

"Yes."

"No … not their whereabouts, yet, but I shall have to tell Basarab as soon as I return to Brasov. You know as well as I do that may be the only way we have to protect the children now."

"Why did you not tell him before this?"

"It was more important for Basarab to stay focused on the task at hand. To have known where his son was would have distracted him, and to have learned there was a second child, well…"

Emelia's voice grew fainter. I could hear husky emotion in her words. "Thank you for your discretion, Vacaresti."

After that, their voices became barely audible, and I only managed to catch the odd word … angry with the way … not blame her … won't sacrifice … in danger … time is of … then silence. I headed toward the office space where I had found the cottage address. A few minutes later Emelia appeared with her satchel.

"Vacaresti is resting," she informed Teresa, who had just returned from outside. "You better, as well; you have a long journey ahead of you tonight."

Teresa handed Emelia a small bottle. "This should keep you nourished until Carla can get you some more. I have two left, one for me and one for Vacaresti." Teresa looked at me and Randy. "Safe journey. I am sure we will meet again—probably sooner than you might want to." Teresa headed down the hallway. "I am going to get some sleep as Emelia suggested."

I thought I had detected a fraction of concern in Teresa's voice when she had wished us a safe journey. But I knew better——she hated me. Was there no end to her hatred for me? Then again, did I actually care anything for her? After all, she was the one person that stood between me and the life I could have with Basarab and my children. I smiled as I walked out the door, thinking. It was I who had given the count, not just one, but two children. He had not killed me when he could have that night. Instead, he had taken me on the wings of hell and planted another seed in my womb. There was no way Teresa could compete against that! I felt a flush creep across my cheeks as I got in the car.

"Are you okay?" Randy asked as he started the motor.

"I am just fantastic," I grinned mischievously.

Randy chuckled. "You are in a good mood all of a sudden … happy to be able to see the kids soon?"

"Yes," I somewhat lied. I could sense Emelia's gaze boring into me from the back seat. Could she read my mind?

"I don't want to stop to eat," I mentioned a few minutes after we got underway. "We can have something once we get to the cottage," I added.

"Okay by me," Randy replied.

After a few more moments of silence, I decided just to plunge right in with my curiosity. "What happened, Randy?" I asked.

"What do you mean?" he returned, obviously not grasping my question.

"At your place ... before Teresa and this Thomas fellow got there ... between you and Ildiko."

Randy grinned mischievously. "Jealous?"

"No! I just want to know how it is that she was taken by Elizabeth, and you were not."

Randy turned serious. "She saved my life. I don't think Elizabeth or the woman that was with her would have bothered to take me back to Radu."

"How so?" I pressed for my answer.

"When we got to my place, we decided to wait it out in your apartment. Ildiko was a chatterbox. She began by telling me how upset she was that Basarab had sent her to Canada with Vacaresti to find Emelia and Santan. She thinks she could have been of better value in Brasov. She clearly hates Teresa, though ... called her a filthy Gypsy several times in the conversation. She seems proud that she is of Basarab's blood, but is still confused as to why he chose Teresa over her, and here she used the filthy Gypsy connotation again. She was also puzzled that Vacaresti hadn't told Basarab about the children ... felt he was betraying his leader.

"She most likely wouldn't admit it openly, but she was quite taken with Samara—didn't say much about Santan, though. She did mention that the children were more advanced than any other children she had known who had been born of a vampire/human coupling."

"There are others, then?"

"Apparently ... anyway, she was quite embarrassed that the old hag, Tanyasin, had caught her off guard ... mentioned that the next time they met, it would be an entirely different story. Added that she didn't know if she really trusted Angelique, even though her father had told her several stories of how Angelique had saved many of the family members from vampire hunters."

"Did she mention anything about me?" I was curious to know.

Randy blushed, and I wondered what she had said to him that would have caused this kind of reaction. "She asked me if I loved you."

When Randy didn't continue, I pushed for his answer, curious to know if he had admitted his true feelings for me to a stranger. "Well?"

"I told her that I did, but also that you didn't return the same to me. I told her I felt you were still in love with the count. She didn't look overly happy when I said that. She said you weren't truly in love with the count—just infatuated. After a while, Ildiko got restless and told me she had a sinister feeling in her bones—something horrific was about to happen. She kept checking the window. Just as she was about to turn back and rejoin me on the couch, she noticed a set of car lights creeping up the laneway. 'They are here,' she said, and then told me I would have to hide—no reason for both of us to go down. I said I wasn't a coward and would face whatever it was that would be coming through the door.

"She laughed at me ... said I didn't stand a chance of coming out of this alive unless I hid myself somewhere. And, she needed me to do this so I could get information to Basarab about what was going on. I kept protesting, but her face darkened. At first, I thought she might just kill me herself; but instead, she walked over to your desk and took a pencil and scribbled something on a piece of paper. She handed it to me and told me it was the information I needed to contact Basarab." Randy paused and cleared his throat.

"Where did you hide?"

"There is a trap door under the kitchen table. Under the door is a set of stairs that go down into the cellar. That is why I have a rug under my table. I prayed the rug would fall back into place when I closed the door. Once I was in the basement, I worked my way to a spot under your apartment so I could hear what was going on upstairs. I still had the intention of helping Ildiko if the need arose. But, I never got the chance. I heard the back door bang open, and then the voice of the woman I assumed to be Elizabeth. She was demanding to know where the children were, but Ildiko wouldn't tell her. Then Elizabeth asked where I was, and Ildiko told her that I had turned tail and left because the whole situation was just getting too bizarre for me to handle. Elizabeth called Ildiko a liar, and then she ordered this other woman to check around.

"Doors in your apartment were opened and shut, and then I heard the crash of the door between our apartments. Quickly, I hid myself in the old wood box by the furnace ... lucky it was empty. When I finally came out of hiding, they were just leaving. I heard Elizabeth ask Ildiko how important she felt she was to Basarab, and Ildiko told her, not very. I detected laughter from two women, and then Elizabeth spoke again ... 'we shall see about that ... if not to Basarab, you will be valuable to someone, so I still have an ace up my sleeve, either way. Radu will know what to do with you.' And then they were gone."

"What did you do then?" I asked. "Did you call Basarab?"

"I waited about ten minutes to make sure I was alone, and then I called the number Ildiko had given me. A guy named Atilla answered. I remembered that he was Basarab's dad, so I filled him in briefly about Ildiko's kidnapping."

"Is that all you told him?" I was hoping Randy hadn't revealed anything to the family about the children.

"No," he replied. "I told him about the children...."

"How could you be so foolish, Randy!" I yelled, frustrated at his stupidity.

Randy looked totally embarrassed. His face blushed crimson. "I ... I guess I wasn't thinking," he stuttered.

"Everything was happening so fast ... I'm sorry ... I didn't mean any harm."

"I am sure Randy meant no harm, Virginia," Emelia intervened from the back seat. "Nevertheless, we will have to take extra caution now that Basarab knows there are two children. I am sure he will be keen to meet his other offspring." After coming to Randy's defence, she directed the conversation back to his story. "When did Teresa and Thomas arrive?"

I knew with everything Randy had been through, he hadn't deserved to be spoken to in such a manner. I backed off and allowed him to continue.

"Not long after the others left. Just the sound of Thomas' voice raised the hair on the back of my neck. It sounded to me like they were arguing, as Teresa had pointed out earlier at the office, and I heard fear in the woman's voice. You know me, Virginia," Randy gave me an impish look, and a wink. "Always the knight in shining armour."

When I didn't respond to his attempted humour, Randy continued. "There was so much commotion that I knew something was terribly wrong, so I burst through the door and attacked Thomas. Of course, as I came through one door, Vacaresti came through another—I was just closer to the action. Vacaresti pulled me off of Thomas. I landed on the other side of the room, and Teresa scrambled out of the way of the fight, taking refuge behind me.

"It didn't take Vacaresti long to subdue Thomas, and he definitely didn't need my assistance. At one point, I stepped forward, but he snarled at me and told me to stay back—called me a boy! Vacaresti told us we had to get out of there; we could fill him in on any necessary details once we were in the car. He chose to leave his rental car in the yard, and we piled into my car. As we drove away, I asked Vacaresti why he hadn't just finished Thomas off, and he said that he wanted him to go back to Radu and tell all, especially the part about how he was overpowered by one of the older members of the family."

"Lucky for you, Randy, Vacaresti came along when he did ... if he hadn't, you and Teresa might have met your end," Emelia stated in a hushed whisper.

I grimaced at the thought of what my friend had been through over the past few days. I had no choice but to see my situation through, but Randy was an innocent bystander. He could have just left. Emelia had given him that option, and so had Ildiko. I couldn't help the warm feeling that crept over me, just thinking about his sacrifice. My fingers tapped nervously on my lap. Randy reached over, and I felt the warmth of his hand close over mine.

"Don't worry, Virginia, we will get through this together."

I looked at him and saw the hope in his eyes, and prayed that he was right ... prayed that we would get through this alive!

~

"This looks like the place," I pointed to a narrow driveway. Randy turned his signal on. I could feel the blood pounding through my veins, just thinking of seeing Santan and Samara. I had thought I might never see them again. I couldn't wait to hold them in my arms—even Samara. Despite her obvious disdain for me, I loved her—she was my daughter.

We were halfway up the laneway when we noticed a car approaching us. Randy slowed down. "Looks like Carla's car."

Both cars stopped, just feet from each other. Carla got out of her car and cautiously walked toward us, stopping on the driver's side. She bent over to look in the window as Randy rolled it down. "What the...?" she exclaimed.

"We'll explain when we get to the cottage," I told her. "It's a long story."

Carla hesitated a moment and then straightened up. "I'll be back shortly. I was just heading out to get some groceries when the security alarm came on and announced there was a vehicle approaching the cottage." She appeared tense.

"Man, that must be some system you have had installed." Randy looked impressed.

"It is. One cannot be too careful, especially with all that is going on. Guess I'll have to pick up some extra food; how long are you guys staying?"

"Not sure … I have no idea what our next move is going to be. Vacaresti and Teresa are returning to Brasov to inform Basarab of what is going on over here. I guess the next step might be up to him, unless we can think of something in the meantime," I answered. "Oh … we need some supplies for Emelia, as well," I added.

Carla raised her eyebrows questioningly at the mention of Vacaresti and Teresa. "When did you see them? And, how is it that Vacaresti just allowed you to leave and come here?"

"Like I said, it is a long story. Right now, it is cold out here, and I want to see my children. We'll talk when you get back. Don't forget the goods for Emelia; she only has one small bottle of blood with her."

Carla nodded affirmatively, and slapped the side of the car. "Do my best on that one, but might not be right away." She leaned down to the window again and peered in the back seat. "Will you be okay if I can't manage to get you anything until tomorrow?"

"I should be fine. I will stretch out what I have as long as possible," Emelia replied.

"Good." Carla slapped the side of the car again. "See you later. I'll phone Adelaide and let her know it's you guys. She and Alfred were worried when the alarm went off. I directed them to take Santan and Samara and hide in the basement until I gave them the okay."

Santan was waiting at the door, his arms outstretched and ready for me to grab him up into a hug. He went from me, to Randy, and then to his great-aunt. Samara hung back, tentatively, but when Santan gave her a look, she came forward and hugged me.

When all the greetings were completed, Santan grabbed my hand. "Come, Mama—you too, Randy—come and see what Grandpa Alfred is helping me build!"

When we stepped into the living room, I noticed a table by a window that looked out onto a three-season room. On the table were the beginnings of wood carvings of buildings. "It is going to be a replica of our cottage, Mama!"

"Santan," Adelaide interrupted the festivities, "I think we should let your mother settle in first before you bombard her with your project."

Santan agreed, reluctantly, and Adelaide showed us into a room where we could put our belongings. "I am not sure how we are going to arrange our sleeping, but we will figure that out later. Right now, I have put on some tea; I am sure you could use a cup. How about some food? Are you hungry? I want to hear all about what has brought you here so quickly. We only just parted ways."

I could tell Adelaide was worried. Why shouldn't she be? Alfred appeared calm, though. "I'm not hungry, but," I pointed to Randy, "I'm sure he is."

Adelaide laughed. "No problem, I'll fix him a sandwich. And, I think you should have one, too."

I knew there was no point arguing, so I followed Adelaide into the kitchen and helped her make two sandwiches. The five of us sat down at the table while Randy and I ate. I wasn't far behind Randy in polishing my meal off—guess I was hungrier than I had thought.

Even though Adelaide was anxious to get all the details, she grudgingly agreed to wait for Carla to return so that we wouldn't have to repeat our story. While we waited, I watched as Alfred whittled away at a piece of wood. Emelia lay on the couch and closed her eyes. Adelaide was busy in the kitchen. Randy and Santan were sprawled on the floor, playing with a Lego set. Samara was scribbling in a colouring book. It was the portrait of a perfect family spending a relaxing winter afternoon at the cottage. I sighed—knowing that representation was so remote from the reality of my situation!

Carla returned, laden with bags. Randy jumped up and helped her carry in the rest of the groceries. Once everything was put away, we sat down in the living room, and Randy and I filled

Adelaide and Alfred in on what had occurred. Emelia remained strangely quiet throughout. Santan listened intently. Samara, eventually, went off to play. Alfred kept shaking his head, but didn't interrupt.

"Not good," he said when we finally finished. His voice was barely audible. "The family is not going to take this kidnapping lightly, either. I know Farkas well, and I know how much he loves his daughter. Farkas means *wolf*, and when he changes, I have never seen a larger or more vicious wolf than he. And, Ildiko's brother, Gara—there will be no place for Elizabeth to hide from his eyes. He, too, was appropriately named—*Goshawk*—Elizabeth will have no idea what has hit her!" Alfred's pitch kept rising, the longer he spoke. "That is just her immediate family. There is no telling what the others will do, once they find out. Dracula's sons have been enamoured with Ildiko for years, but have stayed in the shadows because they knew how she felt about Basarab ... oh dear, this is not good ... it is beginning ... we must protect these children, at all cost, now ... at all cost! I am not sure if there is time to wait for Basarab to decide what he is going to do."

"I think we are safe enough here," Carla pointed out.

Alfred shook his head. "No, my dear. We are not safe anywhere. They will track us down, eventually. You know that, as well as I do. Maybe, it is best that we just wait here, and get down on our knees and pray that the one who comes for the children first, is the one who will protect them with his life!" With those words, Alfred stood up and left the room. A few minutes later we heard a door open and close.

I had never seen Alfred so rattled before. The calm demeanour he had presented when we first arrived had been replaced by a nervous dread. I was amazed, as well, at the amount of knowledge Alfred knew about the family. His relationship to them was clearly stronger than I had been led to believe. And, his statement about praying for the one who will protect the children with his life ... that could be only one person––Basarab! I looked at Adelaide nervously. "Will Alfred be okay?"

Adelaide nodded. "He became quite close to Farkas when he was called to Turkey a few years ago to help with some paperwork. He used to talk a lot about Ildiko, too, what a fine young woman she was, despite being a bit on the wild side. There is a side to my brother that many don't realize. For now, Alfred is probably going to walk down to the beach, and do some thinking. Water soothes him." She looked around, as though she didn't know what to do next. Finally, "Well, not much we can do but wait, I guess … may as well organize the sleeping arrangements for everyone."

~

I slept in the same room as my children. As I lay in my bed, I gazed over at them, eating them with my eyes. I had actually thought I might never see them again, and felt so thankful I was here with them, despite the uncertainty that still loomed over our heads. Finally, I closed my eyes and whispered a prayer to God, asking Him to hold us within a protective veil…

*Virginia … my love … my little bird … are you awake?* I felt a firm, but gentle hand on my shoulder, and rolled over in my bed. And there he was, just as I remembered him from the picture I carried in my mind. I smiled. He pulled my covers aside, slipped into the bed, and wrapped me in his arms. *Ahhhh … how I have missed you.*

I felt the counts fingers tingle over my skin as he caressed each nook and cranny, from my forehead downward, all the while never taking his eyes from mine. We were locked in the moment, and it was a moment I did not want to end. Finally, I could not hold back—I reached out to him and returned the same extraordinary treatment he was bestowing on me. I felt him tremble at my first touch. And he smiled.

Love has a way of making a person feel immune to all the evil in the world, and I was feeling as though nothing could creep into my happiness and steal it away from me. We continued exploring each other—former territories coming alive again. And then, he was inside me, slow and deliberate, moving with the knowledge of what would please me most! I wrapped my arms and legs around him in an iron-clad embrace, never wanting the moment to end. And I heard him whisper in my ear ... *Virginia, my little bird ... how I have missed you, my love...*

~

I awoke with a start and looked around me. The covers on my bed were dishevelled. I pulled the blankets off, and felt the goose bumps creep over me. I smiled. This dream had ended so beautifully—unlike the others. What was I afraid of? Basarab would ensure the safety of his children, and of me. He loved me. He had said so.

But, for some reason, as always, something tried to destroy my happiness. It was the voices inside my head—Teresa's and Max's, and sometimes my own. They kept reminding me the Count Basarab Musat had no heart!

# Basarab

## Chapter Four

*Why are you in my room? Why are you looking at me like that? Do you not realize you are nothing more than a vessel to bear my children? What are you doing now ... why?*

I watched as Virginia slowly disrobed. The breath caught in my throat as the floodgate of old memories came teeming to the surface. A moonbeam found its way through the window, circling around her waist. She reached out and touched the dancing slivers of light, and I shivered as I imagined her feather-light fingers caressing my body. I reminisced about the pungency of her delicacies.

Virginia danced slowly, rhythmically, around the room—for me—drawing ever closer to the chair I sat upon, enticing my passion to respond to the tempo of her dance. Finally, I could take it no longer as she sashayed just beyond my reach, lightly raking her nails across my cheek, sending lightening bolts into my loins. Unable to bear the temptation any longer, I stood and strode over to her, pulling her into my arms, lifting her onto my manhood—dancing with her in the moonlight.

~

I bolted up from the couch where I had fallen asleep. *What the hell was that dream all about!* I gave my head a vigorous shake. *I don't have time to think about such nonsense!* Why had I allowed Virginia to get under my skin so deeply that she was penetrating my dreams as a seductress I could not resist? I was the one with the power, not her, and it was time I took back my control. Mother of my child, she might be, but she was not my seducer. I was the one who did the seducing, the manipulating.

I could feel the fresh blood I had recently taken from a young woman in the park curdling in my veins. I turned my thoughts to the phone message Atilla had received from a young man by the name of Randy, informing us of what had transpired in Brantford. He had mentioned there was more than one child that I needed to protect, relaying brief details of Virginia giving birth to a little girl. I smiled. A little girl. I wondered if she looked like her brother, or if she harkened more to her mother, with curly red hair, milk-white skin, and dazzling blue eyes. Just thinking of such a child, I barely could wait to meet her.

Randy had described Elizabeth to a *T*; and, he had mentioned there was another woman with her. Randy had said Elizabeth and the woman had taken Ildiko. I was furious when my father had informed me of this. *They better not harm a hair on her head!*—had been my first thought. Despite what an annoyance my cousin was, especially in her ardent pursuing of me, she was my blood—like a sister.

However, I knew Ildiko, and I was confident neither Elizabeth nor my uncle would have an easy time with her. I was also sure Elizabeth would have taken Ildiko directly to Radu. I couldn't keep waiting to see what my uncle's next move would be, though, especially now that I was aware of the possible fact that my uncle knew of my son. Elizabeth would not hesitate to share such news, for it would bring her up a rung in the ladder of power that my uncle was climbing toward. I needed to return to the hotel in Brasov as soon as possible. I called Gara and asked him to gather everyone for a meeting; I would be arriving by midnight. It was time to take action.

By the time I reached the hotel, Gara had everything in place. "Everyone should be here shortly," he informed. "Farkas and Tardos will be arriving within the hour; they called and said they hadn't been able to get an earlier flight."

"How have things been here?" I asked.

"Quiet ... some rumblings ... minor, though. And, some strange happenings in the courts, but I will allow Lardom to explain about that when we meet. Did you and your father find out anything of importance? He has not said much since he returned a few days ago. I was surprised when you did not return together."

"There was something I wanted to check out, and he felt I could do that on my own ... and no ... we did not learn anything of any substance that we don't already know. The landscape seemed unusually quiet wherever we went."

"Calm before the storm."

"The storm has already begun, Gara, in earnest, I am afraid." I paused, concerned about what I had to tell him next, knowing my father would not have told him, as per my request. I felt it would be better to speak with Gara in private, rather than raise the subject in front of everyone. "I don't know how to tell you this, dear cousin; you are the closest person to me, next to my father—like the brother I never had. There is no easy way to break this news to you ... Radu has your sister ... at least, I am assuming by now that she is in his hands. Elizabeth somehow managed to get to her..."

"How? How did such a thing happen?" Gara's face turned the shade of volcanic ash.

"We received a phone call from a young man who identified himself as a friend of Virginia. He said he didn't have much time to talk, but that Ildiko had asked him to get a message to me. He said there was 'a lot of shit going down,'—his expression—and that Ildiko had been taken."

Gara pounded a fist into his open palm. I could see his fury mounting, something unusual for my normally calm cousin. "This is not good ... this is not good," he repeated over and over again, anger reeking in his words. "Do you have any idea where she is being held?"

"Not directly, but I have sent out feelers. I have an inkling it is somewhere here in Brasov, close by. I am sure we will hear from Radu soon enough."

"Soon? You think we will hear from him soon?" Gara's frustration was mounting to full ferocity. "This is my sister we are talking about; the other half of my soul. I do not intend to wait to hear from Radu! It may be too late by then."

"He will not kill her," I answered Gara, hoping my words had truth in them.

"You don't know that," Gara spit back at me. "Has he not already done enough to our family? Are you asking me to sit back and allow him to have his way with my sister?"

I understood exactly how Gara was feeling, the frustration of having a loved one in the hands of someone who meant them harm; however, Ildiko, at the moment, was not of my utmost concern. My son was. I knew if Radu got his hands on Santan, it would all be over for the family, and for humankind. I levelled my gaze at Gara. "Ildiko will be fine; she knows how to look after herself."

"You say that, but not with conviction in your words," Gara retorted.

"I say it because I know my cousin. I know she will not give in without a fight. She is the warrior, cunning as any I have known."

Gara scowled at me, and began to pace around the room. He stopped by the window and turned to me. "What of Vacaresti? Have you heard word from him? Has he found Emelia? Or Teresa? She was with Elizabeth, was she not?" Gara questioned.

"No word from my uncle, so I assume he is safe. I know he will be in touch as soon as he is able. No word from Teresa, either."

"Does that not scare you, having no word from either one of them? Your wife is not as seasoned a warrior as my sister. And, I assume this young man made no mention of Teresa, or you would have said."

"No, he made no mention of Teresa. The woman he described was definitely not my wife." I paused, and laid my hand on Gara's shoulder, trying to calm him, despite the chaos that was rolling around in the cavity of my own stomach. "For now, Gara, take a bit of time before our meeting to digest what has just happened, and try to think of some clever way we might be able to beat Radu at his game."

I could tell Gara wanted to respond, but by the hard swallow I noticed in his throat, he couldn't. In place of the anger he had just released on me, was a melancholy sadness. His eyes were brimming with tears. He turned and stormed from the room. I walked over to the window and looked out into the night. A night that was blacker than most—in more ways than one.

~

Two hours after Farkas and Tardos arrived from Turkey, I met with my council members in a conference room down the hall from my quarters. Everyone appeared exhausted. I had instructed the women to be present, as well; the time had come for full disclosure. After filling everyone in on Ildiko's abduction, I continued with the other news I had held back from Gara. I looked at him before proceeding, noting his quiet demeanour. I feared the war that was brewing within him, having just witnessed the rumblings of it.

"There is more, my friends ... there are two children. This Randy informed my father that my son and daughter were safe. Virginia gave birth to a girl last May." I looked around the room, searching for some sort of reaction. Everyone appeared to be in shock.

Dracula was the first to speak, and despite the seriousness of the events unfolding around us, he tried to lighten the mood with his words. "A fertile young woman you chose, nephew; maybe we can have a brood of little ones in the royal household yet! She might be worth keeping around." He laughed softly—sarcastically.

I noticed a few lips curl in the upward direction as I gazed around the table, but other than that, silence. I continued: "This may complicate matters for us. I am sure Radu is aware of the children. I had expected to hear from him by now, about Ildiko, but I haven't, and this gives me the suspicion there might be something else going on in his head. I am thinking that perhaps he is going to proceed to Brantford to try and get the children himself. He is smart enough to realize that if he possesses them, it might be the only thing that will crush me so he can take over the throne. He will think they are my Achilles' heel.

"I have had no word from Vacaresti or Teresa, either. There are too many unanswered questions here. But that matters not, at this point. There is no time to lose; I am going to Brantford to get the children myself; I feel that is where they still are. The blood of my son will call out to me. There is no one who can protect them as I will be able to." I looked around the room at my friends. "With your assistance, of course. There is always strength in numbers, and this is a time for all of us to remain as one in order to overcome this evil."

"Is that really such a wise move with what is happening here, to leave the throne unattended, again?" Bajnok spoke up. I detected a slight edge in Bajnok's statement and assumed he was thinking of the years I had already spent away from the throne.

"I have no choice. If Radu gets to my children first, I fear I will have no resolve left to fight. I need to know I have the support of this council. I will not go alone. Some of you will accompany me. I am not foolish enough to think Radu will make the trip alone."

My father stood. He looked around the room, his face thoughtful. "Maybe, it would be to our advantage if we were to take this impending battle out of Brasov. After all, if Radu has decided to try and track the children down in Canada, then that removes him from here and from the legions of rogues he has been building. The fight would become substantially more equal, levelling the playing field, possibly leading to less bloodshed. The family has never focused on building an army of rogues as Radu has done. Basarab kept the house in Brantford, thinking at some point he might return there. This will afford us safe quarters to set up in."

I searched for a reaction on the faces around the table. Most appeared thoughtful. I noticed doubt in a couple, though. Silence still hung heavily in the room.

Kate, Kerecsen's wife, walked up to the table. "If I might be allowed to say something ... I have just obtained some pertinent information that I think will influence everyone's decision in the direction that must be taken. I have a contact at the airport, and whenever there is something of any great importance that she thinks I might be interested in knowing, she informs me as soon she is able. I received a message that Radu Musat, Peter Stumpp, and Elizabeth Bathory have purchased plane tickets to Toronto. That can only mean one thing; we have little time to act. Basarab's children are in danger ... he must return and get to them before Radu does."

Farkas stood. I had wondered when he was going to speak, especially after me relaying the knowledge of what had happened to his daughter. "I know Radu has Ildiko in his clutches at the moment, but I have complete confidence in her wiliness to get out of the situation she finds herself in. It is somewhat strange to me how easily my warrior daughter was taken by Elizabeth, a rogue ... it just doesn't sit well with me. Possibly, we have missed something here ... could she have been protecting the children by decoying our enemy away, buying time, so to speak?"

I hadn't thought of that particular scenario, but agreed it was a possibility. "Gara, I am afraid I must impose upon you again to watch the throne while I go and find my children. Even though it appears Radu will be away from Brasov, searching for my children, I cannot take the chance that he will not have others continue the onslaught on our home turf."

"My priority now, Count, if you will forgive me for not wishing to do your bidding, is to locate and rescue my sister," Gara retorted, resentment swirling in his words. "If anyone can find her, it will be me. Being twins, we have a connection, despite how different we are."

I fully understood where Gara was coming from, and under normal circumstances I would have been only too glad to have let him have his way, but we were not under normal circumstances. We were on the verge of a war, which had been brewing for too long. My children, young and innocent, were in danger. Ildiko was a grown woman, a warrior—I knew she would think of a way out of her situation and find her way home. And, if she didn't, she was one sacrifice I was willing to make. She would understand my reasoning.

"I must deny your request, Gara," I stated. "Ildiko will be okay," I added.

"If anything happens to her..." Gara's words were pungent with resentment.

"I will take full responsibility."

Gara stared at me, driving his vehemence into my heartless chest. I held my wrath in, for I knew what he was going through. Was I not doing the same thing by trying to save what was mine? However, in my case there was a lot more at stake. Gara did not have the weight of leadership on his shoulders—I did. But with that burden of leadership came the consequences of my decisions. This was the first time in our lives that Gara had crossed me. His father reached out a hand and placed it on his son's shoulder. Gara shook it off, and then swept furiously from the room. Farkas went to go after him.

"Leave him," I ordered. "Once he thinks about the whole picture, he will see it my way."

Farkas's face was tense as he spoke. "This is his sister, the stronger one of the two. She has always been the one to stand up and fight the big battles. He feels he needs to prove he is man enough to save her in her hour of great need." Farkas paused. "I think we should try and free Ildiko. If Radu drugs her, as he has drugged the rogues to keep them under his control, then she is in eminent danger, and so could we be. Who knows what she might say under the influence of Radu's potion."

I looked around the room, studying the faces, and realized I was losing this battle. I saw the consensus in all the eyes as my council nodded toward Farkas, agreeing with his theory. Even my father appeared to be in agreement. He stood.

"I think we should send Kerecsen and Laborc with Gara, and the three of them can rescue Ildiko..."

Suddenly, we were inundated with a loud commotion from the hallway, and then the door swung open. "Rescue Ildiko! Ildiko is just fine; she needs no one to rescue her!" Ildiko stood in the doorway, as fiery as she had ever been.

"Ildiko!" Farkas raced to her side and embraced her. I noted the tears in his eyes, but none in hers.

She acknowledged him with a quick hug and then approached the table. "I have news for you. This battle, if we so choose, can be fought on different turf and involve a lot less bloodshed. I believe Radu will be leaving for Brantford, where your children are, and he will be taking with him Elizabeth, and his right-hand man, a dog named Peter. It should be easy enough for you, Basarab, to defeat your uncle and his two minions!"

I noticed the quaver in her voice when Ildiko said 'Peter.' I also sensed something different about my cousin, something not quite right. Despite her attempt at her usual swagger of confidence, she seemed punctured. I needed to know what it was. "You are correct, cousin. We have just been informed that such tickets have been purchased. Please, sit, and tell us all that has transpired."

Ildiko glared at me. "Everything?"

I nodded.

"I would rather speak with you in private, and let you decide what you want to share with everyone else." Ildiko's lips pursed stubbornly.

"Okay, we will go to my chambers, and I will hear you out. Now that we know you are safe, I think it would be best if we cleared completely out of this hotel. Whoever wishes to stay in Brasov can go to the caves, the rest will accompany me."

The chairs scraped across the hardwood floor as everyone stood. They all nodded respectfully to me. I turned to Ildiko. "Shall we?" She followed me out the door, and down to my room.

"Something to drink?" I asked.

"No thanks … I am not thirsty."

I noticed the doleful look behind the firewall in Ildiko's eyes.

## Chapter Five

"Please, Ildiko, sit." I motioned toward my couch.

"I'd rather stand," she replied, ignoring my offer as she paced around the room.

"What is wrong, my dear cousin? What has happened to cause you to be so agitated? I suspect there is something more to this picture than just being taken by Elizabeth to Radu." I had never seen Ildiko so shaken. When we were children, Gara and I had referred to her as the invincible warrior vampire. Now, she paced before me as though the weight of the world was on her shoulders.

Ildiko paused a moment before turning to me. "Let me ask you something, Basarab, love of my heart … if I had not managed to flee Radu's grip, would you have sacrificed something—anything—to come and rescue me?" Her eyes drove her point home, like a stake in my heart.

I could not respond immediately because I knew what my answer would be … the same as it had been a short time ago when I had made reference to her plight at the council meeting.

"Your hesitation, cousin, tells me all I need to know." Ildiko commenced pacing. "But, of course, because I am here now, you will want to know all that happened with Radu. Am I correct in my assumption?"

I nodded, hoping my eagerness for the information she might have would not display too vividly in my eyes.

"Is it only about your children you wish knowledge, or do you also want to know about their mother, and how she is keeping?"

Once again, I hesitated. My morning dream was still fresh in my mind. Virginia. Did I want to know more about her? She was obviously well … and, she had borne me another child. I looked at Ildiko, realizing she had stopped pacing again, and she was scrutinizing me closely.

"You care for her, don't you?" Ildiko's question struck a chord inside my chest. She laughed loudly. "Does your Teresa know just how much?"

I finally managed to collect my thoughts and return what I felt was a reasonable reply. "I care no more for Virginia than I would care for any other woman I had previously bedded to satisfy the same service for me. She just so happened to be the vessel that received my seed, and she bore me a son, nothing more!"

"And a daughter," Ildiko reminded me.

"Of course ... and a daughter." I paused. "Now, tell me what I need to know about what happened with you and Vacaresti, and how Elizabeth came to capture you so easily. I also want to know, cousin, what has you so rattled." I softened my voice, hoping to draw out of Ildiko what terrible thing had shaken her up so badly.

Ildiko finally settled down enough to sit in one of the chairs across from the couch. "I shall begin with when Vacaresti and I got to the house where Virginia was living."

"Vacaresti knew where she lived?" This was news to me, and I wondered what else my uncle was aware of that he hadn't confided to me.

"Yes, Vacaresti knew of her whereabouts, you will have to ask him where he gained such knowledge," Ildiko sneered. She paused, and then continued. "We were standing outside in the yard when the door opened, and we were welcomed by a female child. I knew, in an instant, she was of vampire blood because she was chanting in our ancient language and her eyes glowed with a burning inferno. Vacaresti went straight to the woman who was pounding on an inner door in the apartment. Another child, unmistakably your son, was standing in a doorway, his eyes glowing red as he took in the scene. When his mother collapsed, he ran to her, only stopping because Vacaresti held up his hand and told the boy that he was not going to hurt his mother. Vacaresti identified himself to the boy as his great-uncle.

"The female child seemed quite smitten with me. As we were taking Virginia and the children to the house, the child sat on my lap and chatted the whole way. Her mother, as we were turning onto the street, started pounding on the car window and screaming out the name Randy. There was a car turning into the laneway; Vacaresti told me to silence Virginia.

"When we got to your house, and had settled Virginia and the children, Vacaresti informed me he was going to search for Emelia. He was worried about her. He had somehow managed to procure enough supplies for me and our guests, and then he left. I tried to enjoy the company of the children, but you know me ... I was never much for hanging out with kids. But, your daughter, Samara, she seemed most eager to please me, and I have to admit I was a tad taken with her." Ildiko actually managed a smile at this point.

"What of Santan?" I asked.

"He remained aloof. I sensed something decidedly different about him, a power like I have never seen before in any of our human/vampire couplings. Samara has some mysterious power, too, but not like her brother's. Something else you might be interested to know is that Samara has no use for her mother; however, Santan is blatantly loyal to Virginia. As for Virginia ... I sensed she is much stronger and smarter than she lets on. I detected the sparks of defiance in her eyes, despite trying to hide them from me.

"However, not long after Vacaresti went in search of Emelia, Tanyasin showed up. Under normal circumstances, she would have been no problem for me, but she caught me off guard and cast a spell that froze me in place. When I was released from the spell, the room was filled with people, Emelia included. With her were some humans—her friends, and a young man named Randy. Angelique was there, as well. I was filled in on all that had happened. Tanyasin disappeared, being thwarted by your female offspring."

"My daughter impeded Tanyasin?"

"As I already told you, your children have powers." Ildiko grinned. "Anyway, a plan was formulated to hide the children, and to decoy Elizabeth. Angelique brought us news that Elizabeth was on her way. It was decided I would return with Randy to the house where Virginia had been living.

"This boy, Randy, loves your Virginia. And, there is something else I noticed. Your son loves him. Stuck to him like glue until we left. You might have a little competition, dear cousin, if you are thinking to keep this Virginia in your life." Ildiko laughed again. This time, I detected a hint of malice.

"This Randy ... he is the one who sent the message to me?"

"Yes."

"And you say he is just a boy."

"Sort of ... he is young ... but he speaks like a man, and has the love of a man for Virginia, although he told me he understood why Virginia could not return his love. I guess Emelia filled him in on some of what is going on. Randy even alluded to the fact that Virginia actually loves you!" Ildiko paused. Her lips curled downward, and a snarl escaped her throat. "How many more women are going to get in the way before you realize who your true queen should have been?" These words were spoken with bitter sarcasm.

"I am married, Ildiko. I made my choice a long time ago, and I have told you many times to get on with your life. Any one of our young men would love to wed you, especially Dracula's sons."

"Ah, I know you are wed, Basarab, but I feel your heart lies in another bed." Ildiko stood and began to pace again. "And it is not your wife's!"

I waited patiently for her to go on, not wanting to say anything because my mind was in turmoil. Was Ildiko right? Did I love Virginia? The dream ... the stirring in my loins when I thought of her ... where was it all going to end? Had I sent my wife Teresa on a suicide mission, knowing Elizabeth would figure out our plan and eliminate Teresa, which would pave the way for me to embrace a new queen—the mother of my children?

"Anyway," Ildiko's voice cut into my thoughts. "When Randy and I arrived at his house, we went straight to Virginia's apartment and waited. I had no doubt Elizabeth would be along soon. When I saw the car lights approaching, I told Randy to leave and hide. I gave him your contact number and instructed him to contact you immediately if I was taken, or killed. He has some fight in him, that boy. He didn't want to leave me; but, I reminded him that if we were both killed, only you could protect those children. Finally, he left through an adjoining door of the two apartments. That was the last I saw of him."

"This Randy seems to be more than his surface shows?" I raised my eyebrows questioningly.

"Possibly."

"Any real need for me to be concerned about him, and what he might do?"

"I don't think he is a physical threat to you if that is what you mean." Ildiko emphasized the word physical.

"But he may be a threat in another manner?"

"Possibly ... however, on with what happened next. I decided to display only enough opposition to make it look feasible, but my actual intention was to be taken by Elizabeth in order to delay her from going after your children. I played my hand well, don't you think?"

I nodded.

"I insisted I had not been made privy to where the children were being taken, asserting that Emelia did not trust me enough to divulge such details. Elizabeth still did not believe me, and she referred me to the woman who was with her, Delphine. Elizabeth pointed out to me how much Delphine loved to torture people, so I had better be truthful. She pulled a picture from her pocket and asked me who it was. I told her it was the young man who owned the house, but he had split soon after we had arrived, saying he couldn't take any more of the drama. Elizabeth didn't believe me. She sent Delphine to search the house. Fortunately, Randy had either left entirely, or hidden himself well because she did not find him.

"Elizabeth asked me again about the children, and if Emelia was with them. I lied, saying she was. That way, if Elizabeth decided to track Emelia's scent, the children would still be safe; and then, maybe, Emelia and I could overpower

Elizabeth and Delphine. However, Elizabeth decided to return to Radu and take me with her to use as a potential ransom ... I think she was counting on the fact that I might possibly mean something to you."

Ildiko paused and stared into my eyes. "I guess she was wrong, eh?"

I said nothing. I looked away from my cousin's piercing stare.

Ildiko laughed. "As I thought ... anyway, Elizabeth is insane! When the cab driver handed her the bill at the airport, Elizabeth's payment to him was to rip his throat open and drain his blood. Delphine took some nourishment, as well. I began to feel apprehensive about my plan, but figured once I was on home soil, I would be able to figure out a way to get word to you."

I stood and walked over to Ildiko and put my hands on her shoulders. I gazed directly into her eyes. "Thank you for buying time for my children to get to safety, but now I want you to tell me what happened at Radu's ... did he harm you in any way?"

"You don't need to know all that happened there, my dear Basarab. Actually, you wouldn't want to know." She tried to look away from me, but I put my hand on her chin and forced her to look me in the eyes again. "Okay," she sighed heavily, "If you insist. I will tell you what you need to know about Radu, first, and then maybe what you don't necessarily need to know about what else happened."

Ildiko brushed my hand away from her chin. She looked up into my eyes, and I noted a bag of mixed emotions—pain, anger, frustration, and the deepest fear I had ever witnessed in her gaze. "Its okay, Ildiko, I am here for you." I persuaded gently.

"Radu was furious that Elizabeth had failed to bring him your son. Even more enraged when he found out there were two children she had let slip through her fingers. He always seemed to refer his comments to the one whom I deem is his right-hand man, a man who goes by the name of Peter. Radu was frustrated, having hoped to use your son as leverage to get to you." Ildiko paused. "But this Peter, he assured Radu that they still had a bargaining chip with me. He said my father and brother might convince you to negotiate. He even mentioned my brother might try to rescue me and that he had heard how pretty Gara was, and said something about keeping certain pleasures in the family..." Here, Ildiko hesitated, and her voice shook when she finished her statement. "And then he had laughed maliciously, and the room darkened with a murky evil such as I have never felt before."

"Radu said he needed time to think. He ordered Elizabeth to take me to a room and make me comfortable. He would tell her my fate once he made a decision. She left me a bottle of blood and departed. I was not thinking as I guzzled the liquid down my throat; I was starving. I began to feel woozy, so lay down on my bed. I heard the door open, and wondered why Elizabeth was returning so soon. But, it wasn't her ... it was Peter."

Ildiko bit her bottom lip, and once again I beheld the trepidation in her eyes. She looked away, eyes cast downward. "I don't think you need to hear the rest ... it is of no importance to what else is going on." Her voice was barely audible.

"Please, Ildiko, allow me to be the judge of what I need to know. What happened?"

"Well, don't say I didn't warn you ... Peter sauntered in, his lips smiling, and asked me if I was getting ready for him. I attempted to get up ... he shoved me back ... I spit in his face ... he slapped me hard across the cheek. 'Wench!' he growled. I ... I tried to put on a brave face ... told him he was nothing but an over-pompous rogue, no match for a true vampire!

"He told me he was the most powerful rogue I ever would have the privilege to meet, and one I should not cross swords with. My head was still spinning. I barely could keep my eyes focused. I felt lethargic ... powerless ... I tried to think how to fight him ... thinking maybe if I gave him what I assumed he had come for ... after all, I've bedded enough men over the centuries ... I fiddled with the buttons on my blouse ... but, I was not prepared for what happened next ... the beast ripped my clothes from my body ... shoved me back onto the covers ... and ... and ... assaulted me ... brutalized me ... like a wild animal ... beating me ... clawing me ... all the while he was raping me, he kept one of his hands over my mouth so my screams could only be heard inside my own head..."

Ildiko could hold the tears back no longer. I tried to reach out to her, to tell her everything was going to be okay, and I would take the necessary revenge on this monster that had dishonoured her in such a manner. She shrugged away from me.

Somehow, Ildiko regained her composure. Her tears shuddered to a stop. "When he finally left, I lay curled on the bed, battered. I could not move for the longest time. I have never been so defiled in all my life. I closed my eyes, trying to will away the vision of his face, but it was still there, leering at me. I tell you, my dear cousin, no human woman would have survived what he did to me!"

"How is it that you escaped, then?" I knew it might be an insensitive time to ask, but I needed to know.

"A saviour. I brought her with me. She is waiting to see you. I thought it best she tell you her story, it is a sad one"

"Radu just let you walk away with this girl?" I hoped the suspicion I was feeling did not ring through in my words.

"It appears so, although, I don't think he intended for either one of us to escape." Ildiko paused. "I must have cried myself to sleep, for I was awakened by a warm cloth wiping the blood from my face. I looked up into a young woman's eyes, and she put a finger to her lips, hushing me. She told me she had seen Peter leaving my room, doing up his pants, and she had guessed what he had done to me. She told me that she wanted out, and then said that maybe we could escape together. She knew the building well.

"She had brought me some new clothes. Once I was cleaned up, we approached the door, opening it slowly. The hallway was empty. Cautiously, we stepped out into the corridor, keeping close to the wall."

"You were not the least bit apprehensive of this mysterious young woman just happening to show up and wanting to help you to escape, as well as wanting to get away from Radu, herself? She is clearly one of Radu's rogues, my dear cousin, which means she would be under his power."

"At first, yes, I was concerned … but, after hearing her story, no."

Ildiko sounded quite sure of herself. I knew from experience that it would take a lot to deceive my cousin, yet I still felt there was something not right with the entire occurrence. It had been far too easy, as though Radu had decided just to let Ildiko go, realizing she was of no real value to his cause.

"Shall I bring her to you?" Ildiko broke through my thoughts.

"Yes."

I realized, until I questioned this girl myself, I would not be able to ease the scepticism I had in my mind. If I felt she was being truthful, her life would be spared. If I had any misgivings, I would not hesitate to end her life—quickly.

## Chapter Six

Ildiko returned a few minutes later with the girl, and then left us alone. She was frail, a ghost of a figure buried deep in the folds of her robe. She pushed the hood off her head, and I noticed the nervous twitch around the young woman's lips. Either she was hiding something, or she had not fed for some time. I smiled, and motioned for her to have a seat. "You have nothing to be afraid of here ... some refreshment?" I offered, holding up a bottle of blood.

She hesitated, at first, and then said she would be appreciative of a glass of blood; it had been some time since she had consumed anything. I watched her gulp down the liquid. She set her glass on the table, folded her hands together, and looked straight into my eyes.

"What would you like to know, Count Basarab?" her voice was barely audible.

"First of all, your name."

"Orsolya."

"Let us begin with how long have you been a rogue; and, how was it that you came to be mixed up with vampires?"

She nodded. "I have been a rogue for less than a year. I came to the city, leaving the family farm, having had enough of scratching out a living in the poor soil. I left under the cover of the night, while my parents slept, not having the courage to face them, for they had been nothing but good to me, despite the poverty we endured. When I arrived in the city, I realized how lucky I had been; at least on the farm I had food in my belly.

"I wandered the streets for days and nights, scrounging for food in garbage bins, taking refuge in dark alleys at night. No job meant no money. Three weeks went by, and still no work. I was either too young, or had no experience, or didn't look strong enough, or ... there was always an excuse to turn me away before I could even step through the door.

"One night, while walking the street, I came across a bunch of young women standing on a corner. They were laughing and carrying on as though they had not a care in the world. One of them approached me. She said I looked lost, and she offered to help me. I noticed how well-fed she looked, and how beautiful she was. She had strange eyes ... eyes that mesmerized me ... at least that was how I felt at the time ... comforted. I nodded my head, staggered into her outstretched arms, and spilled my misfortune to her. She put her arms around me and held me close. Finally, she took me by the hand and told me she could help me ... she knew someone who would give me a job. I would have followed her to hell and back, I felt so grateful.

"We walked down the street and entered a bar. At first, I thought she was going to get me a job waiting tables, but she walked me through the crowd, to the back of the room. I remember thinking how weird most of the patrons appeared to be, but I didn't have time to ponder because the woman ushered me down a hallway. At the end was a large, wooden door upon which she knocked three times before opening it. Inside the room were six men. The smallest one was seated behind a big desk, but he had the aura of being the one in power ... the others stood at attention behind him. He smiled at my friend and me, and asked her to explain what I was all about. I hadn't realized I didn't even know her name yet, until I heard it for the first time—Renata. She told the man my situation.

"He smiled. I detected something unusual about his teeth, but his mouth closed before I could make sense of what I might have seen. He stood and walked over to me, circling around as though I was some sort of prey. I got shivers up and down my spine, but managed to hold my nerves in check, not wanting to embarrass my new friend. Every so often, the man would run his fingers along my exposed skin, and he would murmur how lovely I was, and that Renata had chosen well. She was to bring me to him later, in his chambers. I was terrified. I had never been with a man before; and here, the person I had thought was going to be my salvation had brought me to this man to be used for his pleasure—at least that was what I believed at the time."

The more Orsolya talked, the shakier she seemed to get. I also noticed how she kept her eyes averted from looking directly at me. I decided to be careful with this girl; it was difficult to trust anyone in the times I was faced with, especially someone who had been working inside Radu's organization. "Continue, my dear, what happened next?"

"When I arrived to the man's chamber, I was surprised, and relieved, he did not ask for sexual favours. There was a tray of food set out for me, and he just watched me for a few minutes as I ate. Then, he began to tell me a fantasy story about living forever. He was charming and made me feel so comfortable. His voice was soothing, too, and I found myself being lulled off to sleep."

"So, he did not take liberties with you?"

"No."

I wondered what my uncle's scheme was, then, and now. Of course, knowing him as I do, I am sure he would have preferred Orsolya to be of the male persuasion. "What happened next?" I enquired, noticing the young woman wringing her hands nervously.

Orsolya heaved a deep sigh. "When I awoke the next morning, I was lying in a bed. I looked around the room; it was sparsely furnished, and I noticed there were no windows. The pillow felt damp. I lifted my head slightly and noticed blood on the pillowcase. I tried to get out of bed, but my head started spinning. I felt a stinging sensation on my neck and reached my hand to the spot. My fingers came away bloody. I don't know how long I sat there, in shock, wondering what had happened to me. I felt so strange."

"How long before someone came for you?" I asked this because I knew the importance of giving a newly turned rogue fresh blood within a matter of a few hours from the initial turning.

"I was confused about the actual time, but Renata finally came into my room. I was happy to see her; I guess I would have been glad to see anyone. The strange, sickly feeling that had come over me wouldn't go away. I thought maybe I was just hungry; I couldn't remember when I had last eaten. But Renata was not carrying a tray of food. She asked if I had slept well; I told her I thought so, but mentioned I seem to have been cut, and asked if she could check it out.

"She smiled and said everything was going to be okay now; I was in safe hands. Then she cut her wrist, and as soon as I saw the blood dripping from it, a strange sensation came over me. I felt drawn to the blood, as though I needed to have it. I could feel my body beginning to convulse. Renata's eyes were fixed on me ... she was smiling ... beckoning me to her." Orsolya's voice began to quiver at this point, and it softened to a barely audible tone. "Renata was gentle as she pushed me back down onto the bed. She told me it was time to complete my transformation. She told me the master was pleased with me. She told me to open my mouth.

"At first, as her blood dripped onto my tongue, I gagged; however, before long something overtook me and the blood started to taste delicious. It was as though I couldn't get enough. I grabbed hold of Renata's wrist and sucked greedily. I felt pain and exhilaration all at the same time as my body transformed into what I now am. So ... that was the beginning."

The room was hushed. I wanted to know more. I thought it prudent not to let Orsolya know I knew how she had come upon Ildiko, wanting to see if their stories matched. "Why did you assist my cousin, then, if you were so grateful to your benefactress? Is this not a betrayal?"

Orsolya gazed into my eyes. I saw the burning embers of her pupils floating in a milky film. I thought I detected a hint of desperation. "It was exciting, at first," she began. "But after a couple weeks, the reality of what I had become began to sink in. Renata deserted me. I guess her job was done. I was given a job in the bar, waiting on the male rogues, doing their bidding ... whatever it might be."

I noticed the girl shudder, and remembered the story Ildiko had just told me. I wondered if Peter had violated this girl, as well.

Orsolya continued. "I began to resent Renata for bringing me to such a beast. I guess there was still a bit of humaneness in me, calling out to reconnect. I learned Renata was a rogue, like me, but she seemed to enjoy a lot more privileges. One day, when she stopped by the bar, I cornered her and asked her about her rank. She told me that if I wanted a position like hers, I had to serve my apprenticeship first."

"Did she tell you what sort of apprenticeship?"

"She didn't have to." Orsolya's bottom lip began to tremble. "Like I already told you, I not only served tables; I served whomever the master wished me to serve."

"When you say 'master', I assume you mean Radu?" I wondered why Orsolya had never referred to my uncle by his name.

"Yes ... I ... I was not allowed to call him by name, yet. I learned that any new recruits were only to refer to him as master until he advised otherwise." She paused, and took another yawning, shuddering gulp of air. "I began thinking more and more of my mother, because thinking of her helped me to preserve a portion of what it was like to be human. I began to dream of ways to escape; I wanted to go home and apologize for leaving the way I had."

"So, you bided your time?"

"Yes."

"It must have taken a great deal of cunning on your part to trick a man such as your new master?" I knew I was baiting the girl, but I still did not trust her. The coincidence of her helping Ildiko escape was just too much for me to believe. "And how was it that you said you helped my cousin to escape?" The trap was laid out.

I noticed a trace of shock cross over Orsolya's face. "I d ... d ... didn't," she stuttered nervously.

"Ah, forgive me," I said, a smile on my lips. "So, how did you come to help, then?"

Orsolya's continued hesitation indicated to me that she was weighing her answer. I saw the look of confusion in her eyes, and knew at that point she must be hiding something. Inwardly, I thanked my cousin for telling me her portion of the story. "Well?" I curled my lips sarcastically. She noticed my displeasure.

Hesitantly, she began. "I could not believe my luck when the master called me to his chambers and told me he had a mission for me."

I raised my hand. "So this was not your idea, or anyone else's, to assist my cousin ... you are actually here because Radu sent you?" I could feel my blood begin to surge through my veins. Orsolya's story was already taking a different twist to the one Ildiko had told me.

The girl lowered her eyes to the floor. "Yes ... and no. Yes, Radu sent me to spy on you and to report back to him, but what he does not realize is, I had been waiting for an opportunity to escape from him and his kind." She paused. "He told me you had a soft spot for beautiful young damsels in distress, and he told me I was to stay close to you and report back any relevant information to him. He gave me a cell phone so we could stay in touch with each other."

I laughed. "And you admit this to me? Are you toying with me, my dear? What game do you play? Did you consider how you were going to survive on your own? After all, you are still an emerging rogue, and I assume your nourishment was being supplied by Radu." I was letting her know I would not be easily duped.

"I play no game with you, Count. To you, I will submit my loyalty."

"Why to me, and not to my uncle?"

She hesitated, again. "I ... I just think, from what little Ildiko has told me, you would be my better option. I realize I cannot undo what has already been done to me. I swear on my mother's life that I will communicate whatever information you tell me to give to Radu. He is a wicked man and his intentions are malicious. He needs to be stopped."

"You do not think he will be wise to you?"

"Not if you give me something substantial to alleviate his suspicions."

"I see." I decided I would not tell her how much her story of how she helped Ildiko escaped differed from what my cousin had told me. I was more than aware there was no time to waste, but I also needed to know if Orsolya knew any details about Radu's plans. Surely, as a bar maid, she would have overheard something in passing. I questioned her on this.

Orsolya was quiet for a moment, looking around nervously.

"It is better you speak, girl, than have me find out later that you knew such information. We have our ways of extracting such … if it is not given voluntarily. One of my family members has talons that, if used to obtain information, would make the strongest of creatures tell all."

Orsolya's eyes opened wide with fear, and her words came hesitantly. "He was planning a strike here … very soon … he was going to release all the rogues from his prisons. I overheard him talking to Peter … Peter is his right-hand … an awful man … vicious … and they talked of the child, once Elizabeth brought him to them … to use him as a pawn to get you to do what they wanted … and then Radu had laughed and told Peter the child was expendable … and they would not meet whatever bargain might have been struck with you … Peter asked about Ildiko … Radu said she was of no real value because she was not significant enough to get you to do anything they wanted … he told Peter that he could have his way with her. Radu, Peter, and Elizabeth are going to head to Canada to seek out the child…"

"Children," I corrected.

"They are really only interested in your son, I am afraid … Radu does not think women, in any role, are of much value." Orsolya kept her head bowed, still not looking at me when she spoke.

"I see." I paused. "I thank you for your information. I'll call Ildiko and she will return you to your room. She will keep watch over you until I decide what to do next."

Once I was alone, I pondered upon Orsolya's story. First, what I perceived to be only a partial truth about how she had come to help Ildiko. Second, how it was she knew such pertinent information about Radu's plans. I felt she was holding something back. I needed my father's council.

When I entered Atilla's room, he was standing by the window, staring out into the night. He turned at the sound of my footsteps.

"Basarab ... you appear worried. Come, sit ... tell me..."

I relayed to my father what I had just learned. He, in turn, called the rest of the family council together and informed them of the happenings. I looked around the room, trying to read what was on their minds, knowing what I had to do, and hoping I would have their approval to do it. "You see, my friends, how important it is for me to get to my children before Radu does?"

My father stepped forward. "I think, under the current circumstances, we should vacate the hotel completely. Despite the fact that Radu is heading to Canada, we cannot trust what orders he might give before he leaves. This girl mentioned he was going to unleash his rogues. I am sure Radu has someone here who can be left in charge while he tries to get to Santan."

"If that is the case, we need to leave enough force here to combat any of Radu's plans," Gara spoke up. There was still an edge to his voice that disturbed me, as though he had not forgiven me yet for the line I had taken in regards to his twin.

I did not hesitate to agree with Gara. "That is where you come in, Gara. Once again, you will be in charge while I am gone. As we mentioned before, those who do not come with me, must go to the caves. If all goes well, maybe we can resolve this conflict elsewhere, just between me and Radu. We will take the girl, Orsolya, with us. She will play a crucial part in this. I intend to ask her to set up a meeting between me and Radu."

"Can she be trusted?" Gara spoke up. "I know she rescued my sister, but you yourself said their stories differed."

"I believe she can be trusted to a point, but I am no fool. She will be watched, and one slip ... well let's just say, the world will be rid of one more rogue."

"As long as that one slip is not too costly for our family," Tardos pointed out. "If I might be so bold, Count, where does that leave the humans who live here? There will be a great loss of life if we are not here to protect them against the rogues."

"Gara will know what to do, and if things get too bad, we will return. Unless we stop Radu, there will be even greater carnage—an apocalypse," I emphasised.

"We can send secure messages out to everyone, letting them know what is happening. Many of the family members have safe places where they can go, so I understand," Kate said.

"I'll help you," Melissa stepped up. "We just await your word, Count."

I gazed around the table again, trying to read the feelings of my council, my most trusted few. One by one, they nodded their heads in affirmation of what needed to be done. "Good, it is settled, we leave tonight." I turned to Kate and Melissa. "Can you procure tickets for us?"

Lardom stood up. "I think it better we hire a private jet. I know someone who can help with that. There are too many of us to take such a risk, mingling with the public, and the likelihood that we will all get on the same plane at such short notice is slim."

"Arrange it." I paused. "Once we arrive, I will get Orsolya to send a message to Radu, asking to set up a meeting. Ildiko will watch her. This girl's story was sad, but how true it really is … let's just say, this is not a time for carelessness—or naivety."

## Chapter Seven

The plane Lardom's friend acquired for us could carry enough fuel to take us all the way to Toronto, which meant we wouldn't have to make any stops. I made a mental note to reward that person well, once this mess was over. *Maybe I should send his reward now ... just in case I don't make it back ... ah, there's no time now.* We landed in Toronto at 4:00 a.m., which gave us plenty of time to make it to my house in Brantford before the sun rose. Lardom's friend had also arranged for some limos to pick us up from the airport.

Max, with the assistance of the women, opened up the rooms and removed all the dust covers. I walked up the stairs and stopped in front of the door that led into the room where Virginia had spent most of her time when I had held her captive. I opened the door and stepped inside. Nothing had been touched since that night when I had left her in a defeated heap upon the floor. I walked over to the bed and sat on its edge. She had been beautiful that night, so open, and giving of herself ... so trusting that I was going to spare her life, maybe even set my wife aside for her. A tingling sensation shot through my loins as a vision of Virginia, standing naked before me, flashed in front of my eyes. She had been wanton that night, holding nothing back from me, and she had received my seed into her and given birth to another child. *How is it that you are so under my skin, Virginia?* I stood and left the room, my mind in turmoil.

I left my father in charge of finishing the house preparations while I went out in search of my connection, the man who had supplied our *needs* when Teresa and I had lived in Brantford. I hoped he had not moved. I knew I was taking a chance, and could get caught in the early morning sun, but I had no choice. We had left Brasov so quickly, we had not had time to procure enough supplies. As I approached his house, I noticed a light in the window. I knocked on the door. A voice started yelling, grumbling, it sounded like.

"Who the heck ... Basarab!" The young man looked surprised. "Never thought I would ever see you again. Come in." He opened the door wide and motioned me inside.

"Hello Sean. You might guess why I am here; I will be in need of your services for a while."

Sean cleared his throat. "I'm not sure if I can get you your stuff, Basarab; my contact has moved away."

"Do you know where he went?"

"No, he left town not long after you did. We weren't actually friends—just business associates."

"I see." I had to think of something quick. We only had enough blood to last us a couple days. "Well, when you were getting my supplies, you must have come into contact with other people besides your main fellow. You know I will make it well worth your while." I smiled when I noticed the greed flicker in Sean's eyes.

"So, how do I reach you?" Sean grinned. I assumed he was remembering I had not liked modern conveniences.

"I have a cell phone," I answered. I noticed the shocked look on his face.

"Bit out of character for you, isn't it, Basarab?" Sean smirked.

I held my composure, only because I was in need of Sean's services. I smiled, stiffly. "Have to get with the times, sooner or later. If you have a piece of paper, I will write the number down for you."

Sean went over to the counter and rummaged around until he found a paper and pencil. He returned to the table and handed it to me. I scribbled the number down. As he took it in his hand, I closed my hand over his and looked him directly in the eyes. "This number is for you only; no one else is to be privy to it," I directed. "Understand?"

Sean nodded.

"Good. I expect to hear from you by tonight." I glanced out the window and noticed I did not have much time to get back to the house. "I'll see myself out."

As the door closed, I heard a woman's voice ask Sean who had stopped by at such an ungodly hour. He had answered her, 'just an old friend.'

When I returned to the house, it was quiet. I assumed everyone was resting. As I made my way toward the door that led to the basement, Max stopped me. "Count, I am worried about my daughter."

I was worried, as well, especially since Elizabeth seemed to have returned to Brasov without Teresa. "I don't think you have any need to worry, Max; Teresa can look after herself." I didn't want to alarm Max further, understanding how he must feel not knowing where his child was. I turned, to continue on my way down to the basement to get some rest. There were times when sleeping in my coffin, on the earth from my homeland, was more restful than sleeping on a regular bed.

Max reached out and grabbed my arm, a bold move on his part. "She wasn't with Elizabeth, was she? I fear something horrible has happened to her."

I withdrew Max's hand from my arm. "I told you, Max, she will be fine. Don't worry. She will show up when she is able to. For now, I need my rest so I can think clearly about getting to my children before Radu does."

As I lay in my coffin, I felt a sudden apprehension come over me. I realized I had not heard from either Vacaresti or Teresa. Vacaresti might have returned to the hotel in Brasov, and if that were the case he would get the message that we were in Canada. He would have the sense to use his cell phone and give me a call—I hoped. However, despite my reassuring words to Max about his daughter, I, too, was deeply worried about Teresa and what had happened to her. After all, despite much of her unseemly behaviour, we had had many good years over the centuries. I envisioned when she was a child, innocent and trusting of me, her benefactor ... of the early years when things had been so happy, when she was growing up in my castle...

*Come, Teresa, you will not have your treat until you finish your studies.* I had looked down at her with the sternest look, the one I used in order to get her to do what I wanted.

*I am tired, Count; can I not finish this tomorrow?* Teresa pouted.

I relaxed, as I always did when she begged. *Okay, come to the kitchen and I will have your father give you your treat. What is it you would like today?*

Teresa had sat a moment, thinking, and then told me she would like the grandest chocolate cake, layered with red cherries. I told her that I would see what could be arranged, but it might take a while to create such a masterpiece; so, in the meantime, she should finish her schoolwork. And then I had laughed and left the room.

Later, I had watched with amusement as Teresa devoured the chocolate cake. It seemed to melt in her mouth, the steam drifting through her parted lips. Cherry juice trickled down her chin. I had laughed and wiped it off with my finger, and then offered her the droplets. She had giggled. *You have it,* she said to me, pushing my finger toward my mouth.

*You know I cannot eat the same things as you, Teresa. One day, maybe, you can be like me and we can enjoy our meals together. Would you like that?*

*Very much so! But what of my father? Would he not want to have meals with me, as well?*

*He will not care. Your father serves me.*

*Why does my father have to serve you?*

*I saved his life. His own family left him to die in my forest. He was ill, very ill. I nursed him back to health, and he has been obliged to me ever since.*

Teresa used to ask me about her mother, Lilly, as well. I had always downplayed my role in Lilly's demise, not wanting the child to know it was I who had destroyed her mother. As far as Teresa was concerned, Lilly had never been much of a mother to her. Eventually, she stopped asking.

Then came the day I struck the bargain with Max. He had begged me, again, to release Lilly from the spell I had put her under. Max had said he would give anything to have his Lilly released from her living hell. I had countered with ... *Anything? Even your daughter?* To which Max had replied: *Even my daughter.*

At the time, Teresa had been too young to understand what her father had done; but from that day forward, I began to pay extra attention to her. I told her delightful stories, and told her we would be together forever.

*Forever is a long time,* Teresa had giggled as she wrapped her arms around my neck.

*Yes, it is ... we will have forever to be together ... I will give you immortality ... after you give me a son or two.*

Teresa had looked at me strangely when I said that, but I had brushed the hair away from her face and laughed and hugged her close to me. She would be safe with me. So, thus it was that she grew up in my household, a pampered princess. It did not even faze her when she attended her mother's funeral. Max had been devastated, and appeared to grow old overnight. There were several months, after Lilly's death, when it seemed he had abandoned his daughter, as well—but she had me, and life was good.

Only once, Max tried to take Teresa from me, leaving in the middle of the day, but I tracked them down at night, and snatched her from her father's arms, setting her on the front of my saddle, folding my arms around her protectively. I had ordered Max home, only sparing his life because I did not wish to upset Teresa. I did not want her to know what a beast I could be when it suited me.

Even though the actual wedding papers had been signed when Teresa was but a child, I had agreed not to consummate the marriage until she was of a suitable age. Our wedding, with all the pageantry a young woman could desire, took place on Teresa's sixteenth birthday. She could not have looked happier. I had the most exquisite gown made for her. The inner layer was made of the finest silk, covered by a net of diamonds. I had allowed Max to walk her down the hallway and into the dining room where the ceremony was to take place. I was waiting for her, a bright smile upon my lips. My father, Dracula, Stephen and Evdochia were the only family present at the wedding. My father performed the nuptials.

*Do you, Basarab Atilla Musat, take this woman, Teresa Lilly Vajda, as your wife—to love, cherish, and protect from now and into eternity?*

*I do.* I had looked down upon my bride, and my body had tingled in anticipation of what was to come on our wedding night. Her blossoming into womanhood had not disappointed me.

*Do you, Teresa Lilly Vajda, take this man, Basarab Atilla Musat, as your husband—to love, cherish and obey from now and into eternity?*

*I do.*

I had slipped a gold ring, inlaid with diamonds, on Teresa's finger, and then taken two more pieces of jewellery from my pocket, fastening a diamond necklace around her neck and a matching bracelet on her wrist.

*Do you, Teresa Lilly Vajda, come to this man, Basarab Atilla Musat, out of your own free will, out of love for him?*

*I do.* At the time, she had no idea about the details of the bargain her father had made with me, and she was unaware that to be the true bride/queen of a vampire, the woman had to come of her own free will.

*Then, I pronounce you husband and wife. Who has been joined together here today let no man or woman tear apart. You may kiss the bride.* My father had stepped back, a smile on his lips.

For the first time, my lips covered Teresa's. Later, when we were alone, Teresa informed me that her maid had told her things, and had even showed her some ways in which she could pleasure her husband. The maid had also told my bride that I would look after the rest of the lessons, I was an exceptional teacher. Teresa had asked me how a maid would know such a thing, but I had laughed and changed the subject, and I had dealt with the maid later.

I no longer was Teresa's benefactor, for she had become my life partner, my true love. Until Virginia.

~

I was returned to the present by the sound of my cell phone ringing. I sat up and dug into my pocket, hoping the caller was Sean. "Hello."

"Basarab!" It was Vacaresti. "What is going on? Teresa and I have arrived at the hotel, and everyone is gone."

My spirits rose—Teresa was with Vacaresti—she was safe! "We are in Canada," I stated. "I thought you would have called me before returning," I added.

"There was no time," Vacaresti stated. "And I did not think we would be returning to an empty hotel."

"We had no choice. Radu and some of his people are on their way here to find my children. I had to get to them first. We also thought, since Radu was here without his rogue army, that maybe we could resolve this whole affair without any more bloodshed. But, I want you to get out of the hotel; there is still the possibility that Radu has left some specific orders to be implemented while we are away. Anyone who did not come with me has gone to the caves."

"Do you want us to return to Canada?"

"That would be best," I replied. "But, what I need to know from you, now, is if you have any idea where my children are."

I detected the hesitation in Vacaresti's voice: "I do not know exactly ... I know they are in a cottage somewhere in a place called Port Dover. Carla will know…"

"Carla?"

"The young female doctor the family has employed on occasion."

"Ah … yes … I have never actually met her."

"It is her cottage."

"How do I reach this Carla?"

Vacaresti asked me to wait a minute while he found the number. A few minutes later he returned to the phone and gave me Carla's number. We chatted briefly, and then Vacaresti asked if I would like to talk to Teresa, she was right there. I declined, saying I would speak with her when they arrived to the house. I did not want to waste any more time. I needed to get to my children!

After hanging up the phone, I dialled Carla. She picked up on the fourth ring.

"Hello?"

"Is this Carla?" I needed to make sure I had the right person.

"Yes."

"This is Basarab Musat; I believe you are aware of who I am?"

"I am. How can I be of service to you?"

"I need to know where my children are."

"I am supposed to know such information?" I heard the hesitation in her voice, the mistrust creeping into her words.

"According to Count Vacaresti, you do."

"I see."

Carla was annoying me. I needed to make it clear to her the importance of me reaching my children as soon as possible. "There are people on their way to Brantford that wish the children serious harm. In fact, there is no limit to what they will do to secure Santan and Samara; and, I believe they will not keep them alive once they have what they want."

"They are safe…"

"How foolish of you to even think they are safe! Only I can protect them!"

The line was silent for a few seconds. I could hear Carla's breathing. I began to pace, giving her time to think. It was at that point I realized her loyalty was lying with someone other than me, which could be dangerous. But the more I thought about it, I realized that someone was probably my aunt.

Finally, "I will need to get back to you," Carla said.

I was ready to explode. *How dare she take this situation so lightly*! "I don't think you understand, Carla; I am the ultimate authority in this family; I need to know where my children are, and I need to know now! It would be in your best interest to give me that information, and quickly. I have my ways of finding things out, and it would not be in your best interest if anything were to happen to my children because you refused to tell me of their whereabouts! Time is of the essence!"

There was another moment of hesitation, and then: "One cannot be too careful; I needed to make sure you are who you say you are before I pass over any information."

"Then come to my house; I assume you know where it is?" I was glad she was being cautious. That bode well for her.

"Yes ... what time?"

"How long will it take you to get here?"

"About thirty minutes."

"Then that is the time you should be here. I will be waiting for you." I hung up the phone, and went in search of my father. I needed to fill him in on what was going on, and tell him I had heard from his brother and Teresa, and they were on their way back here.

"I believe your brother's wife is with the children," I began. "She thinks she can protect them, but she has no idea what she is up against."

"She probably fears for the mother, too."

"Radu has no interest in Virginia. I care not what happens to her at this point, either," I lied. "But, at the same time, I wish her no harm. I will make that clear when I have secured my children. In fact, I will even allow her to come with us, stay on as their nanny for a time—at least until this whole mess is over."

"Virginia is a beautiful woman, if my memory serves me correctly," Atilla interceded with a knowing look.

I looked at my father and smiled. "That she is, Father—and fruitful." We both laughed, allowing our guards down for a few seconds. "Anyway, this doctor, Carla, she is on her way here with the information. I can understand her caution, wanting to make sure she is handing it over to the right person."

My cell phone went off. I looked at the call display. It was Sean. I motioned to my father that I needed to take the call. "Hello."

"Basarab?"

"Yes."

"I can have your supplies by tomorrow night; I hope that is soon enough. Shall we meet at our old rendezvous?"

"I'll call you to arrange the time and place." I clicked the off button and turned to my father. "Good. We won't starve while we are here. Now, I must go down and wait for Carla; she should be here any minute."

"Would you like me to accompany you to get the children, son?"

At first I was going to say no, but realized it didn't make any difference if he did come along, so I nodded and left the room. As we stood in the foyer, watching for car lights, I noted the additional creases around my father's eyes. I had never seen him look so tired. Aging was something we vampires were not supposed to do, but I guess stress can take its toll on even the likes of us.

I heard the car approach, but saw no lights. Carla must be taking extra caution, still unsure of whom she might be meeting. "She's here," I informed my father.

A few minutes later a young woman was running across the yard. Even though I had never met her personally, I had heard of her brilliance in medicine, and that she had assisted Count Balenti a number of times. I opened the door as she approached. She appeared to be carrying something behind her back.

"Carla?"

She nodded. "Basarab?"

I nodded. She pointed to my father. "Who is this?"

"My father, Count Atilla." I closed the door after she stepped all the way into the entrance. "Follow me," I ordered, leading the way to the library. Once inside, I did not take time for pleasantries.

"Tell me, were you the one who delivered my other child?"

"I was." I thought I saw the faint impression of a smile.

"I am told it is a girl; is she beautiful?"

"Very."

"Does she look like her brother?"

"A bit, only she has fiery red hair and eyes that could burn a hole through anything, and a temper to go with it all."

I heard my father chuckle.

"Is she as extraordinary as I assume my son is?"

This time, Carla beamed. "Both your children, Count, are exceptional—mentally, they are far advanced for their ages, physically, as well. The physical attributes, though, are more in the mobility area, not so much size-wise."

"I see ... Now if you would be so kind to tell me where they are?"

"It is better I take you there. I have installed a superior monitoring system at the cottage, and unless I say the password and punch in the codes at the final gate, the alarm will activate, and the security company will be at the cottage within minutes, unless they are called and given the password."

"Could you not give me the information I would need?"

"No, the keypad has been set up for voice recognition, as well."

"I see." I turned to my father. "We will need to call a limo in order to accommodate all the passengers we will be bringing back. Can you arrange that?"

Atilla nodded and left the room. I turned to Carla. With my father out of earshot, I was curious to know how Virginia was. "How is Virginia?" I enquired.

Carla looked up at me, and I could see the startled expression in her eyes. "She is ... let me see ... how should I say it ... yes ... she is terrified. Virginia is terrified of you coming for her children; she is terrified you won't come for them and that someone else will be knocking at the door. You see, she knows you will not hurt them, but she also knows you will take them away from her. But, having known her for a while now, I have to say that Virginia is a strong woman, and she will do whatever it takes to protect those children."

I have no idea why I asked my next question, but it had been nagging at me ever since we had heard from the young man who claimed to be Virginia's friend. "Who is this Randy to her?"

Carla grinned. I thought I detected a sly look in her eyes. "Randy is her landlord. Well, technically he is the nephew of the owner of the place where Virginia was living; but, he is also madly in love with her, and with the children."

I stood and turned my back to her. I did not want her to see the fury that had crossed over my face at the mention of Randy being in love with Virginia and my children. *Why should you care, Basarab? You do not love her! Maybe I do ... well, you shouldn't ...* I gave my head a shake and turned back to Carla. "I see."

Carla continued. "Santan is quite attached to Randy—Samara not so much, although recently, she has been warming up to him. She likes me, though."

I thought I detected a hint of smugness in her voice when she mentioned how my daughter liked her. Atilla returned to the room and mentioned the limo would be arriving within a few minutes, and that he had informed Stephen of what was going on.

"I told him we would be returning in a few hours, and hopefully we would have the children with us. I also took the liberty of asking him to contact some of our people in the area, making them aware of your presence here, and that there might be a need of their support should things get out of hand."

~

The trip to Dover was conducted in relative silence. Carla was not one much for talking on the way, and I became immersed in my own thoughts. We had been travelling for about thirty-five minutes when Carla mentioned we were almost there. She pointed to a grove of trees in the distance. "That's the laneway."

I unbuckled my seatbelt and sat forward in my seat, eager to see my children—and Virginia, if I were to be completely honest with myself. I caught Carla glancing at me, from the corner of my eye, but paid no attention. This was the moment I had been dreaming of for months—the moment when I would hold my son in my arms again. *And your daughter*, an inner voice reminded me.

# Virginia
## Chapter Eight

I glanced over at the beds where my children should still be sleeping. They were empty. Panic gripped me. I couldn't lose them again so soon! *Where are they?* Suddenly, I heard laughter coming from outside the room door—Santan and Samara, and Randy. I smiled. He was up early with the children, keeping them occupied while I got some extra sleep. *How thoughtful of you, Randy.* I stretched and got out of bed.

I pulled on my jeans and a shirt and headed out to greet the day. Randy was sprawled on the living room floor, building a Lego house with Santan. Samara was perched on the couch with a colouring book and crayons. She had a serious look on her face. She scowled at me when I entered the room. Was she ever going to come around to liking me? I couldn't understand why my daughter seemed to hate me so much.

Santan, on the other hand, jumped up right away and ran to me. He grabbed my hand. "Come and see what Randy and I are building! Would you like to help?" He plopped down on the floor beside Randy. "It is a replica of our house," Santan added, "Where we used to live with Randy."

"Very nice," I said. "You are becoming quite the architect, Santan."

"Like Grandpa Alfred," he stated with a proud look.

I smiled. Alfred must have told Santan that he had studied to be an architect. "Well, right now, your mama needs coffee and something to eat. Smells like someone is already busy in the kitchen," I added.

Randy smiled. "I would take the credit if I could, but Adelaide beat me to it. I think she is whipping up some pancakes for breakfast, as well. I kind of suggested they would fill the empty spot in my stomach." Randy paused a moment and a mischievous grin spread over his face. "I think she has a soft spot for me."

I giggled. "Who wouldn't have a soft spot for a cute face like yours?" Before Randy could respond, I headed into the kitchen. I was definitely in a chipper mood. "Good morning," I greeted Adelaide who was busy pouring pancake batter onto a griddle.

"Good morning," she replied, not turning around. "The coffee is ready if you would like some," she added. "Help yourself."

"Don't mind if I do." I started to hum as I poured my coffee. I walked over to the entrance of the living room. "Want a coffee, Randy?"

He looked up and smiled. "Sure … you know how I take it."

I noticed the puzzled look Adelaide threw me as I took Randy his coffee. I was still having a hard time figuring out why I was so happy—probably because I was reunited with my children, and, we were safe for now, I reasoned. However, my mind kept flitting back to scenes from my dream … pictures of me entwined in Basarab's arms, his voice telling me how much he missed me, telling me I was his love. I handed Randy his coffee, not daring to look him in the eyes for fear he read my mind. I turned and headed back into the kitchen.

"The first batch of pancakes is done," Adelaide informed. "Can you gather the troops?" She headed to the cupboard.

I jumped up. "Here, let me get the dishes for you, Adelaide … will Alfred and Carla be joining us?"

"Carla left last night after you went to bed. She said she wanted to return to her office and tend to her patients before they found another doctor … said she would be returning later today. Emelia decided to go with her, figuring nothing much would be happening so soon. Alfred has gone for a walk and will eat later."

I set the table before calling Randy and the children to come for breakfast. Randy wolfed down the pancakes as quickly as Adelaide piled them on the platter, but Santan and Samara picked at theirs. After breakfast, I cleaned the dishes for Adelaide, telling her she had done enough already. When I finished, I rejoined Randy and the children in the living room.

"Looks like a beautiful day," I opened with. "How say we take a walk down to the water? I purchased special hats for the children ... you know, those ski mask style hats that cover the face. I think they will have fun watching the half-frozen waves splashing up on the shore."

Randy looked up. "Sounds like a great idea ... and it will help me wear off some of those pancakes, too." He patted his stomach. "Let's set this over here, little buddy, so it's out of the way." Randy picked up the house they were building and set it on an end table by the couch.

Within twenty minutes, we had the children and ourselves bundled, and were headed across the yard to the stairs that led down to the lake. The children were ahead of us, excited to be stretching their legs. Randy reached over and took hold of my hand. I don't know why I didn't stop him. Maybe I was just trying to enjoy the reality of the current moment. After all, a dream is a dream, and I was living in the real world. Randy was real, and, he was human.

"I could get used to this life," Randy said.

"What life?"

"This life with you and the kids."

I withdrew my hand. "Randy, you know we can't go there. I may have to pull up roots in a moment's notice ... maybe less. I can't relax for a second, knowing that there are so many different forces after my children. In fact, I've been thinking, I need to get right away from here—far away."

"We could go together." Randy raced in front of me, turned, and walked backwards so he could face me. "I would protect you with my life, Virginia ... you know that."

"Have you not listened to anything Emelia and Vacaresti said to you? After what you witnessed in your house, did it not get through to you that you would never be able to protect us against these creatures? Randy, sometimes you are such a child!" The words were out of my mouth before I could stop them. I didn't mean to hurt him, but he was being so naive.

Randy surprised me by grabbing me by the shoulders. He lowered his head and his lips found mine, and he drove his passion forward. I was breathless when he finally released me. I staggered back and almost fell into the snow. "There, Virginia … did that feel like the kiss of a child?" Before I could answer, he turned and headed after Santan and Samara who had just reached the top of the stairway.

Despite how shaken I felt from what Randy had just done, I knew I needed to pull myself together. I wiped my hand across my mouth, hoping that would remove the tingling sensation on my lips. It didn't. I quickened my pace and caught up with Randy and the children just as they stepped onto the beach. Randy ignored me as he flopped down in the untouched snow and began to make a snow angel.

Santan was laughing, and he dropped down not far from Randy and began to do the same movements. I watched as the two angels took shape. Suddenly, Samara screamed, and she started to kick snow at her brother.

"No, Santan … no angels … angels bad!" Samara's eyes were gleaming through the tiny holes in the ski mask.

Randy and Santan scrambled to their feet, and messed up the snow angels. Santan walked over to his sister and took her by the hand. Within seconds, Samara was calm again. My mind went back to the past Christmas when Samara had thrown a temper tantrum when the Christmas story had played on the T.V. special.

Randy, once again, saved the day. "Okay! Who is ready to make the biggest snowman ever?" He began rolling a snowball, and the children joined in. As the ball grew larger, Randy turned to me and grinned. "Aren't you going help?" he asked. "How can we make the biggest snowman ever, if you don't help us?"

I hesitated a moment more, and then, to my surprise, Samara called out to me. "Mama help us ... now!"

Randy burst into laughter. "Well, that's a first!"

"It sure is," I returned as I joined the revelry.

Time passed quickly as the four of us got busy making our snowman. We didn't stop at one, though. Samara wanted to make a whole family, and Santan agreed with her. We stepped back in order to view our handiwork ... four snowmen ... one super large one, one slightly smaller, and two little ones—a perfect family.

"Do you want me to run up to the cottage and grab some hats and scarves for our snowmen?" Randy asked.

"I don't..." I began, but Santan cut me off.

"Yes, Randy! Frosty the Snowman always wore a scarf and a hat!" Santan began to sing the Frosty song, and to my surprise, Samara joined him, as best she could.

I shrugged my shoulders. "You heard the children, Randy. Don't be long, though, it is starting to get cold, and it must be getting close to lunch."

Randy took off up the stairs, taking them two at a time. I sighed and touched my lips again. They weren't tingling anymore, but the memory of Randy's kiss still lingered in my mind. I turned to the children who were busy packing snow on the little snowmen. "How say we play a game of fox and goose?"

"What is that?" Santan asked.

"Come, I'll show you," I replied as I began to make some tracks in a fresh patch of snow. "First, we create a bunch of tracks, ending in the middle, which will be the home base. If the goose makes it to that spot, it is safe."

While we finished the tracks, I explained the rest of the game to the children. They decided they wanted to be foxes, and I could be the goose. I managed to outmanoeuvre them for a few minutes before they caught up to me. We tumbled into a pile of snow just a few feet from the safe zone. When we finally stopped laughing, I sat up and checked my watch. Randy had been gone far too long. It should not be taking this amount of time to fetch a few scarves and hats. I noticed Santan and Samara were shivering and decided it was time to head back to the cottage.

"Well, I think Randy has deserted us ... probably for a cup of hot chocolate and some of those leftover pancakes! What do you say we go and join him?" The children ran to me and eagerly grabbed hold of my hands.

"Samara love hot chocolate ... Randy bad for not sharing!" Samara pulled on my hand, trying to pull me to the stairs.

The closer we got to the top of the stairs, the more apprehensive I became. I had a feeling in my gut that there was something terribly wrong. Randy wouldn't have abandoned us for a cup of hot chocolate. By the time we reached the top, I decided to play another game with the children. I had sworn to protect them, and the last thing I wanted to do was walk into the cottage if something was amiss.

"Let's play one more game," I suggested.

Santan looked at me, puzzled. "I'm cold, Mama. Can't we just go in the cottage?"

"We will," I tried to assure him, "But we are going to play a game to get there. We are going to sneak up on Randy and scare him!"

"Fun!" Samara shouted. "Scare Randy ... fun!"

I put my finger to my lips. "Shhhh ... we have to be really quiet. We don't want Randy, or anybody else, to hear us. Now," I dropped to my belly and began to wiggle across the snow, "Follow me. And stay close."

I could hear the children giggling as they wormed their way after me. I was happy for that because it meant they were looking at this as a game. The closer we got to the cottage, the more anxious I became. I noticed the curtains were drawn shut; they had been open before we had left for the beach. I knew, because I had opened them to let the sunshine into the rooms while we were gone, something we couldn't do when the children were there.

I crept over to one of the windows at the side of the cottage, hoping it would not be covered. Luck smiled on me. I inched my way up, motioning to the children to keep down, and telling them to hush their giggling. What I saw through the glass stilled my heart! Alfred and Adelaide were tied to chairs, and it appeared they had been brutalized. I looked down at my children, fear gripping hold of me. Who would do such a thing to these old people? And, where was Randy? There was only one thing for me to do; I had no choice now. I eased back down to where the children were patiently waiting for my next command.

"Santan ... Samara ... we are going to have to prolong this game. Santan, I need you to take your sister over to the shed and hide in there until I come for you. Can you do that for Mama?"

Santan nodded. I was grateful for his lack of questions, but Samara started to open her mouth to speak. Santan quickly squeezed her hand, and she was silent. When I was sure they were safely in the shed, I made my way to the side door. It opened easily, and I slipped inside. The place was quiet. I inched along the wall, heading toward Alfred and Adelaide.

Adelaide saw me first, and her eyes told me how frightened she was. I lipped out the words: "Anyone else here?" Adelaide shook her head, no. Quickly, I went to my friends and untied them, taking the gags from their mouths first.

"What happened here?" I shouted, not meaning to. "Where is Randy?"

Adelaide was rubbing her wrists. I noticed how red they were. "You better sit down for this ... wait ... where are the children?"

"I'll be right back. They are hiding in the shed. I felt something was wrong when Randy didn't come back to us."

A few minutes later, I returned with Santan and Samara. They were both shivering. Despite the fact that I did not want to see my children suffer, I was glad to see the cold actually bothered them. It indicated that they were human, too, not just vampire. Adelaide, despite what she had just been through, had the foresight to start preparing some hot chocolate for the children. By the time I had their coats and hats off, two cups filled with warmth were sitting on the table. She poured a third one for me. I noticed how her hands were shaking.

"What happened?" I asked again, after taking a sip of my drink.

"Wait until you are finished here and we can send the children to their room to play. I don't want to scare them," Adelaide replied.

Santan scowled. "We won't be scared," he said. "Has my father come for us?"

"No ... it was not your father, and I would rather talk to your mama first." Adelaide's lips closed firmly, indicating she would say no more until the children were out of earshot.

Santan's question, *has my father come for us*, bothered me. Was Basarab on his way? Would that be a good thing? Maybe for my children, but probably not for me. I was sombre as I watched my children finished their drinks. I took them to the room we had shared the night before, turned on some music, and took out a couple of books for Santan to read to Samara. "I will fill you in on what has happened as soon as I know," I assured Santan, noting the distressed look in his eyes.

When I returned to the kitchen, both Adelaide and Alfred were waiting for me. I joined them at the table. It seemed like forever before Alfred began to relay what had happened...

"We had just finished our breakfast when the alarm went off. I raced to the computer to see who the intruder was. A small black car was approaching the house. I asked Adelaide if we were expecting any visitors, and she told me, not to her knowledge. At first, I thought to go after you, and tell you not to come up here until we figured out who it was, but Adelaide said she would answer the door and see who it was first. I was to wait by the back door and be ready to sneak out and warn you if Adelaide coughed three times ... that was the sign we had arranged if the person at the door was unsafe.

"As soon as I heard the coughs, I grabbed my coat, but I wasn't quick enough. The voice that stopped me was familiar, one I had heard within the past few days, one I had wished never to hear again. It was Tanyasin."

"Tanyasin!" I exclaimed. "How did she find out where we were?"

Alfred shook his head. "I have no idea, unless, when we were discussing where to take the children, back at the house, Tanyasin hadn't actually left. Maybe she was lingering somewhere close by and heard us speak of this cottage. With her powers, it wouldn't have taken long for her to find us.

"She ordered me to stop. I turned around and saw she had Adelaide. What else could I do, then, but pray you would not return any time soon. She dragged Adelaide to a chair and tied her, and then motioned for me to sit in the one next to my sister, all the while running her nails along Adelaide's neck—a warning to me that if I made a wrong move, she would end my sister's life. I did as she bid.

"When she had us both securely tied, she asked us where the children were. When neither of us answered, she walked behind Adelaide and began to rake her claws around Adelaide's neck again. I noticed a few specks of blood. 'Tell me where the children are!' she screamed, 'or I shall hurt your dear sister!' Adelaide told me not to listen to her, and Tanyasin smacked her across the face so hard a red welt showed up immediately. My mind was racing as I tried to think of something that would appease Tanyasin enough to get her to back off, maybe even leave.

"Tanyasin approached me and leaned over, staring me right in the eyes. Her foul breath overwhelmed me. She asked me where I had been going, and I told her I had been going to go for a walk, something I usually do before lunch. She sneered and said she didn't believe me, and asked me again where the children were. I told her they were not here, they had left a few hours earlier, but I had been sleeping. I had no idea where they were going. She told me not to toy with her, she was no fool." Alfred leaned back in his chair and nodded to Adelaide, who took over the story.

"Tanyasin looked at me and said she figured I had probably been awake when you and the children left the cottage. I told her I was, but you had not confided in me, either. I even went as far as to tell Tanyasin I thought you didn't trust any of us anymore when it came to the security of your children, and I alluded that there was the possibility you might have taken off altogether. She didn't buy that scenario, either.

"She began smacking us, demanding we tell her where you might have taken the children. Surely you would have a base to retreat to; you just wouldn't wander around without a direction, especially with two small children! But we remained steadfast, not giving an inch. Tanyasin appeared about to give up and leave when we heard the back door open, and Randy shouted out a hello. Tanyasin hissed at us, telling us not to say a word. It would not bode well for us if we did.

"Poor Randy … when he entered the room, his face turned white as a ghost. He was quick to take in the whole scene, and he demanded to know what was going on. Tanyasin seemed to be confident in her control of the situation, and she told Randy she needed some information … information she was sure he possessed. He asked her what possible information he could have that would be of value to her, and she told him not to play dumb. Tanyasin struck Alfred and me again, and told Randy not to mess about—she didn't have time for games—he knew where you and the children were, and he would tell her. If he didn't, Alfred and I would not see the light of another day.

"He still tried to evade her question, but after another slap to us, he told her when he had awakened that morning, you had already left, taking the children with you. He had no idea where you might have gone. He didn't think back to his house, but there was a possibility you might have—at least until you could figure something else out. He said you had been going to move and had found another place, but hadn't told him where. Tanyasin still wasn't buying the story, and she told him so. She said that you had been at Basarab's house, and Randy quickly said Vacaresti and Ildiko had shown up and taken you and the children before you could make your move. That seemed to satisfy Tanyasin. She began to pace. I noticed Randy's fists flexing, and I prayed he would not do anything rash.

"Tanyasin picked up on his nervousness and asked him what he had been doing outside. She said, 'You were with the children, weren't you?' He was quick to respond, saying he had been out exploring the Lake Erie shoreline, something he did every morning after breakfast. Tanyasin was still pacing, and, even through my swollen eyelids, I could tell she was caving. Randy settled matters by suggesting to Tanyasin that he take her to his house to see if you had gone there to pick up some of your things. They might get lucky and catch you there. He made one stipulation, though, asking Tanyasin not to harm us any further."

I didn't realize I was crying until I spoke. The words choked out of my throat. "So, what you are saying is, Randy sacrificed himself for us?"

"Pretty much," Adelaide replied.

"What should we do now?" I asked. "We can't stay here. Tanyasin will know soon enough that I am not in Brantford, and she will return. God knows what she will do to Randy."

"I wouldn't worry about him; he will think of something," Alfred piped up. "He's a smart young man."

I stood up and walked over to the sink. "We need to call Carla and let her know what is going on. You said she would be back later this afternoon with Emelia?"

"That's right," Adelaide confirmed.

"We need them to get back now!" I walked over to the phone and dialled Carla's office number.

The secretary answered. "Hello … Doctor Gibson's office."

"Is Carla … I mean, Doctor Gibson, in?"

"I am sorry, Doctor Gibson was called away suddenly," the secretary replied. "Is this an emergency?"

I hesitated, not knowing quite what to say. "Ah … do you know where she went?" I finally asked.

"She didn't say."

"Did she leave with another lady?"

"No, Doctor Gibson's guest is still here."

"Might I speak with her, then, please?"

There was a pause on the line, and then: "I am afraid Doctor Gibson's aunt is still resting, and I was told not to disturb her."

"I need to speak with her, and I need to speak with her now. It is a family emergency!" I could hear the decibels in my voice rising. I prayed this woman would not give me a difficult time.

"Just a moment ... may I inform the lady who is calling?"

"Virginia ... her niece."

The phone went on hold. Classical music filtered through the lines. I waited for what felt like an eternity. Santan and Samara appeared in the doorway of their room—staring at me—demanding with their eyes that I tell them what was happening. I put my finger up, indicating for them to wait a minute. Then, I heard Emelia's voice.

"Virginia?" What is going on?" She sounded tired.

I filled Emelia in as quickly as possible. She told me she had no idea where Carla had gone. "Do you still have a car available to you?" Emelia asked.

"Randy's," I replied.

"Good ... get out of there, then. There is no point in my trying to get to you now; I wouldn't make it before Tanyasin returns. And, you can be assured she will return quickly once she discovers you are not at Randy's house."

"Where should I go?"

There was a pause, and then: "Book yourself and the children into a hotel—preferably a large one. Once you are settled, call me. Use a different name, and pay cash. Do you have enough?"

"Yes ... what about Adelaide and Alfred?"

"By all means, take them with you. Tanyasin will not think twice about killing them when she finds out she has been duped. I hope Randy has a plan of escape, for he might be doomed, as well."

I felt a clutching on my heart at the mention of Randy's name, and the potential fate he might be facing on my account. "Is there nothing you can do, Emelia, to save him?"

The line was silent for a moment. A heavy sigh sounded in my ear. "I will see what I can do. Right now it is crucial for you to get moving. I will await your call." The receiver clicked. I looked around me, at the children, at Adelaide and Alfred who had entered the room.

"Well?" Alfred asked.

"We need to get out of here, now! Pack only necessities and meet me at Randy's car within ten minutes."

"Where are we going?" Adelaide enquired.

"We'll decide on the way. Emelia instructed me to get to a hotel. Once we are settled in, I am to call her." I brushed past Adelaide and Alfred and headed into the room I was sharing with my children.

Santan approached me, an anxious look on his face. "Where is Randy?" His voice sounded demanding, but there was also a hint of worry in his tone.

I turned to my son and knelt down in order to look at him face to face. "Randy is not here right now, Santan … but I am sure he will be okay."

Santan crossed his arms, and his eyes burst with red flames. "I won't leave here without him."

I sighed. "We have no choice. It is not safe for us here right now."

"Why?" Santan's eyes remained locked on mine.

I reached out and put my hands on my son's shoulders. "Santan, I need you to trust me right now. I just spoke with your Aunt Emelia, and she told me to get you and Samara out of here. Grandpa Alfred and Adelaide are coming with us. In fact, by now, they are probably waiting for us at the car. Please, help me gather some things and let's get out of here."

In a normal world, I would not have had to have such a conversation with a toddler. But, Santan was not a typical child. The wisdom that swam in his eyes was beyond my comprehension. Finally, he turned away and began to gather some things together, putting them in his little satchel. Samara left, but I could hear her chattering away in the living room. Better that way. I could pack quicker. Within five minutes, I was headed out the door with my children, and, as I had figured, Alfred and Adelaide were already waiting for me by the car. I threw my bags in the trunk, and then got in behind the wheel, still with no idea exactly where I was going to go.

"Where do you think?" Alfred asked from the passenger seat.

"Hamilton, maybe. We should be able to find a large hotel there where there will be lots of people around. I think that is why Emelia suggested a large one—less chance of anyone trying to cause a commotion. We'll try for one in the downtown, in the hub of activity." I was winging my idea, but as I spoke it through, it sounded like a good plan.

Alfred leaned back in his seat. "Sounds good."

I glanced to the rear seat to make sure the children were properly secured. They were both dressed in heavy clothing, and wearing their ski masks. I hated that I had to bundle them up so much, but they were both still so sensitive to sunlight. Adelaide was squeezed between Samara and Santan. I started the engine and put the car into gear, praying all the time that we would make it out safely.

For some reason, the laneway seemed a lot longer going out than it had been when I had arrived. Possibly because of all the snow ruts I was forced to navigate around. And the trees ... they reminded me of another lot of trees that had always tried to thwart my attempts of freedom. Finally, I saw the road. I decided the best route would be through Dover, and then down Hwy 6. It would be the most travelled. As I put my blinker on, I noticed a black limo approaching the laneway. Somehow, I knew it was headed to the cottage. I wished there were a dark tunnel I could escape into, or a cloak I could throw over the car in order to make it and all those in it invisible. But there was no tunnel, and there was no cloak. There was just the closing space between the Volkswagen and the limo.

I tried to speed up, to get out of the laneway before the limo reached it; however, as though someone in the other vehicle had sensed what I was about to do, it sped up and was at the end of the lane before me. The limo came to a stop, blocking my exit.

I looked frantically each way, hoping to see a possibility of escape through the ditch. Unfortunately, both sides dropped too steeply, and I would never make it through without getting stuck. I slammed my foot on the brakes, bringing the car to a stop. My hands gripped the steering wheel. My heart hammered against my chest, as though it were trying to break free. The pain I was feeling, physically and emotionally, was excruciating. Pins and needles shot up and down my left arm and tingled across my face.

There was no place to run.

## Chapter Nine

A back door of the limo opened and I saw Carla stepping out. I relaxed, but only for a fraction of a second because then I saw a fully robed figure exit from the other side. It strode with intention toward where I was sitting, waiting. I didn't think to lock the doors, not that it would have mattered ... I instinctively knew who was approaching. No door would keep him away from his son—his children. My door opened.

"Virginia ... darling ... what a pleasant surprise." The count's voice cut, like a knife, into my heart. Despite the fact he had said it was a surprise to see me, I doubted it was.

I noticed the count's eyes scanning the occupants of the car, coming to rest on the children in the back seat.

"Santan." I detected the trembling emotion in the count's voice.

"Hello, Father." Santan's voice was strong and steady—detached.

The count reached a hand toward Santan. I noticed in the rear-view mirror how my son shrunk away from his father.

The count did not force the issue. He shrugged slightly, and then turned to his daughter. "And you must be Samara?"

Samara giggle. "Yes, Papa ... me Samara." And she giggled again, reaching her arms to her father.

The count pulled away from the window and opened the car door. He motioned for me to get out. I knew I had no choice. I turned off the motor, and as I stepped out of the car, I dropped the keys in my coat pocket. I noticed Carla on the other side of the car, opening the door for Alfred. The count reached into the backseat and undid the children's seatbelts. He lifted Samara out and held her in his arms. Santan crawled out and ran to me, putting his arms protectively around my leg. Adelaide, now that the children were out of the car, made her way out and waited by her brother.

Carla directed Alfred and Adelaide toward the limo. I didn't have to be told that was where I was to head, as well ... at least, I hoped. I turned and reached for Santan's hand. I felt the firmness of his grip on my fingers. I sensed the closeness of the count, and heard the crunch of his feet in the snow behind me. Santan crawled into the limo and sat beside Alfred. That left only one place for me to sit. I suddenly realized there was another person in the limo—Atilla.

He smiled and patted the seat beside him. "Come, sit beside me, my dear."

The count followed me in and settled on the other side of me. Samara remained on his knee, her arms clutched around his neck, her eyes looking up at him adoringly. However, her father's eyes never left Santan, but she didn't notice that. It was difficult for me to watch, but, on the other hand, I was seeing the count's Achilles' heel—his son. I knew, at that moment, more so than ever before, to protect Santan, Basarab would sacrifice whatever was in his power to surrender.

Basarab knocked on the glass partition between the passengers and the driver, and the car began to move. I knew where we were headed—back to my prison—back to *his* house.

~

Santan sat motionless in his seat, glaring at his father. Carla was between Alfred and Adelaide, her eyes downcast. I wondered if she couldn't look at me because she had betrayed my whereabouts to the count. Then again, the reality was that she probably had no choice. Adelaide was by the window, and she had turned her head and appeared to be watching the scenery through the darkened window. Alfred rested his head on the back of the seat, his eyes were closed. I noticed Basarab closely studying the elderly pair.

"What happened?" he asked with a note of concern in his tone.

"Tanyasin paid a visit to the cottage," I answered. "She beat them, trying to get information about Santan and Samara. Randy and I had taken the children down to the beach area and were building snowmen, and Randy had gone up to the cottage to get some hats and scarves for our creations. When he got there, Tanyasin had Adelaide and Alfred tied up. She turned on Randy, thinking he would have the information she wanted. According to Adelaide, Randy insinuated that I might have gone back to his house to get some of my things."

"Where is Randy now?" Basarab asked.

"With Tanyasin," I replied. "And hopefully still alive. He bought us some time to get the children to safety…"

"Well, there is no place safer for the children to be than with me." Basarab looked over at Carla. "When we get to the house, you will tend their wounds." He nodded his head in the direction of Adelaide and Alfred.

Carla nodded.

We continued on in silence for a bit. I wondered if the fact that Tanyasin was after his children had any impact on Basarab's plans. Of course, I had no idea what his actual plans were. The question was … was Tanyasin working with Radu and Elizabeth, or was she working for her own self-seeking purposes?

Basarab loosened Samara's arms from his neck, although he kept her sitting on his lap, and he leaned forward toward Santan. "How are you, son?" When Santan didn't respond right away, the count continued. "You have nothing to fear from me, Santan. I have come to protect you."

"I know, Father."

I was surprised by the assuredness in my son's voice. He continued to amaze me with his understanding of situations. At the same time, I noticed Santan reach for Alfred's hand. His action did not go unnoticed by his father.

Basarab leaned back in the seat and even though he did not pursue further conversation with Santan, I noted that he continued to study his son. Even though Samara didn't take her eyes off her father's face, she remained quiet. My mind was spinning, and, despite finding myself once more in the clutches of Count Basarab Musat, my only thoughts were of Randy and what was happening to him. As though Atilla was reading my thoughts, he patted my knee and smiled at me. I looked up into his eyes, thinking I saw a flash of warmth there, but that wasn't possible, was it? Was there a vampire on earth that had an ounce of warmth in them—other than Emelia?

Finally, we pulled into the laneway of Basarab's house. Atilla was the first to exit the limo, and I noticed him handing the driver some money. It must have been a substantial amount from the look of surprise on the driver's face. Atilla reached into the backseat, extending his hand to me. *Better his, than Basarab's*, I thought as I accepted the help. The count followed me, still holding Samara, who had once again encircled her arms around his neck. Santan jumped out quickly and ran to me. I took hold of his hand. Alfred and Adelaide came out after Carla, and I saw the devastation that Tanyasin had wrecked on them, now that the beating had had time to settle in. Their faces were bruised and swollen, and my lips trembled as I tried to hold back my tears. I looked away.

As the limo pulled out of the driveway, we were ushered toward the house. Once inside, the count pulled the ski hats off the children. I heard the gasp in his throat as he laid his eyes on Samara, fully, for the first time.

"You are beautiful, indeed, Samara!" he exclaimed.

She giggled and gave him a big, sloppy kiss on the cheek. "Thank you, Papa."

As Basarab set Samara down, I noticed a familiar figure walking toward us. Max. The pain I detected in his eyes was the same as it had always been—denoting the conquest of the ravages of time.

"Max," the count turned to his servant. "You have prepared the rooms?"

"Yes, Count."

"Would you please escort Virginia to her old room; I will attend to her later," the count ordered. "Right now, I would like to spend some time alone with my children."

I was thinking I should protest, however, I realized it would do no good. What the count wanted, the count got. That is the way it had been previously; why would I think anything had changed? I sighed and followed Max. As I was climbing the stairs, I heard Basarab talking to Carla.

"I want to thank you for your assistance, Carla. You will understand, when the time comes, it was the best decision. Please inform my aunt to return here. Tell her no harm will come to her, and also that Vacaresti is on his way. I am sure they will be happy to see each other."

"As you wish, Count. I will leave as soon as I have tended to Adelaide and Alfred."

Basarab nodded. "I would like you to return with Emelia, as well," he added. "We might have need of your services before this ordeal is over. I trust you know what discretion needs to be taken?"

"I do." Carla's response was barely audible at this point because I was almost at the top of the stairway.

I didn't need Max to show me where my room was; I could have found it even if I were blindfolded. "What is to happen now, Max?" I asked when we reached the doorway.

"Why do you always ask me, Miss Virginia? You know I have no knowledge of what Count Basarab will do, or not do. The fact you are still alive is a good omen, though. Of course, I assume he would not have done away with you in front of the children." The chill in his words sent shivers throughout my body. "However, I don't think you need to worry at the moment; the count has more important things to focus on than you." Max turned to leave.

I grabbed his arm, feeling his bones through the fabric of his shirt. He had lost weight. "What of my friends, Adelaide and Alfred?"

"I have prepared rooms for them, as well," was all Max said as he pulled his arm from my grip and stepped out of the room, closing and locking the door on his way.

I stood for a moment, surveying my surroundings. It was as though time had stood still in the room. But, it hadn't. Time had pushed forward. Time had awarded me another child, and just maybe that was a blessing. Maybe the count would see me as an asset and not kill me, even if he had his children now. Maybe he would want more children. I could do that. If I did, it would mean I would be able to remain with the children I already had.

I walked over to the window and gazed out through the bars. I straightened my shoulders and breathed in deeply. I was alive, but for how much longer? I was still at the count's mercy. I walked over to the bed and laid down, the weariness of the day having taken its toll on me.

*"Virginia ... help me...* a plaintiff voice infiltrated my dream world. I gazed around, trying to locate the source. There was a movement in the corner of the room. I walked toward it, unsure who it was. The voice had a familiar pitch to it. *Virginia ... please ... h...h...help me ... No! Don't!* I stopped. *Not you, Virginia ... I need you.*

Out of the shadows appeared a bloodied hand, followed by another, and then Randy's battered face came into view. I ran to him and folded him into my arms. I raked my fingers through his tangled curls, and they came away coated with blood. *Randy...* I gasped out his name. *What has happened to you?*

*Tanyasin.* His voice reeked of despair.

I assisted Randy to his feet and guided him to the bed in the centre of the room. He fell onto the covers. There was still enough light filtering into the room for me to be able to see the whole of the damage Tanyasin had dispensed. I had thought vampires were the most vicious of creatures, but what she had done to Randy! I helped him to stretch out, and then left the room, returning a few minutes later with a basin of warm water, cloths, and towels.

To my surprise, Randy was sitting up, naked and as unblemished as a newborn baby, lounging against the pillows he had piled against the bed's headboard. He was grinning from ear to ear. The basin of water crashed to the floor, followed by the towels. My eyes scanned his lean, youthful body. I felt the heat in my loins—it had been so long since I had been with a man. Randy beckoned me forward with his eyes. I knew what he wanted, what he had wanted for a long time. Hesitantly, my feet began to move in a direction I knew would have no admirable end.

When I reached the edge of the bed, Randy took hold of my hands and gently pulled me toward him. He covered my face with kisses, and then ventured further. He was gentle, yet firm, knowing exactly what he was doing to me—what he wanted from me. Slowly, I succumbed, and began to move with his desire. Time allowed us the exploration of uncharted territory as we discovered what we had kept hidden from each other for so long. We discarded time, plunging forward into our desire for each other, consuming each other with all the pent up fury of lust.

As we lay together, Randy stroking his fingers up and down my body, I could not help but to think how happy I finally was. This was normal. Randy was normal. I would not have a child with him that I would have to hide from the world. We could live a normal life.

Suddenly, the door smashed open, hitting the wall with the force of a typhoon. *Virginia! My darling ... my little bird! What is it you think you are doing?* The count's voice shattered my moment. He strode into the room, heading straight for the bed. Darkness saturated the room. He reached for me and dragged me off the covers. Then, he turned to Randy who had stood valiantly, ready to fight for my honour.

The count threw back his head and roared in laughter. *You think you are a match for me?* He grabbed hold of Randy's raised fists and twisted him to the floor. I could see the pain in Randy's face as he struggled to overcome the powerful creature that was dominating him. The count glanced at me for a moment, and then lowered his head to Randy's neck. Fear propelled me into action, and I lunged for the count, trying to loosen his grip on Randy. The count swept me away with one hand, hurling me halfway across the room. And then, he drained the warmth from Randy.

I screamed ... and screamed ... and screamed...

"Miss Virginia, wake up, Miss Virginia!" Max was shaking my shoulder with a panicked urgency. "What is wrong, Miss Virginia?"

I turned away from his face. "Nothing, Max ... just a dream," I mumbled into the pillow. "Just another dream."

"Can I get you anything?"

"No thanks, Max. I just want to be alone." I was doing the best I could do to hold back my tears. I didn't want Max to see me crying. I heard the door close softly, and the lock clicked into place.

Slowly, I crawled out of bed and made my way to the window. The trees were there, bare of leaves, but still guarding the house. Night was beginning to creep into the day. Soon, *they* would be up. Would he come for me? Or, now that he had his children in his embrace, would he depart, leaving me behind again—dead or alive?

My thoughts turned to the dream I had just had, still vivid in my mind. Randy ... I couldn't let anything happen to him. He was just a young man, who, like me when I had checked out this house, had been in the wrong place at the wrong time. I had ventured up the lane and found him home. He had rented me an apartment, without asking a lot of questions about how I looked––a caped woman carrying a child in a basket. I had allowed him to become entwined in my life, and the lives of my children. Somehow, if I ever saw him again, I had to convince him to leave, to get away before the count realized just how much Randy meant to me and the children—especially, Santan!

## Chapter Ten

I paced around the room, like a tigress, thinking ... thinking. What power did I wield over the count that would compel him to spare my life ... to listen to me long enough that I could reason with him? If Randy should happen to return from wherever he was, I needed to assure the count there was nothing between Randy and me—and, nothing of any significance between Randy and Santan. I knew I didn't have to worry about Samara; she had made her position quite clear as soon as she met her father.

I paused my pacing to steal another look out the window, not that I thought any of the landscape might have changed since my last glimpse. This time, though, I noticed a set of headlights approaching in the driveway. I wondered who it might be. Could Randy have escaped from Tanyasin ... was he coming to rescue me and the children? But, how would he know I was here?

My spirits fell when I caught a glimpse of who exited the car—Vacaresti and Teresa. They strode with purpose across the lawn, heading quickly for the front door. I ran to the bedroom door and turned the knob. Of course, it was locked. How could I have thought otherwise? But, I could still hear sounds from here, and hopefully learn something of value.

I was rewarded with a great deal of commotion from the lower hallway; however, I found it difficult to detect familiarity in any of the voices. Then, I heard Teresa's voice, demanding to see Basarab. Someone told her he was still with his children. I imagined the scowl she probably tried to suppress.

I heard footsteps approaching my door, and I stepped away quickly. When the door opened, I was sitting on the edge of the bed, staring toward the window. Even though the door had been opened, Max knocked to get my attention.

"Miss Virginia, the count requests your presence in his study. Follow me, please." Max turned and headed down the stairs.

What choice did I have? Basarab had my children, and I was determined not to leave this place without them. I hurried my pace. Max stopped in front of the study door and knocked. I crowded close to him, having noticed several figures still lingering in the foyer. All, with the exception of Vacaresti and Teresa, were new to me.

"Enter," came the command from beyond the door.

Max pushed the door open, and we stepped into the room. The count was sitting in one of his large winged chairs, Samara on his lap. Santan sat in a chair across from his father. I was at such an angle that I couldn't read my son's face. The count motioned for me to take a seat.

"That will be all for now, Max. Before you start preparing supper, though, please inform the others I will be with them in a few minutes. I understand my uncle and my wife have arrived."

"They have, Count." Max nodded, turned and left.

"Virginia," the count began, "The children are incredible. You have done a superb job. I am pleased."

Samara glowered at me. "See, Mama, Samara in … in … credible!"

The count laughed, and gave Samara a squeeze before setting her off his knee. "Your papa has some business to look after right now, Samara. You will stay here with your mother and your brother until I return for you."

I could tell, from the look on Samara's face, she wasn't happy about being left with me. Santan, still, had not said anything. The count looked at his son, reached out his hand, and then, as though he thought better of it, withdrew his hand, turned, and left the room. As soon as he was gone, Santan leapt off his chair and raced to me. I was thrilled at the amount of love my son displayed for me. However, his next words deflated me slightly.

"Any word from Randy, Mama?"

Sadly, I shook my head no, fighting the tears that threatened to burst forth at the mention of Randy's name. Just as

I was about to ask Santan how he was, and what his father had talked to him about, there was another commotion at the front door. Despite knowing I probably shouldn't, I walked to the study door and cracked it open. I knew from experience, I would have a clear view of the front entrance.

The first familiar face I saw was Angelique's ... and then, Randy. Santan was by my side within seconds.

"Randy is here," he whispered excitedly. "And he is with Angel."

I was about to ask him how he knew, but changed my mind. He knew because of who he was. I nodded, and whispered: "Yes, it is them."

Before I could stop him, Santan was out the door, running to Randy, shouting his name. "Randy! Randy!"

Now that the door was fully open, I had a clear view of the scene. Despite looking dishevelled, Randy opened his arms for Santan, and my son crashed into him. "How's my little buddy?" I heard the familiar voice question.

"Much better, now you are here, Randy," Santan replied.

I glanced to where the count was standing, scrutinizing the situation. The look on his face indicated he was not pleased with this turn of events. But he recovered quickly. "So, you are the young man that called and spoke to my father?"

Randy, as though Basarab was an old friend, stepped forward. "I am." He shifted Santan to one arm and extended a hand to the count.

The count took the proffered greeting, holding Randy's hand for longer than I felt was necessary. The two men stood, eye to eye. I hadn't realized how close they were to being the same height. Finally, the count released his hold. "Welcome to my home. We will try to make you as comfortable as possible until it is time for you to leave." The count turned to Angelique who was waiting patiently by the door.

"My dear Angelique ... how is it that you have come upon this young man?"

"It is a long story, my count. Could we go somewhere where we can sit? Randy and I both have some information you might best be aware of."

We can use my study," the count replied. "I will have Virginia take the children up to their room."

Boldly, I stepped forward. "I would like to hear what has happened. Randy is my friend, as is Angelique."

I could tell by the look on his face that the count was about to deny my request, but Angelique must have sensed the importance of me being there when Randy told his story. "It will not hurt if she joins us, Count. Surely someone else can see to the children for a short time."

Basarab hesitated, slightly, and then acquiesced. "I will have Max take them to the room he has prepared for them, and he can call upon Adelaide and Alfred to sit with them." The count paused briefly. "Actually, I would like my father and some of the others to join us, as well. That will avoid having to repeat your information to them later. We will meet in the dining room instead of my study. How say, in ten minutes?" Angelique nodded. The count turned to Max, who had appeared in the hallway. He always seemed to just *be there* when the count needed him. "Max, please set out some refreshments for us after you have seen to the children."

"I will bring the tray to the dining room, now, and then return for the children," Max said as he headed to the kitchen. I knew I would not be partaking of the *refreshments*. Nevertheless, I hoped Max might remember me and Randy, and our taste buds. I could feel the grumbling in my stomach.

Samara had followed her brother out of the study, and she was standing by her father's leg, looking up at him adoringly. He reached down and scooped her into his arms, and then turned to Teresa. "Is she not a delight, Teresa?"

Teresa smiled stiffly. I knew she was trying desperately to look pleased. She reached out to Samara, touching her on the arm. Samara pulled away and buried her face in her father's shoulder. "Don't touch!" she screamed.

Teresa backed away, looking startled. The count burst into laughter. "Well, it appears I have a little spitfire on my hands here." He pried Samara off his shoulder and held her out, facing him. "That was not very nice," he said, trying to keep his voice stern. "This is your mother."

*How dare you! Teresa is not her mother! I am!* It was all I could do to keep the thoughts from starting a verbal war I knew I probably would not win. Was the count making sure I was still aware of my place? To my surprise, Santan stepped forward, confronting his father.

"Teresa is not our mother, Father." He pointed to me. "She is." Santan's face had a serious *do not mess with me* look.

Basarab did not laugh this time. He set Samara down and squatted before his son. I detected the tenseness in his body. "Yes, you are correct, Santan. Virginia is your biological mother. But, you are my children, and Teresa is my wife. Therefore, she is your mother."

Santan's next question sent a brief shockwave through the room. "What are you going to do with my mother, then?"

"I will determine her fate when the time comes to decide. For now, Santan, you and Samara will go to your room. I need to speak with your friend, Randy, and with Angelique."

Santan stared into his father's eyes for a moment more, then turned and walked back to Randy. I noticed the angry flicker cross through the count's eyes before he turned to those still in the foyer. "Shall we?" He motioned to the dining room.

Max returned and took the children by the hand. I was surprised at how easily they went with him, especially Samara. Although, she did hesitate at first, but one look from the count, she followed Max. Santan did not hesitate at all, but I could tell from the look on his face that he was not overly pleased.

I watched my children climb the steps and disappear from my sight, before I turned and entered the dining room. Randy had waited by the door for me. I gazed around the table, where many of the vampires had already gathered. The count was seated at the head of the table, Atilla to one side of him, Vacaresti to the other. Basarab motioned for Randy and me to sit in the two empty chairs by Atilla. Atilla patted the one beside him as he looked at me and smiled. As I sat, I noticed the bottles on the table, and the wine glasses at each setting. There was no sign of other sustenance for Randy or me.

The count turned to Angelique, who was sitting beside Vacaresti. "What news do you bring me of your sister?"

Angelique heaved a sigh. "Not good. I have not only had my eyes on the Dracul family, I have closely watched the steps of Tanyasin, Elizabeth, and Radu. Before coming here, the first time, I went to my sister and tried to reason with her. I had heard rumours of Radu's true plans, for not just Elizabeth Bathory, but for my sister, as well. Tanyasin has been so blinded by her hatred and revenge that she has failed to see the whole picture. Actually, they all have their secrets. Rumour has it, Elizabeth has a hideaway that even Radu does not know of—only she and her recruits. Jack is always in the shadows, lurking, playing both sides. He pledges his allegiance to Elizabeth, and to Radu, and believes neither one of them know of his deceit. However, he is too stupid to realize neither one of them has much, if any, use for him. Once he has served their purposes, he will be eliminated. By which one of them, time will tell. There have been moments I have actually felt sorry for him."

Angelique looked directly at Basarab. "As you know, I have also watched over Virginia and the children. They knew me as Angel. I am quite taken with your daughter, Samara, and I can see she is going to be quite a handful," Angelique chuckled. "I realized things were coming to a head in Transylvania, but I felt that before I headed to Brantford to get Virginia and the children to a safer place, I should pay Tanyasin a visit. I knew Radu had sent William Palmer to Greece to fetch my sister back to Brasov. I felt it was my duty to warn Tanyasin about her possible demise.

"As much as there is distaste in my mouth for what she has done to your family, as I mentioned, I know Radu is using her, and once she serves her purpose, he will kill her. Tanyasin is my sister—blood is blood—I had to try and reason with her. As I approached Tanyasin's door, I heard chanting from inside…"

*"Brother Beasts, present yourselves to me*
*Open your portals, allowing me to see*
*Where the child and the woman doth reside*
*Let your infinite knowledge be my guide*
*Brother beasts, I have been your faithful friend*
*Help me bring my tormentors to their final end...*

"I heard the hysteria in her voice, and wondered when she would understand that love was more potent than hatred. She has lived a miserable life because her heart has been filled with hate all these years. I knocked on the door, but Tanyasin did not answer. I decided to leave and try again later."

At this point, Angelique stopped and looked around the table at the vampires I knew she had sworn to protect. I noticed how they all regarded her with looks of respect. It crossed my mind to ask Angelique, later, how she and Tanyasin had lived all these centuries. What were they, if they were not vampires? Gypsy witches?

Angelique drew a deep breath and continued. "I would like everyone here to understand that Tanyasin was not always as she is now. There was a time when she was beautiful and happy, and in love. She was envied by male and female alike. It was a miserable day for many a young Gypsy man the day Tanyasin married Ahren. There never had been a more stunning bride. The day she found she was with child was another day her beauty shone brilliantly. Blaz was born on a cold winter night, a fine, healthy boy that grew up into an honourable young man. How things changed the day the Gypsy wagons turned and travelled through Dracula's lands."

I was watching the count as Angelique relayed her tale. Was that a twitch of impatience, I detected, at her lengthy story? His question to her confirmed my thoughts. "Why do you bore us with this past knowledge of Tanyasin, my dear? Do you try to draw sympathy for her? If that is the case, then you are at the wrong table."

I heard a couple of throats clear, and when I glanced down the length of the table, I noticed some of the vampires nodding in agreement.

Angelique didn't hesitate in answering. "As I said, I need you all to understand her state of mind—what fuels her loathing of this family. If there is some way we can reach her, we might be able to sway her to our side. I have never been able to seek the kind of revenge my sister sought, despite the heartache I felt over the deaths of my brother-in-law and nephew. I never found true love, as my sister had, either. Men loved me, but they left as quickly as they appeared. Finally, like my sister, I delved into the spirit world; but I chose the path of light. It became my salvation, and a means to help those I have come to love."

I couldn't help noticing how Angelique looked at Atilla when she talked of those she had come to love. Did he hold a special place in her heart? Was he the real reason she helped the vampires? After all, according to his diary, when he had sought out Tanyasin to break the curse so his beloved Mara would not die, it had been Angelique who had comforted him. I glanced at Atilla. He had met Angelique's eyes, and I thought I detected tears in his. Would their love for each other be the salvation of the Dracul family? I wondered.

Angelique went on. "I knew my plane for Canada was leaving soon, but I decided to make one more attempt to talk to Tanyasin. This time, she opened the door, but she was not pleased to see me. She asked me why I had come; I said we needed to talk. She said she had nothing to say to me, I had drawn my line in the sand the day I sided with the Dracul family. I tried to tell her that her life was in danger, but she laughed and told me she had not cared about her life since the day she had taken her husband and son down from the stakes they had been impaled upon. She described how she had worn a cloth over her face so as not to breathe the stench of their rotting flesh. Tanyasin reminded me how she had sworn vengeance the day she had laid them in their graves, and she said I had taken the pleasure from her by lightening her curse.

"I told her she has had her revenge, but it has come at a great loss of innocent lives over the centuries. And now, with what Radu was planning, there would be many more lives lost. I told her she not only had Radu to contend with, Elizabeth was plotting her own brand of evil, and that I thought neither one would have a place for her once all was said and done. Tanyasin guffawed at me, and told me Radu and Elizabeth would probably destroy each other, which would leave her right where she wanted to be—in power.

"He will dispose of you, when you have served your purposes, I pointed out to her, but she emphasised to me that Radu was no threat to her; he was just a little man with a big ego. She was going to kidnap Dracula's great-nephew, offering the child up as a sacrifice. She had convinced herself that Dracula would not wish any harm to the child; however, if he cared not, she was sure Basarab would succumb to her will in order to save the boy. He would not choose his uncle's life over that of his son's! Tanyasin is convinced she will sit on the throne of power and watch Dracula, the dog, as she calls him, cower before her. She will make him kneel down at her feet, and cast him the rotted scraps from her table, knowing that even the trash will not sustain him. She was hysterical!

"I tried to convince her that those of your family who had learned to live with the curse, and who wished to exist in harmony, were not dangerous to humankind, but others, such as Radu and Elizabeth, were. I dug for any compassion that might still be in her, playing on the memory of her husband, Ahren, and her son, Blaz. I asked her to reflect on how they would feel about what she was doing. They had been gentle and peaceful men, not vengeful. But, Tanyasin didn't care. She ordered me not to involve her beloveds in this. I had not heard her Ahrens's last words, gurgled through the blood flooding his throat, giving her leave to exact revenge."

"On Dracula, maybe," Atilla intervened. "But on the entire family?"

I glanced at the man sitting beside me and saw the pain in his eyes. I knew he was remembering his wife, Mara. I had also detected the slur of bitterness as he said Dracula's name, and I began to wonder how many times over the centuries Atilla might have thought of destroying the man who was ultimately responsible for the death of Basarab's mother.

Angelique nodded. "Yes, my dear, old friend. It appears that is what my sister thinks. She threw in my face that I had never known true love. I, in turn, told her that she had long forgotten its true meaning. Then I left, but not before telling her I prayed the gods in the After World might inject wisdom in her mind before it was too late. As I closed the door, I heard Tanyasin screaming that she was a witch, a black witch, much more powerful than the white witches. Tanyasin has no idea of the power I have amassed over the last few hundred years—no idea at all."

"This is quite the story, Angelique," Basarab commented, "But what is it you actually thought you were going to accomplish by trying to reason with your sister?

I noticed the continued tenseness in the count's face, the twitching of his facial muscles.

"I had hoped to gain an ally, one with an inside ear to Radu," came Angelique's response. "I was mistaken. So, I did what I have always done; I set out to protect your family—your children. My aim was to get to them before Tanyasin or Radu and his people did. My intention was to hide Santan and Samara somewhere safe until this battle was over."

I couldn't help noticing Angelique had said she was going to get the children to safety, but she had failed to include me in her plans.

"My flight was delayed for two hours in England, but I refused to leave the plane. I thought to use the time to grab some sleep. I dreamed. In my dream, I saw the big house with iron gates, the name on the gate read *Wynarden*. Under the name was inscribed: Previously known as Yates's Castle, built in 1864. I floated outside the house, and then the mist took me inside, down into the basement where I saw Virginia locked in a room. From there, I floated up to the main floor and noted Ildiko in the dining room with one of the children—Samara. Onward I went, up the stairs, to the top floor, to the room at the end of the hall. The door was slightly ajar, and another door beyond that was also open. I heard a youthful voice through the opening, and ventured closer, opening the door wider.

"That is when I saw Santan. He was just standing there, chanting away in the ancient language, staring upward into the stars. He turned as I stepped onto the widow's walk. He welcomed me, and told me he had been calling for me. He asked if I had come to rescue them. I told him, yes. He smiled and said Samara might prove difficult, but he would handle her. I asked if anyone else was in the house besides Ildiko, and he told me there wasn't. He mentioned his Uncle Vacaresti had gone in search of Aunt Emelia. Santan added that his uncle was a good man, but Ildiko was not of the same heart.

"Your son is wise beyond any child I have seen born of mortal women over the centuries, Basarab. Most are much advanced from the normal human baby, but none so much as Santan. There was no specific ending to my dream; it just floated away in the mist that swirled around the widow's walk. But, it had told me everything I had needed to know. When I awoke, I whispered a prayer that I would not be too late."

We all listened as Angelique filled everyone in on what had transpired at the house. I relived each moment as she told the story. Basarab listened intently, his eyes never leaving her face. She said her intention had been to return to Brasov. "I felt it was time you were brought up to speed on what had just transpired because I was beginning to think you would be the best one to protect the children from Radu. Emelia would be able to buy only a limited amount of time, and Virginia would be no match for the likes of the creatures who were about to descend on Brantford.

"Something was nattering at me, though. Tanyasin had vanished from the house, and I began to have second thoughts about returning to Brasov. Where had my sister disappeared to? What was she up to? In the turmoil of everything, she had slipped out, and my inner voice told me she would still come after the children; she would not give up so easily. I told the cab driver to turn around and return to the house. I hoped I would be able to pick up Tanyasin's trail.

"When we pulled up to the house, I got out of the cab and asked the driver to wait for me; I was just going to take a quick look around. The sun was sparkling off the fresh snow. I noticed several other tire tracks in the parking lot—obviously there had been some activity after we had left because I had erased all our tracks. I walked around the house, looking for traces of footprints exiting the house from other than where we had all left earlier. Luck was with me. I found a set of tracks leading out from a side door, and I followed them to a narrow street, and to a set of stairs that lead up to another street. I followed the tracks to the top, and that is where my luck ran out. The tracks had disappeared in the footsteps of daytime pedestrian traffic. By the time I got to the cab, I had decided to drive over to the house where Virginia had been living, hoping Randy and Ildiko might still be there. As we drove up the laneway, I noticed numerous tire tracks coming and going, but when we reached the house it appeared deserted. Once again, I asked the driver to wait. I walked around to the back door and knocked. I waited patiently for a few moments, and then tried the doorknob. It opened easily, and I stepped inside. What a mess!

"I looked around the room and knew there had been some sort of struggle. I walked around slowly, searching for clues. In the living room, I noticed a picture frame facedown on the floor. I picked it up and flipped it over. Santan and Samara smiled at me from behind the cracked glass. I continued my search. I noticed the door to Randy's apartment was open. I called out Randy's name. No answer. I closed my eyes and sniffed the air.

"I picked up the scent of vampires, rogues, and a human. Some scents were fainter than the others, which told me they had not all been at the house at the same time. One scent was particularly strong—a male rogue's. I went outside and studied the foot tracks, getting down on my hands and knees and sniffing each one. The male rogue's were the strongest, but he had left alone. The human, whom I assumed was Randy, had left with the vampires; the female rogues, had left with a female vampire, I assumed Ildiko. I cast a spell, so I could see what had happened.

"Elizabeth Bathory and her friend, Delphine, appeared. Elizabeth was questioning Ildiko. Delphine went through a door and searched through the other part of the house. When she returned, she was shaking her head. The three of them left.

Another vision appeared—Teresa and one of Radu's men, Thomas. It appeared he was controlling her, and then he advanced toward her, a malicious, hungry look in his eyes. I saw the fear in hers. Suddenly two doors flew open, from different parts of the house, and Thomas was being attacked, first by Randy, and then by Vacaresti, who took over after Thomas thwarted Randy's attempt to save Teresa. Teresa was cowering behind Randy. Everything went misty for a few seconds, and when it cleared, Thomas was lying on the floor, and the other three were gone.

"I decided to go to Carla's office in Hamilton to get the address for the cottage. As I was about to climb back in the cab, I picked up another scent, one that had not been in the house—Tanyasin's! I knew, then, that my hunch had been correct ... if she was still around, the children were in grave danger. My sister would not stop until she had them in her clutches. I asked the driver to hurry. However, by the time I arrived at Carla's office, I found it empty, but I could tell there had been a lot of activity there because of the tire tracks. I managed to open the back door, and went straight to the main office where I rummaged around until I found the cottage address. The cabby's smile was bigger than a quarter-moon when I gave him the Dover address.

"When I arrived at the address, I noticed the numerous footprints and tire tracks at the end of the lane, and Randy's abandoned Volkswagen sitting there with its doors still wide open. I ordered the cabby to drive around it and head to the cottage. The alarm was blaring by the time we reached our destination. I raced inside and searched for a shutoff pad. I noticed a computer in the corner of the room, and pictures of the cottage and surrounding area on the screen. I didn't waste any more time, thinking I would most likely need a specific code to shut the alarm off ... I pulled the computer plug.

"As I looked around at the chaos that had taken place in the room, I picked up Tanyasin's scent. I sat down on a chair, closed my eyes, and chanted a spell that would show me what had happened. I couldn't believe how my sister had tortured Adelaide and Alfred. On the other hand, I was proud of Randy for what he did, sacrificing himself to allow Virginia to get the children someplace safe." Angelique stopped and looked over to Randy. "You can take it from here, Randy." She sat down.

Randy stood. I noticed his hands were trembling as he glanced around the table. I wondered if he was thinking the same thing I was. Here we were in a roomful of vampires … what did fate have in store for us? I had come to the conclusion that as long as my children were safe, I didn't care much what happened to me. Did Randy feel the same way? He began to speak, slowly at first, picking up his momentum with each word.

"I knew I had to get Tanyasin away from the cottage. I was hoping Virginia would be smart enough to realize something was out of kilter when I didn't return to her and the children. I don't think I have ever been so frightened in my entire life. Tanyasin was one wicked looking bitch! I was surprised when she took my bait. What I was going to do when we got back to my place, I had no idea; but I knew Adelaide and Alfred would fill Virginia in on what had happened, and they would advise her to get as far away from there as possible.

"All the way to my house, Tanyasin ranted on and on about Dracula, and what he had done to her husband and son. I tried to express sympathy for her plight, and a couple times I thought she actually smiled—hard to tell for sure with all those tattoos she has. Of course, as I knew it would be, my house was empty. Tanyasin stormed through all the rooms, cursing all the while. I thought that maybe I should just get out of there, take the car and flee. But, I feared Tanyasin would try and make her way back to the cottage, and if Virginia hadn't left yet … well, I didn't want Virginia to have to deal with Tanyasin on her own.

"Once Tanyasin realized the house was empty, and that I had duped her, she turned on me like a banshee! She screamed and called me names I have never heard before. I tell you, I was scared shitless! At one point, I thought I was a goner, for sure! But then, she seemed to calm. She came up to me, real close, and told me I would be sorry for what I had done, but that she wanted me to see the full power she could wield. I was to get her back to the cottage and watch what she was going to do with the mother of Basarab's children … before I joined her. She told me what she had done to Adelaide and Alfred was nothing compared to what she had in store for Virginia and me!"

    I noticed the flush in Randy's cheeks. I also realized he was trying to keep himself together. My heart fluttered at what he must have gone through in order to protect me and the children. Randy glanced around the table again, his eyes coming to rest on Angelique. "I listened, as has everyone here, to your story about how you tried to dissuade your sister from her way, but I have never seen or felt such evil in all my life. I can't believe you and she are sisters."  Randy returned his gaze to the count. "The return trip to the cottage was definitely not enjoyable. Tanyasin was cursing … well, it seemed like cursing … I couldn't understand a word … I felt suffocated by her words … it was all I could do to pay attention to my driving.

    "When we arrived to the cottage, and she saw the car at the end of the driveway, she went even more berserk. I was frightened she might have a heart attack because the veins on her neck were popping out so much ... actually, I think I prayed she would have one … but she didn't. When I stopped the car at the cottage, Tanyasin rushed over to my side, dragged me from the vehicle, and pushed me toward the front door. Inside, all was quiet, and I think I breathed a sigh of relief that Virginia and the children seemed to have gotten away. Nevertheless, I was apprehensive because the car at the end of the driveway suggested they hadn't gotten as far as they might have planned to.

    "Tanyasin began screaming at me, telling me I had deceived her in order to allow Virginia and the children to escape … that I had known all along what I was doing. Now, I was going to pay for my deceit. She was coming toward me, madness in her eyes, her hands reaching for my neck. I thought, this is it … for sure, this is where it's going to end for me. I felt the chill of her skin on mine as her fingers gripped my throat. I was aware of her mouth opening, and as I tried to gasp for breath, it was as though she were sucking the life from me. And then I heard her voice…" Randy turned and pointed at Angelique. "She ordered Tanyasin to let me go. The darkness in the room was overcome with a bright light, and to my surprise, Tanyasin cowered before it.

"Tanyasin loosened her grip on me, and turned on Angelique, cursing. I thought for a moment they were going to come to blows, but for some reason, as Angelique approached, Tanyasin backed away. But she was still laughing hysterically, and she told Angelique this was not the end of things ... Radu was on his way to Brantford, and the great Dracul family finally would be brought to its knees. She said Radu had resources so powerful that even the mighty Basarab, cursed leader, would not be able to overcome. Angelique told Tanyasin that her mistake would be to put her trust in Radu, and she reminded her sister of her warnings. But, Tanyasin just laughed again, and as she escaped out the door she said, we shall see, dear sister ... we shall see."

Basarab nodded to Randy, a sign he had heard enough. He stood and faced Angelique. "It appears your sister is a loose cannon. Do you have any idea where she might have gone?"

"Not at the moment. I made it my priority to get Randy to safety, and assumed from the visions I had had, the safest place for him would be here with you and the others," Angelique replied.

"I see." The count looked around the table. I followed his gaze, noting no one was saying anything, as though they were awaiting his command. "I think we have heard enough for now. Up to this point in time, we have thought Radu and Elizabeth were the main forces to be reckoned with, but it appears Tanyasin has an agenda of her own. This means we have more than one front to protect." Basarab sighed heavily. "I believe our human guests must be famished, as am I. Please, gentlemen, pour yourselves a glass of refreshment. I shall personally see our guests to their rooms, and have Max send them up some dinner. When I return, we will make a plan."

I knew that was my cue to get up and follow the count. I had no idea what he had in store for me or Randy; however, I had no choice but to play along. I nodded to Atilla as I stood. He smiled, giving me hope. *Of a friend?*

I followed the count, Randy followed me. At the top of the stairs, the count told me to wait while he showed Randy to his room. I could tell from the look on Randy's face that he did not want to be parted from me, but I sensed he knew there would be no logic to disobeying our host. I watched as he walked away. Even though he was as tall as Basarab, Randy was clearly not a match for the vampire. They rounded a corner, and I tried to tally the seconds till I heard a door. I was hoping I would be able to discern which room Randy had been put in, just in case I was able to get out of my room later. Finally, I heard a door close, and the familiar sound of a lock clicking into place echoed through the hallway. A few seconds later, the count reappeared.

Basarab extended his arm to me. "Ah, Virginia, my little bird. It certainly is delightful to see you again."

I was surprised by the emotion in his voice, the gentleness of his hand as it caressed the small of my back. What was it I was actually wanting here? Was it the count? Or was it Randy? I had thought to play a game, at first, but my heart seemed to be pushing me in a different direction. I didn't want the count to leave me behind again. I didn't want to escape from this man-creature. I realized I was ecstatic to see him. I knew this because the blood was pulsing with feverish speed through my veins.

"It is good to see you, as well, my dear Basarab."

## Chapter Eleven

At the door of my old room, the count surprised me by scooping me up into his arms and carrying me across the threshold. I stiffened, but only momentarily. It felt right to have his arms around me again. I sighed and lay my head on his shoulder. It had been a long day.

Basarab laid me gently on the bed, and stepped back. He just stood there, staring at me. I gazed at him, trying to read his eyes, trying to read his face. I wanted so badly to ask him what his plans were for me, and for Randy, but I dared not, for fear of possible repercussions—especially toward Randy. It was enough the count had observed the close relationship between Randy and Santan. I didn't need to add more fuel to the fire.

The count's voice reached across to me, caressingly. "You are more beautiful than I remember," he began. "Motherhood becomes you."

I smiled. Still saying nothing.

"You have missed me?" His question threw me off guard.

I opened my lips to speak, but no words came out.

"You hesitate ... why?"

I reached deep and found my voice. "Yes ... as much as I thought I never wanted to see you again, or any of your kind, I have missed you. I have dreamed of you. I have dreamed of this moment."

The count's lips curled upward. I was unable to determine if he was smiling at me, or if he was mocking me. When he finally spoke, there was a hint of sarcasm in his tone. "And what is it that you think this moment is going to bring you, my dear Virginia?"

I prayed he could not see my inner trembling as I whispered: "You." I stretched my arms above my head, invitingly enticing him with a full view of my body, clothed though it was.

Basarab's laughter filled the room. "Is it me you really want, little bird, or have you been enjoying motherhood so much that you are wishing for another child?" He approached the bed, sat on the edge of it, and began to run his fingers up and down my arm.

"It is you, Basarab ... it has always been you."

"What of this boy, Randy? I am not a fool, Virginia. I have noticed the way he looks at you. Are you going to tell me that such a vivacious woman as you has remained celibate since the last time you coupled with me?"

"It would be the truth, my count."

"Hah! What do you know of the truth, my dear? You, who attempted every deceit possible in order to rid yourself of this house, and of me!"

"I feared you were going to have me killed."

The count grinned. "I thought of it many times, once I realized you were playing a game with me."

"Why didn't you, then?" I dared to ask.

"Maybe, for the same reason that you say you want me ... maybe, I want you, as well."

For a moment, I felt the count was letting his guard down. Or, was he baiting me? "How so? How can I believe that when you left me in a crumbling heap on the floor that night, while you embraced Teresa, both of you mocking me?"

Basarab sighed. "I could have killed you then, Virginia, but I didn't." His fingers moved up to my neck, caressing my skin with a feather-light touch. "There was always something about you..."

He leaned over me, finding my lips with his own as his hands shoved up under my shirt, his fingers creating magic on my skin. I kept telling myself, as I shamelessly matched his passion with my own, he had to love me, and he would not harm me in any way. I wasn't playing a game of survival anymore—the count wanted me as much as I wanted him. His actions told me so. My life, and Randy's, depended on the outcome of this truth I was trying desperately to believe in.

No, I was no longer playing when I had told the count I wanted him, for my entire body was aflame as the count stripped off my clothing. I heard him gasp, and then he descended on me and filled me to the point of bursting.

My arms encircled his back, and my nails raked across his skin. I felt the stickiness of blood on my fingers. All the pent up passion I had been holding in for months was being released in those moments. I was his again. He was mine. No one else mattered. Not Teresa. Not Ildiko. Only me. The mother of his children.

The fury ended all too soon. The count lay beside me, his body glistening with beads of ice. His eyes were closed. I reached over and traced the contours of his face with my fingers. He grasped hold of my hand, and began to kiss it, reigniting the smouldering flames in my stomach. I crawled onto him, slowly, seductively, and I mounted his waiting lust. We ascended back into our netherworld of longing for each other, fulfilling what was meant to be.

This time, when the tempest was finished, the count left the bed, leaving me cold, despite the cover he had placed over me. How I wanted him to stay, but I knew he couldn't. His people were waiting for him. "I will give you some time to gather yourself together before I send Max up with some food," he said as he pulled his clothes on. "Or are you not hungry anymore?" he added teasingly.

"Some food would be nice, even though I feel quite fulfilled at the moment," I returned.

The count opened the door, paused, and looked back at me. "We will talk later." Then he was gone. The game I had thought I was going to have to play when Vacaresti and Ildiko had kidnapped me had crumbled.

I rolled over and buried my face in the pillow and cried. Hadn't the count told me he had missed me ... told me he loved me? How could I eliminate my competition, because it was there. Teresa was still his wife, his queen. Ildiko would move in quickly and try to establish herself as his queen if anything ever happened to Teresa. There was only one way I stood a chance of remaining with Basarab and my children ... I held the trump card ... I was the mother of his children ... what if I were to ask him to cross me over ... that would put us all on an equal playing field! *Wouldn't it?*

~

I don't know how long I slept, but I was awakened by a gentle knock on the door. As my head began to clear from its sleep state, my nostrils were tantalized with a familiar scent—eggs and bacon. Just as I was ready to get out of the bed and take the tray from Max, I realized I was still naked under the cover Basarab had thrown over me before leaving.

Max was staring at me, and his lips curled in a sarcastic grin. "So, Miss Virginia, you have picked up where you left off? Did you learn nothing from your first game with the count?"

It was difficult to fake innocence, but I tried. "What are you talking about, Max?" My voice shook with emotion.

Max set the tray of food on the table by the window and turned back to me. "The count has no time for your games, Miss Virginia. There is too much at stake right now, and he must focus on the situation at hand. From what I hear, Radu is in town, and he is not alone. Basarab needs to decide whether or not to confront him here on this soil, or to return to Brasov where the seeds of discontent began. He is with his council now, discussing the situation."

I shuffled up in the bed, securing the blanket under my arms. "What makes you think I am playing a game, Max? Did you ever stop to think that it was the count who wanted me? That it was not I who made the first move here? After all, it is I who has given him two children—something your daughter could never do. Doesn't that speak volumes for a man such as Basarab––to have an heir to his throne?"

Max shook his head. "I pity you, Miss Virginia."

"Why is that, Max?"

"Do you honestly think my Teresa will relinquish her throne to one such as you? Nothing will stop her this time from ending your life if she feels threatened by you. And, I might also add, Ildiko will not stand by and see you creep into the count's bed on a permanent basis. There is no wrath like that of women scorned, my dear Virginia. You would be most prudent to remember that."

"Does the count not do as he chooses? Is he not the one calling the shots? The one who dictates who crawls into his bed?" I threw back at Max.

Max's laughter gurgled from his throat. "The count is not always around, my dear. As powerful as he is, he cannot be everywhere. You would be wise to remember that, as well." Max headed to the door. "Enjoy your meal, Miss Virginia; you never know when it might be your last."

I stayed under the cover for a few moments after Max left. Despite my comments of bravado, I was frightened, especially so because of Max's last words to me. Slowly, I cast the blanket aside and gathered my clothes from the floor where the count had thrown them. As I dressed, I noticed the bruises on my body—the aftermath of the rapturous storm that had swept through my room.

I walked over to the table, sat down, and picked at the food on the plate. Would this be my last meal? What of Randy? Was he enjoying the same meal? What did the count plan on doing with him? I felt a flutter in my chest, thinking of my friend. So young ... so undeserving of the possible fate awaiting him ... all because I had knocked on his door one day, and he had opened his door to me, and then his heart. I dropped the fork on the plate, having lost my appetite. I pushed my chair back, stood, and began to pace around the room.

As I passed the door, I checked to see if it had been locked. Of course. My mind went into overdrive. What was it the count had said to me? *Maybe, I want you, as well ... I could have killed you then, my dear, but I didn't ... there was always something about you...*

The memory of his whispered endearments gave me strength. Yes, the game was still on, but it had taken a different path. I would be sweet as honey to Teresa and Ildiko, and when the time came for me to make my move they wouldn't know what hit them! As I have had since the birth of my son, I still held the trump card—this time two of them—Santan and Samara—Basarab's children!

# *Night's Return*

# *Basarab*
## Chapter Twelve

I stood outside Virginia's door for several minutes, pondering on what had just taken place between us. I knew it was foolish to waste such precious time with her as I had, but seeing her again had spawned some unsettled feelings, feelings that had haunted me in my dreams when we were apart. *I cannot allow this to happen again,* I breathed under my breath. I heard footsteps approaching, and turned to be confronted by Ildiko.

"So, my dear cousin, you have succumbed again to the wench who birthed your children." There was a sardonic grin on Ildiko's lips. "And so soon ... you could not wait until more important matters were looked after?" she added.

I drew myself to full height. As tall as Ildiko was, I still looked down on her. "What I do with my time, my darling cousin, is naught of your business. You would be best to remember that."

Ildiko chuckled. "I wonder if the others would feel the same way. I wonder if they would be so tolerant if they knew what you had been doing up here, whilst they awaited your return to discuss a strategy to be rid of Radu. What is happening here, Basarab, is the business of all of us—of *the family*—it would be best you remember that!" Ildiko paused. "Is she really worth what you may have to sacrifice in order to keep her around?"

I couldn't help but to sneer. "By the sounds of what you are actually saying, you are not so bothered about the fact that I am not looking after the family situation as you are about the fact that I took a moment of pleasure from Virginia. Have you not understood by now that you will never be in my bed, cousin?"

"What of your wife, Basarab? Do you think Teresa is such a fool? Do you think she does not know what you are doing, especially after she has risked her life for you and this family by putting herself under the mercy of Elizabeth Bathory? As much as the thought of your marriage to a dirty Gypsy punctures my heart, she is still your wife—and, she is one of us!"

Once again I sneered at my cousin. "My marriage to Teresa has always been a sore spot for you, hasn't it? Do you seriously want me to believe you are trying to protect her interests here? Don't take me for a fool, Ildiko! All I would have to do is open my covers to you, and you would slip in without any regard for my wife. What I do with my time, and whom I choose to spend it with, in all truth is not of your concern, or Teresa's. I think we are finished here," I turned away from her.

Ildiko grabbed my arm. "Not so quickly, Basarab. This is not finished. Too many of us have sacrificed our very existence in order to be here. Remember why we are here—to get your children to safety. That is the priority! Not bedding their mother!" She released my arm.

I didn't respond to her. Basically, because she was right. There was no justification for the time I had taken with Virginia. I headed down the stairway, to the dining room where the others would be waiting for me. However, the only one still there was my father. And he did not look pleased.

He wasted no time confronting me, nor did he mince his words. "What have you been about, my son? There is no time for play. I told the others you must have been tired and decided to rest a bit before meeting with them. They accepted my explanation, but not with their eyes. I could tell they were disappointed and angry." Atilla paused. "Get it together, Basarab, or we are all doomed. As much as I am taken with this woman, the mother of your children, she is not worth the immense loss that will take place if we do not quickly resolve this issue with Radu."

My father, as usual, was right. Not for the first time, did the thought cross my mind that the old Gypsy, Tanyasin, would have been wiser to impose the leadership of our family on my father. He would have been the better choice. Then again, maybe I was chosen for a reason. Possibly, she felt I would be easier to defeat when she decided our time on earth was over. Did she fear Dracula—is that why she had not chosen him? He was the one who murdered her family, not me. I could not help the thoughts that raced through my head, despite the glowering look my father was giving me.

"Basarab!" Atilla's voice was sharp.

I sighed. "Yes, Father ... as always, you are right. I apologize for my behaviour; it will not happen again while we are here." Even as told my father my actions would not be repeated, I knew I may not be able to keep my word.

I walked over to the window. The sun had set in the west. I turned back to my father. "I need to make a call, Father, to the fellow who is supposed to be getting us some supplies." I took out my cell phone and dialled Sean's number. He picked up on the third ring.

"Hello."

"Sean?"

"Yes."

"Do you have my supplies?" I asked.

"Good news and bad news." Sean sounded edgy.

I waited for him to continue.

Sean's voice came hesitantly over the line. "I have some blood for you, but won't be able to get you any more for a few days. Apparently, there has already been a substantial amount taken from the blood bank, and my contact said he couldn't risk giving me what I had requested. He pulled in a bit from another city in order to fulfill some of your needs."

"I see ... did he happen to mention who..." I began to ask.

"You know our clients are all confidential, Basarab," Sean broke in before I could finish my question.

"Of course ... so, where shall we meet? I prefer you not to come to my house."

"How say we meet in the cemetery just down the street from where you are? You know the one?"

I knew. "What time?"

"How say, midnight … does that work for you?"

"Yes. Where, and what will you be driving?"

"There is a mausoleum not far from the entrance across from Buffalo Street. I'll be in a black van."

"Okay. See you then." I clicked off the phone.

My father must have noticed the worried look on my face. "Trouble?" he asked.

I nodded. "It appears someone else in town is getting a blood supply; I am assuming it is Radu. Therefore, we are being shorted. We shall have to ration until the rest comes in."

"What about Carla; can she not get us some? She is a doctor. She must have access to blood at one of the hospitals."

"I never considered her being able to get us our blood … good thinking, Father." I wondered why I hadn't thought of that myself.

"Are you going alone to meet this fellow?"

"Yes."

"Do you think that wise? How much do you trust him? If someone else is dipping into the blood supply, you must consider he might be playing to the highest bidder." I noted the concern in my father's eyes.

"I've dealt with Sean before; he wouldn't dare to double-cross me." Even as I said the words, though, I felt apprehension.

"I would still feel more comfortable if you took someone with you … Kerecsen, might be a wise choice," Atilla suggested.

"Maybe so." I wasn't going to argue with my father. If he felt it best, he was most likely right. I hesitated before speaking again. "Before leaving, I need to speak to the rogue, Orsolya, and ask if Radu has contacted her yet. I am sure he is keen to hear any news she might have for him."

My father looked at me. His eyes were intense as he asked his next question. "Are you sure you can trust her? After all, she was under Radu's influence for some time. I don't buy her story that she wanted to get away from him, and she is willing to betray him. Don't forget, her story differs from your cousin's account.

Think on it, Basarab, and be mindful of this Orsolya. She needs to be watched closely."

"I appreciate your concern, Father. I, too, feel a certain amount of uneasiness around her. I shall be careful. In fact, if it makes you feel better, I shall have Ildiko shadow the girl if she should have to meet in person with Radu. That way we might also learn where he is staying."

"Good idea." My father hesitated before adding: "However, in light of recent events, do you think it wise to use Ildiko?"

I played dumb, even though I suspected the current event my father was thinking of. I wasn't sure how he was aware of it, though, unless he had heard the conversation between me and Ildiko. "What are you talking about, Father?" I still asked.

My father confirmed my thoughts. "Ildiko did not sound too impressed about your most recent liaison with Virginia. You must remember, son, a woman scorned too often may not be a woman to be fully trusted, no matter how you think she feels about you. Ildiko is changed since she returned to us from Radu. I suspect whatever happened to her there might have left some deep scars. And, if I might add, all these years she has only tolerated Teresa because you chose her for your wife; I do not think she will tolerate Virginia, as well ... no, I think it better if you choose another to shadow this girl if need be."

Once again, I knew my father was right. I wasn't secure in how far I could trust Ildiko, either. I had seen the hatred in her eyes when she had confronted me about Virginia. And, I had felt that hatred directed toward me—a first. "If Orsolya should have to meet with Radu, I will have Laborc not far from her side, then."

"I also believe it is better the girl is not aware of your intentions. We do not want her guard up. We must know exactly where she stands—with Radu, or with us."

"As you wish, Father. Radu gave Orsolya a cell phone to keep in contact; so now, I must go and find out if he has tried to reach her. After which, I must go to the cemetery and pick up our supplies. Could you please inform Kerecsen I have need of his company, and also notify the others that as soon as Kerecsen and I return, we will meet here."

My father nodded and left the room. I stood for a few moments, looking out into the night. My thoughts wandered back to the room where Virginia was. *Damn her!* I shook my head and headed to the room where Ildiko had put Orsolya.

When I arrived, I found the door unlocked. I picked up Ildiko's scent before I entered. She and Orsolya were sitting on the bed, their backs to the door, their heads bowed in earnest conversation. Ildiko must have heard my approach, for she stopped speaking. Both women turned and faced me.

"Basarab … we were thinking you might be along soon. Orsolya has just had a message from Radu," Ildiko said. "Apparently, he is curious about what is happening, and would like to meet with her."

I closed the door. "And what did you say to him?" I directed my question to Orsolya.

She gazed up at me, her eyes blank. "I told him I would try and arrange something. I told him you kept a pretty close eye on me."

I hesitated for a moment before speaking. "I want you to meet with him, my dear, and tell him I would like to arrange a meeting with him ... just him and me. Can you do that?"

"Of course." Her voice was feeble. "Where would you like this meeting to take place?"

"Somewhere public, and of course, at night." I paused. "Actually, see if he is willing to meet, first; then we will discuss location."

"I meant my meeting with him." Orsolya corrected.

"Of course." I hadn't considered where she should meet him. I thought quickly. "There is a cemetery not far from here, at the end of the street that runs into our parking lot. I will have the location written out for you so you can give Radu directions."

"Will I be going alone?"

I nodded. "Is that a problem for you?"

"No … no … I just thought Ildiko might accompany me."

"That would be most unwise," I returned.

Orsolya was quick to cover. "Oh no, I didn't mean for her to actually be with me; I just meant that she hides a discreet distance away, in case something went askew."

"No ... you will go alone. As long as Radu thinks you are still on his side, nothing should go wrong. I can trust you, can't I?" I stared directly into her eyes—still blank.

She hung her head. "Of course."

"Good. Now, you will give Radu no information about who is here with me; however, you will try and find out for me if he has any others with him besides Elizabeth and Peter. Your main objective is to have Radu agree to a meeting with me ... do you understand?"

"Yes, but he will want something. He will ask me how many are with you. What shall I tell him?"

I thought for a moment. "Tell him I am here with my father and a couple of my cousins, my manservant, and of course you may tell him Ildiko is here, as well."

"He will not believe me if I tell him your numbers are so few."

"He will believe you if you insist on it. Prove to me, Orsolya, you are on my side, not his."

"Yes, Count."

"Good. I am glad we understand each other. Make your call now, and arrange the meeting for ... let's say, midnight tomorrow."

"Not tonight?"

"I have other business tonight."

"I see." Orsolya took out her cell phone and dialled.

"Put it on speaker," I ordered.

She pushed the speaker button. Finally, after six rings, Radu answered.

"Orsolya?"

"Yes, Master."

"You have something for me?"

"Yes ... and no ... I mean, yes ... Basarab has agreed to let me meet with you."

"He has?" I detected a surprised tone in my uncle's voice.

"Yes."

"Does he suspect you?"

Orsolya looked up at me, and I shook my head no. "No," she replied. "I told him how much you abused me; and, as you said, Basarab is a sucker for a damsel in distress."

Radu laughed. "Okay, then. Where is this meeting to take place, and when?"

"Tomorrow, at midnight. In a cemetery. I will call you later with the directions."

"Okay, then … tomorrow night. I will await your call. I assume you will be coming alone?"

"Yes. I insisted to Basarab, telling him that was the best way for me to prove I was on his side, and not yours."

Radu laughed again. "Good girl. Okay, call me later with directions. Keep up the good work and I shall reward you accordingly." The line went dead.

Orsolya looked at me and half-smiled. "Did I do okay?" she asked.

"You did fine."

Up to this point, other than the greeting when I had first entered the room, Ildiko had remained silent. I tried, when possible, to focus in on her body language, but she had remained aloof—difficult to read—like Orsolya's eyes. "I don't think she should go alone," Ildiko stated.

Before I could reply, Orsolya answered. "I will be all right, Ildiko. Radu will not harm me; I am still of use to him."

"She will be fine," I affirmed. I motioned to the door. "Shall we, Ildiko?"

Ildiko hesitated briefly, and then walked from the room. I shut the door behind me, and caught up with my cousin as she was making her way down the hallway. "Cousin."

She turned. "I have nothing to say to you right now, Basarab. I am still angry with you. Give me some time; I'll get over it. I always do." She smiled then, but I could see it was not genuine.

"As you wish." I turned and headed toward the stairs. It was almost time for me to meet Sean, anyway. I had no time for the games of a jealous woman. I heard a door slam as I made my way to the foyer. As I approached the stairway, I had second thoughts. I turned and headed to Teresa's room.

## Chapter Thirteen

I had no idea what I was going to say to my wife ... what was left to say? My heart belonged to another now. It would take a lot for me to trust Teresa fully again. As I approached her door, I hesitated. Did I seriously need to have this conversation with her at this time? Yes. My father and my cousin were on my back regarding what they thought was my indiscretion. Maybe if Teresa and I talked, we could come to some sort of reconciliation. I knocked on the door.

I was just about ready to turn around, thinking she was not there, when the door opened.

"Basarab!" Teresa looked surprised. "To what do I owe the pleasure of my husband paying me a visit?" Her question had a slightly sarcastic edge to it.

"We need to talk," I replied. "May I step in?"

Teresa opened the door wider and motioned for me to come inside. She sauntered over to her bed, sat down and patted the spot beside her. The last place I wanted to sit was on the bed. I headed to the loveseat that was adjacent to the fireplace.

"I think here would be a much better place for us to have a conversation," I suggested as I sat down.

Teresa laughed. "Afraid of what might happen over here? It has been a while, hasn't it, my beloved husband? How have you been filling your time? It certainly has not been in your wife's bed!" Teresa stood and walked toward me, taking a seat in the chair across from the loveseat.

"Teresa..."

"Don't, Basarab ... I have given you my life ... I have been faithful to you ... I have never looked sideways at another man ... I gave you leave to bed other women in order for you to have an heir ... you have no idea how much I wished it had been me that had been able to give you a son, but it wasn't meant to be."

I felt humbled by my wife's words. "There was a time when I wished it was you as well, Teresa," I began.

"Maybe. Should I believe you? After all, your actions of late have not indicated such a desire."

I knew I was going to have to weigh my words carefully. I knew I had crossed a line with Virginia, a line I had not meant to cross when I considered her as the vessel to carry my child. But, Teresa had changed when Virginia entered our lives. She became jealous and displayed undignified outbursts of temper, unbecoming for the queen she was supposed to be. This had driven me further into Virginia's arms. I enjoyed bantering with her, too, and the more we talked, and I got to know her, the more I enjoyed her company.

"Are you there, Basarab? Or are you thinking of Virginia even as you try to tell me that I am number one in your life?" Teresa interrupted my reflections.

I smiled. "No, I was not thinking of Virginia," I lied smoothly. "I was thinking of you, and how lovely you were as a child, and how you grew into a beautiful woman. I was thinking of the times you saved my life, and of the most recent deed you did, putting your own life in jeopardy by trying to ally with Elizabeth in order to obtain information for me."

"So, what conclusions have your thoughts brought you to?" Teresa's face remained expressionless.

Before I could stop them, the words were out of my mouth. "I want us to work, Teresa, as I have always wanted. We have been given the gift of not only a son, but a daughter, too. We could be happy again."

"And what of Virginia? What are you plans for her, the vessel?"

"She is not your worry," I replied.

"Oh, but she is. Rumours have it, dear husband, you don't seem to be able to stay away from her. Are you trying for another child? We both know by now how fertile she is."

"I take my pleasures where I want to, and when my wife's door is closed to me, I open another one." I looked at Teresa sternly. I needed to regain some of the ground I had just lost.

"My door has never been closed to you, Basarab."

"Some of your actions indicate otherwise; however, I did not come to discuss the past and the problems we have had … I came to discuss how we can move forward." I motioned for her to join me on the loveseat.

She hesitated, and then she got up and came to sit by my side. I gathered her into my arms. At first, her body was stiff, but soon it relaxed. I heard her sigh. I kissed the top of her head. She reached her lips up to me. I met them with a light kiss. I was not willing to give her more than that.

Teresa's eyes motioned toward the bed. I couldn't. "I have to meet with someone, Teresa, the fellow who is supposed to bring us a supply of blood. I am already running late."

She did not look happy as I stood. "Later, then?" Her eyes looked hopeful.

I smiled, but said nothing.

As I walked down the stairs, I couldn't help thinking about what I had just said and done back in Teresa's room. How could I be so manipulative? Did I honestly have any intention of bedding my wife again? Was I not finished with her? Had the conversation I overheard, when she told her father that she didn't care for Santan, not carry some weight in my decision making of setting her aside? However, recently, she had put herself in danger for me.

My thoughts turned to Virginia … sweet, giving, and more beautiful than I deserved—a different beauty than Teresa's. Whereas Teresa's was an outer, exotic beauty, Virginia blossomed from within. The two gorgeous children she had presented me with were testament to that. I had told Virginia how much I had missed her … was that just a ploy to spend a few moments of pleasure? Could I totally trust her? She had left before … would she flee again?

As I headed to the parking lot where I knew Kerecsen would be waiting, I tried to suppress from my head all matters involving the females in my life.

## Chapter Fourteen

Kerecsen flexed his fingers on the steering wheel as we waited for Sean to show up. He was late, and I didn't like that. I watched for a set of car lights, but my ears picked up on the crunch of tires first. I saw a black van approach, headlights turned off.

"Are you sure you can trust this guy?" Kerecsen asked.

"He wouldn't dare betray me. I would rip his throat open and drain his blood on the spot should I even sense betrayal." I think I was trying to reassure myself as much as I was trying to assure my cousin.

"What would the local authorities do with such a body, drained of blood, laying in a graveyard?" Kerecsen chuckled.

"They would never find the body," I returned with a smirk.

Kerecsen didn't say anything more. He shut the motor off and killed the lights on our vehicle. The van came to a stop beside us, and Sean got out and approached. I stepped out to greet him. He appeared edgy.

"Everything okay, Sean?"

"Yeah ... yeah ... cemeteries just give me the creeps, especially at this time of night." Sean looked around.

"Are you expecting someone else?" I enquired.

"Of course not. You told me to come alone, and I did. I understand the delicacy of your situation..."

"And you also understand what I would do to you if you were ever to double-cross me," I interrupted.

I saw the shocked look flicker across Sean's face. "Basarab ... please ... I would never do that!"

"Were you able to find out anything more about who dipped into the blood supply?" I queried, ignoring his plea.

"I told you, my source won't divulge such information to me, no more than I would tell him I am getting blood for you."

"When might I expect the rest of my order?"

"I'll call you as soon as I get it."

I didn't like the way Sean looked away from me when he spoke. There was something up. I felt it in my bones. Maybe my father was right; I made a mental note to approach Carla and see if she could get us the rest of what we might need. I was happy Ponqor had come with us to Brantford; I would have him run a test on this blood before we actually drank any of it.

Sean walked over to the back of his van and opened the doors. "Do you want to open your trunk," he called over to me as he took a cooler out of his vehicle.

I obliged him, not lifting a finger to help him with his load, though. As Sean passed by the car, he must have noticed Kerecsen sitting in the front seat. He nodded his head toward Kerecsen. "Brought some insurance with you, eh, Count?" His tone sounded sarcastic.

I laughed. As Sean straightened up after placing the cooler in the trunk, I grabbed his arm. "Don't ever think for a minute that I cannot handle the likes of you on my own, Sean!" I hissed into his ear.

Sean struggled to release my grip on his arm, but I held tight a bit longer, to ensure he knew who he was dealing with. Finally, I let him go. He rubbed his arm. "Touchy," he mumbled under his breath, but I could also see how pale he had turned when I had dug my fingers into his flesh. He had no idea how close he had come to having me dig my fangs into his neck!

I watched as Sean drove away, this time with his lights on. When I got in the car, Kerecsen was grinning. "Scared the shit out of the little weasel, eh?"

"Hopefully enough so he won't try anything stupid. I am going to have Ponqor test the blood, though, just in case," I added.

"Good idea," Kerecsen said as he started the engine.

Max was waiting for us when we entered the foyer. Kerecsen had carried the cooler in from the car, and he handed it to Max. There was no need to instruct Max on what to do with it. I noticed the others beginning to filter into the dining room. Atilla was standing by the doorway, greeting each one as they went through. My father pulled me aside.

"Emelia has arrived," he informed me. "She would like a word with you, if possible."

"I have nothing to say to her," I remarked.

My father put a hand on my shoulder. "Basarab ... go to your aunt. Make your peace with her. Remember what you once had, how she took you in her arms and nourished you with the love of a mother."

Despite the annoyance I was feeling, I shrugged my shoulders. "Where is she?"

"In your study."

"Tell everyone I will be in shortly; this shouldn't take long," I snapped as I headed to my study.

When I entered, Emelia jumped up from her chair and came hesitantly toward me. "Basarab. Thank you for coming." Her voice was a mere whisper.

"State your business, and make it quick. I have other matters to attend to." My voice was sharp with impatience.

"We have never talked about what happened before we left Brantford."

"You betrayed me. That is the crux of it. You actually did more than that ... you took my son from me!" I snarled.

Emelia bowed her head. "A child needs a mother, and I could see Teresa was not going to be a mother to Santan. She hated the boy. Did you not see that as well?"

If I were to be truthful, I would have to admit my aunt was right. Teresa had never shown an interest in Santan, only a formality of pretence when she had to. My voice softened slightly as I answered Emelia's question. "Yes, I saw that, but it was still not a reason for you to give my son to Virginia. Do you realize how things have become more complicated because of what you did?"

"How are they complicated? If you want to listen to an old woman, what I see is that Virginia loves you. She may not realize it herself; however, I know. She could have made a new life for herself, have kept on the move, despite having a second child. I would have provided her with a means to do so…"

"You see…"

Emelia raised her hand, cutting me off. "Hear me out, Basarab. Eventually, I would have convinced her to return the children to you, which she would have done. Virginia will always do what is best for those children. She would have seen she could not give them the tools or resources to survive in this world as half-vampire children."

I raised my eyebrow. "You honestly think she would have given them up to me?"

"Yes." Emelia paused and gazed up into my eyes. "I hate what has happened to us, Basarab. We are family. You have always been special to me, and it is breaking me apart inside. Can you not find it in your heart to forgive me, even in a small way?" I noticed the tears welling up in her eyes.

The part of me that dearly loved my aunt took over. I reached a finger up and wiped the tears from her cheeks. I sighed and drew her into my arms. "I will think on it, Emelia." That was the best I could do. I released her from my arms and then offered her my hand. "Shall we join the others?"

Emelia took my hand and together we entered the dining room. After seating her, I took my place at the head of the table, I glanced around at the family members who had accompanied me to get my children to safety: Vacaresti, Kerecsen, Laborc; Ponqor and Zigana; Bajnok, and his son, Kardos; my Uncle Stephen and Aunt Evdochia; Tardos and Sebes; and of course, my father, Atilla.

Farkas and Gara had insisted on staying at the hotel in Brasov, and were to get word to Kate and Melissa if there were any unusual activities happening in the city. They, in turn, were to keep us apprised of such events. We had shut down our communication centre at the hotel, so had to rely on the system the women had set up in the caves. I hoped to return to Brasov, though, before anything exploded there. The fact Radu was here in Brantford gave me hope that nothing too much was going to take place on our home soil.

"Welcome, my dear friends," I began. "I am sorry for the delay in holding this meeting, but there were some important matters that had to be dealt with first." I heard a couple of throats clear, but chose to ignore whose. "I just picked up some blood from my source here, but I would like you, Ponqor, to test it to ensure it is not drugged. Sean seemed rather nervous to me, and we cannot take a chance on being duped by anyone. Someone else has recently started digging into the blood supply, and I think it is safe to assume it is Radu. Therefore, it might also be assumed he might, if he had the opportunity, drug any stock that was coming our way. How soon can you perform this test, Ponqor?"

"As soon as we are done here," he replied.

"Good. That is settled. Also, I am not sure when we will be getting the balance of what I ordered; so, as Atilla suggested earlier, we should try and utilize the sources Carla, the female doctor, might have."

Bajnok raised his hand, an indication he wished to speak. I nodded assent. "I have some news you might like to be aware of," Bajnok began. "Dracula is on his way here, and he is bringing his sons with him. Word is, he wishes a confrontation with his brother; he is weary of the games being played and wants to put an end to them."

"I think Dracula must consider the fact that there are more individuals to deal with than Radu," Kardos mentioned. "There is Elizabeth and this Peter fellow, who, I am informed, is an exceedingly dangerous and powerful rogue … and, we must also not forget about Tanyasin … she is still on the loose, and from what we have been informed of by Angelique, the old Gypsy is bent on having her revenge, with or without the aid of Radu. I guess what I am trying to say here is, we must try and reason with Dracula because he cannot be going off half-cocked, trying to resolve matters on his own, especially in a strange country."

"I agree," Laborc spoke up. "We are all on unfamiliar territory here. On our home turf, we know our way around. Dracula cannot be allowed to act on his own, or with Vlad and Mihail, both of whom we know can be as volatile as their father when it comes to situations like this. You and Teresa are the only ones, Basarab, who know this city well enough, having lived here before ... how kindly would the *powers that be* in Brantford be to having a vampire bloodbath on their doorstep?"

"Not so much," I replied. I wondered what my uncle was up to. I knew Bajnok, Kardos, and Laborc were right, and we had reason to be worried about Dracula and his son's actions. "I do have some contacts on the police force here in Brantford, but of course they have no idea of what I am," I continued. "However, I agree, they would not only be surprised, but they would not be pleased to have to deal with out-of-control vampires. In fact, I don't think they would even consider it was the work of vampires, which are nothing more than a myth to people over here. I am sure police from larger cities would be brought in to investigate such heinous crimes, and that would attract unwanted attention to us." I turned directly to Bajnok. "Do you know exactly when Dracula and his sons will be arriving, and if they plan on coming directly here?"

"Word has it they will be here by tomorrow, and yes, my source said they would be stopping here first in order to pay respects to you, and to see the children. Apparently, Dracula is curious about them," Bajnok replied.

Tardos stood. "There is another issue we must deal with, as well, Basarab ... that of the humans under your roof. The sister and brother do not appear to be much of a problem, and I hear the sister has been in the employ of your wife, Vacaresti. Some of us know Alfred from the work he has done for us over the years, so I believe it is safe to say that neither of those two would cause us any problems if we let them go home. However, the other two ... this young man, Randy..." here Tardos paused slightly, as though considering carefully what he was going to say next. "And, the mother of your children, Virginia ... what do we do with them? You have your children now ... maybe we should just pack up and return to Brasov."

"I agree," Sebes intervened. "I don't believe staying here any longer will accomplish anything other than disaster. Free

Alfred and Adelaide, and let us rid ourselves of the other two. They are loose ends we cannot afford."

I needed to be careful not to show how much of a hold Virginia had on me. Randy, I could care less about, although, I was aware Virginia would not want to see him harmed in any way. But, did she care enough for the young man to put his welfare over that of her own? She had always been all about the children—and me. Self-preservation was a game Virginia played quite well. But, there was something else I needed to take care about ... I had a feeling my son would be devastated if I allowed any harm to come to Randy, and that was the last thing I needed when I was trying so hard to gain my son's trust and love.

"We will send Alfred and Adelaide home. I agree they are not a threat to us. As for the other two, I have not yet decided their fate." I looked around the table. "There is one more thing I must tell you. I have asked Orsolya to arrange a meeting between Radu and me. She has a rendezvous with him tomorrow night."

I noticed a worried frown spread across Vacaresti's face. "Do you think that wise, nephew? I agree with Tardos and Sebes; we should go home, take the battle back to Transylvania. Radu will realize soon enough that we have the children, and he has lost this round. We can better protect your children if they are tucked safely away in the caves."

"I appreciate your concern, uncle, but I feel I must do this. If there is any way to reason with Radu before he unleashes his rogues on the world, I would like to try. I don't think even he would be foolish enough to pull anything on unfamiliar territory."

"How will you keep Dracula from his brother?" Atilla spoke up.

I took in a deep breath. I was tiring of all this pressure. Do this ... do that ... don't do this ... don't do that. I just wanted to run up the stairs, open the door to Virginia's room, and take her into my arms again. "I am sure you will be able to keep him at bay, Father, long enough for me to have my meeting," I finally replied.

"You are not going alone, are you?" Vacaresti asked.

"Yes."

"Not wise. You know Radu would never meet you alone; he will have someone close by. If he were to betray the temporary truce you are suggesting, what do we do then? If he overpowers you and captures you, then this trip to get your children will have been for naught." Vacaresti leaned toward me, his hands on the table, his eyes piercing into mine.

I knew I shouldn't have been angry, but I was, and I allowed my words and actions to portray my anger. My fist came down on the table. "I am the leader! I listen to you all, and take into consideration your advice, but in the end, it is I who must decide the final course we take. You are either with me or against me. I did not ask for this role; I was cursed with it! And, forgive me, Vacaresti, but it would not be so easy for someone like Radu to defeat me, or any one of his rogues he might bring along!

"Now, this meeting is over. I suggest we all get some rest." I turned to Ponqor. "I await your word on the blood; bring me the news as soon as you have completed the test." I turned and walked over to the window, turning my back on my family, dismissing them.

Silently, they filed out of the room, knowing they had infuriated me, but probably all seething with their own sense of disappointment at the direction I was taking. Thinking all had left, I turned and saw my father was still in the room. He was studying me, a sad look on his face.

"Where do you go now, Basarab?" My father's question was asked with a hint of sarcasm. "To your wife, Teresa? Or to Virginia?"

When I did not answer him immediately, he walked over and put his hands on my shoulders. I flinched at his touch, as though I knew what he was going to say to me, and I did not want to hear those words. "Go to your wife, Basarab. As much as I like Virginia, she is not one of us."

*I could change that.*

My father must have read my thought. "You are married, Basarab. You used Virginia to give you and Teresa a child. The fact she has given you two children is a blessing. But she has served her purpose. You must let her go."

"Are you suggesting I kill her, and Randy?" I barely could bring myself to ask the question, let alone hear my father's possible response.

"No ... I am not suggesting you kill them. Personally, I don't think either one of them will betray us. Virginia knows if she did, it would put her children in jeopardy, too. As for Randy, he is so enamoured with Virginia, and from what I have observed, with Santan, I believe he would keep his silence, as well." My father paused. "Just leave them. They need not be aware of our going. If you must, leave her enough money to create a new life ... maybe a life with Randy. Give her the opportunity to become human again."

"She is human, Father."

My father's voice was gentle as he replied. "But she has not been allowed to live as a human for a long time now—not since she happened upon you." He paused. "Let her go, son. You have from her what you wanted."

I knew my father was right. But, was I willing to let her go? Seeing Virginia again had stirred emotions in me I thought I would never have for any woman—emotions that even my wife had never been able to stimulate. "I will think on it," was the answer I gave my father as I turned and walked away, my brain exploding with confusion.

I stood at the bottom of the stairs, looking upward, to where Virginia was. Was she waiting for me to return to her, with her arms open and inviting? Or was she plotting how to escape from my clutches, once again ... how to be rid of me ... maybe even to plunge a stake through my heart before she left ... although, in the state of mind I was currently in, her very leaving would do that.

I could not face her right now, especially so soon after my conversation with Teresa. I knew my wife would be waiting for me to return to her bedchamber. Had I promised I would do so, or had I only alluded to such? Was Teresa being honest with me? Would her bed be as inviting as Virginia's? Or, was she waiting to exact her own brand of revenge on me, ridding herself of her husband.

I was confused. Women were confusing. I needed rest. I turned to the door that led to the basement, thinking sleep would revive me, but it didn't ... a dream inundated my sleep ... a dream of a plan gone wrong ... a nightmare of Virginia betraying me...

The cemetery was filled with night shadows, skittering around the gravestones. Radu was late—that worried me. I had a deep-seated feeling my uncle would not come alone. I had decided not to be accompanied, despite the warnings from my council. I had even walked from my house to the cemetery. Now, I wished I hadn't. I paced around the gravestones, reading the inscriptions on them. I was in the older part of the cemetery. Temporarily, I thought of the life I could have bestowed on the departed; however, the thought passed quickly. Why would I inflict such pain on them?

As I passed by a stone bench, and was about to sit down, I heard a car engine approaching. No lights. I slipped behind a tree and watched the vehicle approach and pull up in front of the mausoleum. I watched Radu exit from the passenger side, confirmation he was not alone. I cursed myself for not having listened to my family. Radu looked around. I stayed hidden, hoping whoever was with my uncle would show themselves.

"Basarab ... are you here?" Radu's voice echoed through the darkness of the night.

I hesitated only a moment more, and then stepped out from behind my tree. The clouds released a sliver of moonlight, and as they did, the driver exited the car. The man was huge beyond belief—and feral-looking. He sauntered to the back of the car and leaned on the trunk. When he spoke, I felt the chill of his words.

"I thought maybe your nephew had changed his mind." The man flexed his fingers. "But here he is, crawling out from behind a tree. I think I am in need of some entertainment. It is so dreary in this country." He threw back his head and howled.

"Peter! Enough! Do not draw unnecessary attention to us," Radu admonished. "My nephew was just being cautious."

He laughed. I detected the sarcasm in his mirth. "I wonder if the family knows what a coward their leader is."

My blood boiled. I was no coward. I stepped closer. "At least I am a man of my word, uncle. How is it that you have brought this creature with you when you were supposed to come alone? Is your word not good? Do your people know what kind of man you are?"

Radu's laughter filled the space around us. I shuddered at the insincerity of it. "My people know exactly what kind of man I am, Basarab. And they fear me for it ... not knowing what to expect is a weapon I use to benefit my goals. And, for your information, I have told them how pathetic you are."

"Then you have misinformed them," I began, but Radu cut me off.

"But they don't know that," he said, a sly smile on his lips. "So, nephew, what is it you wanted to discuss with me?"

"I wanted to reason with you, to have you stop this madness you have begun."

"And why would I want to do that? The throne is mine for the taking. You and those by your side have become soft, living too much in the human world, forgetting the old ways ... forgetting our superiority over the lesser beings. It is almost as though you have all grown hearts."

I heard Peter snort and glanced over to him. There was a look on his face that could only be described as pure evil—more diabolical than any vampire I had ever crossed paths with. Once again, I wished I had brought someone with me. Peter stood and began to walk toward Radu and me. I glanced back at Radu and saw hatred radiating from his eyes.

"What do you expect to gain from killing me ... that is, if you can?" I said, backing away slightly.

Radu threw back his head and laughed. "I am not going to kill you, nephew. I am going to enslave you, as you have enslaved me all these years." Radu began to move, as though to circle around behind me.

I stepped back further, almost losing my balance as my foot caught on a tree root. "You were never enslaved, uncle; it was your choice not to join ranks with us. You preferred to walk alone."

"Why would I sit at the same table with the one who brought this curse upon us, with the one who abandoned me in my hours of greatest need?" Radu's voice rose to a screech. "You chose the wrong uncle to drink with, nephew!"

"Dracula never abandoned you—your father did. Your father gave you to the Turkish Sultan as insurance to keep the Turks away from his lands. Dracula was a boy, just like you."

"Dracula was never a boy like me!" Radu retorted. "He was not subjected to the same tortures I was."

"From what I understand, his tortures were of a more barbarous variety," I bantered back. "He showed me his scars. Where are yours?" I tried to push my point home, to hit a soft spot, if my uncle had one.

"Because one's scars are not visible to the naked eye does not mean they are not there!" Radu snapped sarcastically. "However, we are not here to discuss the past, are we? You want to discuss the future of the human race—there isn't one. And you have made it so easy for me, Basarab. In actuality, I never thought you would be this foolish, to meet with me alone."

"But you have only brought a rogue with you."

"Only a rogue, you say! You think Peter is only a rogue! He is worth one hundred of any of your rogues, or for that matter, any family member who might dare to step up against him. Did I ever tell you how I met Peter? I don't think so. I haven't told anyone. Maybe you would like to be the first to know how I came upon my right-hand man."

I put boldness into my words. "I seriously don't care; it is of no consequence to me. Peter shall not be your right-hand man much longer. You think he is so powerful, my dear uncle, maybe you should take care of that power. Dogs have been known to turn on their masters!" I sneered. "And it has been proven over the centuries that no rogue could withstand the absolute fury of a full-blooded vampire," I added.

"No full-blooded vampire has ever met the likes of Peter," Radu guffawed.

I was startled by the sound of a snarling wolf, and as I turned toward the sound, I beheld the transformation. "How is this so?" I hissed. "No rogue has ever been able to change before! Not even the amestecat-singe—mixed bloods—are capable of transformation to an animal."

Peter began to circle, his lips curled back, snarling. Foam from the wolf's open mouth splattered to the ground. The rough on its neck stood straight up, making the beast appear even more massive. I had never seen such a mammoth wolf in all the years I had walked the earth. Once again, I wished I had brought someone with me. I backed away further, stepping cautiously. I needed to get away. I closed my eyes, briefly, trying to will my own transformation. I was all-powerful. I was the leader of my kind. As my eyes opened and I realized I had not changed, I began to panic. Radu must have read my concern.

"What is the problem, nephew? Lost your power?" Radu turned to Peter and raised his hand. "That will be enough for now, Peter. I think we have made our point. This is going to be easier than I thought. I would prefer you show my nephew what it would be like to be conquered by those who are more powerful than he—show him how it was for me in the tents of the Turkish dogs!" Radu laughed maliciously.

I could not move. Peter had transformed back to human form, and he approached me with enthusiasm, a sardonic grin on his lips. "With pleasure, my lord," he growled, flexing his fists as he readied to grip his prey.

"Stop!" A familiar voice rang through the darkness. A bright light appeared, meandering through the gravestones. "Radu, you promised me that you would not harm him." Virginia appeared and came to a halt beside Radu. She turned to Peter.

"You will get no satisfaction from Basarab, I am afraid. He is not half the man you are!"

I could not have been more shocked as I watched Virginia, the mother of my children ... the woman who claimed she loved me, sidle up to the monster, and caress him in places she appeared all too familiar with. How dare she! She raised her head and parted her lips. Peter raised his head, howled, and then thrust an arm around Virginia's waist and raised her up, consuming her lips with his. I could hear her groans of pleasure as the two sank to the ground, intertwining their limbs in a dance of lust. Still, I could not move. I watched the beast take possession of that which I had thought was mine, and I watched as she enjoyed every minute of the possession, giving as good as she was given!

And when it was over, and she lay wrapped in my enemy's arms, she turned to me and smiled. "You see, Basarab, you are not half the man you thought you were!" Her laugh tingled around the graves, sounding like the bells from those who had been buried alive. "Not half the man ... not half the man...

~

I bolted up from my coffin. As cold as the blood was that flowed through my body, I was sweating. What manner of demon had sent me such a dream? Was it an omen of things to come? A warning for me not to be foolish—not to go alone to meet with Radu?

Slowly, I climbed from my resting place. There was someone I needed to see, to ensure her loyalty to me, to me alone. I did not knock on her door, just opened it and entered the room. Her sweet scent tantalized my nostrils. She slept. Serenely. Her long red tresses spread wildly across the pillow. A contented smile was upon her lips. Was she dreaming of me?

I stood by her bed for a moment, then turned and left the room, not wanting to disturb her moments of peace. What had I been thinking? It had been nothing more than a dream. Nevertheless, it was a dream I would take into consideration. I would not go alone to meet with Radu, but he would not be aware of that until it was too late, should he decide to dishonour his word.

The time for playing *nice* was over!

# Virginia

## Chapter Fifteen

I had heard my door open, disturbing my dream. I was grateful for the disturbance, but was not yet prepared to share my anxiety at the crudeness of the visions that had kaleidoscoped through my dream world. I kept my eyes closed. I knew it was him. I heard his breathing, and I felt the stroke of his finger on my cheek, even though our flesh did not actually touch.

When I was sure he was gone, I threw the covers off and sat up. The dream was still unsettling me. Had it been sent to me as a warning? Should I share it with Basarab? Should he be aware that his meeting with Radu was not going to go smoothly? But it was just a dream—not real. I got out of bed and began to pace around the room, going over in my mind the events in my dream…

It had taken place in the graveyard, just down the road … the same graveyard I had rested in when I had made my escape from the house. The scenes were being orchestrated by me. I was surrounded by Radu, Basarab, and a man who was bigger than life itself … a man who was introduced to me as Peter. I was dancing for the men, weaving in and out of their arms, but lingering longer with Peter. I was laughing—at Basarab—as I watched the pain on the master vampire's face as he observed my flirtation with another man.

I was singing, too … a ballad of love whilst gazing into Peter's eyes, whilst being held in his arms … a ballad of betrayal, whilst passing by Basarab. Words of warning spewed from my mouth as I admonished Radu for what he seemed about to do to Basarab, reminding Radu he had promised not to harm the vampire leader—just scare him.

And then, I was on the ground intertwined in Peter's arms. The graveyard was filled with the howling of wolves—victory howls—and howls of defeat! After the consumption, I stood naked before Basarab and told him it was over, he had lost. Radu was giving me refuge—me and *my* children. There was naught he could do about it. Radu and Peter had stepped away, grinning evilly, and then laughing at how easy it had been to defeat the powerful vampire leader, and relating how pleasurable it would be to sit upon the throne.

Basarab reached out to me, misery in his eyes. He begged me not to go with his uncle and the rogue. But I told him I wanted him to experience pain and loss in the same manner I had experienced it the night he had taken me on the wings of hell, and then on that same night, he had left me in shambles upon the floor of my room while he and Teresa mocked me as they had walked off arm in arm. I wanted him to experience a total loss—the loss of his children. As I turned my back on him, I thought I detected tears in his eyes...

I stopped by the window and gazed out into the early evening. The dream disturbed me. I didn't like what I had done in the dream. I knew, deep in my heart, I loved Basarab; and there would be no other who could ever take his place. But he was so unreachable to me, despite me having given him two children. He was married to Teresa. And even if something were to happen to her, I knew Ildiko would be there vying for her place with the count—the place she felt was rightfully hers to begin with. What chance did I stand against those two women? I was not a vampire—they were!

A knock came on the door. I didn't bother to answer, thinking it wouldn't matter if I didn't want visitors, anyway. But the knock came again, so I called out for whoever it was to come in. Emelia entered.

"Emelia! When did you arrive?"

"A couple hours ago ... Carla brought me." Emelia walked over to where I stood by the window and gathered me into her arms. "I am so sorry things did not work out, but you know it might be for the best. The children are here safe with their father and the others. I don't think I would have been able to fight off Radu and Elizabeth on my own, nor the one they brought with them. I hear he is a monster."

"Have you seen the children?" I asked. "... Adelaide and Alfred?"

"Yes, I have seen them all. They are well. Adelaide looks tired, Alfred, too. They are still noticeably bruised from the beating Tanyasin gave them. The children are playing in the nursery. Santan is worried about you, though. He asked me to tell his father that he wanted to see you."

"Did you?"

"Yes."

"And?"

"Basarab gave me the key to your room and requested I take you to the children."

"You have spoken to Basarab?" I asked.

Emelia smiled. "Yes, actually I spoke to him shortly after I first arrived. We talked about what happened when I helped you escape and gave you Santan. I don't think he fully understands, but he seems to have forgiven me a bit."

"I am happy for you, Emelia," I said. "It's a good start."

She sighed. "Yes … we will just have to build from here."

"What of Randy? Have you seen him?" I felt guilty for not mentioning him sooner.

"He is waiting in the nursery for you. Come, we don't have much time before we are all to gather for the evening meal."

"Am I to be present at this meal?" I asked.

"Yes."

A feeling of apprehension flooded me. I wondered if this meal is where I would be told of my fate—if it would be the last meal I was to have. As I turned to follow Emelia, I noticed she had set the key on the table by the window. Quickly, I scooped it up and dropped it in my pocket. I wondered if she had left it there on purpose.

We climbed another flight of stairs, and then took a left turn to a room at the end of the hall. I could hear Samara laughing, and Santan telling her to calm down; then he laughed.

As Emelia and I stepped through the door, we saw Randy on the floor, being tackled by the children. My heart warmed at the sight.

As soon as Randy saw me, his face broke into a broad smile. "Look who's here, kids!" he shouted excitedly.

Santan ran to me and threw his arms around my legs. Samara hesitated a moment, and then slowly made her way over and hugged me, as well. I knelt down and folded my children into my arms, and buried my nose in their hair, breathing in their scent. Emelia stood back, allowing me my moment.

Randy approached, leaned over and whispered in my ear. "I must speak with you in private."

I looked into his eyes and saw worry there. "I am not sure how we can arrange that," I whispered back.

"Ask Emelia if she would mind watching the children for us. Maybe we could go up on the roof to the widow's walk. It would be private there, I think."

I nodded. "I can ask her."

Emelia had sat down on the edge of one of the beds. The children had crawled up beside her, and Santan was handing his great-aunt a book. I approached cautiously. "Emelia…" I began, still trying to think of what excuse I could give her about why Randy and I needed to leave so soon after my coming to see my children. I was conjuring a lie in my head. "Emelia, would you mind so much if Randy and I stepped out for a bit?" I smiled sheepishly.

Emelia glanced at me, not saying anything for a minute. Then: "Of course, dear; I understand you two might want to be alone for a few moments. So much has happened. Where will you go?" I noticed a twinkle in her eyes.

"For a breath of fresh air; I was thinking up to the top where the widow's walk is. It is dark enough that we will not be detected," I added.

"The children and I will be fine, but don't be long. Remember, we are all expected to be at supper tonight."

Randy was already at the door. I turned and followed him out. We quickly found the stairs leading to the uppermost room, the room where I had stayed for part of my captivity. Luck was with us, the door was unlocked. Randy grabbed my hand and pulled me through the room, to the door that led to the outside. Once we were out in the fresh air, we both stopped and breathed in the crispness. I shuddered. Randy put his arm around me, trying to shield me from the cold.

"What is it you wanted to tell me, Randy? Please make it quick. It's freezing out here."

"Your life is in danger," he began.

"No kidding, genius!" I interrupted. "Just when did you figure that out?"

"Don't be sarcastic, Virginia, please. I am not talking about danger from the count. I think he is probably the least of your worries at the moment. I am talking about Ildiko and Teresa."

I felt a moment of shock at the mention of the two women who were my arch rivals for the count's attention. "What do you mean? What do you know? And how have you come upon such knowledge?" I questioned.

"I was wandering…"

"What do you mean, you were wandering?" I interrupted again. "Who let you out of your room to wander about unsupervised?"

"Max came and unlocked the door for me. He told me the count had ordered I was not to be kept locked in. Max said the count knew I wouldn't go anywhere as long as you and the children were here."

"You should have taken the opportunity to get out of here," I said softly, remembering one of my dreams.

"You know I wouldn't do that, Virginia. I would never leave you behind." Randy's face turned red, and it was not from the bitter wind. "Anyway," he continued, "I was approaching a room on the second floor when I heard women's voices. I recognized Ildiko's voice immediately, so I hid in an alcove beside the room. I assumed the other woman was Teresa because I heard the word *husband*. I don't think they were worried about being heard because they weren't keeping their voices down, at all. Ildiko was telling Teresa about how she had caught Basarab coming out of your room, and she knew he had been there for quite some time—she had also seen him go into your room. She told Teresa she had confronted Basarab about what he was up to.

"I could tell, at first, Teresa wasn't buying into Ildiko's story. She asked Ildiko why she cared so much, now, since she had always made it quite clear in the past that she had no use for the filthy Gypsy bride her cousin had married. But Ildiko pushed on, saying you were a threat to both of them, and as much as she hadn't been happy about Teresa's marriage to Basarab, she was even less happy about the count's obvious obsession with you. She said that at least they were both vampires. Then she went on to say you needed to be removed from the equation because as long as you were alive you were a threat to both of them.

"In all truth, at first, Teresa sounded reluctant to go along with any plan that would eliminate you permanently. She suggested getting you out of the house and locking you somewhere until the family had left ... maybe letting Carla know where you were so she could release you when they were well out of the country. But, Ildiko kept pushing, insisting that as long as you were alive, you would be trouble because you would not rest until you were rejoined with your children. She even went as far to say that they would tell the count you had escaped, and they would write a note to the count in which you would tell him you wanted nothing more to do with any of them, and he could have the children. With that kind of knowledge, he would not want to stay and search for you. Ildiko told Teresa that she feared the count had fallen for you in a way even he had no control over."

Randy paused a moment, took a deep breath, and then asked the question I had an inkling had been on his mind even before he had begun to tell me his story. "Is there something between you and the count that I should be aware of, Virginia?"

"What are you getting at, Randy?" I questioned innocently, knowing full well what Randy was driving at.

"You know what I mean. Or, are you trying to play one of your games with me?" I noticed a slight sneer on the edge of Randy's lips.

"If I were playing a game, it would be a game to save us all!" The words were out of my mouth before I could stop them.

"What do you mean ... save us all?"

"Actually, if you want the truth, Randy, it would be to protect you. Do you think, for a moment, the count is going to allow you to live? He is toying with you. He has seen how close you are to his son, and that is a closeness Basarab will not tolerate. I am sure of that!"

"Then it is best we both get out of here," Randy said.

"And how would you suggest we do that?" I retorted.

"Tomorrow, during the day. Somehow, I will pick the lock on your door."

As Randy mentioned the lock on my door, I remembered the gift I had picked up. My hand dug into my pocket, and I drew out the key. "You won't have to pick the lock," I said, holding it up.

Randy looked surprised. "How did you get your hands on a key?"

"A little gift from Emelia, although I don't think she realized she left it on the table." I hesitated before handing the key over to Randy. "I'm going to give it to you. I don't think it works from the inside, and I am sure there is another key around to make sure I am locked in."

"So, you are coming with me, then?" Randy asked.

"Well ... I haven't decided yet. I want to know your plan, if you have one. We just can't leave and have nowhere to go. Your house would be the first place they would look for us ... you do have a plan, don't you?"

"Actually, I do. I called my uncle from my cell phone, and asked him if there was someplace he knew of where I could go to get away from it all for a bit. Told him I needed someplace secluded, but I didn't want to leave the city, or go too far from it. My uncle said he would make a phone call and get back to me. Said he had a friend who was doing some renovations on an old shack at the entrance of Brant Park, and I might be able to stay there for a bit if I didn't mind the mess of the renovations. He called me back within the hour and said it was a go. His friend liked the idea of having someone stay there for a couple weeks because he had to go out of town and didn't want to leave the property empty, especially with all the tools and supplies he had there. He doesn't trust that teenagers wouldn't try and use the place as a hangout if they discovered it was empty. He'd already seen a few young guys hanging around the place, and had noticed several footprints in the snow that didn't belong to him or the workers. He's going to give my uncle a key before he leaves tomorrow."

"How do we get the key from your uncle?" I asked.

"When I call my uncle to let him know I am taking it for the two weeks, he will leave the key for me in a designated spot."

"Does he know I will be with you?" I asked, noticing Randy had not actually mentioned my name when he was relaying to me his conversation with his uncle.

"No ... I never mentioned you ... I really wasn't sure you would come with me ... does this mean you will come?" he asked for a second time.

"I am not sure I can leave the children." I was beginning to get cold feet about leaving, knowing if I did, I might never see my children again. "Maybe it's better that just you go."

Randy grabbed me by the shoulders and leaned down close. "What is it you don't understand, Virginia? You are not safe here! Ildiko and Teresa plan to do away with you, and not just hide you somewhere until the family is out of the city. You will be dead. If that happens, what chance will you have of ever seeing your children again?" Randy drove his point home.

I pulled away from him. I was terrified to go. I was terrified not to. "Surely, there is another way..." I began.

"There is no other way. I will come to your room tomorrow morning after breakfast. Max, I noticed, usually takes a short nap after he finishes his morning rounds. Be ready. You don't have to pack anything. My uncle said the cabin has plenty of food and the owner told him I could help myself. We can stop somewhere on the way, or go out later, to pick up some personal items. I'm sure there are blankets and such already there." Randy hesitated. "Ah, do you have any money with you?"

"In my suitcase, but I don't know where that is at the moment."

"Damn! Okay ... I'll ask my uncle to leave me some money, along with the key, then."

"And you think he is not going to be curious about all this, and ask you for an explanation of why you need to get out of the house, and need money, and are willing to move into a place that is being renovated…"

Randy cut me off: "My uncle never asks questions about my life. I think he will be glad when any obligation toward me is over. You saw how he was … coming around as little as possible."

I knew Randy was right about his uncle, but also felt there was a first time for everything. Hopefully, this would not be the time when his uncle decided to pry into Randy's life. "We better get back," I said, starting to shake from the cold—or was it nerves?

Randy opened the door for me, and we stepped into the room. Despite the fact the room was not heated, without the wind blowing around, it was much warmer than it had been on the widow's walk. I rubbed my arms to get my circulation going again. Randy did the same. Before we exited the room, though, Randy pulled me to him, pressing me to his chest. "I love you, Virginia … you know that don't you? I only want what's best for you. I could never live with myself if something were to happen to you, knowing I could have prevented it."

My body stiffened in his arms. I pushed him away. "I appreciate what you are doing, Randy, but please understand, I can't return your love the way you want me to. I love you as a friend, my best friend—that is all. I am begging you to understand this. There will never be anything more between us. If you expect more, then maybe this is not a good idea that I go with you tomorrow."

Randy was quick to respond: "No … no … I promise to behave. The most important thing right now is to get you away from Ildiko and Teresa." He opened the door, and I followed him back to the nursery.

Santan came running to us as soon as we entered the room. "Mama! Randy! You have been gone so long; I was worried about you … Mama, your skin is as cold as Father's."

I shivered. "Yes, it is, isn't it? Randy and I got carried away walking around the top of the house. I guess it was colder than I thought it would be."

"Me want to see," Samara shouted, jumping down from the bed and running over to us. "Me want to see top of house!"

"Another time, Samara," I said quickly. "Right now, I think we have to get ready to go down and have supper with your papa," I added. "You want to see him, don't you?"

"Yes … yes," Samara squealed. "Samara want to see her papa."

"Shall we then?" I pointed to the door. As we were exiting the room, I noticed Emelia patting her pocket, and then she shrugged. I prayed she did not remember the key, and if she did that she would not return to my room to look for it. Samara was a good distraction, though, for she bounced ahead of us, heading for the stairs. I also prayed Samara would not mention the fact that her mother and Randy had left the room and had walked on the top of the house.

"Someone loves her papa," Emelia laughed, closing the nursery door on her way out.

## Chapter Sixteen

Samara screamed in delight when she saw her father at the bottom of the stairway. I was surprised when he bound up the stairs, meeting her halfway, and scooping her up into his arms. "How is my little princess?" he smiled as he lifted her onto his shoulders.

"Princess Samara good!" my daughter giggled.

How fitting, I thought. Samara had the temperament of a princess—a spoiled one. I looked down on Santan who was still between me and Randy, holding our hands. There appeared to be concern on his face as he watched his father and his sister. Basarab, having settled Samara firmly on his shoulders, reached a hand to Santan.

Santan shook his head. "I am fine, Father. I will come with my mama and Randy."

I noticed the count stiffen at the mention of Randy. "As you wish, son." The count turned and headed back down the stairs.

When we entered the dining room, I noticed a second table had been set up, and that everyone appeared to have arrived, including Teresa and Ildiko. I tried not to look at them, but couldn't help myself. They both appeared attentive to my entrance, but looked away quickly, and began conversing with each other. I wondered whom they thought they were fooling. It was a well-known fact within the family circle that Ildiko had never had any love for Teresa. I noticed Atilla studying the two women, as well, a speculative look on his face.

The count took his place at the head of the table. Samara planted herself on her father's lap, despite his attempt to send her to the table where the women sat, and where the highchair had been set up for her. The count motioned to Ildiko, and she came and took Samara in her arms, and then to the highchair. Samara struggled against her, at first, but a look from her father settled her down. She sat in her chair, a slight pout on her face as she stared adoringly at him.

I hesitated a moment, not sure where Randy and I were to go, and then I noticed a couple empty chairs beside Adelaide, Alfred and Carla—clearly the area where humans were to sit.

As Randy and I headed in that direction, Santan still between us, the count's voice rang out. "Santan, you will sit here beside me." There was such an air of authority in Basarab's voice that the three of us stopped.

Santan gripped my hand tighter, indicating to me he did not want to sit with his father. I knew the worst thing I could do right now was to create a scene. I knelt down so that I was eye to eye with my son. "It is okay, Santan. Go and sit with your father. I will see you after supper."

Santan still hesitated. He looked up at Randy. Thankfully, Randy reaffirmed what I had told my son. "It's okay, little buddy, I'll come and see you later. Maybe even get to tuck you into bed."

*Don't overplay this, Randy, or your wandering privileges will be cancelled!* I smiled and led Santan over to Basarab. "Here is your son, Basarab." I lingered a bit longer than necessary, but I was trying to steer Basarab's attention away from Randy's statement. I pointed to the table where I would be sitting. "Mama will be right over there," I said to Santan, although I was looking at the count.

Basarab looked directly into my eyes. What was I hoping to see? Approval? I had no idea, but one thing I knew for sure, such a statement as I had made was a reminder to the count that I was the mother of his son. It was the icing on the cake that Santan continued to bake—my son's love and devotion for me was not going to go unnoticed! When the count didn't say anything further, I turned, and with my shoulders back and my head high, I walked to my seat, aware of the numerous eyes in the room that were following me. Before I sat down, I embraced Adelaide and Alfred, and whispered in their ears how grateful I was that they were okay. I noticed tears in both their eyes as I released them from my hug. I nodded to Carla and then sat down.

Max entered the dining room, pushing a cart with several bottles on it. He put them periodically along the two tables. When he came to where we humans were sitting, he placed a bottle of *Santa Margherita, Chianti Classico* in front of me. Bottles were opened and poured, and still we waited for our meal. My stomach growled, reminding me it had been some time since I had eaten.

Randy leaned over and chuckled. "Hungry, are you, Virginia?"

"Starving."

Max left and re-entered the room a few minutes later, pushing a tray with several covered dishes on it. I was curious as to what kind of meal the count would deem fit for his children, especially after noticing a small wine glass at my son's setting. I watched in horror as Basarab poured some of the liquid from his bottle into Santan's glass. Santan gazed up at his father; the count nodded and pushed the glass closer to his son. Santan looked at me, as though he was asking for affirmation to drink what his father had given him. I didn't want my son to drink what I knew was in his glass, but what choice did I have to disagree? I smiled to my son and nodded my head, but inside my stomach was churning. I had worked so hard to humanize my children, and it was all for naught, so it seemed. There was no end to his power, no victory over it that I ever would be able to achieve. I reached for the wine bottle in front of me and handed it to Randy.

"Would you do the honours of opening this?"

As Randy opened our wine, Max set plates of food in front of us, removing the cover from each one as he did. I heard Randy breath a sigh of relief at the sight of real food on his plate––chicken breast, lightly spiced; sweet potato smothered with butter and chives; French style green beans with almonds; and a crusty roll.

"If anyone can't finish their plate, just pass it over here," Randy laughed as he was burying his nose in the savoury aroma steaming from his plate.

Alfred smiled. "I'll take that into consideration," he said as he held out his glass for Randy to fill it with wine.

I was surprised at the quietness in the room as everyone partook of their meals. Most conversations were in hushed whispers, with the exception of Samara whose voice rang excitedly through the room. She was sitting between Teresa and Ildiko, and it appeared she was having a wonderful time, despite not being allowed to sit with her father, and despite her previous disdain for Teresa. Of course, Samara had been quite taken with Ildiko, and I noticed it was her that my daughter was more attentive to. I also noticed Teresa had poured some liquid from her bottle into a small glass in front of Samara. I was relieved to see my daughter wrinkle her nose in disgust when she tasted her drink. Ildiko patted Samara's arm, leaned over and whispered something in her ear. Samara giggled, and then lifted the glass to her mouth and took another sip.

I had barely finished my plate of food when the count stood and began to address those in the room. "Tonight, Orsolya is meeting with Radu in order to arrange a meeting between him and me. I know many of you have voiced your concern about me going alone, but I still believe it is the best way to approach this situation."

As the count spoke, my stomach knotted up. I was remembering my dream, and I desperately wanted to stand up and tell him not to go alone. But who was I to demand such a thing, or to be allowed to speak in this room filled with old-world vampires? It had just been a dream. Dreams were not real. I gazed around, searching for this Orsolya the count was speaking of. There were no new women present.

Suddenly there was a great deal of commotion emanating from the front foyer—a door banging, and loud voices. Within seconds, three men strode noisily into the dining room. I recognized the younger two of the group immediately—Vlad and Mihail. I assumed the older gentleman was Dracula, himself. At first sight, there was nothing overly impressive about him. He was smaller than I would have thought, and thin, almost to the point of being a shrivelled version of his sons. But, when he turned his eyes in my direction, the intensity of them burned directly to the core of my soul! I knew at that moment, Dracula was not a man to be taken lightly.

"My dear nephew," Dracula's voice boomed, "I do apologize for not getting here sooner. I was detained trying to gather these two rascals up. I knew they would never forgive their father if I did not bring them along for this event." He laughed, if one could call the sound that came from his throat laughter.

Basarab stood and embraced his uncle. "Uncle, it is good to see you again." He turned to his cousins. "Vlad … Mihail … it has been far too long since we have supped together," he said as he planted a kiss on their cheeks.

"I believe since we attended the birthing and the first initiation ceremony for your Santan," Mihail returned.

"Is the lovely mother here?" Vlad asked, looking around the room. His eyes settled on me, and he grinned. "Ah, there she is—gorgeous as ever. Motherhood becomes her." He turned back to Basarab. "Am I to understand you now have two children?"

"You understand correctly, cousin." Basarab pointed to Samara. "A girl."

Vlad smirked. "A girl … well," he turned to his brother, "I guess we can accept that. Girls do have their uses." The brothers burst into laughter and patted Basarab on the back.

"We are starving," Mihail stated. "I do hope you have enough of this to share," he added as he picked up a half-empty bottle from the table, and put it to his lips.

Dracula grabbed his son's wrist. "Where are your manners, Mihail? I am sure your cousin will share what he has here, but I am also sure he will provide you with a glass from which to drink."

I could have sworn Mihail blushed at his father's correction of his manners. He returned the bottle to the table. As though Max had been summoned, he appeared with three wine glasses. Atilla filled them and handed one to each of the new guests. I glanced at Randy to see how he was taking in this turn of events. He was watching with fascination. I leaned forward slightly in my chair so I could get a glimpse of Carla. Her face was stoic—unreadable. I leaned back and looked over to where Teresa and Ildiko sat. They were staring at me, hatred written all over their faces. I assume it was because it was not them who had received recognition from Dracula and his sons; it was me, their archrival. Despite the reservations I was feeling about leaving with Randy, I began to think he was right. I had no choice but to get away before it was too late, even if it meant leaving my children behind. I turned my attention to Basarab as he began speaking again.

"As I was saying before you arrived, uncle," the count began, "Orsolya will be arranging a meeting for me with Radu."

Dracula scowled. "That should not happen. I have come to deal with my brother. I have been brooding on the situation for some time, and I feel it is time we put an end to him. I also think I am the best one to do that, knowing him better than anyone else does."

Basarab's voice sounded strained as he replied to his uncle. "I am afraid my mind is made up. Orsolya will arrange the meeting; I am giving my word I will go alone."

"Then you are a fool!" Dracula threw his half-full glass across the room.

Kerecsen and Laborc moved quickly to Basarab's side. I noticed Kerecsen's fingers flexing as he glared at Dracula. Mihail and Vlad stepped to their father's side. *Oh great ... a standoff.*

"Settle down, gentlemen," Atilla's voice of reason broke into the silent altercation that was taking place. "We must not begin fighting amongst ourselves." He turned to his son. "Although there is one point I agree with Dracula on ... you should not go alone."

*I agree too.* I could not turn off the pictures from my dream.

Bajnok spoke up: "I have an idea ... let Basarab show up alone, but, in case Radu is not true to his word, let us have reinforcements nearby ... that is, if he even agrees to the meeting."

Atilla nodded his head in affirmation, as did all the vampires in the room. "A wise idea, Bajnok, and one I hope my son will listen to." He turned and spoke directly to Basarab. "I don't think we can take the chance, after all we have sacrificed to get to your son, to have something go amiss and lose Santan to Radu." Atilla paused momentarily, studying the count. I noticed the hard lines on Basarab's face begin to sag in defeat. "It is for the best, son."

Dracula seemed to have calmed down after listening to Atilla. "When you meet with Radu, I and my sons will hide close by," he commented.

"As will I," said Kerecsen.

"And I," Laborc was quick to add.

"However, the girl must not be aware of what we are planning," Basarab stated. "I still do not know if we can fully trust her, despite her tale of woe about how she feels about Radu. That is why I had Max deliver a meal to her in her room." He looked around. "I think this is enough excitement for now. Everyone is free to … oh … one more thing … Ponqor, how did the blood test?"

"I found it to be pure, and even though a couple bottles had a dissimilar taste and odour to them from the others, I could find no properties other than blood that would lead me to think the bottles had been tampered with."

"Dump those two bottles, then," Basarab ordered. "If there is a different taste to them, I don't trust that they are not tainted."

"As you wish, Basarab." Ponqor answered.

Everyone began to get up and disperse. I was not sure what was expected of me, or if I was going to be allowed free reign. Ildiko released Samara from her highchair, and my daughter ran straight to her father. Santan got down quietly from his chair, glanced at his father for a moment, and then walked over to me and Randy. He crawled up onto Randy's lap and put his arms around his friend's neck. The look Basarab threw our way did not go unnoticed by me, or two others in the room—Teresa and Ildiko. However, Basarab picked Samara up, turned, and left the room.

Max appeared and approached me. "I will see you to your room, now, Miss Virginia."

"Might I not visit with my son for a bit longer?" I asked.

"I am afraid not; the count has ordered I take you immediately to your room."

I tensed inside. *Still your prisoner! Why? After the recent moments we have shared ... after you have come to my room and I felt the love of your gaze ... after I felt the gentleness of your touch!* "As the count wishes." I turned to Randy and reached for my son. "Come, Santan, give your mama a hug. I am sure I shall see you later."

Santan transferred to my arms, and I held him longer than I normally would have. I could not believe I was even thinking of leaving him again ... leaving him with these monsters ... for, despite their semblance of normality, that is what they were—monsters who lived on blood! Maybe I wouldn't leave. But, as the thought crossed my mind, I caught a glimpse of Ildiko and Teresa. They were watching me closely; and, if revulsion could be painted on canvas, their faces would have been the perfect models!

I released my son back to Randy, nodded to my friend, and to Adelaide and Alfred, and Carla. Then, I followed Max back to my prison.

~

I was relieved Max had his own key, which meant the key Emelia had carelessly, or maybe not so carelessly, left on my table was a duplicate. I felt my head was about ready to explode. Why was the count locking me up, and no one else? Was it because he felt I was still a flight risk? He had what he had come here for—his children. I knew there was no way they would be out of his sight, or the sight of someone he trusted. Once again, I pondered my fate.

Visions of the looks on Teresa's and Ildiko's faces as they had stared at me in the dining room kept flashing through my mind. Dislike was one emotion I had dealt with many times in my life, but the hatred that had spewed from their eyes ... it was pure demonic! More so from Ildiko, though, which had me thinking Teresa was not the one I needed to be really afraid of.

The more I dwelt on the two women, who both seemed to have their minds set on either keeping Basarab, or getting him, the more I realized I might not have any choice but to take Randy's offer. Would I be ready to go with him when he came for me in the daylight hours? How far would we get if we did manage to escape? And, if we made it safely to this place Randy had arranged for us to go, how long would it be before the count came for me?—assuming he cared. I couldn't help hoping he did. Or would he send someone else, like Kerecsen, to end my life?

On the other hand, what if Teresa, or worse yet, Ildiko found us? I had no doubt that neither I, nor Randy, would leave our hiding place alive, nor that our bodies would be found until the vampires were long gone from Brantford—maybe never. I walked over to my window, sat down at the little table, and peered out into the night. The moon was bright, illuminating much of the area around the house.

I sat up at attention as I noticed a movement in the parking lot. It was Basarab, and he was with a young girl. He towered over her and had his hands on her shoulders. They appeared to be in earnest conversation. And then, he was sending her on her way. I watched as she walked across the parking lot. She paused at the gate and looked back at Basarab. He waved her on, and then turned and headed, not back to the house, but to a small chapel-like building that was half-hidden behind some bushes at the edge of the guardian trees.

Kerecsen and Laborc appeared. The three men stood conversing for several minutes. The count nodded. What I saw next was a first. Even though I was aware vampires could change into wolves, I had yet to see such a transformation. I had only observed Basarab's conversion from a bat to himself in the courtyard when I had made my first escape attempt during my former imprisonment in his house. Within seconds, in place of Basarab's cousins, were two large wolves. They bowed to the count, and then turned and trotted off in the same direction the girl had taken. Basarab watched them until they disappeared from sight. I watched him until he disappeared from my sight.

I stood and began to pace around my room. My mind was a muddle of thoughts. There was too much happening, and I had no time to make a concrete plan. I had to depend on others to see me through this mess, and I hated not having control over my own situation. As I passed by my door, I heard footsteps approaching. They sounded heavy, like a man's walk, and I wondered if Max was coming to take me to see my children. The steps stopped just outside my door. I waited for the lock to turn. But it didn't. The steps moved on. I commenced pacing.

As I passed by my window, I heard the door lock click. The door opened slowly, and the count stepped into my room. I think my heart almost stopped. I hadn't expected Basarab to visit me again.

"Virginia, my little bird, you appear unsettled," he said, approaching me.

I figured I had nothing to lose by being honest with the count. "Why shouldn't I be unsettled? You have seen fit to lock me in this room, yet you allow all the other humans to roam at will."

"There is a reason I call you my little bird ... you do have a habit of taking flight."

I searched for a hint of amusement in the count's eyes, but saw none. "That was in the past, Basarab; my children are here. I will not leave them." I almost choked on my last statement, knowing I probably was going to leave them in the morning light. Or, should I tell the count what Randy had overheard, and take my chances that Basarab would side with me, and not his wife and cousin?

"You look flushed; is there something you wish to tell me?" His voice was alluring.

I hadn't realized that as I had been thinking about telling him of the conspiracy, I had blushed. What excuse could I use for that? I thought quickly. "I have not been feeling well since supper. My stomach seems to be churning. I could be coming down with something."

Basarab reached his hand to my forehead. "You feel normal," he said, a frown creasing between his eyebrows.

I felt the electricity of his fingers as they touched my skin, and I reached instinctively to his hand. The count, as though he understood my signal, covered my hand with his. Gently, he led me over to the bed. "Are you too ill for this?" he asked as he started to undress me.

I shuddered. *Damn! Not now!* "Do you have time for this? Won't Orsolya be returning soon with news for you as to whether Radu will meet with you, or not?"

"I do not anticipate a hurried return," the count replied. "And, there is always time for such delights as this," he added as he undid the jeans I was wearing, slipping them off my waist and down to the floor.

I cannot say it was the most spectacular time I had had with the count, for it seemed he was hurried. Nevertheless, it had been enough to satisfy me, for now. I pulled the covers up to my shoulders and smiled ... not so much at what the count had done to me, but at what he had said to me. *Virginia, my little bird, my love ... you have nothing to fear from me.*

I had nothing to fear from him, so why was I thinking of running off with Randy and leaving my children behind? Surely, anything Teresa or Ildiko attempted to do to me would be thwarted by the count—surely. But Randy's words stormed into my head. Words he had heard Ildiko say ... *I needed to be removed from the equation because as long as I was alive I would be a threat to them both!* But hadn't she also stated she feared the count had fallen for me in a way he had no control over? Hadn't his coming to me tonight been proof enough of how he could not stay away from me?

Or, was he playing a game? Would he, once again, be victorious? I needed to get some sleep in order to think straight. Randy would be coming through my door, soon, in order to take me from this place. My decision of whether to stay or flee had to be made by then.

# Basarab

## Chapter Seventeen

As I exited Virginia's room, I thought I heard footsteps close by, and a door closing; however, when I searched the hallway, I detected no one. I wanted to speak with my cousins before Orsolya returned, so I headed outside. They had all been gone a long time ... *longer than necessary, I think ... I hope nothing has gone wrong.*

My body was still on fire from my recent encounter with Virginia. There were times I found it difficult to understand my feelings toward her, how this human woman had gotten so deeply under my skin. She was a distraction I didn't need, especially at the brink of a vampire war. I had my son and daughter; what did I need Virginia for? She was causing nothing but problems for me. I was aware Teresa only exhibited meagre tolerance toward Virginia, but my cousin, Ildiko, was belligerent when she spoke to me in regards to her ... to the point where I feared for the life of the mother of my children. It baffled me why I should fear for Virginia's life ... if I wanted her removed from my life, I would be the one to make that decision!

The howling of wolves echoed into the night. Music to my ears. I knew Kerecsen and Laborc were close. I leaned against one of the trees, waiting for their arrival. Laborc was the first to arrive, and as he did, he transformed. Kerecsen followed a few seconds later, already changed. I stepped away from the tree.

"Welcome, cousins. I have been worried."

"Radu was late," Laborc stated. "Orsolya had started to return here, but when she saw a car turn into the cemetery, she waited. The car stopped beside her."

"Was Radu alone?"

"No. Elizabeth was with him." Kerecsen took a deep breath. "And there was someone else there, as well. They obviously did not want to be seen because they stayed in the back seat of the car. I circled around, staying upwind, so whoever it was would not pick up my scent. I also noticed Tanyasin hunkering behind one of the large gravestones."

"Interesting," I commented. "Did she see you?"

"I think not. I kept pretty well hidden. The gravestones in the cemetery are large, which was an advantage."

"Did she present herself at any point during the meeting?"

"No. She just sat there, her eyes glued on Radu and Elizabeth. It wasn't until they were gone that Tanyasin came out of hiding, moving quickly to catch up with Orsolya who was almost running to get out of the cemetery. Tanyasin grabbed the girl by the arm and leaned in to say something to her. Unfortunately, she whispered so low that even with our keen hearing we could not discern what she said to the girl," Kerecsen stated.

"One thing, though, Orsolya was shaking like a leaf when Tanyasin finally released her. You will have to ask the girl what the old Gypsy said to her," Laborc added.

"I will do that," I said. "But now, what of the meeting with Radu … did Orsolya follow directions to the letter, or did she possibly add her own agenda?"

Laborc spoke first. "We tried to get in close, but Elizabeth commented that she felt there was something amiss, and she began pacing, circling and sniffing the air. We were forced to back away, out of clear earshot. By the time we thought of changing to bat form so we could get closer, the meeting was over. Radu was giving Orsolya a hug. Elizabeth returned to Radu's side, but she did not embrace the girl."

"And the other person still had not shown themselves?"

"No."

"I assume it was this Peter."

"I assume so, as well," Laborc stated.

"She exudes evil—Elizabeth—and I don't think Radu realizes just how much!" Kerecsen added. "Come to think of it, Elizabeth and Tanyasin should have been sisters!" Laughter bubbled from his throat.

"Yes, I have often wondered how Angelique and Tanyasin could be related," I said. "So, the bottom line is that you didn't really hear much of anything?"

"No … you are going to have to rely on Orsolya to tell you the truth of it—or the lie. Whichever she chooses," Kerecsen answered. "If it hadn't been such a windy night, we would have been able to stay close, but we had to be extra cautious. Our scents are too easily detected by our own kind, even if they are rogues," he added.

"We waited until we were sure the girl would be back to the house before we returned," Laborc said. "Did you not see her come in, Basarab?"

"I'm afraid not. I was otherwise detained." I felt a brief moment of guilt when I thought about what had detained me.

Kerecsen smacked me on my back. "My dear cousin, you live life to the fullest, don't you? Nevertheless, I must be serious here," he said, the smile evaporating from his face. "We need you to focus on the task at hand. If I might be so bold to say something else … if you are so enamoured with Virginia, keep her safe, and then bring her to Brasov with us when we return. You can set her up in a little apartment and visit her whenever the mood strikes you."

"And what do you suggest our dear Basarab do with his wife … you remember Teresa, don't you?" Laborc reminded Kerecsen. I detected a great deal of harshness in his voice.

Kerecsen nodded. "What of your wife, Basarab? Is our Teresa still the love of your life, or has this human wench so bewitched you with her charms that you are ready to forget the woman who has stood by you over the centuries? Does Teresa approve of such a deep relationship as you seem to have with Virginia? After all, it does appear she is more to you than a whore you might pick up off the street in order to partake of a few moments of pleasure, and then discard!"

I took a few moments to contemplate my answer. What I had heard Teresa tell her father that night in Brasov still weighed heavily on me, despite me having gone to her with the pretence of putting the past behind us. She had admitted to her father that she was playing a game. The vision was still clear in my mind …

"I don't care, Father! Don't you get it? I never wanted a child. Basarab was all I ever needed in my life!"

"But, Teresa, Basarab did it for you; you always led him to believe you wanted a child."

"Those are the key words, Father—led him to believe! I hope Virginia hides so well that we never find her—or the bastard child! ... I will play the loving mother ... my dear husband will not want to see me so distraught. I know that beneath his tough, ruthless exterior, there is a man whose heart has holes in it. Some of those holes I have put there, in order to manipulate him! ... He has become so besotted with the loss of his son that I can hardly bear to be around him! Do you want to know who he was calling for in his sleep, Father? It was not me ... it was her!

"My dear daughter, what have you become?"

"Just what you bargained for, Father, when you bargained my hand in marriage in exchange for the release of my mother, Lilly…"

"Basarab?" Laborc jerked me back to the present.

I turned to my friends, my blood family, and heaved a deep sigh. "I am afraid, despite the picture Teresa portrays to us, she is not the woman any of us thought her to be. I know this because I have heard the words from her mouth, and I have kept them to myself far too long. She will have her day of reckoning with me, and she will have the opportunity to clarify her position in my household. As for Virginia, I will decide before we return to Brasov what her fate will be. As you have said, the most crucial matter we came here for has been accomplished. I have my children. Nothing else matters other than trying to dissuade Radu from the course he has set himself upon."

I paused a moment, studying Kerecsen and Laborc, feeling they still were not entirely convinced about where I stood with my wife and Virginia. I smiled, slowly. "In truth, for the time being, and to set you at ease, I am not setting Teresa aside—she is still my queen. And, even though she has not behaved with the grace of a queen since Virginia entered the picture, I understand. Nevertheless, I want to remind you, it was Teresa who agreed to allow me to bed another woman in order to have a child. I know it was a difficult decision for her, but she gave me her blessing so we could have a son." I paused a moment and tried to read what my cousins were thinking. "Please understand, Virginia is just a diversion … it does not hurt, does it, to have a little entertainment?" I laughed, despite the lie on my tongue. *I don't have to justify my actions to you … but there you have it!*

My cousins laughed along with me, but I could tell their laughter was strained. They did not believe me.

"Well, whatever the case might be, keep your focus … at least until we get out of here," Kerecsen suggested. "We will see you later. We'll slip in the back door just in case Orsolya is waiting for you at the front entrance," he added.

"Good idea. Would you like to join me whilst I question her?" I asked, thinking maybe it would be a good idea to have them observe her body language.

Kerecsen took the opportunity to accept. "I think that is an exceptionally smart idea; however, I think she should present her findings in front of all of us. In a room filled with true-blood vampires, I would assume she, a rogue, would think twice about lying."

I turned to Laborc. "Do you agree?"

Laborc nodded affirmatively. "I especially want to see the look on her face when you bring up her encounter with Tanyasin."

"So be it, then." I turned and headed into the house. "Call the others together. We will meet in the dining room within the half hour."

Orsolya was waiting for me in the foyer. She was sitting on a settee, and rose to greet me. I noticed she did not look directly into my eyes, and I took this as a sign of deceit.

However, despite my cousins' suggestion, I wanted to hear her story first, so I began questioning her.

"You have news, Orsolya?"

She nodded. "I do."

"And it is good news?"

"Some."

"Meaning?" I didn't like the way I had to pull the information out of her.

"Meaning, it went well enough with Radu. He agreed to meet with you, alone, tomorrow night. Radu has discovered a quiet restaurant, just outside the city limits. He said it would be better for both of you to meet where there were people around, at least until you heard each other out."

Did he give you the address to this place?" I thought I knew the restaurant Radu was talking about.

"Yes. He wrote it down for you." Orsolya reached into her pocket and pulled out a piece of paper and handed it to me.

I read the writing … Olde School Restaurant … Paris Road … 9:00. Reservation is under Musat. I placed my hand under Orsolya's chin and lifted her face so she was looking directly into my eyes. "Anything else?"

She hesitated. Finally, "Yes … there was another in the cemetery … as I was leaving…" Orsolya began to shake as the words seemed to catch in her throat.

I urged her on. "Who else was there?"

"Tanyasin." Orsolya's voice was a mere whisper.

"Tanyasin!" I maintained surprise in my voice so as not to give Orsolya any indication of my current knowledge. "What did she want with you?"

"She wanted to know why I was meeting with Radu, and what I was doing staying with you. She said she knew I served Radu, I was one of his rogues, and she questioned my loyalty to him. Was I spying for my master, or for you?"

I waited patiently for Orsolya to continue. Her breathing appeared to have accelerated, and I detected nervous twitches at the corners of her eyes.

Orsolya gazed down to the floor. "I told her I was spying for Radu."

"Good," I reassured her. "That was the best answer. It is better she think that, than be led to believe you betrayed your benefactor." *Yet, I wonder if there is more truth in your words than you would like me to know.* "What else did Tanyasin want?"

"She forced me to tell her all I knew about you and Radu meeting."

"So she knows when and where we are meeting?"

"Yes."

"Anything else?"

"I confirmed the children were in the house, and under your protection."

With my hands behind my back, I began to pace. I was sure Tanyasin already knew my children were with me; why would she need to ask Orsolya? Unless, Orsolya had given Tanyasin further information—like the exact location of the children's room. I made a mental note to move Santan and Samara to another part of the house, just in case.

I stopped in front of Orsolya and placed my hands on her shoulders. "You have done well. I am going to take you up to Ildiko now. She will bring you downstairs later if I have further need of you." Orsolya had told me what I needed to know, verbally and body language wise.

She nodded and followed me up the stairs. When we entered Ildiko's room, she was standing by the window, staring out into the night. I wondered if she had observed my meeting with Kerecsen and Laborc, or if she had even gone so far as to sneak out and do a little spying of her own. I also pondered briefly on Ildiko's continued loyalty to me, knowing how agitated she was over my recent liaisons with Virginia.

"Basarab," Ildiko turned as I entered with Orsolya. "To what do I owe this pleasure?"

I detected irony in her words, but ignored the slight. "I would like you to keep Orsolya with you while I gather the others and brief them. I will send Max for you, if necessary."

Ildiko nodded. "As you wish … is all well?"

"I believe so."

As I left Ildiko's room, a feeling of unease raced through my veins, like thunder chasing lightning on a stormy night. She had been too compliant, unlike our last few encounters. I wondered what she was up to.

Kerecsen and Laborc had informed everyone I wished to meet, and there was a sombre atmosphere in the dining room when I entered. Everyone seemed to be lost in their own thoughts. Even my father had a faraway look in his eyes. I welcomed everyone and thanked them for coming, and then took my seat at the head of the table. It was the spot always reserved for me; however, lately, I had had thoughts about how deserving I was of that position. I glimpsed briefly at Teresa, catching her studying me. Her eyes told me nothing of what she might be thinking.

I turned the floor over to Kerecsen and Laborc, allowing them to explain what had transpired in the graveyard. When they were finished, Dracula stood.

"You must let me deal with Radu, nephew. He is not to be trusted ... neither he, nor his high-bred rogue, Elizabeth. Plus, you do not know exactly what this Peter fellow will bring to the table. I have heard rumours of his ruthlessness, and he is loyal only to Radu."

"Everyone seems to be aware of Peter, now, and what he is supposedly capable of, and his loyalty to Radu," I began, "Nevertheless, he is still a rogue, and no match for one of us."

"In truth, that is yet to be established," Dracula replied.

I was frustrated with everyone around me. *Does not one of you think I am capable of ruling? Let one of you step up to the plate and sit upon this throne I have been cursed with! I am so tired of it all!* "It appears, uncle, you want to take my place ... is this your intention?"

I noticed how Dracula stiffened before he spoke. "Of course not, Basarab. You have been an exemplary leader over the centuries ... I ... I just think your priorities at the moment are ... how shall I say it..."

"Straight!" I ordered.

"Very well ... your priorities at the moment are not where they should be. They lie upstairs in the room of one of your guests ... and with your children, of course," he added quickly.

I was aware of the disdain in Dracula's voice. And, if I was aware of it, I was sure the others were, as well. I saw it in some of their eyes. I was losing respect amongst my peers. Dracula was powerful, and he was not a vampire to take lightly. Even though he was my uncle, and had stayed in the shadows all these centuries, I discerned he resented my position of power. I decided to confront my uncle with his absenteeism over the years. "You seem to know more about me than I do." The sharpness in my words could have sliced through thick ice. "But, where have you been most of the time, while we have been dealing with the problems? You dare to show up here with your sons and begin to give me orders!" I was aware of the intake of breath around the table. I was fed up with being second-guessed. I needed to show them all that I was still in control!

Dracula laughed. "So, you do have some of your old spirit left! I thought maybe this human wench had fully castrated you."

My hands curled into fists. I felt the muscles on my face tighten. My lips curled. A snarl emitted from my throat. Vlad and Mihail rose to their father's defence, if he should need it. Atilla stood quickly and stepped between me and Dracula.

"Enough! Do we not have more problems than we seem able to handle without having division within our own ranks?" Atilla turned to Dracula. "It was not Basarab's choice to be our leader. My son was cursed with that position, and in my opinion he has done an admirable job. The stress of your brother Radu's actions has worn all our nerves thin." My father halted briefly, as though reflecting on what he was going to say next. I noticed how his eyes swept around the table, pausing at each member of the family. "If any one of you thinks you can do a better job, step forward now."

No one moved. Some were looking down at the table. Others looked away.

"I didn't think so." Atilla's voice relayed his disgust at what was happening amongst the family members. "Well, now that is settled, I think we should trust in Basarab's plan and hope it works out for the best. Any way we can avoid bloodshed is the approach we should endeavour to take because it will bring less attention to our kind, something most of us have tried to avoid." Atilla looked directly at Dracula and his sons, and then turned to me. "The floor is yours."

Slowly, I stood and gazed around the room, taking in the dour looks. "There may be a different problem that none of us has anticipated. Until now, we knew we were dealing with Radu, and possibly Elizabeth; but Orsolya, as she was leaving the cemetery after her meeting with Radu, was confronted by Tanyasin. It appears, with what we already know of Tanyasin's attempts to get to my children, she might have her own agenda. I do not think if she was to ever get her hands on Santan and Samara that they would be presented to Radu as a tool for him to use to get to me. I also feel there are many secrets and betrayals within Radu's ranks—something that just might work in our favour.

"Kerecsen and Laborc were unable to learn too much because of the weather conditions. Their scent would have carried on the wind had they gotten too close. So, I have had to rely on Orsolya's word for what transpired. She is with Ildiko, awaiting word from me to come down and tell all again, should any of you want to hear the words from her own mouth. I have heard her story; however, if she were to tell it again I would be able to watch her closely and detect anything different in her telling."

I nodded to Max who was standing by the doorway. "Please tell Ildiko it is time to bring Orsolya down."

While waiting for Ildiko and Orsolya, I broached the subject of Peter. "As Dracula and others have said, we should be cautious of this Peter. Even though it appears, on the surface, he is loyal to Radu, he may have his own agenda, as well."

Before I could elaborate further, Ildiko and Orsolya walked through the door. Orsolya's head was bowed, and she did not look up as Ildiko guided her to an empty chair that had been placed beside me. She sat down and folded her hands on her lap, twisting her fingers around each other nervously.

I reached over and lifted her chin with my hand. I looked directly into her eyes. "You have relayed to me what happened in the cemetery ... my friends would like to hear what you have to say ... in your words ... not my translation." I observed a perturbed look cross through her eyes, but she recovered quickly by closing her eyelids and turning her head away.

"You still do not trust me," she mumbled.

"Give me a good reason to," I answered.

# Virginia
## Chapter Eighteen

Sleep tried hard to wrap its arms around me, but it was a fitful sleep, tormented by a multitude of dreams…

I was hiding in the corner of my room. Someone was banging on my door. I walked hesitantly toward the door, not wanting to answer it. I stopped in the middle of the room. I knew it would be Randy coming to get me, and I hadn't decided yet if I would go with him. *How can I leave my children again … will my escaping from here be worth the loss of what time I have left with them? If I do flee, he will still find me, and most likely he will not be so generous with my life when he does! But, on the other hand, why would he care … he will have what he came for … his children.*

When the banging didn't stop, I continued on my way to the door. I leaned against it for a moment, then turned and opened it. Randy rushed in, his face red with anger.

"What's wrong, Virginia? Why did you take so long to answer the door? Someone could have heard me!" He closed the door and looked around the room, a puzzled expression appearing on his face. "Are you not coming with me? You have nothing packed."

I cast my eyes downward. *What could I say to him?*

"Virginia…" Randy laid his hands on my shoulders, forcing me to look at him. "Do you not understand how dangerous it is for you to remain here? Ildiko and Teresa want you out of the equation! I assume they will deal with each other once you are gone."

"I understand," I replied, tears welling up in my eyes. "But, my children..."

"Your children are safe with their father—safer than they would be with you!"

"But..."

"No more buts, Virginia; we need to get out of here now! Time is moving along too quickly; the sun will be setting soon, and they will all be rising." Randy drove home his point of the urgency we needed to deploy.

Suddenly, the door flew open and Basarab strode into the room, his face clouded with rage. "What is the meaning of this?" he shouted. "How did you get into this locked room, Randy?"

Randy shoved me behind him. I knew it wouldn't matter what he did, the count would destroy us both. Randy's boldness, and his courage, surprised me. "Let us go, Basarab. You have what you came for—your children. You have no need for either of us."

"Definitely no need for you, Randy," the count smirked. "But, Virginia..." the count began to circle around, drawing closer to me.

Randy put his arm back, protectively, trying to shield me. I felt his muscles twitching nervously as our skin connected. For all his bravado, I knew he was terrified. "With all due respect, Basarab, you have a wife. Virginia has given you more than you asked of her. Let her go."

The count threw back his head, and the sound of evil filled the room. He didn't stop his circling. "You think you know what is best for me? Yes, you are correct in noting that I have a wife. You are also correct in noting that Virginia has given me more than I asked of her. But, to just assume I would let her go, well, maybe you are missing the fact that I still might have some use for her. Maybe her job is not yet complete. Did you think about that?" The count laughed again, a sound filled with rasping malevolence. "Did it ever occur to you that Virginia actually would prefer me to you ... hmmmm?" The count's words taunted.

"She never would want to be with a monster like you!" Randy returned boldly as he backed into me, stepping on my feet as he did.

As I stumbled from the impact, the count made his move, gripping hold of my wrist and yanking me toward him. I felt an injection of pain shoot up my arm. "Why don't you ask her yourself ... how about it, Virginia? Do you prefer the boy over me?"

The count laughed as he pulled me into his arms. He grabbed hold of my hair and arched my head back. I could feel the advance of his breath as his lips came close to mine. I saw Randy's shadow as he attempted to move forward. The count's arm made a sweeping motion in Randy's direction, and I heard the crash of my friend's body as it hit the wall.

"This is something you have no right to interfere in, boy," the count's voice thundered. "Sit there, and watch. See what it is Virginia, your love, needs—a real man!" The count's lips closed over mine.

Try as I did to free myself from Basarab's hold, pummelling my fists against his chest, it was to no avail. As his tongue swirled into me, my body began to anticipate what was to follow, and it betrayed me by giving in to the assault. My arms crept up around the count's neck. I felt myself being lifted off the floor, and then dropped onto the bed. Randy was totally forgotten as I became all-consumed with the count...

~

I opened my eyes. I was alone. I was fully dressed. Nothing in the room was disturbed. A knock came to the door. Who could it be now? Randy again? This time, Ildiko burst through the door, not giving me a chance to respond. Teresa was right behind her. I sat up in the bed and stared at the two advancing vampire women. I saw the diabolical intent in their eyes, and wondered where Randy was, and why he hadn't come for me in time to prevent this onslaught.

Ildiko went to one side of the bed, Teresa to the other. Ildiko was first to speak. "Your little games are up, Virginia. It is time for you to move on. Teresa and I are here to help you with your move." She laughed. I felt a cloud of evil frosting the air I was trying to inhale.

Teresa reached out a hand and raked her nails down my arm. Her tongue flicked in and out of her mouth, and I detected her fangs. "Shall we do it here, Ildiko?" Teresa's question was like an injection of terror shooting into my veins! I tried to back away from her, but bumped into Ildiko who had crawled up on the bed and was kneeling behind me.

Ildiko's hand grabbed hold of my hair and she pulled my head back, exposing my throat. She was laughing hysterically. She leaned over and whispered loudly enough for Teresa to hear the answer to her question. "No, as much as I would love to, we must take her from here. I fear Basarab would not be happy were he to know what we are about to do to the mother of his children."

*Basarab ... where are you ... please ... come and save me ... surely, I mean more than this to you...*

"Where shall we take her, then?" Teresa asked.

"Hmmmmm .... let me think ... I've got it!" Ildiko made her way off the bed and walked to the window. "We will do the deed in Randy's house. That way, we will kill two birds with one stone. When the police find Virginia's body, Randy will be blamed, and he will be out of our lives forever, as well. The human element will deal with him. Spurned lover ... totally believable."

Teresa sneered as she grabbed hold of my chin and twisted my head, forcing me to look into her eyes. "How is the game going for you now, Virginia? Are you still enjoying it?" She let go her hold on me, and jumped off the bed, joining Ildiko at the window. "We must hurry before we are missed."

As terrified as I was, I made a dash for the door, knowing they had not bothered to lock it. I stumbled as I reached for the knob, but managed to get the door open. I didn't bother to think about which way to run, I just turned to the right and headed toward the stairs, hoping there would be someone in the house that would hear my plight and come to my rescue. Hoping it would be Basarab ... he would stave off the evil that was trying to devour me. Hoping...

The stairs turned into a door. I heard footsteps behind me, and heinous laughter. I pounded my fists on the door. I opened my mouth to scream, but no sound came out. As Ildiko and Teresa descended on me, the door gave way, and a hand grabbed my wrist and pulled me into a room. I heard a clanging sound as the door slammed shut, and voices cursing from beyond.

"Follow me," a voice ordered. A voice I recognized—Randy.

I was running, being dragged by Randy. The snow was deep. It was cold. I did not have a coat on, or boots—my feet were bare. I kept stumbling. Randy kept picking me up. I could hear screaming in the distance. Voices all too familiar to me.

"We need to get to where there are a lot of people around," Randy shouted breathlessly. "They will not dare touch you then. Hurry, Virginia, they are closing in on us."

"I can't!"

"You must!"

"It isn't much farther," Randy encouraged. "I see a church steeple. They won't set foot on holy ground, of that I am sure." His arm circled around my waist, and I could feel my feet lifting off the ground, my toes just skimming over the snow as Randy ran toward the church.

Then, I heard their voices, young and plaintiff. "Mama, where are you going? Why are you leaving us again? Don't you love us, Mama?"

I began to struggle against the hold Randy had on me. "Let me go ... the children ... they are calling to me ... can't you hear them?"

"You're hallucinating, Virginia!" Randy sounded out of breath. "Santan and Samara are with their father, they are safe."

"No!" I screamed. "They are calling for me. I can hear them!"

Randy paused a moment and slapped me across the face. "Get a grip, Virginia! The only ones following us are Ildiko and Teresa, and they want to slaughter you. If you let them get their hands on you, you will never see your children again!"

Randy's slap startled me back to reality. The sting of it was harsh, but it gave me the extra burst of energy I needed to follow him. As we drew near the church, its bells began to ring in the new day. An elderly man was approaching the front door. He was opening it. He turned, a puzzled look on his face, as Randy and I ascended on him.

"Please, sir, let us in!" Randy pleaded.

The man did not hesitate as he opened the door and motioned us in. "What of them?" he enquired, pointing to Ildiko and Teresa who had stopped at the edge of the church property. "Do they wish to enter, as well?"

"They will not enter into holy places," Randy said as he collapsed onto a chair. "Please, shut the door."

My knees buckled beneath me as the door closed out the winter wind, and death.

~

I jolted up in my bed, sweat saturating my night clothes. I glanced to the window, it was still dark. Would the dreams never cease? I needed sleep, especially if I was going to take flight with Randy in the morning. Was I? Realistically, was it the wisest move for me to make? Or, should I listen to my heart and go to Basarab, tell him what I knew? Surely, if he knew what his wife and cousin were up to, it would be the final nail in both their coffins!

I closed my eyes again, willing myself back to sleep—hopefully.

## Chapter Nineteen

I heard my door lock turning. I crawled from my bed and made my way to a corner, crouching there, waiting. *Basarab ... my heart's desire ... please come and make everything better for me...*

It was Randy.

He smiled. "Are you ready?"

Standing, I nodded.

"Where's your coat?"

"Not here. The count took it from me when we arrived here."

"Do you have boots?"

"No, the count took them, as well, and gave me these slippers. They will have to do until we can get something else."

"It looks mighty cold out there, and we have a ways to go. You can have my jacket; I have a sweater on under it," Randy suggested as he pulled his jacket off and helped me into it. I noticed how thin his sweater was and felt guilty.

"Will we not be able to get a cab?" I asked.

"Of course, but I am not sure how soon. Until we are able to hail a cab, we need to keep ourselves warm."

As I fastened the last button on the jacket, a wave of apprehension washed over me. Randy must have noticed the look on my face.

"What's wrong, Virginia? I hope you aren't having second thoughts."

I hesitated. "No ... but ... any way I would be able to see the children before we leave?"

Randy heaved an enormous sigh. "We can't afford the time, Virginia. We might already have waited too long. I'm sorry."

I looked away from him. He took my hand and led me into the hallway. Randy glimpsed to the left, and then the right. "All clear, follow me. Stay close."

We made it out of the house without any problems. When we reached the bottom of the long outdoor stairway, we began to run. I had difficulty keeping up to Randy, but when he noticed I was falling behind he slowed his pace.

"If we cross over these railway tracks, we'll come out at the train station. Hopefully, there will be a taxi there," Randy called back to me. "Do you need help?" he added.

"I'm fine," I answered. "I've been through worse."

I kept glancing behind me, but there was no one following us. I noticed a sign ahead—The Station Coffee House and Gallery. Its lights were on. Randy knocked on the glass door. A young girl came over and unlocked the door for us. "We aren't open for another fifteen minutes, but you guys look cold," she said. "Can I get you a coffee?"

Randy rubbed his hands together. "That would be great. Ah, do you have a phone we could use? I need to call a cab."

"If you wait a few minutes there will be plenty of cabs dropping off commuters."

"How much for the drinks?" I asked.

"On the house," she smiled.

I kept glancing to the door, expecting to see Ildiko and Teresa bursting through. Randy was watching the door, as well. Finally, a cab pulled up. Randy leapt from his chair and headed outside. I followed.

We climbed into the cab. The driver gave me a quizzical look: "No boots?"

"No."

Randy put his arm around me, pulling me close. I stiffened.

He leaned over and whispered in my ear: "It's okay; I'm just trying to warm you up."

I relaxed.

The cabbie finished some paperwork, and then we drove out of the parking lot. I heaved a sigh of relief.

"Where you going?" the driver asked. Randy explained our destination and the driver nodded. "A little winter getaway, eh?"

"Something like that," Randy replied.

I began to recognize some of the landscape from my excursions to the trails. We passed the parking lot at the top of D'Aubigny Creek soccer fields. A few minutes later the cab turned into the entrance of Brant Park. We had only gone a couple hundred feet when Randy told the driver to stop.

"This is it," Randy said. "How much do we owe you?"

"You staying in that place? Doesn't look like much."

I looked at the cabin, as well. It looked like more of a shack than an actual cabin. The taxi driver was right. It was small, with dull-grey aluminium siding and tiny slits for windows. Fall weeds sprouted out of the snow drifts that surrounded the building. I noticed someone must have been around lately because a pathway had been stamped in the snow, and around the doorway.

"The owner plans on fixing the exterior when the snow stops flying ... so, how much?" Randy asked.

The cabbie looked at his metre. "Fifteen."

Randy handed the driver a twenty. "Keep the change." He opened my door. I shivered, when my feet hit the snow. Randy laughed and scooped me up in his arms.

"No sense you walking this short distance," he smiled into my eyes and tightened his grip.

There was a fire blazing in a wood stove and a box filled with canned goods was sitting on the kitchen table. I looked around and noticed a door just off the kitchen. I ventured over and opened it. Inside, was a large double bed with a blue duvet.

"Your uncle seems to have thought of everything," I said to Randy. "But where are you going to sleep? It appears there is only one bedroom, and one bed!"

Randy smirked. "We can put a pillow down the middle of the bed."

"I don't think so!" I snorted.

Randy's laugh roared through the room. He came upon me quickly and grabbed me up in his arms. I struggled to free myself from his grasp, but he squeezed me tighter. He brought his mouth to mine and kissed me hard on the lips.

"What are you doing?" I screamed when he finally loosened his hold on me. I raised my hand to slap him across the face, but he grabbed my wrist.

"Not so fast, my lovely. We have to get along here for a bit, at least until we figure out our next step. I was just playing with you."

"Don't lie to me!" I shouted. "I should have stayed at the house! If I had known your true intentions..."

Randy's face took on a serious look. His voice had a sharp edge to it when he spoke. It was the voice of a man—not a boy. "You would be dead if you had stayed in that house. My only intention was to get you out of there before that happened. I was just so happy we escaped undetected. I guess I was a bit overzealous. I'm sorry. It won't happen again."

"Promise?"

"Promise."

Randy went into the bedroom, returning a few seconds later with a couple of the blankets. He placed them over the end of the couch. "I'll sleep in here," he said.

"Will you fit?" I asked. "You're so tall..."

"It will have to do, won't it?" Randy's voice had a cynical tone to it.

"You'll probably be warmer here," I said. I was trying to justify why Randy should be sleeping on a tiny couch, instead of in a bed where he could stretch out.

"Yeah ... probably."

Randy went about fixing his blankets and pillow. "Think I'll take a nap."

"I think maybe we could both use a nap," I agreed.

"Sounds like a plan," Randy said. Before I knew it, he was under the blanket on the couch and had fallen asleep.

I wandered around the cabin, not looking at anything in particular. I stopped at the largest window and pulled the curtain aside to take a quick look outside. It had begun to snow. *Good, hopefully our tracks away from the house will be covered, not that that will make a difference. I am sure he will find me if he wants to.* I let the curtain drop back into place, and then headed to the bedroom.

I curled up on the bed. *Why Randy? Why do you love me? It only complicates things. I love him! You shouldn't have kissed me...* I touched my fingers to my lips. *What had I been thinking, leaving with him? Now, his life is in jeopardy, too...*

~

I was running through a field of golden grain. Someone was running behind me. I was staggering, my breath coming in gulping gasps. The person caught up to me.

"It isn't much farther, Virginia," Randy's voice sounded out of breath, as well.

"Are you sure they are here?"

"Yes. I saw them in town last night when I went to the store to get some milk for Ally."

*Who is Ally?*

"Ally will be safe with Mrs. Stinson, if that is what you are worried about?" Randy continued.

I had no idea who Ally was, or Mrs. Stinson.

"I see the cave!" Randy shouted, and then grabbed my hand and pulled me through the wheat field.

*Caves ... wheat fields ... Ally ... Mrs. Stinson...* I did my best to keep pace with Randy. Each time I stumbled, he caught me. As we entered the cave, a rush of cool air surrounded me. An opening appeared. He pushed me through it, and then followed. I noticed him looking back into the shadows from whence we had just come. The opening closed.

"We will be safe for now," he said.

"Who is Ally?" I asked. "And who is Mrs. Stinson?"

Randy laughed. "Oh, Virginia, you kill me sometimes. Where does your mind wander off to? Ally is our daughter, and Mrs. Stinson is our friend."

"We have a daughter?" I interrupted.

Randy stretched his arm around me and pulled me close. "You poor thing. I thought you had recovered from your last episode, but apparently not."

I was so confused. "When did we have a daughter?"

"Nine months after we left the count's house."

"Where are we now?"

"Alberta."

"And Ally is your child?" I looked up into Randy's eyes.

"Of course she is mine. Who else's would she be?" Randy's voice was soft.

I sighed and leaned into him. "I am sorry ... I don't remember any of this."

"Its okay, my love. It will all come back to you. It always does."

"Do I forget a lot?"

"Yes, you seem to black things out whenever you are overly stressed." Randy gently took his arm from around me and stood up. "Well, I don't know about you, but I'm hungry. Let's see what I can rustle up."

I made my way to the table and sat down. Randy scooped some stew out onto our plates.

"Tell me what happened," I asked.

"We escaped from the count," he began, "And holed up in a cabin. Soon, you realized how much you loved me. We stayed a whole week there, most of our time spent entwined in each other's arms." Randy paused and smiled sheepishly. "Once we figured we were safe, we contacted my uncle, and he gave me the address of his friend Mrs. Stinson, who lives here. She helped us find jobs. You worked at a law firm until our daughter was born."

*Our daughter? Yes, I remember ... curly red hair ... like Randy ... like my other daughter, Samara. But Ally is sweet-tempered, like Randy. He claims the child is his, but hadn't I been with the count before Randy and I had fled?*

I looked at Randy, a man now, with broad shoulders and a full beard. He was leaning back in his chair, smiling at me.

"I see I have jogged your memory," he stated.

I nodded. *Memories are not always sweet, dear Randy. I dare not tell you how much I think of him...*

~

I awoke with a start. I sat up in the bed, pulling my knees into my chest. *What the hell are all these dreams about?* I sat for a few minutes, rocking. Randy is still a boy ... no, a young man ... not yet like the Randy in my dream. That Randy should never be. I hoped never to know that Randy. I needed to think of a way to release him from thinking he had to be responsible for my welfare. I needed to return to the count and take my chances with him. Didn't I? That is what my mind told me ... but what is my heart saying? Dreams are just what they are, right?—figments of an overactive imagination. And what I had just dreamt was something I had no desire to see come to fruition.

*So, my dear friend, I cannot go with you.*
*I shall set you free.*

Even as this thought went through my head, I had no idea how I would let Randy go, I had come to depend on him so much.

I glanced out the window and noticed the lightening shades of dawn appearing. I was so tired. The dreams had taken their toll on my body. Maybe, I could just close my eyes for another hour before Randy came...

I was running, but this time on a snow-covered trail. Snow was falling in earnest. I heard running behind me, and my name being called. I looked back. It was Randy. He did not look happy.

"Virginia!" he shouted as he bore down on me. "What are you thinking?" He grabbed me by the shoulders.

"I needed to get out for a walk and clear my head."

"How could you be so foolish? I'm sure they are looking for you by now." He grabbed me by the hand and began pulling me, heading back to the cabin.

I stumbled along. *You shouldn't love me, Randy ... You need to let me go! You need to get on with your life! I am not worthy of your kind of love...*

Once in the cottage, Randy peeled off his socks. His feet were red; he was shivering.

"Tea?" I offered.

Randy nodded.

I handed him a large mug of tea, "I'm sorry, Randy; I just meant to take a little walk," I lied. "You were sleeping, and I didn't want to disturb you."

"You shouldn't have gone out so soon, Virginia," Randy replied as he walked over to the couch and sat down. He pulled the blanket around him, making sure his feet were securely wrapped in it. "What would you have done if they found you alone on the trail? What would I do if they had?"

"Randy, there is nothing you could have done even if you were with me. You are no match for them—we both would have been killed. Maybe it would have been better for them to have found me. At least then, they could have ended this miserable life I seem to be embroiled in. Like you said earlier, my children are safe with their father."

"Virginia ... please ... don't talk like that..."

"It's the truth," I cut him off. "I will never be free of the count, or of Teresa and Ildiko. What the count has in store for me, I have no idea. But those two ... I can only imagine it will not be pretty!" I sat down on the couch.

Randy reached for my hand. I didn't stop him. His fingers closed around mine. "Please, Virginia ... give us a chance! I know

I can make you happy. We just need to get away, far away from here. We can have children..."

I pulled my hand away and moved to the end of the couch, out of Randy's reach. "Don't!" I shouted. "None of that is possible! Randy, please, get it through your head ... there is no us ... not as a couple ... we have no future together, no matter what we do, or where we go. Why do you continue to live in this little fantasy world of yours?"

"What makes you think I live in a fantasy world, Virginia? I have made no pretence about how much I love you. I love your children, too, but for now we have had to leave them where they will be the safest—with their own kind."

"Santan is not like them," I interrupted. "He is like me."

"No, Virginia, he is not. Despite the fact that he is of a quieter character than his sister, you have seen the powers he has. He is more inclined to the vampire bloodline than he is to the human part of him."

I looked away. *I know you are right ... my children will be better off with their father.* I sighed. "What do we do now? Do you have an actual plan?" I changed the subject.

"I was thinking that we just lay low for a few days. Once we know we're safe, I will call my uncle and ask him to help get us as far away as possible. He has connections all over the country."

I shivered. My hands began to shake. I gripped them together.

"What's wrong, Virginia?"

"Nothing," I mumbled quickly.

"Don't try and fool me. There is something wrong."

"I don't think I can do this Randy; I can't leave my children." *Or the count...*

"Listen, the vampires have their own problems right now! What better time for us to get out of here?" Randy paused. "You will never be one of them, Virginia ... you need to realize that."

*What makes you think I want to be? ... But, if that is how I can stay with my children ... and with him ...* I got up and poured myself a cup of tea.

Randy threw the blanket off and came across the room to me. He took the teacup from my hands and set it on the table. Then he wrapped me in his arms and pulled me against his chest.

*Why are you doing this? Why are you making things so difficult for me, so confusing? I know you are right ... I will never be one of them ... but, I love him ... I know you can't understand my love for such a creature ... yet, I love you ... how can I not love you, too, the one who has been there for me...*

I gazed up into Randy's brown eyes and felt drawn into their warmth. I did not push him off, allowing the moment to continue. And then, Randy broke his promise to me as his lips sought out my lips. I didn't fight him. He picked me up and carried me into the bedroom.

I felt his lips caress my eyes, my cheeks, and my neck as they swept over my face, always returning to my lips. His hands stroked my arms and my legs, staying away from any vulnerable parts. However, by doing so, he was igniting fires within me that would need to be quenched. I groaned. He took that as his cue to venture further.

Everything was forgotten as Randy made harmonious love to me—innocent love.

~

I awoke to the first rays of the sun creeping through the trees. I picked up my pillow and buried my face in it. I let the tears pour. *What are you going to do now, Virginia? You cannot allow such a thing to happen!*

I went over in my mind the details of my recent dreams ... there was no way I could put Randy's life in any further danger. My thoughts turned to the times at the apartment when Randy had brought me flowers, to all the little things he had done for me, to his close relationship with Santan, to his acceptance of me even after he knew what had happened to me—the kind of creatures I was involved with. I felt a tear slip out of the corner of my eye. I raised my fist and wiped it away. How dare he get under my skin like this! He had no right. The count would destroy him. He would never allow Randy to be part of my life, or the lives of my children—Basarab's children.

If I were to stay with Randy and if we managed to escape from the vampires, what would our lives be like? We would be constantly running. A voice inside me kept telling me the count would never let me go.

Did I truly want him to? No. If I was to be perfectly honest, it was the count I wanted, I needed. No one else, other than my children, mattered. He was my heart and my soul. Teresa and Ildiko would bury themselves sooner or later ... I was positive they would.

I knew Randy would be at my door any time, to take me away from the vampire world. What he didn't understand, as I did now, is that I would never be free from it, and I didn't want to be. Now, all I had to do was figure out how to tell him.

# Basarab

## Chapter Twenty

Later, as I stood watching Virginia sleep, thinking of the moments we had recently shared, I was torn between disturbing her, and leaving her alone. Finally, I turned and headed down the hallway. I would stop in again later. For now, I wanted to pay a visit to my children, they should still be up. After the meeting, Emelia had said she was going to head up and read them a story.

When I entered the room, Emelia and the children were cuddled on the bed. A book was open on her lap, but she wasn't the one doing the reading, Santan was. Samara was listening intently, and staring with awe at her brother as he read the story. Adelaide and Alfred were sitting in chairs that had been brought up close to the bed. It was a comforting scene.

Samara squealed in delight when she realized who had entered the room. She pulled away from Emelia and stumbled across the floor, and into my arms. "Papa! Papa!"

I had never realized what pleasure I could get from such a vivacious child. I had no idea who in the family she took after, but did consider she might have similar attributes to that of her great-uncle, Dracula—and maybe, Ildiko. If that were the case, Samara would have to be watched and nurtured with care. "How is my little princess?" I asked.

"Good, Papa, now you here!" Samara's red curls bounced.

*Red hair like Virginia ... and curls ... lovely. This child is going to be a real beauty ... like her mother.* I looked over to the bed and noted Santan staring at me and Samara.

"Samara!" Santan's tone was sharp and commanding, not the voice of a child his age. "How rude of you to disturb our story."

Emelia reached a hand to him and patted him on the leg. "It is okay, Santan. Your sister just wanted to greet your father. Maybe you would like to do the same?"

Santan shook his head. "I have no wish to."

I could not believe the hatred I saw in my son's eyes when he looked at me. It was obvious he was his mother's son. I would have to tread carefully where Virginia was concerned, and just maybe the only way I was going to be able to have a relationship with my son would be to keep his mother around—and alive. The idea was not totally repulsive to me.

I nodded my head to Adelaide and Alfred. "Good evening. I hope you have not been too inconvenienced with all that has happened. I would like to offer you the opportunity to return to your homes as soon as possible, if that is what you might want to do."

"If it does not matter, then I think we will stay here with Emelia and the children as long as we are welcome." Adelaide looked me straight in the eyes. Her boldness surprised me.

"As you wish," I replied. "We should all be returning home soon, anyway, if things go as planned." I returned my attention to Samara. "So, little princess, shall we join your brother and aunt, and hear the rest of the story?"

"Don't care ... just want to play with you, Papa."

I was torn. It would be a delight to play a game with my child; it would be wiser to allow Santan to finish his story, showing him I was not such a beast as he might think, and I had an interest in what was important to him. "We will listen to the rest of the story," I said firmly, "And then we will play."

Samara pouted.

I sat down on the end of the bed and settled my daughter on my lap. "Please continue, Santan."

Santan studied me for a few seconds, and then he closed the book. "It is okay, Father, you can play with Samara. I am tired of reading."

I knew my son was defying me. I did not wish to challenge him back, so I acquiesced. "Would you like to join us, Santan? What do you like to do best?"

"I would just like to rest now, Father. You play with my sister. She is very happy you are here." I noticed Santan's emphasis on the word *she*.

I was surprised when Alfred spoke up. "Santan loves to build things, Basarab. He is exceptionally skilled at putting Lego pieces together. He can create exact replicas of buildings he has seen." Alfred stood up and walked over to a table that was covered with a white sheet. He pulled the sheet away, exposing the beginnings of a cottage. "See … even Samara helps sometimes, don't you little one?" Alfred beckoned to Santan. "Come, Santan, how say we get your father to help us build some more on the cottage?"

Santan hesitated.

"Its okay, Santan," Alfred continued. "Give your father a chance. He loves you."

I bristled at the statement by this old man, practically a stranger to me, telling my son it was okay to associate with me; telling my son that I loved him. I should never have left Brantford with my father when Santan was a baby. I should have stayed and sought Virginia and my son out before I returned to Transylvania. I would have been more focused, then, on dealing with Radu's attempted coup, instead of constantly wondering about my son's whereabouts.

Santan got off the bed and walked slowly over to the table where his creation was taking shape. I set Samara down, stood, and followed. Samara tottered after me. When I reached the table, I was astounded by the finite details of the building.

"You are very talented, Santan," I pointed out.

Alfred beamed. "That he is, Basarab." He turned to Santan. "Let's lift the cottage up on something, so it looks like it is sitting on a cliff, and then we can make a set of stairs going down to the beach."

I gazed quickly around the room, in search of something to position the house on. "This looks as though it will do," I stated, walking to a corner and picking up an empty box.

Alfred took the box from me and turned it upside down over the house, measuring the size. "Perfect," he commented, setting the box to the side. "Now, Santan, your father and I will lift the cottage, and you can place the box on the table." Alfred paused and looked around the room. He pointed to something on the end of the bed. "Adelaide, be a dear and bring that little blanket here. When Santan sets the box down place the blanket over the box."

The blanket Alfred had referred to was white, which of course would be the colour of snow. Within minutes, everything was in place, and we all stood back and contemplated our next moves. I waited, having every intention of allowing Santan the privilege of taking the lead. After all, it was his project. I would be at his command. Samara had lost interest in the house building and was busy playing with a doll.

For the next hour, we worked together on stairs, and on creating a lake with the blue Lego pieces. On some of the waves, Santan placed a thin white Lego block to give the affect of a whitecap. Samara had eventually climbed onto a chair beside the table and sat there watching us. A couple times, Santan's and my hand would brush against each other. I noticed how my son's body tensed, but I said nothing. Time would heal all. Time was what we had plenty of.

"Time for bed, children," I said, thinking we had spent long enough at play.

Samara complained. Santan nodded. However, instead of going to his bed, he walked over to the door. "I would have a word with you, Father … in private."

"Okay, just give me a minute to say goodnight to Samara," I answered.

Samara didn't want to let me go, but I finally wrested her arms from around my neck by promising I would see her first thing when the sun set. After that, I joined my son who had stepped out into the hallway.

"Is there somewhere else we can go, Father, where there are no ears listening?"

"We can use my study on the main floor." I reached for Santan's hand. He folded his hands behind his back.

"Follow me, then," I said, trying hard to keep my temper in check. As much as I loved my son, his refusal to even touch me was becoming annoying.

Once we were settled into chairs in the study, I waited for Santan to speak whatever was on his mind. He was such a young man in a child's body. Finally, he spoke: "What are your intentions toward my mama, Father?"

The question shocked me. It was the last thing I had expected him to ask me. I had thought that maybe he wanted to know more about me, and about the family ... about where he had come from. "What do you mean, Santan?" I asked, trying to buy some time to think of an answer.

"Just what I said." Santan's face was deadly serious.

"I have not decided yet," I answered at length. "Your mama has been difficult."

"In what way?"

"In the first place, son, she took you away from me. That is something she should never have done."

"Did she not fear for her life? Were you not going to kill her?" Santan interrupted.

"Who told you that?"

"It does not matter. Please answer me."

I leaned forward in my chair. "If she feared for her life, Santan, it was because she was playing a highly dangerous game with me, and she knew I knew about her true intentions. What if I were to tell you that your mama tried several times to escape from here while, at the same time, telling me how much she loved me and wanted to be with me, and how much she wanted to give me another child?" I had no idea if my son, as young as he was, would comprehend what I had just said, but from what I had observed so far in regards to his intellect, there was a strong possibility he would understand.

I could sense the wheels turning in Santan's head. "Do you love my mama, then?"

Did I? Did I love Virginia enough to cast my wife, Teresa, aside? How did I answer this man-child? If I told him I did not love his mother, it would most likely mean I would not have a chance of him loving me ... if I told him I did love her, I would have to embrace her and face the full wrath of my wife, Ildiko, and various other family members.

"Well, Father?" Santan looked at me, a deep frown on his face as he waited for my answer.

I decided to take the middle-of-the-road ground. "I cannot honestly say how I feel about your mama," I began. "There are times when I think about her, and how she has given me two beautiful children, and my heart beats faster with the memories of our times together. And there are other times when I think about the pain she caused me by running away with you, and keeping you from my arms." I sighed, stood, and walked over to Santan's chair. I knelt down in front of him, placing my hands on the arms of his chair, but keeping from touching him. "Whatever my feelings are toward your mama, though, I want you to know this ... I will cause no harm to her."

I noticed the edges of Santan's lips twitch. "You promise?"

"I am a man of my word, Santan."

"What if you were to know someone else was going to harm her?"

"I would stop them." I wondered why Santan was asking such a question. What was it he knew? "Is there something you wish to share with me?" I stood to my full height.

Santan took the opportunity to hop down from the chair and walk over to the window. "I overheard a conversation, Father—one I think you should be aware of."

I kept silent, waiting for him to continue.

"It was a conversation between your wife and your cousin. Your cousin hates my mama, although I have no idea why because she barely knows her. To be fair to your wife, she did try and convince Ildiko not to kill her, but Ildiko said that neither of them would be free to be with you until my mama was entirely out of the picture."

"How did you hear this?" I needed a moment to digest what my son had just informed me of. I knew Ildiko was not pleased with my liaisons with Virginia, but to go to the extent of murdering her, and to drag Teresa into the plot? My cousin had never made any bones about how much she despised my choice of a wife! I also noted how Santan only referred to Teresa as my wife.

"I have powers, Father, which even I do not understand, yet." I noticed a trace of weariness in my son as he spoke now.

Who was it he reminded me of? Who ... yes ... my father! Santan was so much like my father ... his gentle manner ... his firmness ... his wisdom. "Do you know when this plot is to occur?" I asked.

"Soon. They did not say exactly when. Now you are aware of this, can you assure me that you will not allow them to kill my mama?" Santan's voice trembled slightly, and I detected a child-like vulnerability showing through in his eyes.

I nodded. "You have my word; I will deal with this matter."

Santan walked over to me and reached up his hand. "We will shake on this, as gentlemen, then?"

I could not help myself, despite the seriousness of the moment. To see a child making a gentleman's agreement by shaking hands—I burst out laughing as I grasped my son's hand, and then I pulled him into my arms. This time, he did not challenge me, and I knew I had made some headway. Now, I just had to fulfill my promise to him by making sure nothing happened to Virginia.

## Chapter Twenty-one

After tucking Santan into his bed, I headed for my private chambers. I was worried about how to handle the situation I found I was faced with. To confront Ildiko with my knowledge could open another can of worms that I had no desire to deal with, especially at this time. I was to meet with Radu and I knew I definitely could not trust him. My gut instinct told me my uncle would not come to the meeting alone, even though his pretence might be that he was. I was sure there would be someone close by, most likely his man Peter. To call Ildiko out on her actions right now could alienate her brother and her father from me, something I could not afford in the midst of all the trouble the family was embroiled in.

There was also the nagging mystery of what Tanyasin was up to. It appeared she was working on her own agenda, regardless of her professed allegiance to Radu. She was an unpredictable wild card. The fact she had shown up at my house and had tried to kidnap my children was enough evidence for me to know she was up to no good. Then, there was her appearance at the cottage, and again in the cemetery where she had accosted Orsolya with questions about my meeting with Radu, and about my children. She seemed determined to get to Santan and Samara. I would have to up my protection of them; or, maybe, I would send them to Transylvania and ask Gara to secure them safely in the caves. But, it was getting them there that might prove difficult. I realized, then, my greatest fear was to let them out of my sight—my reach.

I needed some wise council, but did not want to talk to my father. I had been leaning too heavily on him as of late, and I did not want the others to think I was weakening any more than they probably already did. Nor, did I need my father to assume the same. There was only one other I trusted to confide in— Angelique. I turned and headed to her room.

At her door, I hesitated, and then knocked softly. I heard her footsteps approaching, and after a few seconds the door swung open. "Basarab," she smiled. "I have been expecting you."

Her statement startled me. "Truly?" It always fascinated me how Angelique just always seemed to know things.

"Come in. Yes, I thought you might seek me out to discuss my sister. I understand she accosted Orsolya at the cemetery." Angelique led the way to a couple chairs near the window. The blind was down. "Please, sit," she motioned to the chair opposite the one she claimed. Angelique folded her hands in her lap. "How might I be of assistance to you?"

"I need to know if there is any way you can find your sister and see what she is up to. Her actions indicate she is playing her own game here," I began.

Angelique grimaced. "Yes, I fear that, as well. Hatred for your uncle has destroyed all she used to be. What did she want from Orsolya?"

"She was demanding information about the children."

Angelique nodded. "Maybe, she thinks if she is able to get the children, she will have more favour with Radu."

"If truth be told, I do not believe it is his favour she seeks, anymore," I stated.

Angelique studied me for a moment, before speaking. "You might be right. Lately, I have noticed a change in her, an urgency to complete her mission to destroy your family."

"Does she tire of life itself?"

"Possibly," Angelique sighed.

"We could remedy that for her," I sneered, hoping the words I spoke were not overly harsh. After all, Tanyasin was Angelique's sister, and I had to consider that if it came down to a choice, Angelique might choose blood over water ... not that she had previously, but there was always a first time. I also had to consider that in spite of everything, Angelique had been attempting to reason with her sister, and she had defended Tanyasin by reminding the family of what Dracula had ripped from her sister's hands.

Angelique looked away from me for a moment. "I wish it were not so that she tires of living; but, I have the feeling her life is slipping away from her, and she wishes to finish the curse she began. There is no remedy you could give her that I would approve of," she added. When she looked at me, I saw the tears in her eyes.

"Then there is only one thing to do, Angelique. You must find her, and try to reason with her again because, I tell you, in all truth, if she raises a hand to harm my children, I will end her miserable existence. You must make her see that it is time to stop her curse, and her alliance with Radu if she still has one. When she does, she will have the peace she deserves, and she can join her husband and son knowing she did the right thing, something that will please them both immensely."

"You are right, my dear count. I will leave now and seek her out. I have an idea where she may be, but the best place for me to start my search will be in the graveyard where her scent will still be fresh. As soon as I know anything, I will notify you." Angelique stood and walked to the door. "The sooner I go the better."

I hesitated before getting up.

"Is there something else you would like to discuss with me before I leave, Basarab?"

I shook my head. "No … no … it can wait. It is not of as great an importance."

Angelique's voice was soft as she spoke. "It must be of importance to you if it is bothering you so much. Take a moment and tell me what has you in such turmoil."

I took a deep breath. "I am struggling with many things besides Radu. I have just learned Teresa and Ildiko are plotting to kill Virginia."

"You learned this from a reliable source?"

"Santan."

"And how did he know?"

"Somehow he heard them … he told me he has powers beyond his comprehension."

Angelique looked thoughtful. "I believe him. He is a special child. So is Samara." She paused. "What else, Basarab? I know there is more."

"I want to make things right with my wife, at least I told her I did; however, after what I have just heard, and what I overheard her say to her father when we were still in Brasov, I don't feel I can trust her. And, if truth be told, I do not love her anymore—not as I used to. I love Virginia. She not only invades my dreams, she has sealed herself in whatever heart I have left! But, for me to cast my wife aside for a human, even if she is the mother of my children, the family will not look favourably on such a move."

Angelique looked sad as she spoke. "I, who have never known true love, might be the last one you should be asking advice from for such a situation. Nevertheless, I think you know the answer, Basarab. It is in your heart, where she is. Of course, you must deal with your wife, and I am sure once everyone is aware of Teresa's betrayal, they will understand."

I reached out to Angelique and gave her a hug. "Wise as always … thank you."

"I had best go now," she stated.

I nodded and followed her out of her room, knowing she had given me my cue to leave. "Good luck," I said as we parted ways. Angelique nodded and disappeared down the hall. I waited until I knew she would be out of the house before setting out after her. As I stepped onto the veranda, I transformed to a bat; it would be easier that way. I flew to the cemetery, knowing Angelique was headed there.

When I arrived, I hid up in one of the giant oak trees. I observed Angelique kneeling on the ground, sniffing the earth. As I settled on an uppermost branch, she looked up, an indication I would have to be extremely careful. Soon she was on the move. I followed discretely, keeping as far back as possible, without loosing sight of her. Despite being on her feet, Angelique was quick. She raced down the main street, and then turned at a set of lights. Once again, she knelt down and sniffed the ground before continuing. When she reached a cement factory, she turned down the lane just beyond it. I followed her to a large house, which she circled around.

I noticed a towering maple tree in the backyard, and settled myself in the uppermost branches. Once again, Angelique gazed upward, and then proceeded to the back door and entered the house. I needed to get inside somehow, if not physically, at least to a window where I would be able to see and hear anything of importance. I flew to one of the large windows at the side of the house and hung from the top frame. I saw two figures inside––Angelique and Tanyasin. I began to wonder if Angelique had known all along where her sister was. Then again, she had not come straight here ... she had tracked Tanyasin.

"What are you doing here?" I heard Tanyasin screech. "How did you find me?"

"Your scent is not easy to hide, sister," Angelique replied.

"State your business, and then leave," Tanyasin snarled. "I told you before, and I will tell you again, I will have my revenge. Nothing is going to stop me from having my final day of glory!"

"At what cost, Tanyasin? Have you not had enough revenge for your extended lifetime? Do you not want rest for your soul?"

"You wish to be rid of me, sister?"

"I did not say that."

"Don't take me for a fool! You have sided with *them* from the beginning. I see through you ... you have a soft spot for Count Atilla, don't you? Don't bother to answer me," Tanyasin paused before answering Angelique's earlier question. "I am as soulless as those creatures are; why would I need to rest? Only my bones have become weary as of late."

"Then end this now ... set them free."

"They will all grow old and die if I do," Tanyasin sneered. "And then you will never have your Atilla."

"So be it. It is better than the darkness you have cursed them with. And, as for Atilla, he will finally be joined with his beloved Mara, as he should be. She was, and still is, the love of his life."

"Never to be yours, eh, Angelique … yet still you are optimistic that one day Atilla might hold you in his arms as more than a friend! Well, let me tell you how it is for me, dear sister … I want to see them all suffer … the darkness I have cursed them with has been my greatest enjoyment all these years."

Tanyasin walked up to Angelique and thrust her face at her sister's. "You had best tread carefully, sister. Even though you betrayed me, the only thing that has kept you alive over the centuries is the fact that you are my blood. In reality, you are as responsible for this blight on the Dracul family as I am, by attempting to diminish the curse, you actually worsened it—not that I mind. Think on that!"

Angelique pushed Tanyasin away. "Do you honestly believe you have the power to destroy me? I have not shadowed you all these years because I could not destroy you. As you said, we are blood."

"Your blood is weak with love for those beasts, though," Tanyasin screeched as she flew at Angelique. "Let's settle this now … let's prove who is the stronger!"

Angelique stepped nimbly aside. Tanyasin crashed into the wall close to the window where I was hiding. She fell to the floor. Slowly, she stood. She raised her head and sniffed the air. "There is one of them close by; were you followed?" she shouted.

"No, I was not followed."

I detected an expression of uncertainty on Angelique's face when she answered Tanyasin.

The old Gypsy began to pace in front of the window. I inched away from the glass, gripping on to the brick. I knew I should leave, but I feared for Angelique's safety, despite her thwarting her sister's first attempt to harm her.

"Sister," I heard the pleading in Angelique's voice. "I am begging you to end this. Leave Basarab's children be. He will kill you if you harm a hair on their heads. And, I will not stop him!"

"So much for blood!"

I heard a blood chilling screech, and what sounded like the banging of furniture. I heard Angelique scream in pain. I reacted instinctively. The window shattered as I flew through it. I was just in time to stop Tanyasin from ripping a semi-conscious Angelique's heart from her chest. I gripped the old Gypsy's hand, yanking her off. Tanyasin looked up in disbelief, but then she laughed. Her delight became obvious.

"The pup of the pup! I gave you your power; I can snatch it away just like that." She snapped the fingers on her free hand.

I dropped Tanyasin's wrist, and shoved her across the room, and then knelt down and gathered Angelique into my arms. As I stood, I turned and snarled at Tanyasin. "Stay away, hag; if you so much as creep near any member of my family again, especially my children, you will not live to see another minute. I promise you that."

Tanyasin was laughing hysterically. "Don't think you are so almighty, Basarab. There is another that runs with your Uncle Radu, who is powerful beyond even his own wisdom. I have read his mind; he tires of your uncle's indecision, of his procrastination. He desires power. He desires the throne for himself because he feels he is more worthy of it than his master. All I have to do is give him a push in the right direction! You think this meeting you are going to have with your uncle is going to end the war that has begun? If so, you are more of a fool than I thought. Radu will not be alone. Peter will be there, somewhere, hiding and waiting to make his move."

"You ramble, witch."

"Do you think so? The one whom I obtained my power from has made a pact with Peter. Radu has no idea of this betrayal, but I do. I was lurking in the shadows when Peter met with her. They will rule together, or so he will think; however, she will be the true leader. Her power is unlimited."

"Where does that leave you, then?" I challenged.

"Exactly where I have been for centuries—by her side. I have served her well, and will continue to do so." Tanyasin's lips curled with laughter, but this time no sound escaped. I felt the sting of her silent mirth.

I made my move toward the open back door. Tanyasin jutted her chin at me. "Go, Basarab ... do what you think you must ... meet with Radu ... think of your precious children while you are there ... will they be safe behind the walls of your puny fortress? There is an old saying, is there not ... while the cat is away, the mice will play..." This time her laughter crowded the room, closing in on me, leaving me with a dull feeling in the cavity of my chest. "Oh, by the way," Tanyasin swept past me as she headed to the door, "Do you know where your beloved Virginia is? And the boy, Randy? Such a sweet relationship they have, wouldn't you say? While you have been so worried about what I am up to, maybe they have slipped from your grasp!" Tanyasin disappeared into the night.

Angelique stirred in my arms. She pushed gently against my chest. "Please, I am okay," she said. I set her down. She looked around. "Tanyasin is gone?"

"Yes." My head was still reeling from the old Gypsy's last words to me, and my facial expression must have shown my distress.

"What is wrong, Basarab?" Angelique asked.

"I fear Virginia has fled again, this time with the help of Randy. I must get back to the house to ensure they and my children are still in their beds."

"Tanyasin could be baiting you..."

"Yes, that is a possibility, but not one I want to take a chance on ignoring." As I headed out the door, I turned briefly back to Angelique. "I will see you at the house?"

She nodded. I looked away, shook my body, and transformed into a wolf.

~

As I approached the stairs of the house, I changed back into my human form and took the steps three at a time. I rushed up the stairs to Virginia's room and threw the door open. Her bed was empty. I turned and headed to the room where Randy was supposed to be. It, too, was empty. I then made straight for my children's room. Emelia was just exiting through their door.

"Shhh ... Samara had a bad dream, and she called for her mother. I took the liberty of fetching Virginia from her room."

"Virginia is with the children, then?"

"Yes."

"And Randy?"

"Of course. He is never far from Santan."

Even though I breathed a sigh of relief that Virginia and Randy were still under my roof, I felt the tightness in my chest at the mention of Santan's relationship to the human.

"Is something wrong, Basarab?" Emelia looked up at me, concern in her eyes.

"There is something ..." I wasn't sure if I should be sharing my new-found knowledge with Emelia, yet; however, despite her past disloyalty toward me, I knew my aunt had acted from a mother's love.

"What is it, Basarab?" She laid her hand gently on my arm.

I heaved a sigh. "Virginia's life might be in jeopardy, and I promised my son I would see that no harm came to his mother."

"Should we go somewhere else to discuss this?" Her voice was shaking.

"Good idea, let's take a walk outside." I took my aunt by the arm and we headed out. Once outside: "Santan overheard Ildiko saying she was going to kill Virginia, to remove her from the equation where I was concerned. My son said Ildiko convinced Teresa there was no other way. I am sure she also convinced my wife it would be the only way for her to be secure by her husband's side, withholding, of course, the fact that is exactly where my cousin would like to be. Ildiko has gone too far this time. I fear, if she convinces Teresa to do the deed, my cousin will inform me of such, thus hoping to clear the way for her ascent to the throne."

Emelia laid her hand on my arm. "Please, Basarab, don't get ahead of yourself. I cannot see Ildiko going that far to secure her place beside you..."

"I can see her doing just that," I interrupted.

"But..."

"No, my dear aunt. My cousin has changed. Even more so since her return from her experience at Radu's. I fear, despite everything Teresa is, she has no idea how well she is being manipulated."

"Teresa knows her place with you, Basarab. She would not do anything to jeopardize her position."

"There is more," I stated. "Tanyasin was the one who taunted me with the relationship between Virginia and Randy, planting the idea that maybe they had fled from the house. I cannot have my eyes everywhere. I have to meet with Radu, and I need all my wits about me."

"I understand, Basarab. Would you like me to watch over Virginia while you are gone?"

"Would you? I will feel so much more settled if you can do so. I don't think either Teresa or Ildiko would come near her if they even had an inkling I knew what they might be up to."

"It is settled then. Put your worries aside." Emelia gazed up at me, a melancholy look in her eyes. "This is the least I can do for you, after all I have put you through."

I didn't respond to her. Even though we had talked through what she had done, depriving me of my son during his infant year, the sting of her deceit still hurt. "Shall we return to the house?" I suggested.

Emelia nodded.

"When you get inside, could you please check on the whereabouts of my cousin; I will go to my wife. If Ildiko is missing, and no one knows where she is, signal me with one howl; I shall do likewise for you if Teresa is not to be found."

Once inside, Emelia turned and headed to Ildiko's room. I spun around in the other direction, toward Teresa's quarters. I approached cautiously, not wanting her to awaken if she was sleeping. The door knob turned quietly, the hinges were inaudible as the door swung open. My eyes focused on the bed. Teresa was there, deep in slumber.

I studied her for a few moments, taking in her tranquil beauty, wondering what had gone wrong between us. Virginia. That is what had gone wrong. Virginia had become more to me than a vessel to bear my son. She had jousted with my mind, daring to challenge me like no other woman over the centuries ever had … arguing her points and making me think outside my world. She had met my appetite with a fuming fervour of her own. She had touched me like no other woman ever had. And, she had given me what no other woman ever had—a son, and then a daughter.

On the other hand, Teresa had been by my side since the day she was born. She had come to me willingly, first as a child, then as a bride. She had saved my life more than once. Lately, she had sacrificed her own life as she tried to prove she still loved me, despite all that was going on between us.

I stepped quietly to the bed, reached over and brushed away a tendril of hair, which had fallen across Teresa's forehead. She smiled and whispered my name, but did not open her eyes. I backed away, and out of the room. As I closed the door, a lone howl echoed throughout the hallways of the old house. I turned and rushed in the direction of Ildiko's room.

When I arrived, Emelia was standing inside the room with a rather shaken looking Orsolya. The girl appeared about ready to cry. "I don't know where she is, Emelia," Orsolya was saying as I entered. "I came to talk to her, but she said she had some business to take care of, and then left."

I strode to where the women were standing, grabbed Orsolya by the shoulders and shoved my face close to hers. "You had best tell the truth, girl!" I shouted.

Orsolya did not miss a beat, despite how taken aback she appeared to be by my arduous approach. "I have no reason to lie to you, Basarab. She did not tell me where she was going, or what her business was. She is very much a mystery, your cousin."

I relaxed my grip on the girl's shoulders and turned my back to her. I was furious. I was frustrated.

Emelia approached me. "Do you think Ildiko will attempt something..." Before Emelia could finish her question, I heard footsteps approaching. I raised my finger to my lips.

Ildiko burst into the room. Her face was flushed. I knew it was a sign she had recently fed, and not from one of our bottles of blood. "Ildiko will attempt what?" Her words reeked with sarcasm.

In spite of the anger I was feeling toward my cousin, I could not help but to breathe a sigh of relief at the sight of her. I hoped the respite would last. I gathered my thoughts together and replied: "Nothing… you must have misheard."

I could tell from the look on Ildiko's face that she didn't believe me. "Is everything okay?" she asked.

"Everything is fine." I answered. "What have you been up to?" I changed the direction of the conversation.

Ildiko smiled beguilingly. "Just out and about."

I knew exactly what she meant, and I was not thrilled. "I trust you were discrete. We cannot afford to bring undesirable attention to ourselves."

"Of course not, Basarab. I would never do anything to jeopardize our family. The body won't be found." Her words had a teasing resonance to them.

I shuddered inside as I stared at my beautiful cousin. What had happened to her? Wild and reckless she had always been, but never to this extent. I feared she was catapulting out of control, and I was terrified she would do something to Virginia. How could I protect the woman I was beginning to realize I couldn't live without?—especially, from one of my own family. The others would never value a human's life over that of a family member … blood was blood!

"Well, then, all is good. Now, if everyone would like to get out of my room, I would like to rest." Ildiko pointed to her door.

"We shall talk again, Ildiko," I said. "Emelia … Orsolya … after you."

"Oh, Basarab, before you leave, have you made a decision about what you are going to do with all the humans under our roof?" Ildiko stopped me.

"Anyone in particular you would like to know of?" I baited.

She laughed. "They are all nuisances—some more so than others."

"I will be sending Adelaide and Alfred home soon. As for Virginia and Randy, I have not yet decided their fate."

"It would be best to reflect on that, my darling cousin. Hopefully, we will be returning home soon. It would be such a burden to have to drag them along."

"It will not be your burden to bear."

"I suggest you should have your meeting with Radu, although it probably won't accomplish anything, and then we should pack up the household and go home. You have what you came here for—your children."

"Yes, I have my children; however, I am going to remind you … Virginia is the mother of my children, and at this point there is to be no harm to come to her. It would be best for you to remember that!"

"Of course, Basarab. Why would anyone want to harm Virginia?"

"Why would they, indeed," I retorted as I left the room.

In many ways, I knew my cousin was right, and now that I had sent her a warning about bringing no harm to Virginia, I relaxed slightly. I needed to be alone with my thoughts. I asked Emelia to escort Orsolya back to her room before I headed to the top of the house, to the room that led up to the widow's walk. When I entered, I made my way to the door that opened to the outside. Once there, I filled my lungs with the crisp night air. I paced from side to side. I shouted to nature's elements…

"Why have I been cursed so? Why can I not have a normal life—to have been born, to have found true love, to die in the arms of my soul mate? What cursed thing did I do in a former life, before I was even conceived and born, that has burdened me with this everlasting hell? She is here, within my grasp, yet I fear I will lose her again! I fear she will turn to the human—the boy. I fear she will see me as a monster, and she will seek refuge in the arms of this boy! I will not allow this to happen, even if I have to destroy him. Do you hear me? For the first time in my long life, I have found true love, and I will not allow anything or anyone to take that love from me!

Damn you, Virginia! You will never be free of me! We were meant to be together. What is it you will have me do? Condemn you to the hell I live in, in order to keep you with me?

… Yes … that is what I will do … I will damn you to my hell so we can live forever in each other's arms!"

## Chapter Twenty-two

It was time to leave for my meeting with Radu. I embraced my father. He hugged me a moment longer than usual, then held me at arm's length, his hands lingering on my shoulders.

"Be careful, son. I am pleased you have decided not to go alone, even though our people will be hidden. As Dracula has always said, Radu cannot be trusted to keep his word, and so far, your uncle has been proven right. Radu did not come alone to the cemetery to meet with Orsolya. You have to ask yourself why he felt it necessary to bring, not just one, but two of his people to back him up. This also indicates he does not trust you. Therefore, he will have someone close by him tonight, of that you can be sure."

I nodded my head in agreement. Despite having wanted to do this alone, I was glad the members of my innermost circle had insisted I have help lingering in the shadows, within arm's reach should I need it.

"Your cab should be here soon," my father said. "The others are already in place. Laborc spoke with the owner of the restaurant earlier, explaining the situation. He arranged a private room, close to where you will be sitting with Radu. At first, the owner was reluctant, not wanting problems in his establishment, saying he had other guests to consider, but Laborc assured him that if a situation arose, it would be dealt with swiftly. I believe the large sum of money for the private room helped things along, as well."

"I do not think Radu will be foolish enough to pull anything in public," I stated as I slipped into my coat. Even though I didn't need such heavy garments, it was always good to keep up the facade of normality when going out amongst the public.

"Be careful all the same," my father replied, patting me on the shoulder. He slipped something into my pocket. "You will need this for appearances at the restaurant since you will not be able to eat their food, or drink their wine." He winked.

A car horn sounded, indicating the taxi had arrived. As I was leaving, I noticed Ildiko and Teresa standing at the top of the stairway. They were watching my departure. Teresa made an attempt to come down the stairs, but Ildiko placed a hand on her arm and shook her head no. Teresa stepped back and waved instead. I nodded to my wife, and ignored my cousin. Then I turned and headed out the door.

"You are going to the Olde School Restaurant, sir," the cabbie more stated than asked. "Pretty snazzy place … the queen ate there, you know," he rambled on. "No lady with you tonight?" he asked as he put the car into drive.

I wasn't in the mood for small talk, but I also did not want to be rude. "No lady," I answered. "All business tonight."

"Too bad," the cabbie laughed. "Nice romantic place ... a little wine ... good food ... a dance or two ... who knows where that could lead to later," he snickered. He was quiet for a few moments, and then: "You been in town long? I don't recall ever picking up a passenger from your address."

I gritted my teeth before answering. "I have been away for a time. My house was under renovations."

"Really? I never saw much going on whenever I passed by."

My tongue slithered over my teeth, lingering on my incisors. I was thinking what a tasty meal this nosey man would make … perhaps another day, though. "It was all inside work," I informed. "Just touch-ups of paint and wallpaper, some flooring. There was no need for a lot of material, or workers to be coming and going."

"I see," the prying cabbie said. "Did you hire a local?"

I knew the driver was just trying to make friendly conversation, but he was annoying me. "No, I used my own people … how much further?" I asked.

"Oh … five minutes."

*Night's Return*

I noticed the man's mouth opening, as though he were going to ask me another question. "Could you turn the radio up, please?" I requested, cutting off any further conversation.

The cabbie's body language indicated he was not pleased with having to be quiet; nevertheless, he did as I requested. A stupid song, I couldn't even understand the words to, came over the airway; but, I wasn't about to ask the driver to change the station. I stared out the window for the remainder of the ride. When we pulled up to the restaurant, I looked at the metre and handed the driver forty dollars.

"Would you like a receipt?" he asked, his eyes bulging at the amount I had given him. "And change?" he seemed to add as an afterthought.

"Neither," I answered as I made my exit. I slammed the taxi door and headed toward the entrance.

Before entering, I stood a moment and gazed around my surroundings. There were not a lot of cars in the parking lot, which was probably a good thing in case of trouble. I wondered if the owner would recognize me, I had briefly met him at a function held in the restaurant a few years ago. I opened the heavy wooden door and entered the foyer. A set of carpeted stairs led up to another thick wooden door. I stepped through and waited. Nothing had changed in the restaurant. Well, maybe the picture of Queen Elizabeth dining there was an addition. It was displayed on the far wall so everyone who entered the establishment could get a full view of it. A gentleman in a grey suit approached me; I recognized him immediately and I noticed the flicker of recognition in his eyes as he reached out to shake my hand.

"Long time, my friend," he smiled.

"Yes … I have been away, back to the old country," I answered as I shook his hand.

"Must be cold out there," he said. "Your hand is freezing."

I smiled. "I am always cold, bad circulation." I withdrew my hand. "Gus, isn't it?" I asked, changing the subject.

"Yes ... and your name is Basarab, if my memory serves me correctly."

"It serves you well."

"How is your lovely wife ... Teresa is her name, is it not?"

"She is well, thank you." I wondered at Gus's recollection for faces and names. "You have an excellent memory. I think we only met for a fleeting moment or two ... and that was quite some time ago," I added.

Gus chuckled. "You and your wife made quite an impression on all the guests that night. People talked for weeks about what a stunning couple you were. Hard to forget your entrance. All eyes were on the pair of you ... especially, Teresa. Please bring her by some time."

"I will do that."

"You have a reservation, correct?"

"Yes, it should be under the name Musat. My uncle was to have made it."

"Of course," Gus nodded as he checked the reservation book. "Follow me. Names and faces I can remember, but if I didn't make the actual reservation, I need to confirm your table location. I believe the waitress mentioned that your uncle asked for a quiet spot, so I suggested a secluded corner on the upper level where you will be able to conduct your meeting without a great deal of commotion around you. You are lucky, early week is not so busy."

We walked toward the back of the restaurant, and up a few stairs. Gus showed me to a table that was nestled in a small alcove. Radu had not yet arrived. Gus pulled the table out slightly, and I slipped into my chair. He unfolded the white table napkin and placed it across my lap.

"Could I get you a drink while you are waiting?" he asked.

"I will pass if you don't mind. I have not been feeling well today ... I think I am coming down with something ... I may not be able to consume any of your delights here tonight, I am afraid." I thought to lay the groundwork ahead of time so as not to arouse suspicion as to why I did not eat or drink. I fingered the flask my father had slipped into my pocket as I had left the house. "Maybe a glass of wine when my uncle arrives," I added, thinking how wise my father had been.

Gus nodded and left me alone. I had taken the seat on the inside of the table, giving me a clear view of the restaurant, and the entrance. It was stunning, what Gus had done with the old school house. I loved the intricate chandelier that hung over the dance floor, and all the world globes that were spread throughout the area. He had kept an antiquated school atmosphere in a modern world. The gentleman at the piano was an added touch of elegant entertainment for the patrons. I also noticed Gus going from table to table, greeting his guests with the familiarity of all being old friends.

Time dragged on, and I began to wonder if my uncle was going to show up. I tapped my fingers impatiently on the table. A young girl came by with a pitcher of water. I held my hand over the glass: "Maybe later," I told her, thinking to keep the glass empty for future usage.

Gus reappeared. "I just received a call from your uncle. He is running a few minutes late, but asked you to wait. He will be along shortly." He paused. "Are you sure I cannot bring you something to drink?"

I decided it better to have something on the go before Radu arrived. "Maybe a glass of your house wine," I replied.

"Red or white?"

I smiled. "Red would suit my palate perfectly."

A few minutes later, the young girl reappeared. "Your wine, sir," she said, setting it on the table. "May I get you anything else?"

"No thank you. This will do."

I waited until she was well out of sight and then scooped the empty water glass from the table and held it down by my side. With my other hand, I withdrew the flask from my pocket, pushed the lid open, and poured the blood into the goblet. I gazed quickly around before returning it to the tabletop. I took the glass of wine and placed it under the table, securely out of reach of my feet. Even if it did get knocked over, no one would notice until I was gone. I leaned back in my chair again, scrutinizing, waiting.

Finally, I saw my uncle arrive, and, as expected, he was not alone.

~

I assumed, by the size of the man who accompanied my uncle, it was Peter. Despite his well-tailored suit, his muscles bulged at the seams, and the man appeared quite discomfited. As he and Radu approached my table, I saw, close up, how feral the man was. His hair, a wiry grey colour, fell uncontrollably to his shoulders. His beard was the same shade, although he seemed to have made an effort to shape it.

Radu smiled upon their approach. "You are alone, nephew," he stated. "I did not think you would be."

"I thought that was our agreement," I articulated through tight lips.

"Yes, I guess it was ... however ... I wasn't sure if you would honour such." Radu gave off a soft laugh and looked around the restaurant. "Are you sure you don't have some of your friends hiding in a corner somewhere?" He leaned over, placing his hands on the table.

"I am a man of my word, unlike you," I retorted.

"We shall see about that, shan't we?" Radu turned to the man who was with him. "I would like to introduce you to my right-hand man, Peter. Peter, this is my nephew, Basarab."

Peter and I stared at each other for a few seconds before nodding our heads in acknowledgement. Up to this point, Gus had been standing off to the side, giving us time to greet each other, I assumed. Finally, he stepped forward and pulled the chair to my right out from the table. He motioned to Peter, who, after fixing me with an obvious disgusted leer, sat down. Gus stepped to the other side of the table and pulled out the second seat for Radu.

"Could I get you gentlemen anything from the bar?" Gus asked.

"We are fine for now," Radu replied, not even looking at Gus.

More seconds ticked away as the three of us seemed to be sizing up each other, and the situation. At length, Radu drawled: "So, dear nephew, what is it you wish to accomplish with our little meeting here?" There was a smirk on the edge of his lips.

"I was hoping we would be able to come to some sort of agreement in order to alleviate a bloodbath," I replied, trying desperately to keep my voice calm.

Peter leaned closer to me. I found myself looking into a blazing inferno. If a police officer were to stop the man on the street, he would be considered to have consumed too much alcohol. I knew better. Peter's eyes mirrored the vile creature he was. I wondered if my uncle was aware of how deeply rooted that depraved vein ran in the man he trusted so deeply.

"What makes you think we aspire to anything less than a bloodbath?" Peter growled.

I was quite taken aback by the fact Peter had answered the question I had posed to my uncle. I decided to tempt fate a little, and, ignoring Peter, I turned to Radu: "Do you let your underling speak for you, uncle? I thought it was you who desired my throne." I bent forward, toward my uncle, a deriding look on my face.

Radu chuckled and threw a quick glance toward his companion. "Sometimes Peter becomes over-anxious in his zealousness to protect me from sabotage."

"You think I have come here to sabotage you?" I interrupted. "You are the one who started this sordid affair!"

Radu's bottom lip protruded into a pout. He ignored my previous statement and focused on what I had first said. "You do me a disservice, nephew, thinking I don't know what you are up to by asking for this meeting. You are loath to give up your throne, yet at the same time you wish to protect all those pathetic humans you so cherish." He waved his hand in the air. "So, what do you expect me to think? Here we are in a strange country, far from our homeland, and you have brought with you a small army. I have but my trusted friend with me…"

"And Elizabeth," I inserted. "And possibly, Tanyasin?"

At the mention of Tanyasin, Radu snickered. "Ah, the old Gypsy crone. What a fool she is! Did you know she actually thinks she is going to sit on the throne beside me?"

"You, if I might remind you, dear uncle, do not have a throne to sit upon."

"But I will soon enough." Radu's grin spread maliciously across his face.

"You cannot succeed," I began.

"Oh, but I will," Radu snapped. "You and your little band of full-bloods cannot stop me. I have created an army such as you have never before seen."

I was feeling impatient with the way the conversation was heading—nowhere. I decided to try and reach him through flattery. "You are a reasonable man, uncle; I am sure we can reach some sort of compromise."

"You are willing to step aside, then?" Radu mocked.

"If you remember precisely how I came to power, it was not of my choice. It was the curse put on our family by the very hag that pleads her allegiance to you. She is the one who foredoomed me to this throne of leadership while I was still in my mother's womb."

Peter spoke up: "Tanyasin is nothing compared to the powerful sorceress who gave her the power she wields. Whatever curse Tanyasin cast upon the Dracul family is of no consequence to us."

Once again, I chided my uncle. "He still speaks for you. Maybe he has an agenda of his own..." I returned my gaze to Peter. "Perhaps it is your desire to sit upon the throne? Do you truly have my uncle's best interest at hand?"

Peter's face darkened with anger. I could tell I had hit a nerve. He made a move to stand, his hands clenching quickly into fists. Radu reached over and laid a hand on Peter's arm. "It's okay ... do not let my nephew aggravate you. He is toying with you ... and me ... trying to incite a rift between us."

Time hung precariously as the big man considered what his superior was saying to him. Slowly, he relaxed back in his chair, but I could tell there was still a storm brewing inside him.

Despite the fact Peter was a rogue, I would not be deluded—he was a treacherous creature.

## Chapter Twenty-three

"Did I ever tell you how I met Peter?" Radu's question startled me. I wondered the importance of such a story; however, I decided to placate my uncle. "No. Is it overly essential at the moment?"

"It will give you an understanding of who he is, and why I know I can trust him." Radu paused a moment, smiled at Peter, and then fixed his eyes on me. "Let me see, how far should I go back ... do you remember when the vampire hunters sought us out in earnest during the first great scourge that swept through Europe in the mid $14^{th}$ century?"

I nodded.

"That is when I met Peter. I had already crossed over Elizabeth, but there was always something about her disposition that gave me an indication she could not be wholly trusted ... but Peter Stumpp ... he was different ... he owed me. I was on the run, travelling through Germany, looking for fresh blood, not having drunk for a number of days. A group of vampire hunters had been hot on my trail, and I had been separated from the family."

"You left the family protection," I reminded my uncle.

He waved his hand in the air in a *whatever* manner. "As I said, I was in Germany. Due to the vampire hunters' warnings, most people kept behind closed doors once the sun went down, and I was finding it difficult to procure nourishment."

Once again, I interrupted. "You should have embraced the strategy the family had, then. We established a different blood source, one which allowed us to keep our identities hidden."

Radu guffawed. "You know, as well as I, it did not matter in what form we took our blood. The vampire hunters were diligent in their pursuit of us, constantly training new people to seek us out, generation after generation ... so, as I was saying ... I was hiding in a forest, waiting for a band of hunters to pass.

When I considered it safe, I ventured out and came upon a farm. The buildings were in severe disrepair, and despite the coldness of the night, there was no smoke coming from the chimney. I anticipated it might be an ideal place to find a warm body, laying conveniently at rest. I approached cautiously, and as I drew near to the front door, I heard someone screaming. And then silence. I decided to enter. What did I have to lose? I was sure I could overwhelm whomever I might find inside ... and I was thirsty. The sight that greeted me would make anyone sick—even our own kind.

"Peter was straddling a young woman. He was wearing a freshly butchered wolf skin—nothing more. The wolf's head had fallen back onto Peter's back, its tongue dangling, still dripping blood. I stood for a moment, silent, my nostrils twitching excitedly because of the smell of fresh blood. I thought of taking the beast first, but I knew I was weak from lack of nourishment, and he looked strong. If he were a rogue, of whom there were many around, he might be more than I would be able to manage in my weakened condition. I stepped back into the shadows of the room, but in doing so, my foot knocked against a wooden box.

"Peter whipped around, snarling, fresh blood dripping from his mouth. I did not see any fangs. He stood to his full height and demanded to know who dared to enter his house. I held my ground. I assumed he was not a vampire, but what then? I thought my best advantage would be to show no fear. I stepped toward him and introduced myself. I told him I was journeying through Germany, in a coach, and it had been overtaken by robbers. I was the only survivor. I told him I had been wandering for days, lost, and as I had come out of the woods yonder, I had seen the silhouette of his buildings. I only wished for some shelter, and perhaps something to satisfy the hunger gnawing at my belly."

The waitress approached our table. "Is there anything you would like me to get you, yet? Would you like to see the menu?" She spoke with her head down, and her voice was barely audible, as though some sixth sense inside her told her she should beware of those sitting at my table.

Peter reached out and took hold of the girl's wrist. I noticed her face turn red as she tried to loosen his grip. "How about you, lovely? You look as though you would be a delectable dish."

I noticed Gus approaching. "Is there a problem, gentlemen? I hope Laurie has not offended you in any way."

"Oh no," Radu replied. "My friend, Peter, gets a little overzealous when he sees a pretty young girl, don't you Peter?"

Peter laughed and released the waitress's wrist.

I felt, by the look on his face, Gus wished to say something more to Peter, but he just looked around our table. His gaze stopped at me before he spoke. "Laurie, you may go ... there are other tables you can serve ... I will tend to these gentlemen."

"Thank you ... you are most kind, sir." Radu smiled at Gus.

I knew it was not a genuine smile, and I think Gus knew, as well. I could tell by the look in his eyes before he turned and walked away. I reached for my wineglass and took a sip.

"I see you brought your own refreshment," Radu noticed. "How wise."

I said nothing, so, glancing around to make sure we were alone again, Radu continued his story. "Peter told me there was nothing in his house that would be of interest to me, and as he said this he began to circle around, like a wolf stalking its victim. I stood my ground, and as he moved away from the woman, I inched toward her. I needed to show this monster what we had in common, before he attacked me. I calculated his size and decided, due to my slight stature, I would be quicker. I made my move. Within seconds, I had scooped the woman into my arms and planted my teeth into her neck, drawing life from it. Peter advanced. I looked up and snarled, my fangs dripping with the blood of his victim. He stopped and demanded to know what I was.

"I told him I was a beast, like him, only I was more powerful than he ever would be. Peter roared with laughter, disdain written all over his face as he told me there were none more supreme than he. However, as he stepped closer, I could smell his fear. I decided to tell him our family secret. After all, he was not going to be alive much longer. I could feel the woman's fresh blood surging through me, giving me strength. I asked him if he had heard the legends of bloodsucking vampires that swept through cities and towns, on the wings of the night, leaving their victims behind, drained of life's blood ... he acknowledged he had, but he didn't believe the stories to be true because he had never met a vampire.

"I asked him what manner of creature he was, drinking the blood of a beautiful woman. I even went as far to joke, telling him that I hoped he had pleasured himself with her before he took her life."

At this point in the story, Peter leaned his chair back and scoffed. He grabbed hold of his manhood. "Of course, I told your uncle, what woman would not want to be satisfied with this?"

I remained silent, disgusted at his vulgarity.

Peter took over the story. "I told Radu I was a werewolf, asking him if he had heard of my kind. He told me he had heard rumours of such creatures, but never met one. So, I asked him what made him think he was more powerful than me then."

Radu laughed softly as he gave Peter a look, and then he continued the telling: "Logic, I told Peter. I elaborated by telling him that whereas he had to wear the skin of a wolf, I could become one! I circled around him, exposing my teeth, growling viciously. I noticed his face go white as I stood on my haunches and towered over him.

"It was at that moment an idea occurred to me—what if I were to ask Peter to join me? I had few friends within the family, none actually. What if I started my own family, where I would be the ultimate authority—not having to cater to some snivelling little pup as had been our curse to accept!" Radu grinned at me, possibly hoping for a reaction.

My voice was controlled as I answered my uncle's intended insult. "You were always welcome in the family, Radu; it was your choice not to be part of it."

"Really ... was it? I had had enough of bowing to you, Basarab, and your chosen privileged few. You never genuinely allowed me to be part of the hierarchy. If you want the truth, I think it had a lot to do with the sage advice of your father, Atilla, and your Uncle Stephen ... and, of course I must not leave out my dear brother, Dracula. He always had it out for me." Bitterness crept into Radu's voice. "I have waited a long time for this moment. I was cheated out of what was rightfully mine. Even though I sat on the throne of Walachia from 1462 until 1473, and then again in 1474, due to the circumstances that befell our family, because of my brother's actions, I had to fake an illness. History was cruel to me, recording my death in 1475, as the result of syphilis. Whose idea was it to suggest such a disease—my brother's? Dracula is responsible for what became of our family, and for what became of me as a result of our imprisonment in Turkey!"

"You cannot blame him for that," I intervened. "He was a victim, too. It was your father that sent you and Dracula to the Sultan, in order to ensure the Turks did not attack his lands."

"No, it was not just what our father felt he had to do ... Dracula forsook me. Because of my brother's insolence and rebellious behaviour to our Turkish hosts, we were separated, leaving me at the mercy of the Sultan's son's revolting behaviour. If I wanted to survive, I had no choice but to acquiesce. I played the game well, educating myself with all I would need to get back control of my life—but it has been a long time in coming to me."

"Dracula endured his own form of torture," I informed my uncle. "Maybe different than you, but all the same, he learned to survive and play his own game. And then, unlike you, who became a Turkish puppet, Dracula turned his knowledge on the Turks, using it against them."

Radu laughed again, this time with malice. "Do you remember the day I tried to bury the hatchet? How I came and embraced my brother, my cousins, and you? But, as I said before, I was never made to feel part of the family, and I knew the reason was because my dear brother didn't want me there. So I left. And, as I was telling you in my story of how I met Peter, this is when I truly began to formulate my plan to take back what was rightfully mine. I saw in Peter someone whom I could create such a hold over that he would do anything for me."

I heard a low growl exhale from Peter's throat. Radu looked at his right-hand man and smiled. "Don't be sensitive, my friend ... you know what I mean, and you also know what you mean to me." Radu looked back to me. "Would you like to hear the rest of my story?"

In truth, I did not care to; however, if he let slip information I could use against him, it was worth it to hear the rest. I nodded.

Radu smiled again, barely. "I asked Peter how he would like to be able to change to a wolf for real. He was curious, so I explained what would happen. He agreed, saying he was tired of the way the townspeople treated him, he wanted revenge. I assured him that was a possibility, but it would have to be under my astute guidance. However, and this is where the situation became difficult, prior to the transformation, Peter insisted on going to town to settle some affairs. Unknown to him, the law had finally gathered enough incriminating evidence against him, and they had decided to end his reign of terror. They had a long list of heinous crimes Peter had committed, the latest addition coming from an overheard conversation ... he had been bragging to someone in a bar about his having had intercourse with a succubus sent to him by the Devil! I laughed at the thought that this was what tipped the good town's people over the edge—the women and children Peter had ravished and murdered were not enough.

"I began to worry when he had not returned that evening, so I went into town, and sat in the corner of a local bar. While there, I heard the buzz of the upcoming trial. Peter had been captured and put in jail. Everyone was discussing the demise of Peter Stumpp. One man, over-intoxicated, was boasting how he had once escaped from Peter's clutches, and dealt him quite a blow before the leaving. He bragged how that blow had left a mark that should still be visible for everyone to see at the execution.

"A woman sat down at my table, and I struck up a conversation with her. As you know, Basarab, we vampires have our ways of obtaining information when we need to. The woman was more than pleased to tell me anything I wanted to know. She also suggested that if I was up for a little something more, she would be only too happy to oblige me when she finished work. She told me where Peter was being held, and when his execution would take place. She didn't think it would be a lengthy trial—everyone knew he was guilty! I thanked her for her time, and asked her when she would be finished work. She giggled and thrust her breasts a little closer to me. Little did she know that it was the blood pulsing through the veins in her neck that I was more interested in.

"I searched the bar for someone who looked similar to Peter. My eyes kept returning to the braggart. I decided he would do, after a bit of roughing up. He was close to the same size and build. I left the establishment and lurked in the shadows, waiting. Finally, the man staggered out the door and headed my way. It didn't take long to subdue him. I slung him over my shoulders and headed for the jail. Entering the front door, I pretended to walk unsteadily, due to the weight of the load I was carrying. I ordered one of the keepers to open up the cell in the back so I could dump the filthy, drunken swine I had found on the street in it. He hesitated, but only a moment, once he looked into my eyes.

"After that, everything fell nicely into place. Peter was surprised to see me. Luckily, he was the only one there at the time, which made my task easier. I laid my victim down on the mattress in the corner of the cell and then turned to the keeper. I took him by the shoulders and stared into his eyes, burning into his mind what I wanted him to do and remember. Within a few minutes, I had Peter's cell open, and we made the switch. I let Peter bloody the man's face so much that it would not be recognizable. I ordered Peter to strip and exchange clothing with our victim. As we were leaving, the man began to moan. We walked out of the jail, unseen, because of the spell I had cast on the guards. Peter was astounded. I told him he still had a lot to learn, but I was sure he would be an astute student.

"As we passed under the cell window where Peter had just been, we heard the man screaming that he was not Peter Stumpp, he was Albrecht Brauer, owner of the town brewery. We heard the guard yelling, saying that he was no fool, and would not be hoodwinked by the likes of Peter Stumpp. Then, there was a thump, and all was quiet.

"I ordered Peter to go on ahead; I would meet him at his house shortly—I had to retrieve a package. He did not question me. I felt good; I already had him under my control. I returned to the bar, and the woman was waiting for me. I told her I lived a short ways out of town, and asked if she minded walking. She didn't. When we arrived at Peter's house, she was hesitant, but I crossed her palm with a few pieces of gold, and she stepped eagerly through the door.

"I said to Peter: 'Look what I have brought us, my friend.' The woman looked at me, frightened, but I assured her everything was okay ... that my friend would pleasure her first. I laughed and told her I had seen his jewels, and I guaranteed she would not be disappointed. I pointed to the gold in her hand and told her there would be plenty more if she performed well.

"What transpired next energized me. I could not wait until I had Peter totally under my control, and I got to taste a little of what he gave that unfortunate young woman. When he was finished with her, I moved in and took what I needed. Then I turned to him and informed him it was time. Peter Stumpp has been by my side ever since, my number one.

"I educated Peter about what had taken place at *his execution*. Civilization considers sadistic Dracula's methods of torture, but those were not worse than what was supposed to have happened to Peter. Peter, or should I say, Albrecht, was positioned on a large wooden wheel in the centre of town. The executioner used burning tongs to slowly tear the flesh from his body. Then, he took an axe and severed his arms and legs, followed by his head, after which all of the body parts were heaped onto a pyre and burned. Next to the pyre, a pole was erected, and someone nailed a wolf pelt around it, and placed Albrecht's severed head on top of the pole. I heard a woman cry out that the man they had executed was not Peter Stumpp, it was her husband, Albrecht Brauer; but no one believed her, and she had been hushed. As a result, after hearing such a story, Peter has been forever grateful, and faithful, to me." Radu leaned back in his chair, a pleased grin on his lips. "Haven't you, Peter?"

Peter nodded stiffly. I had the impression he did not take kindly to having to sit through Radu's story of conquest.

"Peter, would you go out to the car and bring in our bottle? I am thirsty, and it is not polite that my nephew should be drinking alone."

Once Peter was out of earshot, my uncle turned to me. I sensed that he had sent Peter away so he could add something more to his story. "You are wondering how I know I can trust such a monster, are you not, Basarab?"

"The thought has crossed my mind."

"I'll tell you then ... and let this be an indication to you of the nature of the power I wield. One day, when Peter and I were alone, after a meeting with some of my other key people, I told him it was extremely critical that he be my constant eyes and ears, as well as being my friend. I re-affirmed to him how long we had been together—a long time—longer than anyone else, with the exception of Elizabeth, whom I knew could not be wholly trusted. I informed him that some of my closest men also needed to be watched.

"Peter agreed. He told me he had observed some discontent with certain individuals in our ranks. You see, nephew, Peter is loyal to me. Of all around me, it is him whom I can truly trust. Even so, I needed to test him. I am a careful man. I poured a glass of blood for each of us. I watch Peter gulp his down. Mine remained untouched. I poured another for him. Suddenly, he noticed I was not drinking, and he asked if I was not thirsty. I told him, no. He then asked me if there was something he should know about the drink. I asked him if he trusted me. His answer was, with the life I had granted him. I then told him not to ask me such again, that he of all who were close to me, was safe. Only then, did I pick up my glass and down the liquid, satisfied that even my most trusted man feared me." He paused. "So, have I answered your curiosity as to how and why I allow this man the liberty to answer on my behalf sometimes?"

"You have," I affirmed, even though I knew, probably more than Radu did, Peter was his own man—he was nobody's puppet.

At that point, Peter returned. He pulled a bottle from inside his suit jacket and sat it boldly on the table. I glanced over to where Gus was working the bar. If he had noticed the sudden appearance of a bottle of wine on our table, one that had not originated from his bar, he said nothing. I made a mental note to make it up to him later, financially.

Radu waved his hand toward the bottle. "Please, Peter, pour us a glass. Would you like yours topped off, Basarab?"

I shook my head.

"Don't trust me?" he hissed venomously.

"As you can see, I brought my own," I returned tersely. I paused, studying my uncle, wondering exactly what his goal had been in telling me his story of how he had met Peter. Was he trying to intimidate me? "So, here we sit … you reminiscing about Peter, and me wondering where this is all leading to."

Radu laughed softly, a hint of contempt rippling through the sound. "Oh, dear nephew, I did not stop with Peter," Radu stated. "I became restless after a number of years. I wanted the power that had been stolen from me, but knew I had to plan carefully, and I wouldn't be able to defeat your numbers with just Peter by my side, despite how powerful he is. I recruited several more key people, all criminals of the vilest kind, some of them doctors who have been instrumental in creating the drug that allows me to control my army of rogues. One of them had connections to the North American continent, which suited my purposes because, I knew I would need to expand beyond Europe, eventually."

I was growing impatient, and I was also wondering what my friends in the back room were doing. They must be getting restless, by now. "What is the purpose of you telling me all this, Radu? Did it ever occur to you that I might use some of your information as a weapon against you?"

Radu laughed. His eyes narrowed. "You flirt with me, Basarab. I am telling you this so you will realize how powerful I am, how I have created an army so formidable that you will not stand a chance against it, even with your pure vampire bloodline."

"Are you sure of this?" I taunted.

"Very."

I had begun to wonder where Elizabeth Bathory fit into Radu's plans. From first hand knowledge, I knew she had sights on being on the throne beside my uncle. I decided to ask since my uncle was being so forthcoming with information. "What of Elizabeth?"

"Elizabeth ... she has had her use ... she is a wild creature, sometimes to the point of being uncontrollable, but she did prove to be quite an asset for me when we were travelling around Europe and the British Isles. Even though I don't trust her, I feel I will still be able to use her ... what better front than to have a beautiful woman by my side?

"While she was in London, she picked up Jack—The Ripper—and began to use him to do her bidding—her dirty work, actually. I remember the first time she introduced him to me. I knew, right away, what kind of man he was. A clever plan began to formulate in my mind—one that would give me the inside information on Elizabeth. Jack played right into my hands, and for the most part, he has been invaluable. I find his snivelling annoying, but for all the time I actually have to deal with him, I am willing to put up with the aggravation—and he does serve other purposes on the odd occasion, as well." Radu chuckled.

"Then, a stroke of luck came my way; Elizabeth told me you had a son." Radu hesitated, and smirked: "It was delightful to see Teresa again, too, I might add, even though my gut tells me she is not being honest with Elizabeth. I do not believe, for a moment, Teresa ever would betray you, would she?" Radu did not give me the opportunity to respond to his question. "I figured

I would allow Elizabeth to decide whose side Teresa was actually on. Elizabeth has not survived this long by being anyone's fool—not even mine.

"My original intention was to have Elizabeth bring your child to me, so I would be able to make you and the family bow to me, with less bloodshed—maybe. Of course, I can still have the child, the throne, and the battle—my choice. My inner circle was becoming restless, so after Elizabeth left with Teresa, I informed them it was almost time ... once I had the boy in my clutches, we would make our move. I would send a message to you, Basarab, and how quickly, and what we did, would depend on your reply."

I needed to take my uncle down a peg. "I guess I thwarted your plans, then, didn't I?"

"For now."

We were interrupted by Gus as he approached our table, looking at his watch. "I just wanted to let you know we will be closing in about half an hour." His eyes flitted toward the back of the restaurant, to the door of the room where I knew my people were waiting. I glanced at Radu and Peter, hoping they hadn't noticed and become suspicious. They didn't appear to have.

"Thank you, Gus, I think we are almost finished here," I said, even though nothing had been accomplished more than me learning how my uncle had recruited Peter and his army.

Gus nodded, and left.

"Well," said Radu, "I guess this conversation was not what you expected, was it, Basarab?"

"Not exactly. I was hoping we could have reached a compromise."

"There is nothing to compromise, nephew. I want the throne, and I will have it, one way or another." He leaned forward, his elbows on the table. "It is in your hands, Basarab. If you value these humans so much, you can save them by handing over the power to me, by submitting to me. The family has become lenient over the years, hiding what they are, allying with humans. I will not be so inclined." He leaned back, giving me time to absorb his full intention, which I did.

I knew now, more than I had before, there was nothing I could say to dissuade Radu from his intended path to my throne. He had waited a long time for his moment, planning and scheming, and building a rogue army he felt could not be defeated. I began to wonder if his coming to Canada to get to my son had been nothing more than a decoy to get me out of Transylvania. Was something going on there now that I should be aware of? Was Gara safe? Surely, he would have notified me if there was activity on the home front.

"What's the matter, Basarab? Already feeling the sting of defeat?" Peter taunted.

"Never! Especially, not from the likes of you," I sneered. I had accepted the fact that the only way to stop Radu was to eliminate him and his followers—every last one of them.

Radu pushed his chair back from the table. "I believe it is time for us to leave, Peter. It has been lovely chatting with you, Basarab. Too bad we couldn't have reached a compromise. In truth, though ... and I definitely want to be truthful with you, nephew ... I only came here tonight so I could see the look on your face once you realized that no matter what you do, it will be futile." He lingered at the table a moment longer. "Would you like to walk out with us?"

"No ... thank you for the offer; I would like to straighten up with Gus. He has been most generous allowing us the use of his restaurant, even though we did not partake of his hospitality. And, I need to call a cab, as well," I added.

"We could drop you home," Peter suggested.

I noticed the hunger in his eyes. "I think that would be unwise of me to accept such an invitation."

"You do not trust us," Radu enquired.

"No."

As Radu and Peter left, I heard them chuckling. I waited until they were well gone before heading for the room where my family awaited.

# Virginia

## Chapter Twenty-four

I paced around my room while waiting for Randy to show up. I'd had no way of stopping the dreams that kept invading my sleep. The dream I most feared was the one where Ildiko and Teresa had accosted me, and I pondered if it had been sent to me by someone as a warning for me to take extra care. But how did I battle such creatures? There was no way I would be able to overpower them. My only salvation was to tell the count, and I would do so as soon as he returned from his meeting.

I heard the key turning in my door. I prayed it was Randy, not Max with my morning meal; or worse yet, Ildiko and Teresa. The door creaked open. Randy stepped inside, an urgency to his entrance.

"Are you ready?" he whispered. Randy must have noticed the look on my face, a look I tried not to show. He came hastily to me and took hold of my shoulders, peering down at me with his warm brown eyes. "What's wrong?"

I looked away from his intense gaze. "I can't go with you," I garbled.

"No! Don't do this, Virginia. You are insane to want to stay here! They will kill you! If not Teresa and Ildiko, the count will slowly destroy you. Don't sell your soul to them!"

"Don't put it that way, Randy."

"What other way is there to put it? Think of your children, Virginia. Think how hard you have worked to make them more like you than like their father. And it has worked with Santan … there is still hope for Samara…"

"Stop, Randy! I just cannot go with you. I can't leave." I wiggled from his grasp and turned away.

I wished Randy would say something, anything, but he didn't. I dared myself to turn and glance at him, thinking he might have left so quietly that I may not have heard him. But, the look on his face told me all I needed to know about what he was going to say next, even before the words were out of his mouth. "You can't leave *him*! It is the count you cannot leave, not your children! You are in love with a monster, no matter how hard you tried in the past to convince me and yourself that you weren't!" The accusation spewed from Randy's mouth. "Tell me this isn't true, and I will try and believe you."

I couldn't speak. I couldn't tell him what he wanted to hear. I turned away from him again.

"Wow!" The word was spoken with a questioning wonderment. "I feel so used … is that what our relationship was all about, Virginia? You just used me as a back-up…"

I spun around, and even though I knew I shouldn't be angry at Randy, my words were sharp with reproach as I cut him off. "How many times, Randy, did I tell you there was no *us*? But you kept coming at me … you kept trying … I never asked you for more … you were just there all the time … offering help … worming your way into my children's lives … expecting that one day we would be a family … taking advantage of my loneliness, my vulnerability … how many times, Randy, did I tell you?"

"Your vulnerability? I am wondering now if anything you have ever told me has been true."

"What did I always tell you, Randy? I told you that you were my friend—that is what I told you—my best friend. Nothing more. Can you deny that?"

I noticed Randy's shoulders slump slightly. His lips barely moved as he whispered: "No … that is what you always said … we were just friends."

"Then continue to be my friend, Randy. Nothing has changed for me in that area. I still do not know what the next few days, or few hours for that matter, hold for me—for us. Maybe I am wrong about everything. Maybe I am mistaken even to consider the count will protect me, but that is a chance I am willing to take. He is where my heart lies. I cannot lie to myself or anyone else any longer. He is the father of my children, and if I am to have any chance of remaining with them, it will be through him. I know he loves me, too … he has told me as much."

"And you believe such a monster has a heart with which to love?"

Randy's statement brought old memories back of conversations with Max and Teresa, conversations where they continually told me the count had no heart … he did as he pleased, whenever he pleased. But none of them had seen the side of him I had—none of them!

"Yes," I breathed. "Yes, I believe he has a heart. I have seen it, and I have felt it beating against mine."

The pain in Randy's eyes was almost too much for me to bear; nevertheless, the words were out, and my feelings were in the open. I had confided my dark secret to my best friend, and I know it had hurt him to the core, but he was young—he would get over it. Now, I had to do the only decent thing I could do at the moment, despite my having almost asked him to stay. I had to tell him to get out while it was still possible.

"You go, Randy."

His face was as sad as his reply. "I can't do that, Virginia. I still can't leave you, despite how you feel. Besides, I will not leave Santan."

"Do you honestly think the count will allow you to continue to be around his son?" I asked pointedly.

"He will have no choice … Santan will demand it. And, if I know anything about the count, he will do whatever it takes to win the heart of his son. At the moment, I have his son's heart!"

There was no way I could dispute what Randy was saying. Santan loved him. And why shouldn't my son love him? Randy had been the one who had been there for Santan, and even though my son had always seemed to know Randy was not his real father, he loved him, and was as devoted to Randy as he was to me.

"So, what will you do now?" I asked.

"Just what I have been doing all along. I will spend time with the children and wait for whatever is going to happen next." Randy headed for the door. He handed me the key. "I guess I won't be needing this. Maybe I'll see you later in the children's room, if the count allows it."

As Randy quietly closed the door his final words stung my heart. I dropped the key into my pocket. I would return it discretely to Emelia next time I saw her. I had no further need of it. I walked slowly over to my bed and sat down on the edge of it. What had I done to my friend? He was so undeserving of the fate that I knew in my heart might lie ahead of him.

Not long ago, he was just a young man struggling to find his way in the world … orphaned at too young an age … left in the care of an uncle who was too busy with his own life. He had embraced me and my son at a time when I had no one else, and he had become so dear to me, so indispensable! He had grown and matured … and when he had found out my true story, he still stayed … because he loved me. And what did I give him in return … a death sentence?

~

When Emelia came into my room, I was still crying. Not hard. Just enough to drain some of the pain I had caused Randy from my soul, to wash away the guilt I felt. Emelia came over and sat down beside me. She put her arm around me and pulled me to her. I laid my head on her shoulder. She patted my back.

"Everything will be okay, dear," she whispered.

I breathed in deeply. "I hope so," I gurgled, and then swallowed the rest of my tears. I wiped my eyes, rested a moment more on Emelia's shoulder, and then pushed away. "I am afraid I have hurt Randy more than I ever meant to," I began.

Emelia looked at me with a knowing smile. "He will be okay," she assured me.

"How can he be okay? He loves me, you know."

"I know. He is a strange young man, your Randy. Santan clearly loves him."

I nodded. "And that may be the only thing that saves his life." I paused. "I told him to leave, you know ... but he won't go."

"I don't think he will ever leave you or the children," Emelia stated.

"Basarab will not be pleased. I cannot see him keeping Randy around. Randy's bond with Santan is too much for the count to tolerate for any great length of time, I am afraid."

Emelia laid her hand on my leg and patted it. "Santan will come to know his father, and he will accept what is to be. He is a wise child. All will be well—for both of them." Emelia stood and walked to the window. She sat down at the little table where I ate my meals. "Come, Virginia, sit with me. I have something important I must tell you."

As I walked to join her, I decided I would tell her about the plot Ildiko and Teresa were scheming. "I have something to tell you, as well, and something to confess. Please allow me to go first." I sat down.

Emelia smiled and nodded.

"I was ready to leave this morning. Remember when Randy and I went to the widow's walk? He had overheard a conversation between Ildiko and Teresa. They are planning to get rid of me. Randy devised a plan for us to leave here, and he came this morning to get me."

"How did he get in your room?" Emelia asked, and then her eyebrows rose questioningly. "Wait, your door was unlocked when I came to you ... how is that?"

I dug into my pocket and handed Emelia the key she had left in my room. "This is yours, I believe. You forgot it the other day."

"I see ... continue, then," she encouraged as she took the key and slipped it into her pocket.

"I told Randy I loved the count, and that I couldn't go with him. I told him I was going to go to Basarab and tell him of the plot, and that I was sure Basarab would protect me."

"Basarab knows." Emelia reached over the table and took my hands in hers. "He knows, my dear, and that is why I am here now. He asked me to guard you until he returns and can deal with the situation."

My heart must have skipped at least three or four beats. He knew! And he was going to protect me! "He knows," I breathed.

"Yes ... Santan told him."

"Santan told him? How did he know?"

"The child has powers that even we vampires do not understand. He went to his father and ensured your safety, embracing his father once he promised nothing would happen to you. This was a step Basarab desired more than anything, and Santan knows that." She paused. "He loves you."

"I know my son loves me," I said.

"Of course, Santan loves you, but I meant Basarab ... he loves you," Emelia clarified.

I swallowed hard.

"However, at the moment, I think we have to be exceedingly careful. On the way here, I bumped into Ildiko in the hallway. She, too, was headed in this direction. She seemed flustered, angry really, when I told her I was going to see you and would be sitting with you for a while. She changed her direction and stomped off."

"So it begins," I sighed. "Emelia, tell me truthfully, will this turmoil never end for me?"

"Basarab will deal with Ildiko and Teresa; you can be assured of that."

"I hope so ... but then what? What does he do with me ... and Randy? What place do two humans have in the vampire world?"

Before Emelia could answer me, there was a knock on the door. Max entered with a tray of food. "Ildiko mentioned you were here with Virginia, Emelia," he said. "So, I thought you might like to join Virginia as she has her breakfast." Max placed my plate of food on the table and took the cover from it. He placed a glass of blood in front of Emelia. "Is there anything else either of you might like?" he asked.

Emelia smiled. "This is lovely, Max, thank you."

Max turned and shuffled out of the room. As I watched him leave, I noticed how much slower his movements were from when I had first met him. He seemed weary beyond what weariness should be. At the doorway, he turned briefly and looked directly at me, and then closed the door.

"Shall we?" Emelia waved a hand at the food.

My stomach rumbled, indicating it would not refuse the morsels in front of me. I dug my fork into the scrambled eggs and took a bite of toast. Emelia sipped at her nourishment. Suddenly, Emelia gripped her stomach, and a frightened look came into her eyes.

"Virginia ... stop ... don't eat anymore!" And then she slumped over, her head crashing to the table. The glass of blood went flying, splattering onto the floor.

I spit the last mouthful I had taken onto my plate. "Emelia!" I screamed as I got up and raced to her side. I tried lifting her from the chair, but my head began to feel woozy and severe pain shot through my abdomen. I crumbled to the floor, grabbing hold of my stomach. I closed my eyes, trying to blot out the pain. I heard the door open, and footsteps approaching me. I kept my eyes closed ... better that way ... better that whoever it was did not know I was still alive ... *oh God ... dear Emelia ... Basarab ... we need you ... where are you...*

## Chapter Twenty-five

My greatest fear was realized—it was Ildiko and Teresa. The footsteps stopped just before where I was laying, and I could feel their shadows hovering, waiting to drain the life from me and send me to an everlasting hell. My dream was coming to fruition, and Basarab was not here to save me. I squeezed my eyes tighter, praying they wouldn't notice the slight movement of my eyelids.

"You see, Teresa, my plan has worked. Drugging the food was a genius move. Max is not aware of what you did, is he?"

"No."

"Good. Now we need to get her out of here until we can finish her off."

"My husband will come to her rescue; I know he will."

"We will just have to make sure Basarab never finds her body, then." Ildiko's laugh filled the room with evil. "Besides, even if he does, he will be too late to do anything about his beloved Virginia. She will no longer be his problem, or ours, and you and your husband can have your happy little family."

"And what of you, Ildiko? What are your plans? You have always had aspirations for my standing in the family. Am I to find myself in the same situation one day as Virginia is at the moment? And what of Emelia? She was not supposed to be involved."

Ah, yes, poor, dear Emelia ... what were they going to do with her ... kill her, too? Or, was she already dead? I could feel the heaviness of my pain trying to drown me. I fought to remain conscious. If I could hear what they were up to, maybe I stood a chance of surviving ... somehow ... if they didn't kill me immediately. I wished I could speak ... that I could dig away at the rift between the two vampire women, possibly giving me a chance to get away and find Basarab. But my pain was too great, and I dared not take the chance of having them see I was still conscious.

A diabolical laugh echoed through the room, followed by a sarcastic sounding retort. "That is a chance you shall have to take, isn't it? As for Emelia, she will awaken eventually. I am sure what we used will just buy us enough time to deal with Virginia. How foolish of Basarab to think Emelia would be able to thwart our plans."

*Good ... Emelia is still alive ... maybe she will awaken and call for help ... better she doesn't ... probably.*

"Do you honestly believe Basarab knows?"

I could hear the fear in Teresa's voice.

"Of course ... he must."

There was a brief silence, and then I heard footsteps walking past me. Something dropped to the floor, a clinging sound.

"There you go, Emelia ... sleep well."

Ildiko must have carried Emelia to the bed.

"You mentioned, Ildiko, I must take my chances with you, but I would like to remind you of something. Don't underestimate my power, or my position with the count. I am only in on this with you so that we both can be rid of her."

Of course, I knew they were talking about me.

"I think we should we just do it now!" Ildiko sounded overly eager. "Finish her off and then dispose of the body somewhere where it won't be found. We can't take a chance that she awakens and screams out for help."

"I don't think we should do it here. Basarab will smell the blood, he will smell her death."

*Oh God! Where are you? Basarab ... Randy ... anybody!*

My brain was trying to absorb what was going on around me. Teresa was reluctant to kill me, this much I was gathering. Likely because she feared if the count found out she was involved in my demise, her role as his queen would no longer be. Ildiko just wanted me dead—whatever the cost!

"Do you not think he will know either way?" Ildiko replied to Teresa's statement. "Whether we do it here or somewhere else, he will know."

"It will be easier to hide damning evidence if we do this elsewhere." Teresa sounded firm in her conviction. Was she buying time, so as not to kill me?

"Are you getting cold feet, Teresa?"

I heard Teresa laugh. "Should I be, Ildiko? After all, it has crossed my mind that you might make it look as though this was all my idea. That would pave the way for you then, wouldn't it—to get what you have always wanted—my husband. Don't think for a second that I have not forgotten the number of times you have referred to me as a filthy Gypsy!"

I was fighting desperately to stay conscious. The pain in my gut was excruciating, and it took all of my strength to keep from crying out.

Ildiko's laugh, if I could call it that, filtered through my fogginess. "I guess you could say, dear Teresa, I would rather see my cousin with a dirty Gypsy, than see him with a snivelling human!"

Teresa was not backing down. "It seems to me that everyone wants a piece of my husband. I just want to remind you, dear Ildiko, many have attempted to take him from me over time, but not one has succeeded!"

"Until now … until this human came into his life!" A foot nudged me in the back.

"Truth be told, I don't fear either one of you."

"You should," Ildiko retorted.

Momentary silence.

Then: "Well, I guess once this deed is done, I should have nothing more to fear then, right?" Teresa's voice had risen, and I detected anger ripping through her words.

"I guess not." And Ildiko laughed again.

I was slowly losing control … my mind was becoming foggier. I realized I was totally at their mercy; there would be no making a run for it this time.

"Like I said, Ildiko, I will not do it here." Teresa was speaking with conviction. "Enough time has already passed. Neither one of us wants to deal with an angry Basarab, and I fear he will be back from his meeting with Radu soon. We can secure Virginia somewhere away from here, and then return to the house with the hope our absence was not detected."

"And if it was?"

"We will be able to explain it. We will tell the count we were feeling pent up and just went out for a bit of fun."

I felt a cold breath by my ear. "Ah, sweet Virginia, always the game-player, weren't you? Well, consider your game over." There was a pause. The coolness left. "I know just the place to hide her until the way is clear for us to finish this," Teresa commented.

"Where?"

I was fighting hard to maintain my ability to hear where they were going to put me. It might be my only salvation, if I had enough strength left to escape.

"In the cemetery near the house, there is a mausoleum. The walls are so thick, once she awakens from the drug we gave her, she can scream to her heart's content, and no one will hear her. Plus, it will be close by so that when the time is ripe to do the deed, we won't have far to go." There was a few seconds of silence, and then Teresa added: "Maybe we won't have to do anything, when I think on it … if we just leave her in the crypt, she will starve to death!"

*Oh God! There would be no escaping from such a place!*

"You can get inside this mausoleum?" Ildiko enquired.

"No problem. It is full and not used anymore. The bodies inside are all so old that no one who cared at the times of their deaths is alive to visit. I used to entertain the occasional guest in there. Of course, I am sure there is nothing left of them now but a few bones." Teresa laughed.

I felt a set of arms reach under my back and my legs. I knew it was Ildiko; I knew she would be the one to carry me. I allowed my body to go limp, which, at this point, was not a difficult task. As Ildiko began walking, I heard her tell Teresa to get the key that had dropped on the floor ... the door must be locked ... things must appear normal for as long as possible. I heard Teresa ask about Emelia ... I did not hear Ildiko's response.

~

I have no idea how long I had been out, but I was slowly coming around. My stomach still hurt like hell. I thought of screaming, but what would the point in doing that be, at least until I knew where I was, and if they were gone. I could smell the staleness of the air surrounding me, and death. My mind began to clear a little, and I remembered Teresa saying they were going to hide me in a mausoleum. Is that where I was?

My eyes were trying to adjust to the darkness. The floor I was lying on was stone cold, with an earthy smell. I swallowed the screams that were trying to get out. There was no light anywhere, not even a sliver. I began to crawl, searching for a wall, or a door, where I could pull myself up and lean against.

Not a sound, other than my body scraping on the ground as I moved along. I was alone in the dark with the ghosts of the past—ghosts that I would be joining soon, whether Teresa and Ildiko came back for me or not. I kept inching around until I reached a wall. I managed to push my body into a sitting position. I vaguely remembered Teresa saying she had brought her victims here. There was no way I wanted to venture further into the crypt, to come face to face with any human remains. I closed my eyes and thought back to when this whole nightmare had begun, and my tears flowed freely. What a foolish young woman I had been ... how had I ever deemed it possible to play, let alone win a game against such creatures?

And now, what of Randy? An innocent in this entire web of evil I was caught in. Randy loved me ... he loved Santan ... and Samara ... he was honourable ... he had tried to save me ... but there was no saving ... not from these creatures! Would Emelia come to my rescue again ... she couldn't ... or Angelique? Would she use her unique powers and find me before it was too late? Would Basarab remember our moments together ... would he remember that it was I who had given him, not just one, but two children … would he save me in order to obtain the love of his son … would he care enough? He might, if he had a heart … but Max and Teresa had always told me he didn't have a heart … he was not to be trusted … he did as he pleased … when it pleased him … but, I loved him … despite … yes, it was the count I loved … not poor, innocent Randy … so, I am damned … either way, I am damned!

    With that realization, my mind shut down again.

# Basarab

## Chapter Twenty-six

The ride back to the house had been silent, the way I wanted it. Dracula had wanted to know the outcome of my meeting with Radu right away, but I told him I would fill everyone in when we got back to the house. By the look in his eyes, I knew that he knew it had not gone well. I made a quick phone call to my father, asking him to gather everyone in the dining room for a meeting.

"It did not go well," I opened once everyone was seated. "Radu did not come alone, Peter was with him. Radu told me the story of how he recruited Peter—all the gory details of it— and he mentioned some of the others he has on board. Peter is a beast, and if you want my opinion, Radu should watch his own back. I got the impression Peter has an agenda of his own and is just biding his time."

"So what now?" Sebes enquired.

"Now we pack up as quickly as we can and return to Brasov. I don't think there is more we can do here. We have what we came for. We must protect the home front before Radu unleashes his army."

"What of the humans, cousin?" Mihail asked.

"The humans are not to be harmed," I replied firmly.

"What of the mother of your children?" Mihail continued. "Does she return to Brasov with us, or do we leave her behind to go to the authorities?"

"I have yet to decide if she stays or comes with us. But, there is one thing I know, Virginia will never go to the authorities."

"How can you guarantee that?" Dracula joined the conversation. "Plus, don't forget the boy, Randy."

"I do understand the concern here; however, neither one will betray our secret because they both love the children and would not do anything that might bring harm to them." I paused and looked around the table, hesitating briefly at each family member, demanding their allegiance with my eyes. I continued: "You will know my decision on Virginia and Randy before we leave. For now, let's start closing the house."

I stood up, turned and headed out the door—my way of dismissing the meeting. I was anxious to get to Virginia. As I headed up the stairway, I was confronted by a frantic Randy.

"Basarab! I can't find Virginia!" Randy shouted.

"What do you mean, you cannot find her? She should be in her room."

"I have been knocking on her door, and she doesn't answer."

"She cannot get out of her room," I stated. "What is the meaning of you going to her room?" My suspicion was raised as I recollected what Tanyasin had said.

"I just wanted to talk to her." Randy looked away, not wanting to look in my eyes, I assumed.

I pushed past Randy, heading to Virginia's room. My heart was thumping. What if she was missing? What if somehow she had gotten out of her room and she had fled, leaving everyone behind, including her children? But how? How could she get out unless someone had been careless with one of the keys? I would check with Max and Emelia—they both had keys.

The closer I approached to Virginia's room, the more urgency I was feeling. There was something wrong. I didn't wait for a key. My foot rose up and hit the wood with a loud crash. As the door swung open, the first view I had was of Emelia sprawled on Virginia's bed.

"Virginia!" I howled.

Randy was right behind me, pushing his way into the room. I heard footsteps running up the stairs. I scoured the area. No sign of Virginia. I heard Emelia's moan and raced to the bed.

"What happened here, Emelia? Where is Virginia? Did she do this to you?" My questions were delivered fast and furious.

Emelia looked at me, her eyes hazy. I felt bad pressuring her, but I had to know. Randy was standing by my side, practically breathing down my neck. It irritated me. Others rushed into the room—I cared not who they were. My only thoughts were to find Virginia.

"Emelia…" I could hear the desperation in my own voice.

"I came here to watch over Virginia … as you requested … on the way I met Ildiko … she was not happy … Virginia and I were talking … she told me Randy had overheard Ildiko and Teresa plotting…"

I turned and glared at Randy.

Emelia continued: "He wanted to take her from here … but … but…" Emelia raised her hand to her head. She closed her eyes for a moment. "Oh, yes … Virginia said she could not go with him because she was in love with you. I told her that you already knew." Emelia heaved a deep sigh.

"Go on, Emelia," I encouraged.

"Max came … brought us some food … I told him it was very thoughtful of him … oh, Basarab, I am so sorry … I am so sorry I could not protect Virginia. There was something in the blood … I began to feel unwell … I remember telling Virginia to stop eating … I don't think she had eaten much, yet … I remember loosing control of my body … Virginia screamed my name … that is the last thing I heard." The words stuttered out of my aunt.

Despite my desperation to locate Virginia, Emelia's statement about the blood bothered me. Why would someone want to harm Emelia? Why would Ildiko or Teresa want to harm her? Because I had asked Emelia to watch over Virginia, and that had interfered with their plans to do away with the mother of my children. What had they done with Virginia?

My eyes scanned the room again, searching for a possible clue of a struggle. There was nothing. Was Virginia already dead—drugged to make the killing easy, and clean? "Are you sure you didn't see or hear anything else before you passed out?" I questioned Emelia.

Emelia looked away, toward the window. "Nothing, Basarab. I was falling ... Virginia screamed my name, as I already told you ... and then I came to when you entered the room ... that's it."

I turned and pushed my way through the crowd of vampires that had gathered in the room. No one said a word as I rushed out. When I reached the top of the stairway, I screamed: "Max!"

My faithful servant appeared in the foyer. "Yes, Count?" His voice was barely audible. Was he hiding something? Was it fear I detected?

I literally flew down the stairs, and when I reached Max I grabbed hold of his shoulders. "Do you know where your daughter is?"

I could feel Max shaking under my grip. "She came by not long ago and told me that she and Ildiko were going to take a walk around the enclosed courtyard. I haven't seen her since."

I didn't wait for more. I headed to the doorway that led to the courtyard. As I ran down the steps, my mind was remembering another night I had gone down these same steps—the first night Virginia had tried to flee from me. I pictured her in my mind, desperate to get away from me, groping at the stone walls, finding the door, and then the latch. I pictured her as she turned around at the sound of my voice, how she faced me, the rain pouring over her. And then, how she fell into my arms, and how I wrapped her in my cloak and led her back up the stairs, into my house. I could have let her go, but there was something about her…

I smelt them before I saw them. They turned as I approached. They appeared shocked to see me. "What did you do with her?" I could hear the animal in my voice.

Ildiko was the first to speak. "With whom?"

Teresa looked away.

"You know exactly who I am talking about, Ildiko. Do not toy with me!"

"Basarab! What are you talking about? We have been here for the past couple of hours, talking."

I snorted. "You two? Talking? Friends? Don't take me for a fool! What would you two have to talk about?"

Ildiko grunted. "Maybe your infatuation with Virginia? Wouldn't that be an interesting subject for your wife and cousin to discuss?"

Her statement infuriated me. I grabbed both women by the arm and propelled them up the stairs and into the house. They did not resist. I pushed them into my study and then turned to the crowd that had gathered in the foyer. I barked out four names: Atilla, Vacaresti, Emelia, and Max. I was a bit surprised to see Emelia up so quickly, but knowing how vampires heal, I should have expected it.

"Are you sure you should be up yet?" I directed my question to Emelia as I shut the study door.

"We must find Virginia," Emelia's words were still coming slower than normal. Vacaresti moved to her side and helped her to a chair.

Teresa and Ildiko stood about three feet from each other, flanking one of the windows. Teresa appeared subdued ... Ildiko defiant. I turned to Max. He was standing by the door, visibly shaken.

"Max," I began, "Was anyone else in the kitchen while you were preparing the tray for Virginia and Emelia?" I noted how Max glanced quickly to Teresa, and then dropped his gaze to the floor. "Max, it will only bode well for you if you tell me the truth," I added.

Max's voice was scarcely audible: "Teresa." I noticed a tear drop to the floor. My servant quickly wiped his eyes.

I turned to my wife. "What did you do? What did you use? What have you done, Teresa? Where is Virginia?"

Teresa remained silent. She could not look me in the eyes. Ildiko stepped toward me, her eyes flaming.

"We did nothing, Basarab, as much as we would have liked to. Do you honestly think we would jeopardize our stations in this family for the likes of your human incubator? No, you will have to look elsewhere for whoever is responsible for your precious Virginia's disappearance. You have no proof to show that we had anything to do with this." She paused. "Did it ever occur to you that she is the one that drugged Emelia, and then fled? Emelia had a key to get in the room—ask her if she still has it."

 I turned to Emelia. She was patting her pockets, a puzzled look on her face. "What's wrong?" I asked.

 "I don't have it … it was in my pocket … Virginia had just given it back to me…"

 I raised my eyebrows. "Virginia had just given it back to you? How so?"

 Emelia crowded in closer to Vacaresti. "I must have left it in her room the last time I visited with her. She returned it to me because she didn't want to leave. She wanted to stay here and tell you what Randy had overheard. She was putting her faith in you that you would protect her."

 *Virginia was willing to put her faith in me to do the right thing—to protect her.* I should have been furious about Emelia's carelessness, but I wasn't because, in the end, it had helped to confirm how Virginia truly felt about me. She could have fled. But she didn't. I would have let her go—if that was what she desired. I returned my attention to Teresa and Ildiko.

 "I ask you again … what have you done with Virginia? Answer wisely!" I knew Ildiko was not ready to talk, so I focused my gaze on Teresa. "If I were to search your things, would I find the key to Virginia's room?"

 As Teresa opened her mouth to speak, the door of my study burst open. Angelique stood in the doorway, Santan on one side of her, Samara on the other. Santan and Samara's eyes were burning flames! The children's stature was solid as they pointed toward Teresa and Ildiko: "They lie!" they shouted in unison.

 Ildiko laughed hysterically. Teresa was silent.

 I motioned to Angelique to bring the children forward. I nodded to Santan. He returned the greeting. I reached my arms out for Samara, who would normally have run into them. This time she didn't. She stayed holding on to Angelique's hand, her eyes blazing as she glared at Teresa and Ildiko.

"What is it they lie about?" I asked.

Santan looked directly at me. "They know where Mama is. We will show you what has happened." With those words, Santan took hold of my hand. "All of us, except Max, must form a circle around Teresa and Ildiko."

Atilla, Vacaresti, and Emelia stood and joined the circle. Ildiko was no longer laughing, but she still held a defiant look in her eyes. Teresa stared at the floor. Angelique and the children began to chant…

*"Oh great spirits, hear our plea*
*Bring these women to bended knee*
*Show us their mind, their foul deed*
*Bring these women to bended knee…"*

The chant was repeated over and over.

Teresa and Ildiko fell to their knees. A great ball of fiery energy appeared in the centre of the circle, hovering over the two cowering women. And the deceit was revealed … first, Ildiko giving Teresa a potion to poison the food … Teresa, in the kitchen, slipping the poison into the blood, and putting some of it on Virginia's dish while Max's back was turned … the scream from Virginia as she ran to Emelia … the terror on Virginia's face as she knelt beside Emelia … the two of them entering Virginia's room … Ildiko wanting to kill Virginia right there … Teresa, hesitant … and then the visions became faint … Ildiko placing Emelia on the bed … a key falling to the floor … fainter … Ildiko picking Virginia up … fainter … the women leaving the room … fainter … out the front door … fainter … running now … darkness!

The ball of energy dissipated. We released hands. I turned to Teresa and Ildiko, the fury building inside me like an unleashed volcano. "Where is she?" I bellowed.

They remained silent.

## Chapter Twenty-Seven

"**You** leave me no other choice, then." I turned to my father and Vacaresti. "Please escort them to the basement and lock them in their coffins. Watch over them for me until I return; I will deal with them once I find Virginia. For their sake, she better be alive!" I turned to Emelia. "Please take Santan and Samara back to the nursery."

I knelt down to my children and gathered them into my arms. Samara snuggled deep into my chest. I could feel her tiny heart beating rapidly against mine. Santan remained the *little man*, but that was okay—he was in my arms, and that is what counted. "I will find your mother and return her to you," I assured them, despite the fact I wasn't sure I actually could deliver on this promise.

"Mama is still alive," Santan said.

Samara nodded the affirmative.

"How do you know?" I asked.

Santan shook his head. "I dreamed of a dark place, with heavy stone walls. There was a lot of death in this place, but, there was also life." Santan paused a moment and then looked up at me. "What of Randy, Father? What are you going to do with him? He is my friend."

I noticed the desperation in Santan's eyes, and I knew, at that moment, I would not harm Randy in any way. "For now," I began, "How say he accompanies you and Samara and Emelia to the nursery? He can help to keep you safe until I return."

Santan smiled.

I released my children to Emelia and Randy. My father and Vacaresti escort Ildiko and Teresa out. Ildiko glared at me as they were leaving; Teresa turned her face away. I motioned to Angelique, the only one left in the room with me.

"I have an idea," I said. "Follow me." I led the way out of the study, and out of the house. "Santan mentioned a dark room with stone walls, and death. There is only one place I can think of that might have both—a cemetery. And there is one close to here. If they were short of time to put Virginia somewhere until they could get back to her, then that would be the most logical place."

Angelique knelt down in the snow near several footprints, some large, some small. She sniffed the snow. "They were here … these are their prints," she said pointing to two sets of prints that appeared to be walking side by side, one heavier than the other. Of course, the heavier one would be Ildiko. Not only was she larger than Teresa, she would be the one carrying Virginia.

We followed the prints to the edge of the property and down the sidewalk as far as the street, where they disappeared in the tire tracks. We didn't have to say a word more to each other; we just set off toward the cemetery. "Hopefully, we will be able to pick up the tracks in the cemetery and save some time, in case there is more than one building where they could have put her," I mentioned, lengthening my stride.

When we reached the edge of the cemetery, Angelique dropped to her knees again. She pointed to the tracks she had noticed. "It's them," she said standing and heading in the direction the steps were leading.

I followed behind, allowing Angelique to lead. My thoughts turned to Virginia. Now that I knew she had professed her love for me, and I had willingly admitted to myself, and to others, how much I loved her, I felt the ache in my chest at her possible death. I swore if we found her alive, I would never let her from my sight again.

"Over there," Angelique was pointing to a large mausoleum in the centre of the cemetery.

We rushed to the building. The door was not sealed shut, evidence of recent activity. I placed my hand in the slight opening and pulled. Death wafted into my nostrils. "Virginia!" I howled as I stepped inside.

Something, or someone, in the far corner moved and emitted a groan. "She's here!" I shouted back to Angelique as I raced to the sound. I fell to my knees, and just as Virginia's name was on the tip of my tongue, I realized it was not her. "Tanyasin?"

Angelique was by my side within a second, kneeling beside her sister. She gathered the battered body of Tanyasin into her arms. Tanyasin's breath was coming in gasps; her eyes already had death in them. "What happened, sister?"

"E...e...lizabeth..." I could barely hear Tanyasin's voice, it was so weak.

"Where is Virginia?" I asked anxiously.

Tanyasin gasped. I heard the blood gurgling in her throat. "She ... took ... her." Tanyasin tried to shift in Angelique's arms.

Angelique stroked her sister's hair. "Be still, Tanyasin. We will get you help."

"T ... too l ... l ... ate." She coughed and blood spilled from her mouth. Angelique wiped it away.

Despite the condition Tanyasin was in, I was desperate to know if she knew anything more of Virginia's possible whereabouts. "Do you have any idea where Elizabeth might have taken Virginia?"

Tanyasin's eyes were emptying of life. "My sister is dying, Basarab. Allow her to die in peace. She will finally be with the ones she loves, with her husband and her son. I know she has wronged your family, and she has not done you a service with the burden she bestowed on you, but she has suffered enough. We will find your Virginia." Angelique began stroking her sister's hair again, and she hummed an ancient Gypsy song I recognized.

Tanyasin was trying to speak again. Angelique leaned over and put her ear to her sister's mouth. Tanyasin whispered something, and then her body began to convulse and a massive ball of black smoke emitted from her mouth. Angelique held her tight, rocking her sister, her own tears raining through the smoke. After a few minutes, Tanyasin was still.

I could not believe the sight in front of me. Tanyasin was indeed beautiful, as Angelique had always told her sister once was. She looked soft, at peace. "What did she say?" I enquired, still hoping Tanyasin had given some clue.

Angelique swallowed the rest of her tears. "She asked me for forgiveness … she said to tell you she was sorry … and then she told us to beware of the great sorceress … she is the one to fear more than anyone."

"The one whom she attained her power from?"

"Yes." Angelique stood, lifting her sister in her arms.

I reached out: "Here, let me carry her. We will take her back to the house and make arrangements for her body to be returned to Transylvania, to be buried beside her husband and son."

Angelique placed Tanyasin in my arms. She was light as a feather. We headed back to the house. Despite the grief I knew Angelique must be feeling because of her loss, her pace was quick.

~

Dracula met us as we entered the foyer. "What angel have you brought to the house?" he asked when he saw Tanyasin in my arms.

"It is Tanyasin," I answered.

"Tanyasin!" Dracula's voice was filled with surprise. "Don't play games, Basarab. This beauty cannot be that ugly hag!"

I noticed how Angelique's body stiffened.

"Elizabeth murdered her," I informed my uncle. "When her final breaths left her body, her beauty returned."

Dracula looked thoughtful. "Did Elizabeth take Virginia, then?"

I nodded.

"I assume she is taking Virginia to Radu."

"That would be what I assume, as well."

Some of the others were approaching us. I motioned to the dining room. "Please … I am going to put Tanyasin to rest in one of the rooms, and then I shall be down to fill you in on what appears to have happened, and to figure out what our next move needs to be."

When I returned to the dining room, everyone was milling about. No one had taken a seat. There was an air of nervous tension in the room. Dracula approached me.

"Some of us have been discussing the situation, and we think it might be best if you were to allow me to go after Radu and save your Virginia." His voice softened. "Basarab, I know what it is like to have lost a beloved, and I know my past actions were the reasons for the curse our family has been burdened with. Please, allow me to do this for you; allow me to put my brother's atrocities to rest, and to restore your love to you."

I noticed Dracula's sons nodding their heads in agreement, and Kerecsen and Laborc, as well. I was slow to speak, but when I did, my words were firm. "I do appreciate your offer, uncle, but I am afraid I must decline. I believe it is better if we go as a group—a united front of power to be reckoned with! We have no idea how many Radu might actually have with him … you cannot fight them all yourself." I looked around the room. "I suggest we take Mihail, Vlad, Kerecsen, and Laborc with us. I would like the others to stay here and prepare for our leaving back to Brasov." I scanned the faces in the room. "Is everyone in agreement with this plan? We will take Angelique with us, as well. She may be able to help us discover where Radu is hiding."

Everyone voiced their agreement.

"Thank you. Now, time is of the essence more than ever. We must save Virginia's life. I promised my son—my children— I would bring her safely home to them. And I am a man who keeps my promises."

# Virginia

## Chapter Twenty-eight

I was cold, so cold. The past few hours had been draining. First … having to tell Randy I couldn't go with him because I loved Basarab, and then seeing the look of defeat in his eyes. Second … learning from Emelia that Basarab knew of the conspiracy against my life and that he was going to protect me. Third … watching Emelia crumble before me, and there had been nothing I could do. Fourth … listening to Ildiko and Teresa as they plotted my demise. Fifth … awakening in the crypt, skeletons scattered around me, death in the air.

And finally, when I heard the door scraping open, I had prayed that it was my love come to rescue me. Instead, I had heard a familiar voice, one so ugly and filled with venom that I had just wanted it all to end right there and then! I had wondered why Teresa and Ildiko would send Tanyasin to do the deed, especially when Ildiko had seemed so eager to kill me herself.

As the door opened further and the night shadows crept into the room, I detected someone else with Tanyasin, someone I had not met before.

"You see, Elizabeth, I told you I knew where she was! The count loves her, you know."

If I could have crawled away, I would have. But to where? Just the thought of touching one of those skeletons was enough to raise the bile in my stomach.

"Does he, now?" Elizabeth walked over to me and squatted down. "Lovely creature," she said as she reached out and lifted my face with her fingers.

I found myself staring into the eyes of madness itself. I had heard stories of Elizabeth, stories of her magnificence, but I saw no beauty in her. I tried to shrink away, but her fingers clutched around my face as she slowly pulled me to a standing position. I feared my legs would not hold me.

I noticed Tanyasin wringing her hands as though she were worried. "Have I done well, Elizabeth?" she cackled.

I was trying hard to understand what was going on. Why did it appear that Tanyasin was *bowing* to Elizabeth?

Elizabeth had released her hold on me at that point, and I crumbled back to the floor. She turned to Tanyasin, and the words, as she spoke them, filled me with dread. Not just the words themselves, but the sound they made as they bounced off the stone walls. They sounded like death.

"You have done well, Tanyasin. I am sure Radu will be pleased when he gets his hands on this little gem."

"So, you will meet your part of the bargain now?" Tanyasin's voice sounded strained.

"And more."

What happened next happened so fast, it was over almost before it had begun. Elizabeth turned on Tanyasin, and with the strength and speed of a wolverine, she mauled her and then threw her into a corner. Blood splattered everywhere, painting the stone walls with fresh death, painting me with death. I have never heard or seen such horror in all my life! I had remained frozen in the terror of the moment.

"Radu asked me to give you this message ... you are no longer an asset to him!"

When Elizabeth was finished with Tanyasin, she smoothed the layers of her cape, grabbed hold of my wrist and dragged me out into the night air. The last sound I heard from Tanyasin was one of gurgling pain as she screamed out Elizabeth's name.

*So, now what?*

I felt the stickiness on my arms and my face, and rubbed at my skin trying to remove some of the dried blood. I gazed around the room. The walls were a smoky colour, and the smell in the room was pungent, as though there had been a recent fire. There was no furniture, no windows, and I had yet to see a door, although I suspected there was one. Cautiously, I stood. As I stepped forward, a voice, from somewhere behind me spoke up.

"Ah, finally, you are awake."

The voice was smooth, almost seducing.

"Who are you?" I asked nervously. "Where am I? Where is Elizabeth?"

The man came into view. He was of medium stature, and not unpleasant to look upon. "Which question would you like me to answer first?" He laughed. He didn't sound evil. Before I had the opportunity to respond, though, he answered me. "My name is Jack. Perhaps you have heard of me … Jack the Ripper?"

*Oh God! Will the horror never end?*

"Elizabeth will be along shortly. She asked me to watch over you while she went to inform Radu of her prize."

Jack began pacing, nervous baby steps. There was enough light from a couple of candles that had been lit in a corner of the room that I could detect the twitching of Jack's shoulders. Why did he appear to be nervous? Was he afraid of something … or someone? Was he afraid of Elizabeth? *He should be*, I thought to myself as I remembered what I had witnessed in the crypt.

I tried to think back to the story Basarab had told me about how Jack had come to be what he was today … yes, it was Elizabeth who had turned him … at the hospital where he had worked … Elizabeth had watched Jack slit a young girl's throat … the girl he was going to perform an autopsy on, and when he realized she was not dead … and Basarab had said Elizabeth had used Jack … that Jack already had the seeds of darkness within him … he had become her puppet.

Was this prior knowledge the fuel I could use to get under Jack's skin and distract him?

"So, I hear you are Elizabeth's bitch," I started my assault.

Jack stopped pacing and spun around to face me. I could feel the nerves in my stomach and prayed they stayed where they were.

"And who told you such a thing?" he spit.

"You forget, Jack, or maybe you just don't know, I have been around for a while now. I have read the history of the demise of the Dracul family. I had incredibly in-depth conversations with the count ... conversations where he acquainted me with various circumstances within the family. You just happened to be one of those circumstances."

"Basarab told you I was Elizabeth's bitch?" Jack's voice was taking on a disgruntled pitch.

I leaned against the wall, trying to look as though I was in charge. Jack didn't have to know how many of my nerve endings were on fire. "Yes, and he said more." I was on a roll. Why not make some of the stuff up as I went? Jack didn't know what I actually had been told. Just looking at him, I could tell he was not of strong character and could most likely be used by anyone if they offered him more than someone else did. I had noticed the greedy look in his eyes, too.

I continued: "He said anyone could use Jack. He said you were weak. I believe one of the phrases he used to describe you was *a snivelling weasel of a creature not worthy even to be a rogue*! Yes, those were his exact words."

Jack was in front of me before I could move away. He grabbed hold of my shoulders and threw me across the room. "I'll show you I am not a snivelling weasel!" he bellowed as he charged toward me.

Somehow, I quickly regained my feet and scurried out of his way before he attacked me again. "Yet you still serve Elizabeth!" I sneered as he hit the wall where I had just been.

Jack's hiss echoed around the room. "Oh, I just don't serve her, you pathetic little human; I serve the master, as well. He is much better to me than she has ever been!"

"You are a traitor, then?" I smirked. "Are you sure Elizabeth is unaware that you are playing two sides of the sword? Are you sure Radu is not using you for his own purposes, as well? After all, he doesn't trust Elizabeth; so, what better way to find out what she is up to than have her trusted little puppet bitch report back to him?" I had no idea where my courage was coming from, but from my side of the room it sounded convincing. My only hope was that whatever was coming out of my mouth was getting under Jack's skin.

Jack seemed to sober for a moment as he gathered himself from the floor and walked toward me. "You have no idea." His voice was just above a whisper. "I have never forgotten what she made me do ... my first kill as a rogue vampire."

I had no idea who that might have been, but I was willing to bet it had been someone Jack might have been in love with. "Was it your love ... your wife ... your sister ... your mother ... someone very dear to you?"

Jack walked over to me. I stayed firm where I was, feeling I had defused the initial anger he had shown. He reached a hand to the wall beside me and leaned in close. "Let me tell you something, Virginia ... there is much not known about me, much I keep hidden. That day when Elizabeth came upon me in the morgue ... the day she turned me into what she is ... well, let's say I have learned to play her wicked game as well as she, maybe even better! Elizabeth assumes she has me under control and I like her to believe that because it suits my purposes.

"Rogues do not have the full power of the bloodline, but we do have other attributes. We do not have to sustain ourselves fully with blood, although Elizabeth does—she is obsessed with blood. A rogue is able to tolerate small amounts of sunlight, which makes our movements in human society easier. Brilliant doctor by day, sadistic murderer by night! I thoroughly enjoy my mention of fame in the history books."

"You think what you did was recorded as fame? You were a monster!" I interrupted.

"Of course I'm famous. People still talk about me," Jack beamed. "Many a night, I would joke with Elizabeth about how the police had never been able to discover who the *Whitechapel Murderer* was. I was a celebrity, and I relished in the spotlight, even though, eventually, I had to remain hidden. That is part of the game I love to play. I wonder how many theorists would be shocked to know I still walk the streets, how many cases police forces around the world are still baffled about?

"One thing does bother me, though—the police only blamed five or six of the murders on me. They claim the other thirteen women found in the East End area from December 1887 to April 1891 were not the *Ripper's* victims! Stupid fools—what did they think—I was going to keep the same MO with all my victims? I have changed my techniques so many times over the years. If the brilliant detectives were as smart as they thought they were, certainly at least one would have figured me out. A couple got close—but Elizabeth would move us away from the area before things became too heated."

"You still haven't answered my question, Jack … if you were in such league with Elizabeth, why is it you decided to betray her … who did she order you to kill?"

Jack stood straight and turned away from me. He walked halfway across the room. "Why should I tell you?" he asked.

"Because maybe it is time you got it off your chest. Maybe in doing so, you can take control back over your life instead of being someone else's puppet, whether it be Elizabeth's or Radu's," I responded.

Jack slowly pivoted around to face me again. He seemed to have a lost look in his eyes. He hesitated a moment more. I remained silent, waiting. And then he began to tell me the story I had been waiting for, the one I hoped I could use to manipulate him into letting me go.

"My first victim, as a rogue vampire, was Martha. She was young and beautiful, and I had been with Martha several times before Elizabeth turned me. Martha was comfortable with me—happy—she knew my needs. I was always gentle with her because she seemed so innocent, despite the profession she had been driven to by her atrocious stepfather.

"The turning created in me a thirst for blood that I was unable to quench. I didn't intend to slay Martha for Elizabeth; I was going to keep her on the side for me. But something went terribly wrong that night. Elizabeth had not given me enough time to adjust to my new way of life before she sent me out onto the street to seduce young women for her needs. Martha lay on the bed, smiling sweetly, and eager to please me. She was excited that night, telling me she had finally saved enough money to be able to get out of the city and start a new life. She told me she would send word to me once she was settled, and I could join her if I wanted to.

But, something inside me snapped when she turned her head, exposing the blue veins pulsing with blood. I could feel the fangs growing inside my mouth. My body twisted in frustration as I tried to calm the demon that was unleashing within me. I remember the look of horror on Martha's face as I approached her. She asked me what was wrong. I answered her with a snarl, just before I attacked her … my lovely Martha. I shall never forgive Elizabeth for her death! But, I never let Elizabeth consume my Martha's blood—nor did I mutilate Martha's body as I did the rest.

"My medical training was helpful when it came to restraining the women before transporting them to Elizabeth for her to have her way with them. That is the reason the police never found semen on any of the victims—I was not the one defiling them. Once Elizabeth procured what she wanted, she allowed me to take a trophy, a little something for all my trouble. I missed working in the morgues, dissecting and extracting body parts, so for the first little while I would remove an internal organ as my trophy. The novelty of that soon wore off, and I began to take other things—more personal items, always changing it up, so as to throw the police off my trail."

"Like you said … always changing your MO." I articulated.

Jack smiled nervously. "Of course … I had to." A pause. "Then, Elizabeth introduced me to Radu. I looked into his eyes and saw my way out of her clutches. Over the years, with all the disgusting things I was doing to female bodies, for Elizabeth's pleasures, I had developed a propensity for men. What I saw in Radu's eyes revealed he was of the same mind. I noticed the scowl on his face when he brushed the back of Elizabeth's hand with a kiss. I could feel the extra tightness in our embrace, and his hardness, before he let me go."

"So, not only are you Elizabeth's bitch, you truly are Radu's? Are you the bitch or the dog?" I dared to ask.

Jack snarled and started to advance on me again. I leaned into the wall, realizing I might have taken things a step too far. "Would you like to discover which one I am?" he growled.

I shook my head. "Sorry ... I didn't mean to offend you," I quickly articulated. "Please, tell me more of your story."

He stopped and studied me for a moment before continuing. I breathed a sigh of relief.

"Radu and I kept our relationship discreet, especially from Elizabeth, which has been tricky. She is an astute woman; actually, wily is a more accurate word to describe her. She has taken her place beside Radu, and he has allowed her to believe she will be his queen once he takes Basarab's throne. I know better. Many nights he and I have lounged on the bed after a passionate coupling, joking about how we are deceiving her and how she will never realize the supremacy she thinks she is going to have." Jack's expression turned thoughtful.

"I am not sure if Radu is strong enough to overpower Elizabeth, though. Evil he is, yes ... a match for her, I'm not certain. There are too many things Elizabeth keeps secret. She trusts no one. I don't even know where she sleeps. Her apartment is nothing but a front; her actual lair is unknown to any. I tried to follow her once, but she caught on to me, circled around, and came up behind me—threatened me within an inch of my pathetic life if I ever attempted such a thing again!

"It has become more and more difficult for me to acquiesce to her—especially, as my relationship with Radu strengthens. I wait for the great battle, for it is coming soon. Radu's rogues are ready. He has promised me that I will be by his side, a leader he knows he will be able to rely on, be able to trust. I can taste the power, it is so near-at-hand. Elizabeth will not know what hit her when Radu unleashes *me* upon *her*! And I will, at long last, have my revenge for Martha ... I can hardly wait."

No sooner were the words out of Jack's mouth, the door burst open and Elizabeth stormed into the room. "Just as I expected!" she screeched as she advanced toward the shocked

Jack. "I gave you eternal life, and now I shall take it away from you … your time on this earth ends now!"

I wished I could have taken the opportunity to flee through the open door behind Elizabeth, but I remained frozen against the wall. I watched in terror as Elizabeth opened her fury on Jack, ripping his throat open and thrusting her hand into his chest, pulling his heart from his body. She raised the heart to her mouth and drained the blood from the dripping veins onto her tongue. Jack's body was crumpled at her feet, his limbs still twitching. His eyes were open, the disbelief in them apparent. She was roaring in a language I did not recognize.

She threw the heart to the corner of the room, leaned over, put her hands around Jack's neck, and lifted him off the floor. With one quick twist, she severed his head from his body. "This, Jack dearest, is how I deal with traitors!" Her barbarity crowded into every corner of the room, even extinguishing the candles. I heard the thud of his body as it hit a wall. She lifted his head high in the air, and then threw it across the room. It rolled, coming to rest beside Jack's still corpse.

My body caved to the floor. I buried my face in my arms and closed my eyes, not wanting to see anything more, not wanting to see what Elizabeth had in store for me.

## Chapter Twenty-nine

"It's about time you woke up. You humans are so weak." Elizabeth's voice penetrated into the fogginess of my awakening. "It is time for me to take you to Radu. I told him that I have a special gift for him, and he is becoming impatient."

I tried to find my voice. The congestion in my throat was choking me—I wished it would. Anything would be better than what most likely awaited me with this creature. I coughed. My throat cleared. "What good am I to Radu?" I managed to ask. "I am no one the count would bargain for."

Elizabeth approached me and squatted down. "Oh, but you are, my dear. I have it on reliable authority that the count loves you, not his wife. I have been told Basarab intends to set her aside, and he will be embracing you as his new queen. His children slipped through my fingers, but you shall not."

She gripped hold of my arm and pulled me to my feet. I wasn't sure my legs would hold my body, but I didn't have to worry about that because Elizabeth basically dragged me across the room to the door. I tried desperately to focus on my surroundings. As we entered the hallway, I was able to confirm the building I was being held in had been in a fire, and it had been recent because the smell was still overwhelming. We reached the end of the hallway and turned. We came upon a set of steep, charred stairs, and Elizabeth set foot on the top step.

I tried to pull back. "They don't look safe," I muttered.

Elizabeth just laughed. "Safe enough," she said. "We will only be using them once, anyway," she smirked. "Don't worry, I won't let anything happen to you … yet," she added sarcastically.

I had no choice but to continue. The steps creaked as we descended. My foot almost went through the board on one of them and I stumbled. Elizabeth tightened her grip on me. At the bottom, we turned and headed down another hallway. More charred walls. I heard voices coming from close by. We turned into a room that appeared to have been set up as an office of sorts. There was not much light in the room, just a few flickering candles.

"Finally," a man clapped his hands in delight, "You are here with my surprise." I assumed it was Radu.

Elizabeth released my arm and pushed me forward. "This is the woman Basarab is in love with ... the mother of his children."

As I stumbled across the room, almost losing my footing, I felt another set of powerful fingers grip hold of my arm, which saved me from crashing to the floor. I looked up into the most horrifying face I had ever set my eyes upon—pure evil—if evil ever could be considered pure! I felt my stomach revolting at the sight, churning, and then, before I could stop it, the contents of my belly exploded out of my mouth and onto the floor. The man holding me laughed and released me. I landed in my vomit.

That was not the end of it, though. He squatted down beside me and grabbed hold of my hair, pulling my head back so I had to look him in the eyes. Red-black eyes with streaks of yellow and orange they were, with no white showing at all. His hair was a steel-grey with thin strips of black and red running through it, and it hung uncontrollably around his shoulders. His eyebrows matched, bushy and unkempt. He had a beard that matched the hair in colour, and it cascaded across his oversized chest. As if that wouldn't have been enough to scare anyone, when he opened his mouth, his tongue flicked across a set of oversized, sharp teeth. He was leaning over me now, as though he were going to take a bite of my flesh. I tried to close my eyes against the assault. However, whatever remained in my stomach found its way out.

"Peter!" Elizabeth's voice rang out loudly in the room. "Let her go. I did not bring her here for your pleasure. There are plenty of other delicacies out there to satisfy your needs. This is Basarab's new chosen queen, the one who will be used to negotiate for the throne our esteemed leader, Radu, desires to take control of." Was that a hint of sarcasm I detected in Elizabeth's tone?

Peter released me and stepped away, and once again I sprawled upon the floor. This time, Elizabeth was the one to help me up. I barely managed to move my feet. My gut still pained from the vomiting. My veins were still frozen with terror at what was happening to me—or going to. Elizabeth led me to a chair across from the man whom I assumed to be Radu. He was sitting behind a small table that had most likely belonged to some children at one time. From the look on his face, he was not pleased. Elizabeth shoved me onto the chair, and then went around and stood behind me, resting her hands on my shoulders. As much as I was repulsed by her touch, I was also grateful for it. I don't think I could have managed to keep sitting had she not been supporting me.

Radu stood. He walked over to me. I recognized a modest facial resemblance to his brother Dracula, but otherwise, he was nothing like his older brother. In fact, his features were more that of a spoiled child, pouting because he couldn't have more candy, or the toy he desired. Plus, his body was soft and podgy, not indicative of a warrior's build. He put a finger under my chin and lifted my face to look at him. I peered into pools of lifeless darkness.

"So, you are the woman who bore the intended heir to the vampire throne. Well, my dear, your son shall never sit on that throne." He removed his finger from my face and wiped his hands on his shirt, as though he were trying to rid his skin of my human scent. "The throne is mine for the taking." Radu walked around to where Elizabeth was standing.

I dared not look around, but I could feel the tension in the room. Peter was skulking by the wall, watching.

"My lovely Elizabeth," Radu started saying. "What makes you think I need this woman to obtain what I want? Basarab knows where I stand. He has met with me and Peter. He knows the power I wield, the armies I have behind me. I have no need for her, or the children, for that matter. They will be nothing but a hindrance now."

"But…" Elizabeth started.

"No buts!" Radu bellowed. "Get her out of my sight! Do what you want with her, and when you are finished, return here immediately. We will be leaving for Brasov as soon as you do. I have already sent instructions for the armies to be prepared. As soon as I return, I will unleash my rogues and the throne will be mine!"

Elizabeth released her hands from my shoulders, and walked toward Radu, stopping right in front of him. I did my best to keep my balance on the chair. Deep inside I knew this was the end. There was no way Elizabeth would allow me to live. I closed my eyes. I heard her voice, ear splittingly harsh with insinuations.

"The throne will be yours?" she hissed. "How is it you assume such a pathetic creature as yourself ever could sit upon such a throne, hold such a powerful position? I have been biding my time for years, waiting for the moment when I could put an end to your inflated ego. I am of royal family as much as you are, but I am the one more deserving to sit on the throne! The leadership should come from someone who has intelligence, strength, and wit, not someone who drops to his knees or bends over to every pretty boy! While you have been creating your little army, I have been building my own forces—something Jack was unable to tell you because I never trusted him enough to allow him into my innermost circle." She paused. "Oh, by the way, your Jackie won't be able to provide you with anymore tidbits about what I am doing; he has met with an unfortunate accident. If you don't believe me, just ask Virginia; she witnessed the entire event."

Elizabeth moved quickly to the side of my chair and roughly grabbed hold of my arm, jerking me to my feet. As she dragged me from the room: "We shall see who will ascend to the vampire throne!" she shouted as we left.

She pulled me out of the building and shoved me into the backseat of a car parked by the entrance. The street lights were on, and I noticed we were at the end of a row of derelict buildings. Elizabeth reached over me and grabbed a piece of rope from the floor. She wound it tightly around my wrists, and then ripped a piece of cloth from the lining of her cloak and bound my mouth.

"Lie down," she demanded. "Not a sound or a movement of any kind, or I will end it all for you right here and now!"

I wondered what difference it made when my life ended. I knew for sure, now, there was no hope for me. My biggest regret was I had not been able to hold my children in my arms one last time—or Basarab. I heard Elizabeth get into the car, and the engine started. The car idled for a few moments. What was she waiting for? Was that Delphine woman Ildiko and Randy had spoken of in the vicinity? I heard the passenger door open. The weight of the passenger, as they sat in the front seat, told me it was not Delphine.

I focused my eyes to the front and watched as Elizabeth and Peter embraced. "He wants you dead," Peter was saying, and then they both laughed.

"Little does he know."

"I told you we shouldn't have bothered with her."

"Yes, you did, didn't you? But it has been fun." Elizabeth threw back her head and laughed. "Did you see the look on Radu's face when I told him what I thought of him?"

Peter's answer was a hearty chuckle.

I watched as Elizabeth stroked her fingers through the beast's hair, and raised her lips to his. "Just a taste of what you will soon have, my love," she chimed sweetly. He growled. After a few moments, she pushed Peter away from her, put the car into gear and pulled out onto the street. I closed my eyes as my hearse drove me to my final destination.

# Basarab

## Chapter Thirty

Angelique had a serious look on her face. "We need to start at the crypt," she suggested. "Obviously Elizabeth has taken Virginia, but we were so caught up with my sister…"

"Yes, you are right." I interrupted as I turned to the others. "There will have to be a set of tracks leading away from where we found Tanyasin, either foot or tire. Let's go. We have no time to waste. Every second counts now, and the less we waste, the better the chance we will have to find Virginia alive."

I didn't have to repeat myself. Everyone followed me to the cemetery, and when we reached the crypt where we had found Tanyasin, Angelique circled around, searching for tracks. "Over here," she called out, and when I reached her side, she pointed to one set of tracks leading to the cemetery roadway. However, that is where they stopped.

Dracula came up beside us. "Looks as though there have been a number of vehicles in and out of here. How are we going to determine which one Elizabeth might have left in?"

Angelique laid a hand on his arm. "I will do my best." With those words, she closed her eyes, raised her arms up over her head, and began to chant.

*"Oh great spirits, hear my plea*
*Bring the vision direct to me*
*Show me the place where Virginia be*
*Bring the vision direct to me…"*

The chant repeated over and over.

# Night's Return

I was getting impatient. Snow began falling, large wet flakes. If Angelique could not get a vision, all would be lost. The tracks would be covered over. Finally, she began to speak.

"I see a bridge ... over a river of ice ... a lot of old, rundown buildings ... a sign ... Zorba's ... and ... yes ... Zorba's restaurant ... there is a building beside that ... it looks like there was a fire ... yes ... the front is charred brick ... boarded up windows ... I see some letters ... t ... h ... e ... theatre ... now, I am seeing debris and weeds behind these buildings..."

"I know where this is," I shouted. "When Teresa and I were living here in Brantford, there was a fire in an old theatre downtown. It was beside a restaurant called Zorba's. They are located on the south side of Colborne Street, not far from the Lorne Bridge that goes over the Grand River." I reached over and hugged Angelique, breaking her trance. "Once again, you have saved us. Please return to the house and help prepare for our leaving." I turned to my other companions. "Follow me, it isn't far," I yelled as I transformed into a wolf. The howling behind me told me they had followed suit.

I raced back to West Street and headed for the downtown. I cared not who might have been out and about, who might notice a pack of wolves in the city. It didn't matter. The only thing that mattered was getting to Virginia and holding her in my arms again ... and returning her to Santan and Samara as I had promised. When we reached the end of Market Street, I turned right onto Dalhousie, and when I reached Queen Street, I swung left. I could feel the blood pumping swiftly through my veins as I swerved right onto Colborne. The burned out theatre was within my sight. As I approached, I returned to my human form, as did the others.

"A couple of us should scope the place out and see how many Radu might actually have with him," Dracula stated.

"I agree," Kerecsen said. "Let me and Laborc go in. We will take the form of a bat for a better view on things."

I knew they were right. It was the wisest thing to do, check out the building before rushing in. Kerecsen and Laborc could locate the area where Virginia might be being held, and I could go straight to her. My two trusted men transformed and disappeared inside.

I paced back and forth in front of the theatre. My nerves were frayed. *What is taking them so long?* Finally, they returned.

"Did you see her?" I couldn't wait to ask.

"She was nowhere in the building," Laborc informed. "We did see the lifeless body of Jack in one of the rooms, though. Someone ripped his heart from his chest and severed his head. A real mess. It appears Radu is alone."

"He was pacing in one of the rooms, mumbling something about being betrayed by the one he most trusted. I have a feeling his beloved Peter has taken on an agenda of his own," Kerecsen said.

"And you didn't see Elizabeth anywhere?" I queried.

"No ... just Radu," Laborc replied. "Maybe, she and Peter were in on things together," he added.

I noticed Dracula clenching and unclenching his hands. I guessed he was eager to see his brother, to confront him. I headed into the building, hesitating a moment to allow Laborc and Kerecsen to take the lead.

Radu looked up in surprise when the six of us entered the room where he was. It was a tremendously satisfying moment for me. I beheld the coward he truly was. "Where is she?" I demanded, striding right up to him and shoving him into a chair. I leaned over and glared into his eyes. "Tell me before I rip your pathetic heart from your chest. It appears there is no Peter here at the moment to protect you!" I stepped away from him.

"I'm not telling you anything!" Radu seemed to be digging deep for some courage to stand up to me.

I threw my head back and howled! The walls echoed with the fury of the sound. When I returned my gaze to Radu, he was shaking. I advanced again. Radu gripped his arms around himself, attempting to still his quivering body. Suddenly, I felt a hand on my arm, pulling me away from Radu.

"Not yet, Basarab. He still has to tell us where Virginia is." Dracula stepped in front of me and faced his brother. "Well, brother, here we are. Face to face. You have been trying to disrupt our family anonymity ... your greed for the throne has put us all in jeopardy." Dracula leaned over and grabbed Radu by the throat. "I will not allow this to continue, brother." He threw Radu across the room.

Despite his initial shock of being attacked, Radu gained his feet quickly, and turned to face his brother. His lips curled back, exposing his teeth. He charged. Kerecsen stepped between Radu and Dracula, his talons greeting Radu, stopping him short. He grabbed Radu by the neck and deposited him back on the chair.

"I could let your brother finish you off; he has been anxious to do so for quite some time now," Kerecsen informed the now cowering Radu. "You should be thankful to our esteemed leader, Basarab, for it is he who has kept Dracula under control." Kerecsen raked his talons across Radu's cheek, and down his neck, breaking the skin just enough to allow the blood to drip slowly onto Radu's clothing.

"We should just end it here," Dracula stepped forward. I detected the contempt on his face, and something else—he appeared irritated that he had been stopped from killing his brother.

However, the fear of Kerecsen inserting his talons into him again must have loosened Radu's tongue. He turned and fixed his eyes on me. "Basarab, I swear, I do not know where Virginia is. It was not my idea to take her ... this is all Elizabeth's doing ... she brought Virginia to me." Radu licked his lips nervously. "I told her I had no use for your woman..."

"You had no use for her, yet somehow you did not think to protect her from one such as Elizabeth?" I shouted furiously. "Do you know what she did to Tanyasin? And Jack? She is out of control, Radu—totally! And yet you saw fit to let her go, to take Virginia and minister whatever fate Elizabeth saw fit!"

Radu's voice reverberated with the panic he was feeling. "Yes ... I admit ... I let Elizabeth take Virginia ... but ... I sent Peter after them ... he was to finish Elizabeth ... kill her ... and bring Virginia back to me ... I was going to let her go ... honestly ... please, believe me..."

"So, where is Virginia, then?" the question spit from my mouth.

Radu looked away. "I fear I have been betrayed by the man I thought I could trust beyond all others ... Peter has not returned."

Dracula burst into laughter. "So your faithful dog betrayed you! How fitting. Or, there is another possibility, isn't there ... maybe one you would prefer to believe ... Elizabeth killed him, as well. After all, she seems to be piling up the bodies around her."

"My guess is that others in your camp have had their sights on my throne ... so unfortunate for you, uncle. But, if you come clean now, and tell us everything you know, I will spare your life. You must have an idea of where Elizabeth might have taken Virginia." I was still hoping Radu could give us at least an indication of where we could start.

"I have no idea. Elizabeth has been shrewd. Even Jack could not get me concrete information on her lair ... in fact, he never supplied me with much information about her. Sometimes I had the feeling even he was playing me."

"So, you have nothing further to say to me?"

Radu shook his head. I saw the trepidation in his eyes, in the way his body went limp.

"Then we are finished here." I turned to my companions. "Let's get out of here. We need to go back to the house and see if Angelique can once again summon her visions to tell us where Elizabeth and Peter have taken Virginia. My only hope is that Virginia is still alive because they plan on using her as a bargaining tool to take the throne from me."

I headed toward the door. I assumed everyone was following me. When I stepped out into the night, I turned and noticed Dracula had not exited with us. "Where is my uncle?" I asked, looking around at everyone.

Mihail and Vlad smiled knowingly.

"I believe he wanted a word or two with his brother," Vlad grinned.

Mihail laughed. "A conversation he has wanted to have for a long time."

I had not intended to leave Dracula alone with Radu, knowing what he most certainly would do. Nevertheless, at this moment my chief concern was rescuing Virginia. What was between the brothers, was between them. "He can join us when he is finished his *conversation*." As I headed in the direction of the house, I transformed once again into a wolf. My companions followed suit. There was not much night left.

As we raced off, Radu's voice echoed out into the night. "No! Dracula … I am your brother … please … noooo…

Then, there was nothing but silence.

## Chapter Thirty-one

In the driveway of the house, we all transformed back to our physical selves. I burst through the front door and screamed out for Angelique. I didn't wait for her to emerge from wherever she was; I assumed she would be with the children in the nursery. I don't think I had ever moved so quickly up the large staircase before, and within seconds I was in the room where my children were playing.

"Angelique, we require your services, once again. Radu did not have Virginia. She has been taken by Elizabeth and Peter."

Angelique quickly came to my side. Randy, who was sitting with Santan, jumped up, his face turning red. Emelia was shaking her head, looking distressed at this new revelation. Adelaide and Alfred both gasped in horror. Carla, who was sitting with Samara, went pale. It was obvious from the traumatized looks on everyone's faces that they all knew the seriousness of the situation.

Santan stood and walked toward me. He appeared calm, despite a slight worried look on his tiny face. "Time is running out, but I know in my heart that my mama is still okay. They have not harmed her yet. They want to use her to take over your throne. They know you will not allow them to kill her."

My son's words stopped everyone in their tracks, except for Samara. She was sobbing on Carla's shoulder: "Monster … bad monster … hurt mama!" I didn't have time to contemplate the change in my daughter's attitude toward her mother, but it was good to see.

I turned to Angelique: "Please…"

"I will need the children again; they both have a connection with their mother that might make the visions come faster," Angelique commented.

She held her hands out for the children. They came forward and placed their little hands in hers. A hushed calm echoed in the room. Angelique began to chant. The children did not join in this time. A vast cloud emerged, blacking out the ceiling. We all looked upward. I saw a bridge and a river … a road leading out of the city … another road … a hairpin turn … a sign … Brant Park … a forest of snow-laden trees … the cloud swirled onto the road leading into the park … it stopped … hovered over a shack … smoke from a chimney…

Angelique's body twitched and she released the children's hands. "I know where they are!" she shouted.

"Lead us," I ordered, my voice tense with emotion.

Randy rushed to my side and grabbed hold of my arm. "I am coming with you," he stated emphatically.

I didn't have time for such nonsense. There was no way the human would survive if Elizabeth or Peter got their hands on him, and Santan would never forgive me if I allowed something to happen to Randy. I laid my hand on his shoulder.

"I think it better if you stay here with the children. This business must be dealt with by vampires, not humans."

I noticed how Randy's facial muscles tightened. He was not pleased to be delegated to nursery duty. I knew he still loved Virginia, despite her confession to him about her feelings for me. Santan came to my rescue. He put his hand in Randy's.

"Everything will be okay, Randy. Please stay with me. My father will return my mama to us."

Randy heaved a deep sigh, giving into my son. I was somewhat unsettled by Santan's words, though—how he had suggested I would return Virginia *to them*. I was bringing her home to *me*. I led the way out of the room and headed down the stairs to where the others were waiting. Angelique was right behind me. Dracula was just coming through the front door, a satisfied look on his face. I didn't have to ask him about Radu … I knew he was not going to be a problem for us anymore.

"Angelique will lead us to Virginia," I informed. I turned to Dracula. "Is it still snowing?"

"Very heavy," he replied.

"I will form a cloud," Angelique began. "I think it best if you all take the form of bats so we can take the shortcut by flying over the river."

"How will you lead us?" I asked.

She smiled. "I will be the cloud."

For the second time that night, I set off with Dracula, Kerecsen, Laborc, Vlad, and Mihail. We formed a V-flight line, with me as the leader. The winter air was frigid, not that it mattered to the cold-blooded creatures that we were. I recognized the shack as we approached, and my wings flapped faster. We returned to our human bodies as we landed a short distance from the building. Suddenly, a blood chilling howl echoed from within its walls ... followed, by a woman's scream.

There was nothing that could have stopped me at the sound of that scream! "Virginia!" her name howled from my lips as I burst through the door of the shack. The sight that greeted me sickened even I, who has seen the worst of humanity and vampire.

Virginia was spread upon a wooden table in the centre of the room. Her arms and legs had been bound with ropes that were tied to the table legs. Her body was streaked with blood, which was oozing from several deep gashes. Her face was lined with tears. She was shaking uncontrollably, and I knew it was not from the cold. She was petrified!

Peter was straddling her body, his feet planted on each side of her. He was naked, crouching down and swinging his manhood along my beloved's flesh. Elizabeth, too, was naked, dancing around the table, clapping her hands in delight. As I made my move, I transformed, mid-stride, into my wolf form, leaping across the tabletop in a blind frenzy and knocking a surprised Peter to the floor.

It didn't take him long to regain his feet. He stood and faced me, baring his teeth. I snarled, lifted my head and howled. I could hear Virginia screaming, but my only objective, at that moment, was to destroy the monster in front of me. Never had even a vampire been as vile as this Peter. I lunged. We met in mid-air. My teeth sank into Peter's arm ... his teeth into my front leg.

But, I had the advantage of being grounded with four feet, and long claws that dug into the wooden floor, enabling me to keep my balance as I swung his body through the air. His teeth gouged my flesh as they loosened from my leg. Peter smashed against a wall unit, and it toppled to the ground covering his body. He shoved it off, shook his head, and stood ready for my next attack. He was laughing at me as he spit fur from his mouth.

"Is that all you have?" he guffawed.

I didn't bother to answer him as I advanced. My focus was on his neck, on the large blue veins pulsing just beneath the skin's surface. My target—his death! From the corner of my eye, I saw Elizabeth beginning to circle around, heading in Peter's direction. I wondered where the others were.

As though in response to my thoughts, the room filled with the sound of snarling wolves. A soft light illuminated the area around the wooden table where Virginia lay ... Angelique. Elizabeth was stumbling away from her approach toward Peter, trying to run for the door, which was blocked instantly by my companions. I returned my attention to Peter, just in time. He was trying to creep around behind me, flexing the muscles in his huge, python-sized arms—arms that could quickly squeeze the life out of a mortal man.

I attacked again, swiftly, this time grazing his neck with my teeth. He jumped nimbly out of the full impact of my connection. I didn't give him occasion to focus on his next move. My body swung around, and I aimed for the other side of Peter's neck. This time my aim was accurate. Peter let out a chilling scream of shock. He went down. I did not stop. The wrath that was inside me, at what he had been about to do to my beloved Virginia, unleashed! My fangs ripped at Peter's flailing body until his head severed from his body.

I stood with my paws upon the still heaving chest of the creature in the throws of its final moments of life. I gripped Peter's head in my jowls and flipped it across the room. It landed at Elizabeth's feet. She screamed. I saw a piece of kindling by the woodstove, grabbed hold of the wood with my mouth, and then shoved it into Peter's black heart. I raised my head and howled my victory for all to hear.

I stepped away from my conquest and slowly approached the table where Virginia was now sitting up, cradled in Angelique's arms. Angelique had wrapped her cape around Virginia's body. I transformed into my human form, but I could still feel the stickiness of Peter's blood upon my skin, the scorch of my vengeance still racing through my body.

As I reached out a hand to Virginia, she shrank from me, her eyes wide with horror. "Please … little bird … my love … do not be afraid of me," I begged of her.

She dug deeper into Angelique's arms.

Angelique looked at me, pity in her eyes. "Give her some time, Basarab. It is not every day a human witnesses such a sight as what your Virginia has just seen. This has been a horrendous time for her, and even though the biggest peril she has ever faced in her life has been destroyed, she fears the one who destroyed it."

"I must hold her," I insisted, reaching for her again. "Please, Virginia, I will never do you any harm. Come to me, my love."

Behind me, I heard a snarl. Elizabeth had made another move toward the door. Her naked body was glistening with sweat. The snarling increased, and the pack closed in around her, awaiting my command.

Angelique whispered something into Virginia's ear. I noticed Virginia dip her head, hesitantly. Angelique nodded to me. I stepped forward and gathered my love into my arms. Her body was shuddering with nervous energy, with fear. She looked up at me, and I beheld the terror in her eyes. My heart shattered as her body stiffened in my arms, and then she lost consciousness. It was better for her. She would be all right when she came to; when I was once again the man she had come to love, when the sight and smell of battle was not glistening on my flesh.

I turned and began to head out of the shack. I hesitated in the doorway as a voice, I am not sure whose, asked me what they were to do with Elizabeth.

"Finish her," was my answer. "I have what I came here for."

As I walked away, Elizabeth's shrieks were drowned out by the feeding frenzy within the shack.

# Virginia

## Chapter Thirty-two

I have no idea how long I slept, but for the first time in a long time, it was a dreamless sleep. I awoke in the house, in my bed, snuggled under a duvet. Emelia was sitting in a chair not far from my bedside, and Carla was leaning over me, checking the bandages on my arms.

"You are healing up nicely," she smiled when she noticed my eyes open. She replaced the gauze she had been checking. "Quite a time you have been through," she added.

I looked away. "Yes," I whispered. "It has been that." I didn't want to think about what had been about to happen in the shack.

Elizabeth and Peter had laughed and carried on during the ride to the shack. I had tried desperately to get my bearings of direction, in case there was any chance of my escaping. But I couldn't focus, and there had never been an opportunity. When they reached the shack, Peter had pulled me from the car and deposited me, at first, on a couch inside. He and Elizabeth had danced around and joked some more about how they had duped Radu, about what a fool the little tyrant was. I almost felt sorry for him as I listened to the malice that echoed in the room.

Then, things had quickly gotten serious. Elizabeth had walked over to me. She said they didn't actually need me … asked Peter if he agreed … he nodded and said that between the two of them they would have no problem taking the throne from Basarab, who was nothing more than a besotted fool in love with a weak human. Peter had suggested they have their fun with me, and when Basarab found my lifeless body, he would go mad with despair, leaving them to walk in and take the throne. How they had laughed!

Elizabeth dragged me off the couch and over to the table. She unbound my hands and took the cloth from my mouth. "I want to hear your screams," she had whispered as she ripped the clothes from my body. "Get the ropes," she ordered Peter when she was finished stripping me naked. She lifted me with ease and placed me on the table. I didn't fight, what would the point in that have been?

And then they ... I closed my eyes and tears oozed out of their corners, flowing down my cheeks. Emelia was immediately by my side. She reached over and gathered me into her arms and stroked my hair. "Everything will be okay now, my dear," she whispered. "You are safe with us."

"Oh, Emelia ... they were so horrible! Elizabeth is the most horrid creature I have ever seen, and Peter ... they are so powerful."

"Hush, child. They are no more."

Despite Emelia's assurance, I wasn't comforted. I tried not to visualize everything that had happened in the shack, but it kept pushing forward in my mind. How they tied me ... stripped their clothing ... how they had danced around the table, both of them raking their nails up and down my body, flicking their tongues over my skin, catching the droplets of blood from my wounds ... how Elizabeth had suggested Peter have his way with me first because the only thing she was genuinely interested was in drinking the blood from the mother of Basarab's bastard children.

Peter had leaned over me, before climbing up onto the table. He had stroked my face with his tongue and moved his lips to other more intimate places. That is when I had prayed for a deliverer to come and either rescue me, or, at the very least, end my life, taking the pleasure of my death away from the monster that was straddling me, running his penis along my flesh. He taunted me ... mocked me ... told me I had never had such a man as he was ... that not even my beloved Basarab could match what he was about to bestow on me. I gathered whatever strength I had left, and screamed … and then, Basarab had crashed through the door and attacked the creature looming over me.

*Basarab. He too is a monster.*

"He is not the monster you think he is," Emelia said softly, as though she knew exactly what I had been thinking. "And he is waiting to see you," she added.

"But…" I was envisioning what he had done to Peter, the beast the man I loved could become.

"He did what he had to do to overpower Peter," Emelia said. "You must not allow what you saw to undermine the love you two have for each other. I have never seen Basarab so rattled as he was when he knew you were in danger and he could not reach you immediately."

"Where is he now?" I asked.

"I believe he is with the children, waiting for you to awaken."

I thought for a moment more. Finally, I nodded. "I am ready to see him, I think."

Emelia motioned to Carla, who left the room, I assumed to convey to Basarab that I would receive him now. Emelia assisted me to sit up. She propped some pillows behind my back. After a few minutes, a knock came on the door, and Carla and Basarab entered the room. I stiffened at the sight of him, but then remembered how much I loved him. And, how much he loved me.

Basarab took Emelia to the side and whispered something in her ear. She shook her head no, and then left the room, joining Carla who was waiting for her in the hallway.

"What was it you asked Emelia?" I enquired as Basarab approached the bed.

He hesitated, as though he didn't want to tell me.

"If it's about me, I want to know," I pushed for an answer.

Basarab sighed. "I asked her if you had been compromised."

"Compromised?"

"I needed to know if they had bitten you," he stated in a flat voice.

"And?"

"Emelia saw no sign of punctures that would indicate such."

Basarab reached across my covers and drew me into his arms. I began to cry as I laid my head on his chest, still amazed that I was in his arms. I looked up long enough to ask: "Did I hear Emelia correctly when she told me that you loved me?"

Basarab stroked my cheek, and then my hair. He brushed his lips across my forehead. "Yes, my little bird, I love you." He paused. "And, am I to understand that it is me you love, not Randy?"

I nodded, unable to communicate through the tears that were choking my throat.

He pulled me closer.

"I want to spend as much time with you as possible," I began. "Until this frail human body of mine is of no use to you anymore. Even a few years with you will be better than none at all."

"We will cross that bridge later," Basarab said. He covered my lips with his, gently, not with the fiery passion I was used to from him. But this was nice, comforting. "For now," he continued, "We have something more important to do. I want you by my side when I proclaim you as my new queen."

I gasped. He was going to announce to everyone—his father, his uncles, his aunts, his cousins, and his family—that I was his new queen. "What about Teresa?" I needed to ask. As far as I knew, she was still alive. "And Ildiko?" I added.

Basarab heaved a sigh. "They will learn their fate after I have made my announcement about us." He brushed a piece of hair off my forehead. "Now, are you ready to go downstairs with me?"

"Not just yet. I am still so tired. Could I rest just a bit longer, before facing Teresa and Ildiko?"

"Of course." Basarab lifted the duvet and slipped underneath. He lifted me and nestled me into the crook of his arm, and that is where I fell asleep, soothed by the sound of an ancient melody of love.

~

I awoke still cuddled up to Basarab's chest. His eyes were open, shining, staring at me. "Are you ready, now?" he enquired.

I smiled and nodded. Basarab cast the duvet aside, stood, and lifted me from the bed. "I can't go down dressed in a nightgown," I mentioned.

He set me down and went to my closet, returning with a red velvet housecoat. He helped me slip into it, and fastened the belt around my waist before offering me his arm. "Shall we, my love?"

"We shall," I returned.

~

On the way downstairs, Basarab explained to me that several of the family members had already left, returning to Brasov. I asked him about Orsolya, and he told me he had given her the choice to stay with the family, she had earned his trust, but she had said she would like to see some of the world. She had promised to keep in touch. Only Atilla, Vacaresti, Kerecsen, Laborc, Emelia, Carla, Randy, Santan, and Samara remained, and Teresa, Ildiko, and Max. When we entered the dining room, everyone, with the exception of Teresa and Ildiko, stood. They remained seated, with Kerecsen and Laborc next to their chairs. Basarab stopped at the head of the table, gave a nod, and everyone sat down.

I studied Teresa and Ildiko. Teresa was subdued ... Ildiko as insolent as ever. Basarab and I remained standing. Santan was beside Randy, Samara with Carla. The children made a move to approach us, but Basarab motioned for them to stay where they were. They obeyed, even though Samara pouted. I knew she wanted to be with her father.

"Before we head home, I would like to thank all of you for your patience while waiting for Virginia to recover from her ordeal. Now, there is something else that must be dealt with before we leave." Basarab looked directly at Teresa and Ildiko. "Stand up," he ordered.

Teresa slowly rose from her chair. Ildiko remained sitting, an insolent look in her eyes as she stared at her cousin. Basarab nodded to Kerecsen, who took hold of Ildiko's arm and forced her to a standing position. She tossed her head and sneered at Basarab.

"What is it you have in mind for us, Basarab?" Ildiko challenged. "Do you honestly think the council will abide by this decision you are making, to cast your wife and your cousin aside for the likes of that human whore that stands beside you? Maybe Radu isn't the one who will dethrone you after all!"

"Radu is dead." Basarab stated flatly. "And Elizabeth and Peter. They are no longer a threat to me, and after tonight, neither will you or Teresa be a threat to me and the woman I have chosen to stand by me side."

"And how do you plan on getting rid of us?" Ildiko was glaring at me.

"I have explained to your father what you and Teresa plotted against Virginia, and almost got away with. I told him how you even poisoned Emelia in order to be able to get to Virginia. I told him there was no place in our family for such betrayal. He will be waiting for you when we return to Brasov, and he will take you into seclusion. Maybe, one day, I will find it in my heart to forgive you, Ildiko. You are family, and because you thought to betray me, I have to admit, a part of me has died. You were more than a cousin to me, you and Gara were like the siblings I never had. I want you to know that it is only because Virginia still lives that I spare your pathetic life."

"You are banishing me from the family?" Ildiko looked shocked.

"Yes."

"And my brother, Gara, he is going to go along with this and still serve you?"

"That will be his choice. Your fate has been decided." Basarab turned to Teresa. She bowed her head. "Teresa ... you whom I took under my wing as a child ... I gave you everything a child could desire ... things you would never have had if you were living in a Gypsy wagon, always on the run, always considered a criminal. I saved your father's life, and looked after him well all these years ... I set you as my queen, not a whore I bedded and discarded ... I found Virginia, and she gave us a child, something you always told me you wanted. But you were so jealous you could not contain your hatred for her, or for Santan. So I spent more time with her, at first because she was more pleasant to be with. I grew to care for her, and was set to let her go, knowing she would not betray our secret because she would see no harm come to her child. What you did not seem to understand, back then, was that I would never have set you aside as my wife—my queen—had you not been so prone to see the mother of my children dead!

"How do you think I felt when I overheard you tell your father how much you hated Virginia, and that you didn't care for Santan? I couldn't believe my ears! Then, here, Santan approached me, upset with what he had overheard you and Ildiko discussing ... how you were plotting to be rid of Virginia so you could secure your place as my queen. Well, my dear Teresa, by your actions, you have removed yourself!

"I banish you from my life, from my world. I never want to see your face again. However, because I was informed that you actually didn't want to kill Virginia, I will give you one token of gratitude. Your father, Max, will be released from my service so you will have his company. However, his companionship will be short-lived because I will be taking away the immortality I bestowed on him, so he can one day be reunited with his Lilly, your mother—my gift to him for all his years of service to me."

"You are sentencing my father to death?"

"No, my dear, you did that. You wrote his death sentence, as you did your own." Basarab turned to Max who was standing by the door.

I felt a moment of sadness for the old man, but then I thought about what Basarab was saying. I knew Max would embrace this turn of events as a blessing. He would be with his Lilly, something he had always yearned for.

Basarab motioned to Max to step forward. "You have served me well, Max. It is time now for you to leave me. I will make sure you have enough funds to last you for whatever life remains in you."

"And what of my daughter, what becomes of her?" Max's voice was shaking with nerves.

"I assume she will be with you until your final breaths. After that, I care not what she does as long as I never have to lay eyes upon her again." Basarab waved Max away from him. He turned to Teresa. "One thing I would like to make clear to you, Teresa … I do not ever wish to hear news of you going rogue. You know how to live discretely in our lifestyle. If you should try to do otherwise, I will see to it that it will be the last thing you ever do!"

One could have heard a pin drop on the carpet, the room had become so hushed. I glanced over to Randy and Santan. Santan had taken hold of Randy's hand, and he was staring challengingly at his father. I knew what he was thinking, and I prayed Basarab would come through for his son.

"Now, for you, Randy," Basarab faced in his direction. "You have made your way into the lives of Virginia and my children and have risked your life to save them. My son loves you; my chosen queen holds you in her heart as a dear friend. So, having said this, I want to give you the option of either leaving, or of coming with us. If you choose to leave, I will make sure you have enough money to start a new life, and I will expect discretion … likewise, if you come with us. I promise you will never have to fear for anything from our kind, and you will always be welcomed in our home. What say you to this offer?"

Randy blushed, as I knew he would. "You honour me, Basarab. I think I will come with you. I have always wanted to travel to Europe, and I couldn't bear to be away from the children, they have been such a part of my life over the past couple years. I wouldn't know what to do without them."

I noticed how Randy left out any reference to me. Probably a wise move.

Basarab nodded. "Well, that was a quick decision." He turned to Carla. "And what are your plans? I understand you have served the family on occasion, and you were also the one who delivered Samara. You went out of your way to protect Virginia and the children. You have my deepest gratitude for all you have done."

Carla smiled, a rare display for her. "I think I will take a trip to Europe and stay with Adelaide and Alfred for a while. I notice how frail they both have become, and I feel I owe them to tend to their needs in their golden years. Adelaide took me from an orphanage when I was a child, and she raised me up in her home. Emelia was a large part of helping me along, as well, by paying for my education so I could become a doctor. If you or any other family member ever is in need of my services, I will make sure you know where to reach me."

"If you are ever in need of anything, do not be afraid to call upon me," Basarab returned.

"Thank you."

Once again a silence came over the room. Angelique stood. She gazed around the room, at each one of us, resting her eyes upon Atilla for a moment before finally looking directly at Basarab. "I have a request to make of you, Basarab."

"Go ahead," Basarab responded. "How could I refuse anything you might desire after all you have done for this family over the years?"

Angelique glanced to the children, then back to Basarab. "Your children have exceptional powers, greater than any I have ever witnessed of vampire-born offspring. They are going to need a good teacher, someone who will help them to understand their powers, and who will teach them how to use those powers properly. I would like to come with you and be part of your household."

Before Basarab could reply, Atilla stood. He smiled directly to Angelique. "So you wish to become a tutor to my grandchildren … how would you like to be the tutor to your own grandchildren?"

At first, Angelique appeared confused. Basarab burst into laughter. "Well, well," he remarked, "I do believe my father is asking you to marry him, Angelique. By the sounds of it, there will be two weddings taking place when we return to Brasov!"

Emelia clapped her hands in delight. Her face was beaming. "How enchanting," she said.

"Well?" Atilla smirked. "Your answer, fair maiden."

"Yes … my answer is yes! Oh, Atilla, I never thought the day would come when I would find such true happiness."

"It has come, my dear Angelique." Atilla walked over to Angelique and embraced her. She nestled into his arms as though she had always belonged there. Looking at them, and knowing what I knew, I think she had.

Basarab looked around the room, his eyes coming to rest upon Santan and Samara. "Now, what would my little princess like to do?" I looked up and saw the twinkle in Basarab's eyes.

Samara jumped down from her chair and raced to her father. He opened his arms to her, and she jumped into them. While holding his daughter in one arm, Basarab extended his other hand to Santan. Santan hesitated a moment, looked up at Randy and smiled, and then walked with dignity to his father.

Basarab took his son's hand and knelt down. "I have kept my promise to you, Santan. Everyone you love dearly is safe." Santan looked at me and smiled. He glanced over to Randy and smiled. He looked into his father's eyes and smiled.

"Thank you … Papa."

# Epilogue

Three years have passed since it all happened. My wedding day was shared with Atilla and Angelique, and I could not have asked for a better day, or the night that followed it.

We took up residence just outside Brasov, in the Transylvanian countryside. Basarab decided to sell the house in Brantford. He had asked me a couple times if I ever would like to return there, just for a visit. But I can't. Even though things have ended well for me, too much bad happened there. For the first year, after our leaving, my dreams were nothing but nightmares. Visions of what Elizabeth and Peter had done to me constantly disrupted my sleep. Eventually, the horrifying dreams became less and less, until they stopped altogether.

After the house was sold, Basarab took me on a trip to Scotland. We left the children in the care of Atilla and Angelique. The scenery there was breathtakingly beautiful and I fell in love with the countryside. We visited a great many castles and before we returned home, Basarab surprised me by handing me the deed to one of the castles we had walked through. "A summer getaway," he had smiled.

Basarab spent some time away, after he settled us in our home, to deal with cleaning up the rogue army Radu had created. He didn't give me any details when he returned, only telling me it was over. Truthfully, I didn't really want to know anyway.

Randy, after a few months of travelling around Europe, enrolled in university to continue his journalism studies, which was what he had said he had wanted to do when I had first met him. Basarab, as promised, paid for his tuition and all his living expenses. Randy visits us every chance he gets, much to Santan's delight. Even Samara is excited when she finds out Randy is coming. I wonder, sometimes, if the cause of her joy is because of the presents he showers on her. He has one more year before he graduates, but is already doing freelance articles for several magazines and newspapers throughout Europe.

    I believe Randy has finally come to terms with our relationship. We have had several in-depth conversations, reliving much of what has happened since I walked into his life, and he tells me he understands, especially when he sees how much Basarab loves me. I keep telling Randy it is time for him to move on and find someone to share his life with. The last time he visited, he did bring a charming young woman along. I like her. Santan approves, as well, which makes Randy happy.

    Teresa disappeared, as was ordered, with the exception of a letter we received two years after leaving Brantford. She informed us that Max enjoyed the time they had together, but he was now in the arms of his Lilly. She said nothing more about how she was doing. I noticed the look on Basarab's face as he read her letter, and after, he seemed distant. I can't say I blame him for that, she had been a significant part of his life for so many centuries, first as a child under his care, and then as his wife and chosen queen. I know he had loved her at one time. We have talked about it because he wanted me to understand.

    Ildiko is still in seclusion. We get periodic reports from her father. Gara, at first, was furious with Basarab, but when it was explained to him what had happened, what his sister had done, he acquiesced, although he comes around less often now.

    Emelia and Vacaresti traveled around Europe for a few months when we first arrived home. Emelia had giggled and told me it would be like another honeymoon, of which they had had several over the centuries. Emelia was absolutely devastated when she received the news of Adelaide's passing, followed by Alfred's a few months later. I know how much Emelia loved her friends. Since Adelaide's and Alfred's deaths, Emelia and Vacaresti have been dropping by more often for visits. The obvious strain that had been between Emelia and Basarab has dissipated over time, and Emelia has confided to me how happy she is to have her nephew back in her life.

After Atilla and Angelique's honeymoon, which lasted six months, they returned to our home and Angelique began tutoring the children. They love her, and she has been instrumental in teaching them how to harness their powers.

Santan is still as serious as always. Over time, he has relaxed with his father, and there are occasions when Randy visits that I see the three of them building something and laughing together. Samara remains *daddy's girl*. That has not changed. However, Samara has warmed to me considerably, and we have enjoyed many sweet moments together. Shortly after arriving in Brasov, the initiation ceremony for Samara was performed. This time, unlike when Santan's was carried out, I knew what to expect.

Basarab and I have tried to add to our family, but I guess it isn't in the stars for us. When I think about it though, Santan and Samara are quite the handful for me, despite all the joy they bring. In reality, the children, Basarab, and the rest of our family are all I need. I feel complete.

~

I set my pen down, not knowing what else I could write. My life has finally come together. I am happy. For how long, I have no idea. After all, I am still human. My love is not, and neither are my children. I am determined to enjoy every moment with them that I am blessed to have.

I heard the door to my study open. I knew it was Basarab. He had a way of coming in and surprising me with delights.

"You are looking very thoughtful today," he said, coming up to me and wrapping his arms around me.

I leaned back and looked into his eyes as he towered over me. "Just thinking about how long you are going to keep this human wife of yours. I will get old one day, you know, and I will die."

Basarab picked me up from the chair and walked across the room to the daybed that was nestled into the window nook. He sat down, keeping me on his lap, his arms holding me tight. "We have not discussed that issue for a long time," he began. "You don't have to grow old, Virginia. I am happy with Santan and Samara; we could not be more blessed. It seems we are not going to have any more children, so maybe it is time for you to join us, so you can remain with us for eternity."

He stroked my hair and kissed my forehead. He had offered me this immortality of his before, and I had always been hesitant. Maybe, because I had thought to give him more children … maybe, because I was afraid of taking that step. But now, as I gazed up into his eyes and saw the love radiating from them, I could think of nothing I wanted more than to spend an eternity with my children and the one I loved.

I sighed, and he held me closer, waiting for my answer. Finally: "Yes, my love, perhaps it is time."

His lips closed over mine, igniting the fire within me. As his tongue brushed across my neck, I waited with bated anticipation for the new chapter of my life to begin.

*Mary M. Cushnie-Mansour*

Books in the

## NIGHT'S VAMPIRE SERIES

Night's Gift
Night's Children
Night's Return
Night's Temptress
Night's Betrayals
Night's Revelations

# Author Page

Mary M. Cushnie-Mansour is a freelance creative writer who resides in Brantford, Ontario, with her husband, Ed.

In March 2006, Mary completed a freelance journalism course at Waterloo University, Waterloo, Ontario, after which she wrote freelance articles and a fictional short story column for *The Brantford Expositor*. Mary has published several poetry anthologies, collections of short stories, biographies, youth novels, and children's picture books, some of which are bilingual (English/French). Mary is most infamously known for her *Night's Vampire Series*, and the *Detective Toby Series*. She also writes a blog, *Writer on the Run*.

Mary believes in encouraging people's imaginations and spent several years running the "Just Imagine" program for the local school board. She has also been involved in the local writing community, inspiring adults to follow their dreams. Mary is available for select readings and workshops. To inquire about a possible appearance, contact Mary through her website—

http://www.writerontherun.ca
or via email
mary@writerontherun.ca

Mary's Moto—To live without a dream would be like living in a house without windows … how many of us will fulfill our dreams before the cobwebs of time cover the caverns of our minds.